COMMONS

COMMONS

Calum Cumming

STONEWALL PRESS
PAVING YOUR WAY TO SUCCESS

Published in the United States of America

ISBN: 978-1-64460-001-6 (*sc*)
      978-1-64460-000-9 (*e*)

Library of Congress Control Number: 2018957022

Published by Stonewall Press
4800 Hampden Lane, Suite 200, Bethesda, MD 20814 USA
1.888.334.0980 | www.stonewallpress.com

Short Stories
18.09.20

CONTENTS

CHAPTER ONE

There is a burn that runs down through the city. It originates in the west somewhere. No-one knows quite where it springs from but suffice to say there is something in it wholly corrupt. The water is opaque as if it contains some toxic substance leached from the waste of mankind. Yet the smell of the Denburn isn't of effluent but of something that forebodes the trouble that is coming. The burn's winding, seemingly innocuous, course through the city of Aberdeen suggests another unknown pattern of existence beneath the rawness. This is what underpins the physical strangeness of our lives.

When I was a kid I used to play among it, at the water, and once I went down there with Ernie and his cousin Billy Joe from Canada. We walked the burn west from Albert Street towards the pitch of the underground weir. Billy Joe was 16 and from Ontario. She was dark, with piercing blue North American eyes, her teeth were white and her smile was enriched with calcium. We stopped before going into the darkness. I could hear the noise of the water as it tumbled over the weir, conjuring up images of drowning in my mind. But the birds were singing on the trees above the bank and this gave me some confidence. Scratching at my face to get rid of the midges crawling on my skin, I looked down at Billy Joe's baseball boots. There was red gum stuck to the sole of one boot. Ernie asked her if she wanted to go up with him, and she said, "Yeah." She seemed bored, listless. They went on alone. Ernie put his arm around her.

I was feeling ravenous, I went up the bank to eat gooseberries from a bush. It was that time of the year when the fruit was at its best. Suddenly I noticed on the branches the chrysalis of butterflies. It was such a strange thing to behold, those eggs hatching into adults, that I became frightened and jumped down off the bank and shouted up to Ernie and Billy Joe at the weir. Ernie came running down panting and asked, "What the hell is wrong?" I told him about the butterflies and he started laughing. Ernie said, "Don't mind about that. BJ wants to see you up at the weir, Cal." He had an envious look on his face. His closed mouth was twisted. I went on alone up into the darkness the hundred yards or so towards the weir, the air smelling of the burnt, evil water and of damp lime mortar. Stalactites, formed from the cement deposit, hung from the tunnel ceiling.

Billy Joe was standing there smoking a cigarette. It was a Carlton. She asked me if I would like one and I said, "Yes." I liked the flat, cellophane, royal purple packet, the two sections of ten wrapped in gold paper. I found the whole mechanism of smoking cigarettes exotic, attractive. I was too young to smoke, but you didn't get punished in those days. Ernie used to steal them from his Ma's press.

We both stood there silently smoking, and she said that she liked me. She put her hand in my thick, curly brown hair. She was leaning against the tunnel. She was taller than me. She said I was more grown up than the other boys of my age. She was wearing a blue, zip up leather jerkin that fastened across the collar. It was unbuttoned, and I could see the clear outline of her meikle paps. Billy Joe asked me if I had ever been with a girl before, and I said, "No, I haven't." I knew then at that moment, that women would appreciate my honesty.

The noise of the weir was roaring in our ears, and the opaque water frothed as it tumbled over the fall on its journey to the sea. She said I could kiss her if I wanted to, so I did. I put my arms around her circumference, and drew her towards me in an embrace. She suppled into my arms, and, suddenly as though a shiver were running down her spine, she asked me if I would always be her friend. I said that I would, and then my hands touched the mounds of her breasts. Billy Joe said I could put my hands down her jeans. She felt wet and warm. I fumbled for what seemed like an age until BJ said I was still too young for anything more adventurous. She told me to wash my hands in the water, but the scent, her pungent sexual smell, was still there. It would be there for days. Together we came down the tunnel towards the exit and Ernie, who was jealously guarding the light. I never saw her in my life again.

It was an August day in 1993 and I woke early, put on my clothes and drew the curtains apart. The North Sea had turned the colour red. We were working down in the village for the water board, testing the village sewerage outfall, and the men had been putting dye down the outfalls since 6am. We were doing this to establish the flume of the effluent in the sea and taking water samples to discover the location and direction of the flume pattern.

That morning I walked along past the harbour wall towards the North Sea outfall. Painted in large blue letters on the harbour wall were the words, "Scots shit out," as if in antagonistic response to the infamously miss-spelt Nationalist slogan painted on the footbridge further down the coast: "Scotland free or a dessert". I approached Billy and Sandy in their orange boiler suits. I looked out at the outfall ending in the sea at high tide. The local fishermen had their cobble nets out to catch the sea trout. This was the place to catch them, amongst the warm effluent and the shit. The fish had a keen sense of smell, coupled with a natural instinct, and were fooled into thinking this is where they would find fresh water. I thought about the Denburn, which discharged into the River Dee estuary, and I wondered if the trout congregated there, swirling and shoaling like curved fluid bars of silver, anxious to be on their way upstream to the spawning pools.

My job as technician was to take samples of seawater and label time and location. It was an easy job requiring only physical dexterity and a certain fleetness of hand. The red dye contained a radioactive isotope which enabled the laboratory to establish the discharge pattern of the out falling sewerage. The sea was the colour of blood now, and I could imagine what Homer had meant when he described the wine dark sea overflowing with the fresh blood of Greek manhood.

It was about three in the afternoon when we finished the dye test and sampling. Billy and Sandy had been putting dye down the manhole for the past nine hours. I looked down the manhole one last time before Sandy shut it securely and I saw it was clogged on the walls and in the channel with thick white human fat. It would need pressure jetting. We finished up and got out of the boiler suits and protective boots and gloves. I packed my samples and checked the paperwork was correct and then the boys took me up to the Stonehaven depot in the van. I reported to the engineer with the information, which would be checked and sent down the line to the laboratory for analysis. It was Friday, and I was going on holiday that night.

I waited for my train to Aberdeen. I had always been an imaginative person. I was used to being by myself, caught up sometimes in a dream. In this sense I retained the innocence of a child. This did not always make life easy for me as an adult. I was a changing man, like the proverbial chrysalis, twisting and turning in its case on the branch. Or rather those past few months I had been like a lonely Sibyl, trapped inside a wine bottle in a cave. My only outlet had been my work, and this did not satisfy me, which is why I would lapse within myself in a reflective effort to escape to another imaginary place. Like a coil spring, I had been depressed to the point where I could sink no lower but merely, ground out, score the earth.

I had been married. It had been a rushed tryst, a structural disaster. Subsequently, hard on the heels of this, I had had an affair that had served as a microcosm of the failure of my marriage. I blamed myself somehow for it all and everything that was to follow. That had all happened in the period immediately before this job had begun. I had been clinically depressed.

My wife Eva had been American. She was Californian, and sought out the poetry of folk. I realised only after I had married her that she had metamorphosed a few times before I came along. She was only ever learning guitar, she was only ever thinking about playing it. There had been something there though, however briefly. You know, I never could bear her hand writing, it says something about a person's character, I thought. It was fragile, it was weakly traced. Like one time when we were married in the USA, and we went to give blood for money, we were penniless, and the doctor couldn't find a vein in her arm. Like her handwriting, all waving ellipses and turned around letters. I felt that I had been cruel to her, and she would burst into tears like a child.

Then came Ruth, from Dundee. She was gallous, she was the schist flecked with grain and mica that was used to grind down the sand stone of Eva. To mix this with cement, that would make a mortar that would bind us together. That was it, I confused their two characters, Ruth and Eva. I found Ruth's hard edged personality attractive, sexual. But Ruth's parents had discovered that I was still married. In good Scots Presbyterian fashion the Mother turned against me, she turned away from me to the TV when I entered the room. There was I so lusting for the Daughter that it was as if I had contracted syphilis. Even then when the Mother had effectively killed things I wondered if she were any good in bed. Yet a hard rain was going to fall, and turn all that pounded bone to dust. I was told to end the relationship with Ruth, or they would, which of course they did. So that was it, this was the setting out point from which all else would spring forth, as I waited for my train to Aberdeen.

The train came, the Inter-City from London; a 20 minute ride. I got a seat and decided to get a drink from the bar. At the buffet was a Scotsman dressed in kilt, brogues, skean dhu, and sporran. He looked like a movie star. He was drinking whisky steadily. I looked at him while I waited for my beer. The man was smoking a cigarette and his drink was rocking gently with the motion of the train. He suddenly directed his sage gaze at me and asked, "What the fuck are you looking at?" I at once burned with shame and indignation, at this outburst of Scots machismo, this downright medieval parochialism. What gave so many Scotsmen a barb for a tongue? In the absence of anyone else, I looked at the barman for some kind of empathy. I may as well have gazed at the moon, as he smirked back at me whey faced. The drinking culture in this male country we call home: react, and you are in a fight. I took my drink in a shaky hand and went back to my seat.

I had almost finished my drink as the train wound around the long bend like a slinky ferret. Nigg Bay and Aberdeen came into view. This city is built, largely and incredibly, of one of the most enduring and indestructible building materials in use on our planet: grey granite. As the train crossed the River Dee towards Guild Street station I looked at the city outline. Scrubbed immaculate and unforgiving.

There are basically three parts to Aberdeen. The west end, old money that was once new money. The fish processing area, Torry, South of the Dee. And where I lived, the agricultural centre to the North East: Kittybrewster. There was once a mart at Kittybrewster, and an abattoir. The souls of many hundreds of thousands of animals have been transmuted here to feed our burgeoning stomachs. There is more than just a trace of this farming stock in the character of the people in this part of Aberdeen. It is most apparent in the men. Great haunches of fuzzy, brown forearms. Empurpled pictish faces. A rigid coldness of personality, coarseness of tongue and wit. Flaccid bullish cocks that are more used in pishing copious amounts of alcohol into bar urinals than making imaginative love. The whole city is spattered with severe housing estates, that is the hallmark of the urban Scottish picture. You can't help notice it; they are grim, out on a limb. Severity, poverty has no peer. Last exit from the black panes of Northfield. Imagine that. Try erasing it from your mind like graffiti from a wall. In truth like most Scottish cities Aberdeen has its own indigenous culture, some would say inbred identity. At the end of the day it means that we are all tramping on other people's souls in our old homes in our old stone world. The existence of the west end is governed and dictated by the same rawness that inhabits the east. The atmosphere, the dialect is common. The tramp between one mercantile extreme and the other is not insurmountable.

I got into my flat on Belmont after straking up through the town. I looked at my reflection in a shop window. I had lost so much weight. I was like a scarecrow with a belly of corn.

I lived in a tenement. Along with the haddock-filleting machine, and the down-hole drilling bit, the tenement was one of the staple institutions of Aberdeen. The guy above me in the tenement was Nigel. He was like his name. He never went out, had no friends or visitors and yet he was only 30. I used to hear his washing machine grinding away all the time. And his fastidious creaking. He used to maintain a sense of decorum if you saw him on the stairs but he was hiding some awful hack within that had led to this. Bill lived next door to me on the landing with his wife and step-daughter. He was a window cleaner. His skin had a sallow permanent yellow pigment. He was a reformed alcoholic and the household were all Jehovah's witnesses. Bill had just had a colostomy. He had the wiry build and complexion of an Asiatic primate and the rubbery sleekitness of a stoat and you could always smell his strong body odour. He used to clean my front window sometimes and he was philosophical about his illness as he dunked the chamois. Bill said he was quite happy to work away with the side passage. Underneath him was Willy the vagrant. He had no curtain on his front window and I used to spy in on him there like a character from a Francis Bacon painting, sitting on the armchair amongst the squalor. Great pools of eyes filled with a combination of fear and searching intelligence. He had no left arm, having lost it in a mincing machine. He had been a butcher boy. I had been in his flat once, I had let the police and ambulance men in, after Willy's mother died and Willy realised he had no one left in the world that cared about him, and so he gave up. He had starved himself for weeks, until someone raised the alarm. In the kitchen was a pile of used tea bags scattered into a mound on the bare boards. Sitting like a tepee. His spare false arm was on the mantelpiece in the living room, like part of a dummy. Of course the social services kicked in at that point. Sent him to hospital to be fattened up. Cleaned up his flat, and stuck him back in it with a TV to stare at now. They even thought about net curtains, but omitted the spiritual fabric that Willy craved for, that we all crave for, and some even take for granted. Across from Willy lived Tiger. He had been a trawler man all his life. He was built like a stick of liquorice, with a core of bendy wire. His arms were covered with crudely drawn tattoos, and sometimes I used to change a light bulb for him, and take a drink with him. I was a good hearted person that way. I have the common touch. Tiger smoked and drank on enthusiastically until the day came when they carted him away and amputated his legs. He is dead now. In the pub across the road they always go on about what a character he was. Which I suppose even old Tiger was by comparison to their parochial grue. Margaret was up the stairs next to the manicured banker Nigel. She was from the metropolitan capital of "Edinburgh" and was of somewhat dubious virtue. She used to spend her days up in the social club of the mental hospital. She was middle aged and she used to pick guys up in there and bring them back. I didn't trust her. One time I went up and knocked on her door to ask about a key for the communal shed we shared. She opened the door in a rag worn dressing gown. The smell of rancid beef dripping wafted out the door, or perhaps it was Mazola. The guy was in there, he grunted at her and asked if she wanted him to come to the door. But I didn't have to face up to him. She used to have a Rottweiler, and she exercised it out on the graveled drying green. It paced round and round, and in the same direction, kept going clock-wise round. Methodically, unemotionally. Without showing any sense of affection. Margaret would go around after it and pick up its shit in a plastic farm food carrier bag.

I looked at my watch. The one my Dad had given me on one of his yearly visits. I didn't know my Dad that well. I had never spent any time with my Father. I dwelled upon that increasingly as I grew older and my own life took a spiral downwards. I came to realise I had been profoundly damaged by the physical absence of my Father's love. It was 6pm, and I was meeting Elaine in an hour. I shaved, washed, and changed from my work clothes. I put on my black and white patterned Indian shirt, black jeans, white socks and black boots. I brushed down my Dior navy blue double breasted jacket, and put a green and red paisley pattern handkerchief in the breast pocket. Just a dash of colour. Black was the sartorial dress of the day. It gave you power, an aura somehow. I was moving up the gear box, I was gaining speed as the evening now approached. I felt an empty pit in my stomach, but it wasn't food my stomach was anticipating, it was something else unknown. I ate some food and watched TV for a bit. Iraq was in the headlines, and the part the West was playing with systematically starving it to death. I toyed with the ricotta and spinach tortellini on my plate. This was being done under the flag of the United Nations. I thought of John Lennon's line, who sang, "All we are saying is give peace a chance," and I realised Lennon had paid with his own life for uttering such a rare ideal. After all "peace" just means food, any child can point that truth out. I wondered if there was any difference at the end of the day between being shot by an obsessed fan in the safety of New York, or hanging publicly from a lamppost in Baghdad.

I left the flat and walked into town to meet Elaine at The Wild Boar. Or as someone euphemistically had once coined the place, "The Bored Whore." It was where I had met Eva some 4 years ago. She was pulling pints, and it really is true: service is part of an American's identity. It must come down to space I thought. Here we couldn't expand anymore. There wasn't much of the road trip experience. We felt hemmed in by our small island coastline. There was some sort of co-existence in the UK where we all just had to rub along together. Unlike here, in the States, the modern infrastructure was there, (they had poured some serious cement), but there was also space. Of course it doesn't help that people who work in Bars in this country earn a pittance.

But it was more than just that somehow, service identikit didn't seem to be part of our culture. It was ironic, seeing as service industry formed such a large part of our economy. I supposed service workers everywhere had plenty to feel disgruntled about. I walked down towards the pub. I thought about America when I had first visited the country with Eva. We travelled from Seattle down to Mexico and back up again. I remembered the guys on Haight Ashbury in San Francisco pushing their shopping trolleys down the street, probably stoned, drunk, or both, but desperately poor. Their belongings were heaped up, in the carts, in a mound. Eva and I visited this really famous bar at the City Lights bookstore where Kerouac and Cassady would meet. Outside a hobo is enjoying a little pipe of grass. Defying the astringent identity of a corporate America. Perhaps then, it was just a brief window of enlightenment when people really did wear flowers in their hair in the post war period, but the thought of the old hobo having a toke in the sunshine at the door of the bar cheered me up. It is true that drugs and drink do not create an artistic enlightenment in the individual; the reverse is true: they are an intoxicant. The pain is there though, the time ahead of you. The dullness of that and the ordinariness of reality. The Beatnik Hippy culture of America was still clinging on. Eva and I were sitting in this bar, and Kerouac's dark brooding handsome face is staring down at us. They have turned him into some kind of Icon here. A parody of himself amongst the mobile phones, and exclusive, cigarette smoke free atmosphere. The cultural wilderness of white Anglo Saxon America was excessively clean and bland. There was a TV on in the corner. Hollywood mostly doesn't create that gap between ultimate truth and the perceived reality of say me and Eva sitting in this bar-a homage to the Beat writers, who lived life to excess-and we are the only people drinking alcohol. That in Europe would be perceived as ironic. America was a country that seemed on the outside so clean, but dig some and you hope to come across distinct identity. I had hoped not to be disappointed in this regard even then when my marriage was disintegrating. I had looked across at Eva, sucking on her cider.

I had thought that I admired something about Americans. They seemed to have mostly non addictive personalities; their physique, their rational intellect, their sheer candour. However there seemed to be an absence of dialect there, everything seemed the same. Like it or lump it that was what unified the UK, the cultural variations of the people amongst the physical infrastructure of the country. Eva once said to me when we returned to her Homeland after an absence of four years. The thought of 250 million other Americans backing up, welling up inside her. She said, "There is no poetic spirit in the world I live in." And her pretty corn blue eyes burst into tears.

I was at the Wild Boar. I concluded, "I'll just take my coffee with plenty of milk. In the morning, after the night before." I went inside. It was the only bar in the town that approached something cosmopolitan. The ceiling was high and classically vaulted, and the bar was done out in warm greens and pitch pine. Paintings hung on the wall, and there was a continental feel to the place. It was where the bright young things liked to congregate for food, drinks, and intellectual conversation. All the other bars in the town were either ancient, wine red dark, or ersatz copies of the metropolitan model. The oil industry had only served to heighten the atmosphere of medieval atavism that inhabited the pubs of Aberdeen. I looked around, it was 7pm, and Elaine wasn't here yet. It was quiet. Wendy was on the bar on her own. She bowed to me and held her hands up in prayer. She was Vietnamese, and she had come to Europe as a refugee, as a child. There was an intuitive grace about her. A timelessness. I asked for a pint of Stella, and asked Wendy how she was, as she poured the pint. She said, "I am waiting for my final exam results." She seemed confident of herself; she had just finished a languages degree. I wondered if hardship when you are growing up was more akin to the generation in this country that returned from the war and returned to study. The maturity of their experiences seemed to make them more able to disentangle their own egos from the competitiveness of academic life. I asked Wendy, "What is the difference between mediocrity and meritocracy?" She looked at me in an intelligent frown, a trace of a smile playing across her oriental lips. She placed the drink in front of me, and I gave her the money. I looked at the brew; I was ready for a drink.

Wendy came back with my change; the view outside was unchanging and glacially still, in the clear light of a late Northern summer. Wendy said, "So what is the difference between mediocrity and meritocracy Cal?" I replied that, "In the world the second was a prerequisite to finding a decent job, but the first was the right of the rich." She said, "You are so rich in cynicism," and she was done with me, and went to put some more music on. It was Herbie Hancock, "Taking Off." I took his cue and moved to a table with my drink. Opposite me, in front was a painting of an ancient Haddock, a "John Dory." The painting of the fish was spiny and archaic. A simile for the Scot's character I thought, swirling in a small ever-decreasing pool of water. I took a long draught on my pint.

"Hi Cal," I looked away, towards the light. It was Elaine. She looked great, circa route-66, 1954, heading south West towards the sunset. She came and sat down opposite me, barring the fish. We were platonic, start out as you mean to go on. She had gold and sapphire studs in, black Tee shirt, shiny navy blue Fliers jacket on, black jeans, white socks, and lace up working beat boots. She was like something from the carnival, blue eyes and corn blonde hair. I asked Elaine, rising like the gentleman, what she was drinking, after I said Hello, and gave her a peck. She said, "I'll have Baileys on ice," lighting up a fag from a ten pack of Regal. Maybe she was nervous, we were just kids, not in the glare. I went to the bar and got her drink. I liked Elaine and asked her if she liked the pub's exhibition. "It is a bit of a con, a bit old and decrepit looking," she said as she descended on her drink. I sat down again; the bar was starting to mingle a little bit now.

Elaine was living in London with Dave. I asked her, "How's London?" She replied, "Oh it's alright matey, still going round and round." She was up visiting family. I asked her, "What was it in Scotland that gave young adults the feeling that we had to leave in order to achieve some kind of potential, what is it that constrains us here Elaine?" She replied, "If you stay here and don't express your potential, you feel worthless, on the margin of society, and you will go off your head." I wondered if that included me, I said, "Scotland isn't a very easy place to feel liberated in, in an expressive sense." She sipped her brown creamy Baileys, and looked at me with her tough blue eyes. She said to me, "Well if you are going to stay Cal make a difference then, don't feel as though it is your national identity that makes you feel obliged to remain locked in obscurity." I thought about it and said, "Being Scottish was predominantly about being part of a scabby margin. The majority of the population who lived here felt as though we had been primed to fail, we were doomed in a sense; it was what gave us discipline, a sense of survival. Our dour identity." Elaine looked a bit prosaic; she toyed with her now almost empty glass. It was time to change the subject. I excused myself and went to use the bar toilet downstairs. The urinal was filled with red tablets of disinfectant. The colour red and the smells of urine and disinfectant seemed to seep into my head, cloyingingly, combining with the heat. The strangeness of the "Water Key" occupation I was employed in had rubbed off in me in some non-concrete, imaginative sense. Spirituous liquor was transformed into golden dark yellow, warm liquid, frothing from my penis. Alcohol and the abuse of it was the definitive way Scots choose to identify themselves. I thought of the circular, creative tun used in brewing. The point of germination, the distillation of the argument. The first sprouting of the maltlet, that was common to all creation. Dali said the sum of all existence is what swirls around in our testicles. Only the Scots had chosen to distil this truth in a particular way. Curious. I finished, washed my hands, and went back upstairs.

The bar was getting busier now, filling up with the generation after mine. They seemed more sophisticated somehow, not so eager, but more confident than I was. Not so much waiting or even hoping. Choosing to drop off their branches.

Elaine said, "Come on Cal lets go and smoke a joint before the band." We went out the door and across the granite sett street to a car park. It was good for me to be in the company of a woman once more. It was mild and infinitely blue. A light warm wind was blowing. Elaine shivered from the base of the column of her spine. I asked her if she was cold and she replied, "No, it is just that happens to me sometimes". I said, "It's a reminder of our fear of death, the limited potentiality of our lives". She said, "Oh God you aren't back on that again are you." She burst out giggling and said, "Don't speak such crap Cal!" Elaine produced the joint from the arm pocket of her jacket, and I sparked her up. Elaine passed me the joint and I took a few hits. I asked Elaine how her back was just now. Like me she had fractured her spine as a teenager. We shared this in common, we both realised that even what is bred in the bone is not indestructible. She said she had been getting massage recently. I looked at my own hands. They were good, knowing hands. Elaine said, "You and I have realised the fragility of our own bodies, that's all." I passed her the joint. I said, "What does endure then on the human plain? Is it only a memory of the dead in the minds and hearts of the living." Elaine ground the roach out under her boot and said, "Ashes to ashes, dust to dust Cal, let's hit the gig." We walked up to the venue, it was a former church, and was now called the Ministry of Sin. I wondered what our idea of faith was now in the face of our secular existence. What did we believe in?

The Artist was Gill Scott Heron, he was a radical poet/musician. He was seen as some kind of black subversive underground figure. He had an international credibility that made him hard to pin down to any one culture. Elaine and I went into the venue, and I got us some drinks at the bar downstairs. The place was heaving with people. I recognized a lot of faces I hadn't seen in a long time. Elaine said, "The band will be on in about 15 minutes, we'll have this drink downstairs then go up to the concert." I raised my glass in assent. It was hard to make the leap from quiet bar to this cacophony of noise. The speakers were blasting out "The Beastie Boys." I was a bit stoned; it seems to make me more thoughtful. I was on a train of thought and forgot the art of conversation for a second. Elaine leaned towards me with her beer clutched in her hand, and looked up into my face. She said, "So what are you thinking about then Cal?" "Oh nothing really," I replied defensively. She could tell there was something I was lying about. She looked at me in the eyes, intuitively, and asked me, "So how many girls have you been out with then?" I looked back at her in faint amusement. The question served to fan my ego. I had a sardonic grin on my face, and I replied, "Oh not that many, perhaps 40 women." She burst into a giggle; it made me imagine that sexual encounters were different if you were a woman. Perhaps women's sexuality was the key to understanding the power of attraction between men and women. She was curious now, she said, "Have you ever had a gay fling?" I felt as if I was being set up for something. I replied honestly. I said, "Just once, I was at a party." Elaine let out a giggle and asked me, "Did you enjoy the experience?" I said, "It was neither here nor there, the experience. It was just meat. Afterwards though when I left the party, and this poor guy, who was totally unable to come, I think because he was afraid of my heterosexuality, I was filled with anguish. As if it mattered somehow. I felt guilty."

On that note we went upstairs to the venue to see the band. There was a familiar fug of sweat, dry ice and smoke. The band was coming onstage without any fanfare, unannounced. The stage was in a pit lower than the auditorium, it was intimate, almost intimidating. The band were all dread locked black, rastas. As they performed their first song, they were almost in supplication, to the mainly white audience. Gill looked small, relaxed, wearing mirror shades. I looked behind myself; the guy on the mixer desk was also a Rasta. He was beginning to groove to the beat. He shone me back a warm smile full of Caribbean gold. Elaine and I began to dance euphorically. The hypnotism of the beat began to affect me. My pelvis swayed, my arms moved in time. I thought of how at the Bacchanal people became ecstatic under the influence of the atmosphere and the music. It was a religious experience. Amongst the wave of the crowd, I kept looking around. I was sweating profusely. Everywhere people were smoking joints openly. Even the band was passing round reefer. But black man can take it, white man can't. Time was sped up; the band was well into their set. Elaine went to get us more drinks. The next song was a gangsta rap/hip hop number. Gill sang, "I don't wanna be a new jack hustler." I sat on the stairs leading to the stage; I needed to ease this hysteria. Elaine came back with the drinks from the bar. I stood up. I said to Elaine it was true that white men can't jump. "Why is that," she shouted back. "Because," I shouted back at her, "We are inferior in almost every respect to black men, both physiologically and poetically. We don't know how to rap." At once the music stopped and the band went to take their break. Soothing Calypso music came over the speakers. There was a tiny silence while people returned into the physical plain.

Elaine said, "I was thinking about what you told me about your gay fling, it makes me feel better about you Cal. I think it is important for Scotsmen to debunk the myth of heterosexual virility. I think Scotsmen are about the most repressed sexual beings in the Universe." I gave her a limp wristed wave, and said in a mincing accent, "Shut that door." Elaine asked me to go down to the toilet and roll a joint for her. She gave me the skins and the dope. I went down to the toilet. I went into a cubicle. I could hear the cistern, the noise of water coming out of the faucet. It made me remember when I was a kid, and I lifted the lid off the cold water tank in my Granda's house, and looked in. The dark cold depth of the water, spiders crawling. The noise of flowing water rising into the float valve made me feel strange, afraid somehow. For in truth we are water born. And here I was now working in the water board, amongst the strangeness of creation. The experience had been like a premonition somehow. First I took a pee, and then rolled up.

Afterwards I decided to have a quick drink at the bar downstairs, before heading back up to the gig. It was empty; the solid curved font was carved from ash grey granite, dressed and polished. I ordered a whisky. I could see the stairs behind me in the bar mirror. I noticed a girl in a white front split dress coming down the stairs. I noticed her hair; it had a blonde sheen that lent her something of a golden girl appearance. Her dress was virtually translucent, and you could see her white bra and knickers underneath. Her legs were bare and nut brown. She was wearing stacked black open toed shoes. Expensive shoes that gave you poise and height. Unlike the kind that the kids in Aberdeen wore. They made you look like Boris Karloff. She had on a diamante bracelet, and that is all. I looked into her eyes as she passed me, they were grey/blue; they had appeared brown at a distance. She looked at me over her shoulder as she disappeared into the ladies. I drained my drink and went back upstairs.

Elaine was talking to the owner of the place, Bob. She knew him from her childhood in Torry. He was from a fishing family. At least half of this town had been constructed on a box of old fish. He gave me a customary nod, then disappeared. I was neither kith nor kin to him; to me he was just another punter. Elaine said, "Have you got the joint Cal?" I passed it to her, and gave her a light. This was the most liberated dope night I had encountered in the whole history of Aberdeen. Elaine was toking on the joint and she indicated to her right over my shoulder. I looked over and there was the girl standing on her own at the balcony rail. Elaine passed me the joint, and said in dead seriousness, "Any time you are ready Cal." Maybe I misunderstood her, I was blowing hard. The band suddenly came back on stage unannounced and fired into a Bob Marley song, "Redemption".

I turned to go up and speak to the girl, Elaine had her hand on my arm, and she was beseeching me. She said, "No Cal don't go over there." You cannot put a paling where there has been a post; there was no stopping me. I felt strong and confident. I strode over. I said to her, "Hi my name is Cal." She gave me a cool look. She said she couldn't hear me, would I like to go and sit down in the seats behind. It was dark way back there. She said, "My name is Selina," and she held out her hand. Her hands were small, the painted purple finger tips rubbed down somehow, it wasn't in keeping with the rest of her image. I kissed her hand. Inside me there was a lot of hurt, a lot of loneliness. I was in the mood to channel my emotions sexually. I said to Selina, "You are gorgeous," and kissed her mouth. Incredibly she didn't resist, but seemed to be encouraging me. I put my arm lightly around her. I kissed her mouth passionately. I kissed her neck, her chest, stopping abruptly at her bra. I looked up muzzily. "Drink", she said hoarsely, holding my head in one hand and a half full glass in the other. She said, "It is champagne." I took a draught of the wine and looked at her realistically. "How did you know it was me," she said in a broad Mancunian accent. "Did you just take a chance?" I could see she had on too much make up; it was either a sign of gaucheness or the stage paint of the harlequin. The band rushed onwards in a spin. I didn't reply to her, I just kissed her mouth again, our teeth enameling and bumping like dogs. I heard a Mancunian accent to my left. A man's voice. He said, "She is an ex model you know, only 23." I looked around and expected to be confronted by some kind of pimp. Selina introduced him as Alastair, her older brother. I felt as though he had intruded upon our relationship. The intangibles of a brother and sister. Were they in love with each other?

I had always found the character of the people from the urban industrial centres defined by their own industrialism. Their characters were like their deep accents, densely constructed and influenced by the identities of more than just one nationhood. There was little or no indigenous identity in any of England if you stopped to consider it. Elaine came over; my burst of energetic passion had subsided. She looked down at us both pointedly and said, "Cal what are you doing?" Selina replied plainly, "It is alright my love he is with me." Linking my arm with her badly drawn, painted fingers. Alastair showed some tactile sense and said we should all go down stairs for a drink, Elaine was happy again. It was not nice to feel excluded by the scart of others sexual attraction. We went and sat at the bar. The music seemed like a backdrop now, almost a distraction. Selina ordered champagne for all of us, and her brother paid discreetly. I couldn't stop kissing Selina, I was addicted to her pheromone. I asked Selina what kind of music she liked, and she said, "Soul, northern soul melts my heart." She said to me her parents were from Aberdeen originally. She lived in a little village in Cheshire. That is about as much as I ever discovered about her. Elaine and Alastair were engaged in polite conversation, small talk. People were starting to come down the stairs, paired off into couples. I felt non-zombified again, part of the majority, with Selina on my arm. I said to Selina that the band would be over soon. She looked at me and said, "I go from the heights to the depths Cal," and she drew an imaginary circle with her hand. I was puzzled at that, but before I could reply, she asked me, "Do you like dancing?" and she did a pirouette under the instinctive outstretch of my hand. She was animated and gay once more. She said, "Let's go back upstairs and hear the end of the band."

The four of us went back upstairs. The band were at the end of their set. We all went up to the balcony, like a gang, to catch the final songs. Selina was cradling an unopened bottle of champagne to her chest like an infant. The last track was a heavily overdubbed song. Gill seemed to be in an ecstatic trance as he sung in a pan African dialect that seemed incoherent. The dubbing laid down an infinite techno beat. Selina was grinning on in determination. I felt she looked at me as though she was in some sense superior. I looked down to my scuffed feet. Momentarily I felt like some kind of disco victim. I looked across at Elaine, if I could have read her mind I would have known she was thinking, "Gangs will play harmless pranks upon one another Cal." The lights came on and finally Gill stuttered, "Suffer not the little children to come unto me". He bowed, and a spontaneous applause broke out. Finally he seemed humble and human. It was as if he finished where he had begun, in supplication to us. The world was not at the stage where we could rejoice after the entertainment was over. The politics of his music was not just about looking good, but also feeling good. Anticlimax. I kissed Selina again.

We decided to go to my flat and drink the champagne. The crowd was dissipating into the warm August night. We got a taxi; we were amongst the lengthening window of darkness that cloaks temporarily the eternal light of a Northern Summer. Selina sat beside me in the back of the taxi. Seemingly languid, exotic in the black, punctuated by the pattern of white shadow, moving under the neon. The car smelled of vanilla, I opened my window, and warm air flooded in. We got to the flat, I put some music on and we drank champagne from mugs. Selina and Elaine started chatting about Aberdeen. Both their views of the area was crystallized in the moment when they had left, they were both nostalgic for the place. Alastair said to me, "You know how women like to chat, a bit more lip smacking is required," he seemed to be bidding me on to do something. I turned to Selina, they were both sitting on the floor. I felt reckless and uninhibited. I clutched her hand. Her shapely brown legs were gripped tight. I noticed she had a snaggled front tooth, it overlapped the other. I kissed her again, our bodily fluids exchanging, I was infected by her. In the same way animals carried bacteria in their mouths, somehow my attraction was caught off her teeth. Before drinking the last of her drink Selina nudged me to drink the dregs together in a toast. As if we had drunk of one another. The bottom, the end result was more important than the beginning. I got up and put on another tape. I went to use the toilet. I could not find water. It was as if there was a padlock on my bladder. I was acutely conscious of the relative strangers next door. It was as if they could divine my thought pattern by some kind of telekinesis. What I had drunk I could not impart. It was now part of me fluid and diffusing throughout my beating body.

I rinsed my face and went back next door. Elaine was holding up two books to me, one was "Big Sur," by Kerouac, and the other was "Difficulties with Girls," by Kingsley Amis. It was some kind of two-card tarot reading that was based upon what Elaine knew of me, prophesying my own beginning, middle, and end. My destiny. It made me feel paranoid as if my guests were conspiring against me. She said, "This is the deal." I frowned in confusion. Selina looked at me and said, "What goes around, comes around." I replied, "Yes I know that," my hands were still mottled with dye from the day's work. Alastair had fallen asleep on the floor. He was like a rag doll gone awry. Thrown out of a tenement window. The bones of his feet and hands were in a strange contortion. He seemed almost lifeless. Selina was rolling a joint with her painted little fingers. I went to make some tea for us all.

I brought in the tea and asked if anyone would like to hear my poetry. It was starting to get light again. I noticed the peach fuzz on the nape of Selina's brown neck, in the sunlight. I read a poem that was about the experience of hepatitis. Suddenly Alastair woke up agonizingly, and interrupted my reading. He asked me if I had injected heroin. I said, "Yes, a few times when I was a teenager." He said, "That is not such good news for you Cal." Selina looked dismayed, it was the cardinal rule amongst young middle class people today. Do anything you want, but don't touch smack. It was infradig, it was anti-social. You were branded as an outcast if you took it. The severe values of today's middle class generation with regard to heroin, were post Aids consciousness, the antithesis of what I had believed to be hip. There didn't seem to be a middle ground to stand upon.

I read another poem about a man and his peasant mother on an island community in Scotland. This poem seemed to appeal to Selina's bucolic humanity. She said it was exactly right. I noticed her nose was slightly hooked over and out, like a bird of some kind. Probing for a kernel of wisdom. I read a couple of other poems, and then Selina looked over at her brother. It was as if there was some kind of secret sign between them. The spell between them broke up the familiarity of the party. Elaine said it was time to phone a taxi and go home. I asked Selina if I would see her again and she said she had left me her address and number. Elaine could see what was coming, so she said, "Excuse me I have to go to the loo before the taxi comes." I kissed Selina again and rubbed her curvy thigh. Selina's brother seemed taken aback, embarrassed. He stared down at his long slender surgeon's hands. My hands felt her knickers underneath. I knew Alastair didn't like it but I didn't care. I whispered in her ear, "I love you," and she replied flatly, "I can't say that on a first night." I needed to fill in the gap in my life with another's human touch. The buzzer sounded for the taxi, Alastair and Selina were on their feet, and Elaine came out of the loo. I went with them downstairs to the car. Alastair immediately got in the front seat of the car. He didn't say goodbye. He just shrugged at me, turning towards the driver. Elaine wished me a goodnight, and said she would phone. She seemed afraid to kiss me goodnight. I said to her, "I don't bite you know." Selina crackled at that, she found it funny. Elaine said, "Enjoy yourself in Germany," she zipped up her jacket and got into the car. I embraced Selina and kissed her. Her spine was rigid, her body unsupple. She seemed to be retreating from my advances now. In the light of the morning, she said, "I had fun Cal." She got into the back of the car next to Elaine. Both girls waved to me as the car sped off, their hair shining like sheaves of corn and barley. The hard dawn light was rising steadily, picking out the sharpness of the grey granite buildings. I stood for a couple of minutes watching the memory of the car. Alone now I felt emptied and washed out. I was exhausted by the entire cycle of events. I went straight upstairs, locked the door, pulled off my clothes and fell into bed.

CHAPTER TWO

I fell into a deep coma like sleep. My body was incubating. I must have slept in exhaustion for 5 hours or so. Finally I began a dream where I was dancing with Selina. It was a slow languid dance, and she beckoned me towards her with her hands. She had a look of sexual intimacy in her face. Her eyes were heavily lidded. She smiled at me, and her bitched snaggle teeth glinted at me in the subdued light. We came together in dance; I was in expectation of sex. Abruptly, she grabbed my testicles, and I suddenly woke up. Momentarily I howled at the pain that had entered into my testes. Sunshine was pouring in the window, I was conscious of that, I was awake. The pain subsided to a dull constant ache. Like flesh thawing out in the heat. I felt hot spots pin point my body, as if some kind of foreign matter was causing a chemical reaction in me.

I tried to use my rationale. I wondered if I had recognized something of myself in Selina. As if we were of the same pattern but of slightly different tread. The soulful symmetry of staring at someone, and the mirror is staring back at you. Had we eaten of a forbidden fruit? Had we transgressed some kind of paradigm of existence? Modern society was so inbred and reckless. For that reason we are given individual names to differentiate us from one another. Health, virtue and sanity were something most of us took for granted.

I could hear Nigel creaking above me, beginning his daily, solitary, routine that filled in the wasteland of his life. He was like a rat in a cage, gnawing at the bars. We all were, in this block, part of an experiment that was about how to cope with, and get through life without going insane. Soon I would hear the dial of the washing machine scrunching. Doing the first of many cycles of the day. I rose and went to the bathroom to pee. My balls felt leaden, as if some kind of weight had sunk down to the bottom of my soul. I finished peeing and looked in the mirror at my face. I was brown from a summer outdoors. I had strong wolf features. High cheekbones, a straight nose. My teeth were strong and yellow white. I turned on the tap and rinsed my face. My eyes smarted from the chlorine in the water. I dried my face and looked into my eyes closely. They were vividly blue, the kind of eyes that demanded attention in a gaze. I knew that. The iris in my right eye had a peat-coloured fracture in it. I wondered if I had inherited this flaw from my Grandmother, who was a Celt.

I went through to the living room and saw Selina's address lying amongst the debris of the previous night. I sat down and began to doodle on the back of the paper. I began to think about her again. I was lending weight to a meaningless encounter. Except that pain descended to my testes in direct proportion to how much I thought about her. I wrote the word 5 on the paper. I equated this with the universal colour blue, used to demark potable water. I then wrote down the word red. It was the universal colour for demarking sewage. I got the idea for a series of abstract paintings. They would depict the world from the 1930s' until the 90s'. Green and yellow would represent fertility and hope. Red; hope dashed, the world at war. Blue; the sadness of the world, musically reprieved. Yellow; a world of idealistic hope. Brown; retreating back into organic parochiality. Green; riven with avarice and jealousy. And now the 90s' are blue and black, the bruised spirit of our times. It didn't seem a grandiose idea, but something genuine. I had been unaware of my own thought pattern. My doodle had become garrulous and incomprehensible. It was not that my glass was still half full. Rather that I had just drunk too deeply from the cup of life itself.

I made some coffee, I smoked a fag vacantly, and I put on my clothes. I phoned Ewen in Dundee, he was coming up tonight with Katie before we got the flight to Amsterdam tomorrow, and on by car to Krefeld, near Dusseldorf in Germany. Ewen was an artist, and Katie worked for an airline. They were ex-pat Scots. I decided to take a leap into the unknown and send flowers to Selina. I walked up to the flower shop in Rosemount. I walked past the old Co-operative site. It had once represented one of the founding pillars of the movement. The butcher, the baker, the candlestick maker, had all been part of this institution. The infrastructure of the site stood abandoned and empty. Waiting for the bulldozer, waiting to be razed to the ground. The ghosts, the fabrics of so many people's lives, their toil, seemed to utter a silent reproach as I walked past the site. A slice of working class history that was to be replaced by the false god of our new labour consumerism; a computer retail park. All that was left of this centre of urban necessity was the food supermarket. It too would soon be a thing of the past. In this upwardly mobile society, consumer analysis perceived that the majority was not interested in cheap, low quality foods any more. And the rest? Well to hell with the rest. The social Diaspora increases, the margin upon which we exist grows ever narrower, and more crowded. In the winter the working class, poor people who shopped in the Co-op would trudge past my window with their laden bags, in the snow and the slush towards the bus stop. Like the shoppers of Petrograd, searching hard for some hope within our beaten down hearts. Old before our time, hunched against the bitter Scottish weather.

I got up to the florists and decided on a reckless gamble. I bought a bouquet of orchids. I sent a message with the flowers. My intuition told me that what I was saying was correct. Of course intuition can be a flawed logic. I wrote, "We share old gold in the soul, blue at 5, love Cal." I wished someone had told me then I was barking up the wrong tree. I was like a squirrel doing a spiral upwards. Then repeating itself down to the base of the tree trunk. I walked quietly back to my flat through Royal Cornhill Mental Hospital. Black smoke was belching out of the Victorian red brick, belted chimney. When I was a kid, the complex had been secure, surrounded in barbed wire. I still had the scar on my left thigh where I had cut myself badly trying to get in. The persistent thought that dominated my mind was the need to be cared for, and not just that, to be cared about. There was a fine line between individuality, and loneliness I reflected. I had been veering to the latter too much recently. Like a wounded animal I had retreated to somewhere infinitely slight within myself. The sun came out from behind a cloud, and then it shone very suddenly, brilliantly. Some of the patients were out in the grounds with nurses. You could always tell the patients, their distress serves to stigmatize them. Holding themselves together, in a fragile place deep within. The nurses were calm and reassuring. The source of distress, the patient's illness had led them to become materially distressed. That was obvious. I played a game with myself. Spot the nurses, spot the patient. It was as if society, not content with having dished out a dose of bad luck to you in the form of mental illness, it was hurting you more completely with this. In some way these people were being punished in all sorts of degrading discriminating ways for having become mentally ill. In effect what society was saying was that in some way you are guilty for your own crime. That is the punishing factor I thought, that no one could really care about you if you were mentally ill. Society did not care. This point of self-realization must be behind a large number of suicides. I thought this choice could often be excluded if people were given the social and spiritual fabric to lead dignified lives in the mainstream of life. Happiness.

I felt profoundly depressed at the notion of how people with mental illness are treated in this country. I got back to the flat, and locked the door. As if that would somehow make a difference. Keep all the badness outside my home. Semi heroically I was thinking about suicide, how would I do it? Was there confusion between self-pity and anguish? I laughed out loud. I realised I couldn't, Ewan and Katie were coming round. The only way I knew how to make a protest about the demise of my own life was to wave despite the fact I was drowning.

I made myself some food, toast and eggs. I wasn't very hungry. I had had no appetite for food since my humiliation by Ruth some months ago. I was sick of the sight of food. It couldn't tempt me, there had to be something wrong. I had been humiliated by the narrow-minded preconceptions of the British middle class, through my split with Ruth. She and her family's values were liberal as long as the pattern of my behavior conformed to their own view of life. That would have been condoned. There is always a hidden agenda in this sort of structure. The things that aren't talked about are the things that could serve to liberate our souls from the corseted restraint of our own lives. At the end of the day people like that don't want their children to stray from a narrow career/creative path. They want to maintain and pass on their status quo. Continuing on ad infinitum. Continuing on ad nauseum. I thought about Ruth. One time when all is still rosy, before her parents discovered that I had a history. A lucky escape. But there was still the question of a burgeoning sexual libido between Ruth and myself. That is what I missed, that is what had been wiped out at random by her parents. I remember Ruth and me were in this nightclub, and Ruth goes to use the toilet. She comes back upstairs. The place is stifling, heaving. There is a heater on the wall. I lift her up to turn it off. She climbs up on my shoulders, and turns it off. I get the waft of shit straight from her bum. I don't suppose it was her fault there was no bog paper, but still it is a litmus test for someone's character. It was a metaphor for the values that she and her parents regarded as being at the core of respectability. Behind the façade they have erected for themselves lies the fact that they have levered themselves not so long ago from the urban dung heap. The façade was to hold the back draft at bay, to maintain your standing in the community and recreate your own character. But as Ruth herself might have commented, gesticulating with her long slender, capable hands; you can only pish with the cock you have got Cal. There is no changing that physical truth.

I looked at my watch. Ewen and Katie would be here soon. I went to wash the dishes and hoover before they arrived. My domestic routine, boring but safe. I packed my bag for my 5-day holiday. That didn't take very long. I went and had a crap, and performed a few other ablutions. I popped the black heads I could see on my face. I always got caught up in this activity. The white fat, squeezing out from my nose. You are what you eat; your face is your social barometer. High pressure, low pressure, meridian. Maybe it was the ablutions that the middle class found revolting. Was this what led to secret behavior? I was finished with my face, in the windowless, airless cocoon of my bathroom, I rinsed my hands. Suddenly the whole floor shuddered violently. Nigel's washing machine was going into fast spin cycle. Removing the final dregs of dirt from his grey flannel trousers. The last traces of frustration from his bed linen. Everything clean and pristine once more, until tonight comes around. Suddenly I felt sorry for Nigel, again, and I hated him simultaneously. The buzzer sounded. I answered the intercom. It was Ewen and Katie. I buzzed them in, and opened the door to welcome them inside.

Ewen came up the stairs at the head. He looked the restrained, retentive artist, conservatively holding onto the banister. He looked an archetype, almost a parody of the way a painter should dress. He was small and dark with a close shaved beard, gold wire glasses and just a hint of dissipation in his face. He was wearing a tweed jacket, white shirt, and pressed linen trousers. A meerschaum pipe bowl was poking from the breast pocket of his jacket. Katie brought up the rear. She was wearing an enormous straw hat, like a character from a Van Gogh canvas. I said to her, "Are you ready to bring in the harvest Katie." And she replied that, "All I have is the body God gave me." Holding out her hands. Her wedding band glinted. It was an unusual rose coloured gold. That colour, that bond had been unlucky for me I reflected ruefully. I welcomed them both in, and quietly turned the mortise behind us. Ewen looked around the living room before deciding to sit down. It was the first time that either of them had been here. The late sunshine was streaming in the living room window now. The day was in decline. There was just that tiny feeling that summer was not endless after all. "Well fit like then?" I said, Katie replied, "Gutten tag mein herren." Ewen still seemed taken with the decorum of my flat. His own material circumstances had been pretty precarious until he had met his wife Katie. She was the rock to which he was firmly, immovably anchored. Perhaps his own ambition was what he misunderstood as his own creative worth. It must be hard to disentangle creativity from the need for food, warmth, and shelter. Ewen said, "This is a real piece of gold this flat." I felt a bit edgy about that, I didn't agree with him, I just said nothing. The silence hung in the air for a bit like an unclaimed fart. Then Katie produced a bottle of Hungarian wine from her bag, and we all began to relax into the situation. Ewen sat down next to Katie on the couch. I went into the kitchenette and got glasses, and a corkscrew. I uncorked the bottle and poured us all a glass of wine. I raised my glass and said, "Here is to us three, and the next week, "Slainte." We drank together, that first slug of alcohol that tastes so invigorating. Katie took off her hat and laid it under the coffee table. I put on some jazz music, in the background, low.

Ewen said he felt like celebrating. He produced a pink £100 note from his breast pocket. He said, "I sold a drawing today to a gallery in Dundee." I replied dryly to him, "That money was only dirty paper anyway." Ewen let out a raucous throaty laugh. His chest was gurgling with delight. Ewen said, "I want to take the three of us for a meal tonight." I thought Ewen was trying to recreate some of the atmosphere of when we were all students in Glasgow. When we had first met. In those times we were more innocent, eager to sample life. Like strutting Bohemian figures from 1920s' Paris. But of course as anyone can vouch living on the edge in Glasgow is nothing like Paris, except life doles out the same cuts to the poor. Glasgow's West end seemed like a post-industrial, stagnating pool. Inhabited by a migrant population of students, academics, working people, and charlatans. Sodden in alcohol. Aberdeen didn't seem such a decadent place. It was honest at least, a certain plainness of character.

Katie disappeared to the toilet. It looked as though we were going out for a meal. Ewen shouted through to her, "Are you away for a Kurt Schwitters darling." He laughed hard at his own joke. With the same chesty, raucous gurgling. Without any feeling. I said, "We can go down to the restaurant in The Boar. You can check out the paintings Ewen." He was rolling some Condor tobacco in his palms. The pipe was out on the table. He was obviously contemplating a condor moment. He said, "It is alright Cal, the future of Scottish painting is safe in my hands." If I had thought he was being ironic I would have laughed, but as it was I misunderstood him, his ponced up ego was sticking in my craw already. Before I could reply Katie returned from the toilet. She had left the light on. Katie asked me, "How is your work going, you must be glad to be away on holiday." I told her about what I had been doing on Friday. She genuinely did seem to be listening. Ewen was pulling on his pipe in self-satisfaction. I was getting a sore throat. I could feel the glands swollen and tender. I said, "I think I am getting a cold." Katie said, "Who gave it to you Cal?" I replied, "That was last night, that would be telling". Ewen suddenly perked up, he was listening now. I threw a catalogue of Henry Matisse at him, and he picked up on it avidly. I said I would order a taxi for us to take us to dinner. I topped up everyone's glass, finishing the bottle. I put the dead man with the rest in the small kitchenette. I washed and shaved and came back and ordered the taxi. The cab came, we all got in. It made its way into town. It was a real grey overcast night. The granite seemed listless and without any sparkle of mica. However it was still picked out by its own sharpness, its hardness.

We got to the bar and I paid off the taxi. Inside it was between busy and empty, nice and relaxed. Alex was on the bar. He was Polish. He was the bar manager. He once told me that he had read "Mein Kampf", when he had been on "the broo". He was a bit older than the rest of the staff. The Polish were even more anti-Semitic than the Germans. While he was away getting us drinks, I told this to Katie and Ewen. Ewen asked me, "I wonder if he enjoyed it." There was a touch of menace in his blue eyes. "Oh well fuck the Pope and the IRA, and the third world debt," I said. I started to cough a bit, a dry hacking cough. We went downstairs and got a table in the restaurant. Ewen did a customary tour of the exhibition that was displayed. It was still fish. The paintings were all dark ochre reds, browns, and green. It seemed they had been conceived in such a way to lend them a distressed and ancient quality. As if the fish had just been hauled in from the murky depths of a vast, inky, North Sea. Ewen came and sat down; he seemed a bit humbled by the experience. He burrowed into the resume of the Artist. A local painter called Craig Prempeh. I looked across at the bar; the barwoman was talking to someone who was holding a vast pile of sparkling clean bar linen. He was literally dwarfed, almost obliterated by the pile. It was Nathan.

He was the local launderette king in Aberdeen. Linen wasn't the only thing he was good at laundering. I shouted across to him. He looked across at me, dropped the linen on the bar, and after a few words with the barwoman, came over and joined us. I introduced everyone. Ewen was still perusing the resume. He had a slightly worried furrowed look on his face. Nathan was the typical South mouth. He had more front than South End pier. I once had lived in one of his properties when my marriage had split up. I discovered then how adept Nathan was at bending the system to suit his material ends. He seemed to be able to measure life down to the last penny. Everything and everyone within his orbit had a monetary value. This confirmed his conservative politics. I couldn't say I disliked him, but I felt uneasy in his company. Nathan had become fatuous, and he knew it. His was the individual world of the upwardly mobile society, the 90s' had created. To paraphrase J. F. Kennedy. The way Nathan thought was, "Do not ask what you can do for someone else, but rather ask yourself, what they can do for you." His Dickensian, olde England values believed devoutly in a self-help society. As a result of this he might as well help himself to what he wanted. Burrowing on, thinking ahead, unaware of the people he had trampled upon. I had realised long ago not to take anything from him that would have to be returned as a favour at some point in the future. The waiter came to take our order. Nathan said he wasn't staying long, he was working. He got a drink from the bar. Ewen asked what the special was. The waiter replied, "Calf's kidney in a Burgundy sauce, with colcannon." Ewen's eyes positively brimmed with delight, he said, "Yes I'll have that please. Delicious!" Katie ordered the Caledonia chicken, and I just had onion soup. The waiter took the order and disappeared. Ewen said, "You have to eat you know Cal. You look like some kind of rock n roll refugee. You could do with putting on some weight." I glossed over the remark and said to him, "Eating has been like a kind of mechanical activity to me of late, I can't seem to find any enjoyment in food."

"And you such a bodily, sensuous person as well." Said Katie, nudging me intimately.

Nathan came back from the bar. He had Perrier water, with ice, and a twist of lime. A clean, refreshing drink. As if that could cleanse the grime that clung to his soul. He was fleeing from the shadow of his past, which he tried to ignore. I started coughing again; my throat had become sore and hoarse. Nathan asked me what I did last night. In keeping with the upwardly mobile groups of individuals of the 90s', Nathan shared in common, an arrested emotional development. His sense of fair play encompassed having a steady girlfriend sitting at home, while you went out and indulged in drink and drugs, and tried to get off with any girl that came along. Just like your average duplicitous Calvinist. Except it was wrong, it was leading us into the inferno. I said, "I went out with a friend and we saw a gig. I met a girl at the gig, and we all went back to my flat." Everyone started chuckling suggestively. That was it I supposed, there was more innuendo than there was sex going on at the moment. It was unhealthy. Nathan asked me the name of the girl. I replied her name was Selina and described her to him. Nathan seemed a little taken aback, he said, "I know her."

He looked up from his drink. He was like a small creature, its face emerging into the sunlight for the first time.

Nathan said, "That girl is part of the Whitbread brewing family, they own breweries throughout Britain." Somehow I wasn't surprised when I heard this. It was some kind of fait accomplii. Nathan said their association with the distillation of alcohol goes back to medieval times, and the Norman conquests. This piece of empirical evidence that involved me directly had Ewen's ears straining. He was always looking for some kind of slant for his next canvas. Something original to latch onto. I said to Nathan, "My own breads aren't feeling too sweet after my encounter with her." He tapped my half full pint glass of lager and said, "Well that is where it all starts if you think about it." Nathan looked at me now with a new sense of maturity; he had shifted me onto a higher plateau of human understanding. I coughed again violently. Katie said I should get something for that cold tomorrow at the airport. The food arrived. Nathan drained his drink, and said he would excuse himself. He wished us, "Bon appetit" and disappeared, via the kitchen door.

Ewen and Katie attacked their food with gusto. Particularly Ewen. There was no conversation, no chat, just staring at the plate with fork and knife attacking. I thought I could detect a faint growling deep in the back of Ewen's throat. I ate my soup delicately, almost distastefully. I broke the rhythm of fierce oral masticating. I said to Ewen, "Has the kidney got the correct tanginess of urine for you Monsieur?" He purred back positively, "Bloody delicious." I said to them both, "There has to be some kind of connection between artists and offal." They finished their food in silence. I lit a cigarette while the other two were still eating, and blew the smoke in an indiscriminate direction. I asked if anyone wanted another drink. They both replied no. I went up and got myself a whisky and ice. When I got back, Ewen was asking the waiter for the bill. I said, "Maybe we should get an early night, we have to be up early tomorrow." Katie nodded in agreement. Ewen seemed a little disappointed. He said, "That's not like you Cal!" He was smoking his meerschaum pipe, digesting his dinner. The bill came and Ewen proffered the soiled pink £100 note. When the change came he left a meagre tip and stuffed the rest inside his jacket without checking it. Ewen took the catalogue of the "fish" artist with him. We left and got a taxi home. I pulled the settee out for Ewen and Katie and said I was going to bed. I said, "Just help yourselves to anything you need, I'm off to bed." We wished one another goodnight. I woke in the morning. I had slept like the dead. I rose, had a pee and went back through to the bedroom. I put some clothes on. I drew the curtains apart. To the rear of the building was the constant hum of air conditioning from the chiller store of the Co-op. The noise was like a nocturnal companion to me in the small hours. I could hear the noise of traffic from beyond the living room. Where Ewen and Katie had slept. It was harsh and intrusive, unreassuring and polluting. I heard them next door talking, I knocked on the door and they shouted, "Come in." They were both up and dressed, the settee was folded back. They were drinking coffee. I made myself some. I said to them, "I'm sorry, I must have slept in". My throat was painful. Katie said it was all right we had 2 hours to catch the flight. I said I would pay for a taxi to take us out. Ewen was insulated inside his Art, he was reading the catalogue on Matisse, and he just nodded in absent agreement. Maybe travelling wasn't so exciting if you were ex-pat and you were just returning to your foreign location. Katie said she was going to get herself ready and she went to the bathroom. I took my coffee and sat down beside Ewen. I asked him if he had slept well. Ewen replied, "Fine except for the traffic in the morning." I took a hit on my coffee and lit a cigarette. Ewen looked at me briefly, rather distastefully, and said, "You like the two together in the morning, eh." I said, "In the morning my body craves nicotine and caffeine like a child craves its mothers breast." Without looking up from his catalogue Ewen said to me, "You should pack in the fags for a bit and look after that cold Cal."

I phoned and ordered a taxi to take us to the airport. My keys, my airline tickets, passport, and wallet were all together on the table. Katie came back from the bathroom. She forgot to turn the light off. I washed and shaved. I got myself ready, and we were set to go. The taxi came. We piled downstairs with the luggage. I got in the front. The driver asked me where we were flying. I replied, "Amsterdam." The driver said, "That is something worth getting up for in the morning," and gave me a knowing wink. Out at the airport things were pretty quiet. It was Sunday. I paid off the taxi. He wished us, "Bon voyage." We checked in for our flight. Katie and Ewen took their bags onboard as cabin luggage. Going through customs Katie and Ewen got the full treatment. Katie bore up to it stoically, but Ewen seemed a little outraged and priggish. Of course they were looking for dope. I looked on in frustration. My own view was either legalize the whole lot and take it within the establishment or screw the nut of law enforcement even tighter. Almost everyone now has smoked dope at some point or other, yet that common consensus did not seem to inform the law. There was no choice in the matter. Eventually customs were satisfied and we boarded at the gate for the flight. I had a window seat. Ewen and Katie were parked in the aisle. Next to me was sitting a young Belgian man. He introduced himself as Jean Luc. He said his group had been on vacation in Scotland. Suddenly the plane prepared for takeoff. The cabin staff made their safety announcements. The turbines whined increasingly louder as the plane taxied to take off. All at once we were thundering down the runway, gaining speed, until the plane levered itself up and into the air. The aircraft gained altitude and banked over Aberdeen. The city looked uniform and set out, grey and puritanical. We headed South following the coast. I looked out of the window. Streaks of rain riveted the Perspex. I thought I could make out a smudged red colour somewhere in the North Sea. Drinks were served and everyone relaxed into the short flight. Ewen spilt his drink. Jean Luc said, "Your friend has spilt his drink, watch he will do it again." And he did, it was uncanny. I asked him what he did. He said, "I am part of an international community that is concerned with the world peace movement." He made a gesture with his hands and wrists forming the wings of a dove.

Dinner was served, and we both ate solemnly. The trays were cleared away and we were passing over a beach. A long endless strip of dirty brown sand. We were over Holland. The captain announced that we would be landing shortly. Jean Luc patted his chest and said he was relieved to be arriving safely. As if flying was a little sketchy somehow. I had never questioned it before, but I would dwell on the safety of air travel in years to come. We were on our final approach for landing.

The plane touched down with a rubbery squeak at Schipol airport. The aircraft shuddered and snaked as the pilot applied the air brakes. The flight was over. We taxied to the disembarkation gate. The whine of the engines reduced to a whimper. We got ready to disembark. I looked out the window; it was a hot blue day. Jean Luc wished me well and shook my hand. I said, "I am going on to Germany." Jean Luc said, "Don't go," and started laughing. I looked out of the window finally, at the sticky black tarmac. We all made our way off the plane. In the gate tunnel I was reunited with Ewen and Katie. I was overcome with a paroxysm of coughing. Katie said, "Here, I got these for you at Aberdeen," they were lozenges. I took one and things calmed down a little. I thanked her and said, "That was thoughtful of you, cheers." We snaked through customs and then onto the baggage reclaim. Schipol airport was a tribute to ethereal modernism. It was beautiful architecture. In the secular world we had created for ourselves, places like this had become the new citadels in which we pray to mammon. As we were making our way out of the airport, someone high up on a balcony was filming us with a camcorder. He was wearing leathers and had on wraparound sunglasses. He looked like a rock star. "Tosspot," muttered Ewen under his breath, barely looking up from carrying his bag. His pipe was jogging up and down in his breast pocket. He was wheezing a bit.

We got out of the terminal building and arrived at the long stay car park where Katie's car was parked. We all got in with the bags. We made our way out and away from Amsterdam heading South East into Germany. We stopped at a MacDonald's just before the border for a burger. It was true these places were just like Hollywood had portrayed them. A Big Mac was a Royale, and they served beer too. We crossed over the border onto the autobahn. Ewen had buoyed up a little after his refueling stop. He said, "There is no limit now Cal." He seemed a little excited, gnawing on his cold pipe. The car sped up to 100mph, keeping up with the flow of the traffic. The countryside seemed to pass in a blur. The fields were flat and filled with yellow ripening maize and corn. This colour was interspersed with fields of green kale and cabbage. All under the perpetual blue sky, and the hot sun. Eventually we reached the exit for Krefeld. We pulled off the autobahn, and slowed back into normality after our high-speed ride.

We were on a rural road, but unlike in Britain, the road was modernised and well maintained. The tar macadam seemed slicker somehow. I indicated to Katie that the roads seemed better maintained in this country. She replied, "That is the key to understanding the economic miracle that is the German powerhouse Cal, to reinvest your wealth back into a sustainable infrastructure." I replied to her laconically, "Yeah, living in the UK is a lot of fun." I looked into the face of a farm labourer who was tending a horse in a field. He stared back at me. The man's face was brown and lined, full of bucolic character. There was a simple poetry, a dignity in rural manual toil. It didn't seem to matter where you went in Europe, farming folk had the same outlook on life. This was only altered by regional variation, language, and dialect. Somehow the essential honesty remained the same. We were approaching Krefeld. All the houses had window boxes with brilliantly coloured flowers of mauve and blue. There was a pervasive organic smell in the air. A farmyard smell of livestock. The reek was similar to that of rural Scotland but different. Unique to this indigenous culture. We arrived at Krefeld where Ewen and Katie stayed. Ewen seemed relieved. All the tension and excitement drained out of him. I said to him, "Krefeld coming home Ewen," he replied, "Bloody right mate." This part of Germany had been destroyed in the war. All the architecture was post war and modern. They had a top floor apartment in a 3-storey block. It was fastidiously clean and ergonomic inside. The flat was done out in warm pastel shades. Ewen's abstract canvases were on the walls. There was a balcony leading out from the living room. I walked out onto the balcony and looked at a magnificent strong wintergreen tree. At its base was a stone filled cupola. I sat and looked at the superb tree, composing myself in silence. Ewen came out with a beer for me and sat down beside me. Ewen had taken off his jacket. The sun was starting to lower in the West. Everything seemed clean and ordered. More prevalent than the chaos that had rained down here not so long ago. Ewen said, "The story goes that that tree was planted after the war by Joseph Beuys. He was born near here and planted trees all over this surrounding countryside." The swallows were making high-pitched screaming sounds. They were weaving and diving in the eaves of the surrounding apartments where they nested. I said, "I know a little about Beuys, he declared all men are born artists. Some of his critics declared him as a kind of shamanistic figure who freely accessed the spiritual world, but did not present a message that was truly good, truly compassionate." Ewen was lighting his pipe, I noticed he inhaled on the tobacco slightly. He coaxed the meerschaum into life. He took a swig of his beer and said, "Did you know he was a Stuka pilot in the war Cal? His plane was shot down on the Russian Steppes, and the natives found him badly burnt and injured. They wrapped him in goose grease and felt; they saved his life. The dome of his skull had been fractured. It was reassembled with gold wire by Russian surgeons. That is why he wore, what became his personal trademark, his fedora. It was his experiences in the war that mythologized his character. In a sense he was elevated from being just a mere mortal into some kind of demigod."

I looked down at the cupola of the tree and sipped my beer. After a moment of reflection I asked Ewen if he admired Beuys. Ewen turned towards me and said, "I think that Beuys intended his art as part of an ongoing manifesto to effect environmental and social change. Locally his action was a gesture towards social renewal. For that he is universally respected by the local community."

The sun was setting; it was a bold red native sun. When I used the toilet I noticed the water was incredibly hard. Packed with mineral salts. The white powder smeared the washbasin like talcum powder. Katie was relaxing on the couch, watching cable TV. The British Rhine Army was close by. It was possible to get all the UK channels here. Out on the balcony Ewen had lit this great red candle. It was diamond shaped. The spent wax was spewing on to the table enthusiastically. It seemed to give off a brilliant, incandescent light. He was rolling a joint on the table. "Where did you get that from," I said. He replied, "I always keep a little in the house." It was nearly dark now, the candle lit up our faces like piratical masks. Sitting, hunched over the table in a dark medieval, Scottish conspiracy. All the surrounding houses seemed shut up and in darkness. Ewen said the German people liked to retreat within the body of their houses at night, turn in from the world. There was an intense feeling of foreboding, as if the streets were unsafe now. Ewen lit the joint and smoked with exaggerated sucking sounds. I drank my beer and looked at the traffic lights in the distance changing uniformly on an abandoned street. Ewen passed me the joint and I had a few hits on it. I asked him if Katie smoked, and he replied, "No never, but she tolerates it in me if it gives me some kind of artistic enlightenment." I replied to him that I thought all dope did was dull the senses.

"But it does create a certain abstract thought pattern," said Ewen. I said, "For some people dope is fatal. It can make you psychotic." I explained, "I don't think any mind altering drugs should be taken lightly, least of all cannabis. Ewen said, "If that is the way you feel you should stay away from it altogether; for me it is just something I use to relax, and I usually smoke on my own. I suppose I like to explore my paintings themes under the influence of dope." I said to him, holding up the joint, "There is a cache that surrounds drugs because they are illegal, that is why we want them, and why we crave them once we have become hooked." Ewen replied finally, he had finished his beer, "Yes I think for some people drugs are a crutch, in the same way alcohol can get a hold of you and wreck your life, but everyone is different. It is unfortunate that some people have addictive personalities, and others, the mainstream, do not." I said, "I think physical addiction is a genetic flaw in your make up. You are predisposed for example to having a psychotic reaction to cannabis." Ewen stood up and picked up the empty bottles, he said, "Who knows Cal lets go inside." He snuffed the candle. At once it was pitch black and still. I followed him inside, and closed the doors on the night. Katie had gone through to bed; Ewen said she was tired after the journey. She had pulled out the couch for me to sleep in. Ewen said he was going to bed also, if he was stoned it didn't show. I realised what a pampered life he led. Katie was the rock to which he was firmly attached all right. Perhaps it was artists preordained right to lead selfindulgent lives, blinkered from the mundane realities of everyday life. If that were so what sort of reflection on life was art? When I thought about it I couldn't think of one painter who could drive a car. They all had a woman to do it for them. I thought that perhaps that was it. What separated the also rans like Ewen who were more obsessed with the idea of being a famous artist than a painter of originality was that the latter had learnt more completely the lessons of having to stand still in life sometimes. They had been forced more completely to plumb the depths in order to achieve scaling the heights. But of course in this bent, corrupt world of fake celebrity, that was not altogether true either. It was not enough to just have originality anymore. Art was a business. The trick seemed to be to learn the rules of the game.

Ewen wished me goodnight, and disappeared quietly. I took my clothes off and lay down. My cough started up. I couldn't stop coughing. I didn't manage to sleep very well. At last though I was alone with my own thoughts in a dark quiet room. I thought about Selina, not as a person but the sexual ideal of her. I got an erection; I wanted to masturbate but the loneliness of the idea made my hard on wilt. I had a headache after smoking the dope. I had a fleeting dream of a surgeon scoring a halo round my shaved skull. The surgeon was smiling at me with gold fillings. He lifted the dome of my skull and peered in on my brain. I still had a dull headache the next day. We all got up early. I was filled with hope for the day ahead. I was putting my clothes on when Katie came in with coffee for me. I felt totally uninhibited; I had no sense of modesty about my near nakedness. "Sorry Cal," she blurted out, red faced, and disappeared. I drank the coffee with relish. It was strong German coffee and had a hint of corn flour in it. I scrambled for my cigarettes, to share that tandem experience. We had some breakfast in the kitchen. Ewen came through, he seemed a morning person, where as I took a few hours to wake up. Ewen had shorts and a summer shirt on. He said we could go on the bikes to the butcher some 8km away. He wanted to get some meat. I thought perhaps I had been wrong about him not doing any chores. Ewen said, "There is nothing I like more than the different butchers in different parts of the world. I could spend all day staring into a butcher's window. The cuts of veal, the links of sausage, the German bratwurst. The fresh blood draining from the board, the sheer juiciness of it all just makes you want to step inside and steep yourself in the smell of fresh meat." This obviously was his ceremonial chore, it all added up to his art. I replied feebly, feeling rather queasy, "I prefer the curve of the fishmonger for artistic stimulation Ewen." I went to the toilet and locked the door. I undid my trousers dropped my underwear then sat on the toilet seat. My bowels evacuated themselves almost immediately in a firm but fast motion. It was a German toilet; you could examine your shit sitting moist high up in the bowl until you flushed it away with water. I looked at my effort. I felt extremely proud of myself. Not only bodily but as importantly in my own mind. I flushed the toilet. It made me happy, being able to defecate in the host's home for the first time. I took my time and washed and shaved. The talc powder stuff was everywhere. I thought of the soft water of Scotland. I thought that in this sense my homeland was more sharply defined somehow than here. The outlines seemed blurred somehow.

I said I would like to get some cigarettes first. Katie asked me if I would manage myself without any German, I replied, "No problem." She gave me directions to the local shop. I walked leisurely to the shop. It was a beautiful dappled morning. I went into the shop and confidently pointed towards the cigarettes. I asked for them in English. The girl started laughing at me, speaking in German. She didn't speak English. I had insulted her without realising it. I said finally, "Marlboro red bitte," and she gave me the cigarettes and I paid. When she gave me the change, after I thanked her she seemed to have a look of benevolence in her face. I came out and returned to the flat. Ewen had the bicycles out for our ride to get the provisions. He had his sunglasses on, and we set off on the bikes. The roads were almost flat, excellent cycling conditions. We were at or about sea level here. I pedalled along, pumping the cog and wheel energetically in the warm sunshine. I had been an amateur cyclist in my teenage years and it was as if that confidence had returned to my legs. Ewen soon dropped off the pace. He was in a more mundane frame of mind, preferring to observe the landscape. A British army land rover passed us in the other direction. He was flying the Union Jack, and another camel logo flag flew below it. He waved to me and I waved back frenetically. There was a new road being built ahead and I waited there for Ewen. He finally caught up and stopped. Ewen reached in his pocket for a ventolin puffer. He inhaled deeply on the puffer. He suffered from asthma. He spluttered, "Slow down Cal you have the strength of ten men." I shouted back at him in a mock Cockney accent, "8th Army mate, ordnance datum," and made a horizontal motion with my hand. I said, "It all levels out." Ewen looked back at me, he seemed benign behind his glasses, like a humble man. I had a fresh windblown smell about me. The short competition was over. We cycled into Tonisvorst in pedestrian fashion. Two by two. Ewen went into the butcher to get his meat. On the opposite side of the square was a church. There was a massive stained glass frieze on the gable end. It was composed entirely of figures making different symbols using their hands and legs. It formed the code for some kind of communication. I was reminded of the choreography of pop singers. The difference was that our modern world searched for a meaning in symbolism where in fact there was often no meaning intended at all. Whereas this did have an intrinsic belief. It had all been jumbled up now, we had become so casual. Ewen came out of the butcher, he seemed happy with his purchase. We cycled off and Ewen said, "Lets go and get a beer, I know a good bar with a pool table."

When we went into the pub two guys were doing something to the table. Ewen asked them in German if we could get a game. The guy replied, "It is almost ready for you." Ewen said, "Let's get a beer and wait till the table is ready for us." We got beers and went and sat under this image of the world. The map was old and split into two spheres. The polar caps were coloured in white, and written in the North Pole were the words the "north frozen sonne," and in the South Pole the words the "south frozen soul." I looked at it for a few seconds. Ewen had lit a bowl of tobacco, and was staring straight ahead from behind the dark presence of his sunglasses. I indicated to the map on the wall and said to Ewen, "I wonder why God gave us two testicles, I mean we only need one to reproduce." Ewen chuckled and puffed rhythmically on his pipe stem. He said, "Maybe he was feeling generous, it is a back up system, if one is firing blanks you have the other ball to play with, it's a balance." I said, "Maybe it is symbolic like that map behind us, it represents the dualistic nature of our character. Maybe male reproduction is an admixture of our character, the whole in part, where the sum is greater than the two parts." The guy fixing the table indicated to Ewen that it was ready for us. Ewen said, "That is enough talking balls Cal lets play some." He rose and took some change from his pocket for the pool table.

The pool table was a big American table, baby blue baize. I wondered if it was a legacy from the war. I picked up the cue ball and rolled it down the table towards the bottom rail. It bounced and finished exactly on the break off line. There was a sharp intake of breath from behind the bar, and someone shouted in English, "Oh such touch." We had a few games of pool. I was no match for Ewen's competitive streak. It wasn't just a question of winning with Ewen, it was proving that he was better than me. Perhaps it masked a deep core of inadequacy within him. I wasn't disappointed with my mediocre, uninspired performance. I was more interested in observing Ewen. He didn't seem in the least bit triumphant; it was the competition that had spurred him on to victory. Ewen retreated once more behind the anonymity of his cop shades. We said goodbye and left on the bikes for Krefeld. On the way back we came across a large of group of elderly cyclists going in the opposite direction. The cyclist's faces seemed full of animation and enjoyment. I said to Ewen, "You wouldn't see that on Princes street in Edinburgh." Ewen took up the cudgel of perceived Scottish consciousness. He declared, "Scotland, wha's like us, not very many and they're all dead." I said back to Ewen, speeding up, "I don't think the Scots really gather in groups that much. Unless it is for the football or the pub. I mean even the idea of the family congregating in Scotland is becoming a fallacy these days." Ewen was speeding up to keep up with me, He replied, "Aye we are just groups of lonely individuals co-existing with one another, society is dead." I shot ahead of him and shouted back, "That is the blue print that has been stamped on our foetal consciousness, but we still keep trying to lever ourselves out of the dung heap." We were almost back into Krefeld. I slowed down and we cycled together back to the modern apartment. Everything was calm, still, and unperturbed. Katie had gone to work in Dusseldorf. We had some lunch. Ewen said he was going to do some work in the afternoon. The artist he was penning his ideas from at the moment was Francis Bacon. He had photographs of his work all over his small studio. Over lunch Ewen explained to me that one of the techniques he had copied from Bacon was gluing corduroy to wet painted canvas and literally "ripping it off" when the glue had dried. It left behind a distinctive tread mark on the canvas. Ewen said that at the moment he was exploring "crudity" in his work. I asked him what that meant. He said that his aim was to conceive an abstract canvas in such a way that a symbolic meaning could be critically interpreted as universal. But the means by which he conceived the canvas was all about making, "A mark on the canvas that could be perceived as crude or even childish." Ewen said that he was convinced the combination of a disciplined ideology and free artistic originality would bear fruit for him, in his next exhibition. Ewen said gloomily, "Art is criticised far more severely in Scotland than on the Continent." I said, "Surely that is a good thing, it distinguishes more readily between the chaff and the corn." I said, "Scotland is the school of hard knocks period Ewen." He seemed a little angry now, even bitter with the system. Ewen said, "I could spend my whole career in Scotland, and not achieve any recognition beyond a couple of shows a year, whereas here…" I decided to lighten the atmosphere. I said, "You could always become a pool hustler." Ewen started smiling and said, "I'll just work with the balls I've got Cal."

I left Ewen to his work and went out and sat on the balcony. The tree was shimmering silently in the sunshine. I wrote a card to my mother and brother in Scotland. Finally I wrote a letter to my Father in The Western Isles. I reflected on my family; we were a group of people now living silently apart from one another. Like trees uprooted from the forest floor where we had originally taken growth. Our proper place was grouped together. It was impossible to blame any one person for my parents' separation when I was a young child. Enough to say that it had done more damage than good. It had created a deep sense of unhappiness in me. This schism in my infant character was translated in my adult life into a sense of unfulfillment. I had a deep need within myself to be nurtured. In turn my Father had been unable to translate his own sense of unfulfillment into care when he had married my Mother. He had turned away from her and their children back into the cycle of depression and, the momentary, false joy that alcohol had provided him with all his life. Norman used alcohol to mask his feelings. His sobbing tears really were the tears of a sad clown. When my Parents split my Father resumed the journey of running away. The journey he had briefly suspended when he had first met my Mother. Except now Norman felt in total damnation. Stuck in purgatory, thinking he had done more harm than good to his own children. In a cerebral sense, in a physical sense he loathed himself. My own and Norman's pattern of communication had been set in stone all those years ago. All the tearful farewells where the emotions had welled up inside both of us, coming out like an endless flood. As a child I was powerless to stop my Father running away back abroad to some awful arid disciplined life, teaching the language of English. Children are powerless in a marital breakdown, they are the evidence. For my Father was a product of Empire. He was of that era and grouping, which spent all their working lives abroad. Empire may have set out to be benign in concept, but the evidence I lived with seemed more like invasive cancer. Now, we have increasingly retreated within the shores of this small parochial Nation. Norman returned only briefly, laden with whisky and gourmet food. Cutting a dashing, witty, romantic figure. He unwittingly or not had passed on his creative sensitivity of character to me. Of course the mask slipped. The person that was the centre of attention in the bar was not the exile also. What I saw of him when he was here was that Norman spent his entire life either drinking or recovering from the effects of drink. Masking his inner core that had been damaged when he had been a child in need of nourishment. This was continued now. My Father lived in one of the most isolated places in Britain. Norman was continuing to act out the tragedy of his life. Continuing to dole out cuts, not only self-inflicted wounds, but to the rest of his post nuclear family also. Norman was plagued with guilt and self-pity. He was a human being who doubted himself.

I still idolised the heroic proportions of my Father's life. I stood by him. I wondered if I would have stood by Norman if the roles were reversed. Or would I just dismiss him as a washout. I thought that in a sense I had in some ways painted myself into the same corner as my Father. I could be taciturn, arrogant, and verbose. I could also be charming and romantic. Like some kind of cardboard cutout? Ephemeral, fleeting and of no substance. I wanted to destroy the mould somehow. Shatter forever the notion that the sins of the Father should be visited upon the son. I wanted to be a real person that existed in normality for all the time. Not just opening hours.

I wrote the letter to my Father. It was brief; it was not inhabited with the social niceties and coded references that filled my correspondence with him. I was done with that. I wanted to tell the truth. I told him I had discovered a great Artist, here in Germany. Joseph Beuys, a man who had literally unearthed the seeds of truth, and honesty in his work. I wanted to appeal to my Father's soul. I craved some kind of recognition for the person I was. I wrote to him that if only Norman could see beyond our familiar relationship and try to get to get to know me, as a person things could be better. I wondered if it was too late for that. My Father had already turned inward into a foetal ball, away from the light. Norman's instinct was less strong than his vice like grasp of mortality. He was at the point of no return. The point of giving up. Yet I wanted to give us one more chance to become whole. The tree stood strong and immutable. I said to my father that he had never taken much enjoyment in his own life, rather he had endured. But now I wondered if Norman still had any interest left. I said it must be difficult to feel trapped by decrepitude. But we are all part of the domestic condition. I said Norman was paying the price for a full, careless life. Norman had reaped as he had sown. I finished the letter by saying that if Norman felt neglected it was only because of what he had chosen to neglect in himself. In a sense what I was saying was the opposite of what I wanted to say. That was, to recreate my lost childhood, and play with my Father, in his arms. To turn to Norman for paternal confidence and advice. To be cared for, and feel complete. To be part of a happy family. I could not find a way of saying that.

I re-read the letter, sealed the envelope and wrote my Father's name and address on the front. I felt with this letter I was taking a sharp rap on the door of the unknown. There is no going back. We exist moving forward in some kind of downward motion, attached to the Earth by gravitational pull. If life tends to pull us down we have to push against that force, and in some sense rise above ourselves. Much as our characters are pulled by the contradictions within us.

I heard the front door open and close, it was Katie back from her work. It abruptly brought to an end my solitary train of thought. I went inside, Ewen had finished painting for the day. The TV was switched on. It was MTV and bands of the 80s'. Steve Strange was singing, "Let's fade to grey." Ewen's soul was stripped bare; he looked worn out, as if the cares of the world were resting on his shoulders. I wanted to disentangle Ewen from his session of painting. I said, "We are the grey people Steve," to the TV. Ewen replied back abruptly. He said, "Speak for yourself Cal." Ewen's competitive edge was honed by two hours of meticulous work. He badly wanted recognition, I could see that. I wondered what if any difference it made. I said, "It only makes a difference, if you effect some change for human good Ewen." Steve Strange was still warbling on insipidly. I thought of Aberdeen, grey buildings, and grey sky. Reflected in grey personalities. Ewen seemed confident of his own preordained route. He said, "All my work is an attempt to colour back in what has been erased by life. To reclaim by creative experience what has been almost forgotten." Ewen was serious, that was what defined a lot of Art; as either subversive or mere whimsical pish. It was worrying that society was increasingly more duped by the triviality of the latter. That was the statement Steve Strange was making. Ewen seemed irritated. He abruptly flipped the channel. I had been picking at the scab that was his creative potential. The limit of his worth was what hung on the walls. Ewen was not content with that. His steady output was an evolvement of his life. He wanted to be somebody.

Katie came into the room, the expression on her face indicated she was not of the visionary frame of mind, at least not today. It was her stolid ness, her concrete view of the world. That which was in view, kept Ewen's feet on the ground. He may have concerned himself with the last detail, but she painted in the blocks of colour that held their life together. It was the most rotten cliché in the book, but they were a team. She came and sat down. She could sense there was a little tension in the air, but she chose to ignore that. Katie asked me if I wanted to go for a meal in town tonight and see something of the city. Before I could reply Ewen shouted back, "Yes," sulkily. His ego naturally placed him at the centre of attention. The place where I had once sat. I was more obliged now to sit on the periphery of a situation. I no longer wore my feathers so brightly. I was plumbing those depths of subconscious and conscious awareness. I thought I must appear thoughtful, diffident, and afraid of life itself sometimes. Head slightly tilted downwards, an apprehensive expression in my mouth and eyes. The deformation that happened at a stage of infant immediacy in my past.

The film on the TV was "Dr. Strangelove," it was the end of the movie, the end of the world. The bit where the USAF pilot of the plane straddles the bomb, and rides it towards nuclear holocaust. Endgame. He shouts, "Ride em' cowboy," waving his Stetson in the air and chomping a cigar in his mouth. I said to Katie that the nihilistic message of the film didn't seem to have as much impact now. It was as if we had almost forgotten the lessons that history had taught us. Ewen said, "We are more concerned with postponing the inevitability of our own existence these days." I replied, looking around, "That is not to say that a Bohemian existence is preferable to a world of Ikea furniture, because as every poor person knows it is not." Katie had been silent; she said thoughtfully, "Mankind finds a watered down version of the truth more palatable. All you can do is lead your life honestly, with care." Ewen piped in from behind the vision of his gold trimmed glasses, he added, "And intellectual discipline and fastidiousness." I said almost apologetically, "There is also compassion and tenderness, somewhere left in the world." Silence. We were no further on. I looked out at the balcony. It was beginning to get dark. The physical infrastructure, the line and level seemed ordered. As if somehow it was built with foresight, to endure. A light whispering wind was blowing in constantly. It felt ominous, in keeping with our nocturnal mood. Katie went to shut the doors. She said, "You get used to that wind here after a short while."

We took the car into Dusseldorf. There were still a few imposing buildings left standing that had survived the war. The city was a centre of banking in the country. We parked up and walked down a long broad pedestrianized avenue, into the heart of the city centre. The street was crowded; there was a positive atmosphere of youth and vitality. Regeneration. There was an organ grinder standing with his monkey, and a tin cup on a chain. He was Yiddish, and he had a long plaited beard. It was like being in pre-war Germany. This was contrasted at the end of the road. The stripped trunk of a tree was set into the pavement. A natural totem rising like some phallic object. A symbol of male virility. We stopped at an Art Gallery, and looked into the window. A metric surveying staff was cut up into zigzag sections, and set against a rural landscape of crops. It seemed to comment upon our need to impose nurture upon nature. I said to Ewen, "That is one of the reasons the Empire went phut, we measured things in feet and inches." I pointed to the staff and added, "Whereas metric measurement is closer to the truth, more simply universal." Ewen replied, "I suppose that is true, but imperial measurement has given Britain a certain identity if nothing else." Following ancient patterns of boundary instead of creating straight lines of existence. The installation piece seemed to comment on our deep need to civilize, and to cross ancient boundaries, in a way that was uniquely and specifically German. Efficient and well designed. Something completely different from the ugliness of the "Heath Robinson" compromise that seemed to define the British way. The idea was appealing to me; it seemed attractive and seduced me.

We stopped at a Chinese restaurant and sat at a table outside. We ordered drinks and looked at the menu. It was cheap. We had a meal and all pitched in for the bill. After dinner we went to a bar. It was the oldest pub in the city. It had ceramic murals on the wall depicting the traditional artisan crafts of skilled manual labour. The place had a dark ambience, an organ city. The other Patrons looked at us in faint amusement as we spoke in Scots dialect. We were a novelty. We got back to the apartment about 11pm. Katie said she was off to bed, she had to be up for work the next day. I wished her goodnight. Afterwards Ewen whispered to me, as if in some sort of conspiracy, he said, "Do you fancy a beer and a spliff before bed?" I said yes eagerly. That was it, I thought, I was weak and spineless. I had no self-control, I couldn't say no. I said to Ewen the only way I could avoid dope was by not being around it at all. I went out onto the balcony. The wind blew in constantly, lightly. As if it was cutting at something, calling to me. Ewen put some music on, "The Fall," and he came out and joined me with the beers. The music had a resonant, plaintive quality. The moment seemed important somehow. I strained to listen to every beat, every word. Ewen rolled up the joint. We both smoked it leisurely. I asked Ewen how our generation in Germany felt about the Holocaust. I was beginning to feel stoned. My mood was turning to the spirit, delving for the truth. The dope in some sense just refined the atmosphere. It made it more accessible. My frame of mind reacted to the cannabis in a way that reflected my physical and mental state. Ewen said, "Our generation don't see how they can fully bear the blame for something that happened before they were born." I blurted out, toking on the orange embers of the roach. "It is as if the sins of the Fathers are being perpetuated, visited on the sons and daughters." Ewen thought for a little, and he replied, "I think Germans should always feel responsible for the act of the Holocaust, but memory fades, the light flickers and goes out. We forget what suffering has taught us. That is the point in history when it could happen again." Ewen added finally, "War is not commemorated in any way in this country. Only the act of war, the crime, is marked here against time in a sense that forces people to cherish the liberty we British take for granted." Ewen said he was going to bed now. He wished me goodnight. I looked out at the Wintergreen tree, I wanted to go and stand under it. I waited until Ewen had retired and I walked through the apartment, everything was quiet and dark. Only the different colours of the micro lights of the TV and Hi-Fi broke the dark pitch. I opened and shut the front door quietly; I went and stood under the tree. I touched wood, as if it could pass on to me some good spirit. I could smell the purely healing amber, oozing from the pine. I stood still, held my hands in prayer and looked down at the cupola of stones. It was as if I could distinguish an individual face in each stone. A seething mass of condemned humanity. Drowning in their own lungs. Gasping for some air. Their faces full of anguish and fear. I closed my eyes, trying to black out the suffering. I willed myself into a meditative trance. I almost lost consciousness. I came to, there were tears in my eyes. I recomposed myself, and looked at the porch light in the apartment opposite. Theirs were unseen, unknown eyes observing my gesture from behind the dark sweep of the windows. The light dimmed to nothing and then shot back up in brightness again. It confirmed my strangeness, but not in context of the present tense of this place. More the human behaviour that had already been acted out in the past.

I went back upstairs from the street. It was totally silent and deserted. I pulled out the bed settee, and got into bed. The constancy of the positional glow of the micro lights reassured me, made me feel secure in myself. The light wind whispered under the balcony doors. I was woken frequently by my own coughing. It was a deep whooping cough that produced no substance. In the morning my back was sore from the effort. Katie came through with a large glass of orange juice for me. She said, "We heard you coughing, this will help." There was no mention of my strange behaviour. It felt like something best left unsaid. She opened the balcony doors and warm, therapeutic sunshine streamed in. The ominous tension of the night had receded. The mood was totally different. Where there was cloying darkness now there was joyous light.

That evening Ewen and Katie were attending a meeting of an Artists group which they were part of. They said I was welcome to come if I wanted. It was being held in a private room above a bar in the town. I just said I would wait for them in the bar. Ewen said, "Come on Cal give it a go," I demurred and said to him that, "If I were an artist being creative I would enjoy contributing to such a gathering of fellow creators, but since I am not, the idea of it makes me feel bad about not being creative. Therefore I avoid these situations like the plague. I don't want to be seen as some kind of dilettante, I am more honest with myself than that." Katie said,

"Quite right Cal just you stick with a fag and a pint meantime."
The Bar was empty except for two old guys in the corner. I decided
to break out a bit and have a wander around the town. I went into
the foyer of a small cinema; they were playing "Brighton Rock."
I started to chat to two young guys about the film. They spoke
perfect English. It was strange to think of English speaking films
being regarded as a foreign genre. They seemed almost excited to
be talking to me. I went and sat in a small park facing the street.
Lots of cars filled with young people drove past him at high speed,
moving in convoys. The same cars would reappear every few
minutes. I thought, "Boy racers of the world unite." They obviously
had nothing else to do; this was their leisure pursuit, in the hot
hatches. They stared at me as if I was some kind of foreign body.
I went back to the bar, the two old men had moved to the font.
They were deep in conversation. I ordered a glass of beer, which
was about the sum of my German. They say you can get by in a
foreign language if you can order a drink and tell someone you love
them in their own tongue.

It seemed like the best beer I had ever tasted. Served in a deep
crystal goblet, it was golden yellow, with a frothy blonde head. "Here
is to Bacchus," I murmured to myself. A middle-aged man came
into the bar; the barman seemed to pay him deference. The man
ordered a beer, and stood beside me. It is difficult to understand
people by mere physical gesture, without language gesture takes on
the meaning you want to give it. The man looked at me. I raised
my glass and said back to the man, "Cheers." The man asked me
my name and I introduced myself. We shook hands. I noticed he
was wearing an ornate fraternity-jeweled gold ring on his wedding
finger. He looked at me deadpan, serious and said in English, "You
enjoy the cult of the stranger in this town tonight." I thought so,
parochiality exists wherever you traverse, but at least here they
weren't content to let it ride. They showed a warm interest in you.
People liked to say what was on their mind. I replied back to him,
"I usually like to slip in unnoticed, without any fanfare, and then
slip back out again. I don't feel it is necessary always to make any

comment. I have come to enjoy my own company. I like to reflect with my drink and cigarette in unperturbed solitude." He bought me another drink without asking if I wanted one, he was above that, and he was calling the shots. He said, "My name is Thiessen, I live in a castle, they call me Teezy round here." The barman placed the drink in front of me. I felt willed on and drained the first. The two old men were more animated now; they had developed an interest in me. Thiessen said, "Those men are veterans of the war you know." I nodded in empathetic recognition. I showed them a matchbox. It was "Scottish Bluebell" matches. One of the veterans said to me in English, "It is good to know that some things never change." I said to Thiessen, "So we are all God's children at least we have established that truth." Thiessen made no remark to the comment. It was regional; it was specific to his own identity. The aristocratic air about him could not be pierced; perhaps it was lost in the translation. I thought it must be difficult to imagine in such a guttural language like German. To describe the transparency of emotional response. It was just that I reflected, imagination was beyond price like humour. It could not be bought and sold. It did not have any material value.

As soon as he had arrived Thiessen was gone. I turned away to the light then turned back to him, and all that was there was the froth sliding down an empty glass. Teezy didn't say goodbye, but he had left money on the bar for all the drinks. The barman came to gather the empty glasses and the money. He viewed me now with something approaching awe, as if I had entered into some kind of pantheon. Germans seemed to like specifics more than I did. The short sharp intensity of an experience. I wondered if there was a word in German for boredom, which in a sense is just a way of trying to define the length of time ahead of you. Perhaps the war had taught Germans to seize the moment because they realised there wasn't much time left.

Ewen and Katie came into the bar. The meeting was over. We all had a drink together; I was back on familiar linguistic territory. We went back to the apartment. It was getting late, starting to turn to dusk. On the walk back to the apartment I was quiet and thoughtful. I felt confused as if all the elastic that bound me together was coming unravelled. It was slightly unsettling to be thought of as a cult. I wanted to take one step back and examine the situation in a cold sober light. I could not, I felt propelled forward by the impetus of the moment, the context. I was filled with a mixture of excitement and anticipation.

Ewen was placatory, he said I should try and get some rest. It was dark now. There was thunder not far away. I went outside on the balcony to look. Suddenly a violent lightning storm began. It was rod lightning. It was as if the heavens were communicating their conscience. It began to rain, heavy steady rain, damping everything down. There was a fresh wet smell in the air of concrete, tar macadam, and earth. In the distance pelting rain flooded the neon street. The overhead traffic signal swung wildly in the wind like a lantern. We all went to bed; weather like this was like a depressive force. It placed you indoors. It forced you to retreat inside yourself to a warm safe place. I tried to sleep; I tried to stifle my cough that had returned like a foe. I lay writhing on the bed for hours. My mind was active with associated thoughts, which I couldn't switch off. I couldn't shut down. Finally it was 5am and it had stopped raining. There was just a constant dripping noise. The birds had started singing so dawn could not be far away. I thought the daily cycle we take for granted was one of daily survival if you were a wild creature. Each moment is precious, and that is why the birds sang. Rejoicing at the coming of the daylight. The end of the potential deadly danger of the night. I got up, used the toilet, and put the light on. I felt zealous, not burdened by the effects of sleep. I put my clothes on. I wanted to get some exercise, escape from the claustrophobic interior into an open exterior world. I felt as though I was searching for something, some sign that would inform the search for identity within myself. I felt primeval. I could hear Ewen snoring next door. Like Ewen's paintings I wanted to make my simple mark. I wanted to discover the answer to the question I had set in my own mind. What was the source of devotion within me?

I let myself out of the apartment quietly. I was not conscious that my behaviour was strange. I had to make a physical journey. I walked up the road and retraced a route back towards the Dutch border. It was still dark, there was no sign yet of dawn. I arrived at a large crossroads. At the side was a stone with the value 0 inscribed on it and a datum line. I took this to be an ordnance bench mark. I imagined it was the lowest point, I was at sea level. I couldn't go any lower. The benchmark by which I could judge myself. I laughed out loud at the notion. My mind was accentuated and as highly tuned as it could be, yet I physically couldn't go any lower down, without swimming in the sea. I walked on into the countryside unaware that I was leaving the village behind. I sang to myself, "Are you high or are you low," to dispel my fear of the dark. There was a shrine to the Virgin Mary at the roadside. It was an icon, and was protected by vertical steel bars. I looked in on it, there were fresh flowers. I suddenly thought of Selina, I imagined that the look of love is as close as we can get to a religious experience. I seemed to have come a long way in what were a few days. I marched on rapidly. There was a crack of sunlight appearing in the East. Defining the spiny fanning form of the trees. I came to a stone track veering off West into a wood. I stopped and decided to take it. I couldn't stop and turn back. I had to go on, I had no time to waste on indecision.

Dawn had risen to a rosy glow. Ahead of me a railway track bisected the path diagonally. There was a signal box above the track. Everything seemed abandoned and quiet. I felt as though I had been here before, the premonition of a dream. The rails gleamed blue in the strengthening light. I walked ahead further into the wood. The air had an organic smell, it was pervasive. The trees were beech, their branches and foliage fanning out either side of the metallic path. Their shiny smooth bark was grey like the hide of an elephant. I came to a bridge and crossed it; a small burn was flowing underneath. The route of the path ran parallel to the burn. To my left the wooded area cleared, replaced with corn growing in huge flat fields. Every 100m or so was a manhole on the other side of the burn. There was a sign saying, "Fern Gas Danger," at each manhole. The dawn had now become ubiquitous, daylight. The sky was painting itself in blue. I came to another bridge across the burn. Painted on the abutment of the bridge was an arrow pointing downwards with a question mark above it. All that was lying there was an empty cigarette packet. I picked it up as if it contained the answer to the question I had set myself. In a sense it did. I opened it; inside it was crawling with centipedes. Writhing with hundreds of legs, sharp pincers, and shiny orange bodies. I dropped the packet in fear. I was horrified at the strangeness of nature. I was terrified of what was spilling out of me. I went and sat under a tree on the other side of the bridge. I felt paranoid; I was convinced that someone was watching me. I looked around there was no one there. I could hear the sound of a car engine. I stood up and looked in the direction of the noise. A small van was approaching from the West. Its wheels were throwing up dust into the air. The van stopped an older man with glasses was driving. He didn't speak any English but beckoned me to get in. I accepted the lift and got in. The van was stacked with crates of beer. Within five minutes we were on the public highway. The man was talking all the time in German.

We stopped at a diner with an American car; a Cadillac stuck on its roof. It seemed like some kind of sculpture. There was a small town ahead. The man dropped me here. This was where he wanted to let me off. I got out thanked him for the lift, and the man drove off. I walked through the streets of the small town. The morning was beginning to come alive. A newspaper vendor was opening his shop, and a café/bar was open. Judging from the laughter coming from the dark recesses it had been open all night. I came to a central green. On one side was a nightclub, The Apollo 13. On the other was a hotel. What I would have given to pass an Amex card and slip between the clean sheets of a hotel bedroom with some coffee and a croissant, followed by a strong toasted tobacco cigarette. The mere thought of it, decadent paid for luxury. Suddenly I was overcome with exhaustion. I sat on a bench and closed my eyes. I fell into a disturbed sleep. I could hear voices in my head whispering in

German. I opened my eyes and looked around there was no one there. I closed my eyes again and slept a deep recuperative sleep. I was woken by the noise of banging, close at hand. I looked to my right, in the direction of the noise. It was a breakfast vendor taking down his shutters. I had no money, I was hungry and thirsty. We have come to take the enabling factor of cash for granted until we have none. I cleared the sleep from my mental and physical state. I pushed my hands through my hair and felt the grizzle on my chin. In front of me was a statue of Christ on the cross. He was looking over me, taking pity on my confused soul, but he couldn't do anything to feed the hunger in my belly. I wondered what Faith translated into our secular world meant if you had nothing and you were hungry. You can't feed off hope, you need substance.

I rose to go, I could only place my faith squarely behind myself. I wanted to find my way back to Krefeld. I thought of all those thousands of miles I had driven with Eva in the USA, and the signs, "gas, food, lodgings" would repeat themselves seductively. That was all I wanted now. I was deflated; my search for truth had ended in disappointment. I walked to the edge of town and came to a signpost. I didn't see the sign for Krefeld. I thought about it instinctively, rationally, the direction I had come from. My sense of direction was good. I took the road heading South East. Within a couple of miles of walking I was on a busy highway. The road was thronging with cars moving at high speed. I was the only pedestrian on the road. It made me feel vulnerable and stigmatized. I just walked on looking and thinking ahead. I came to another small town, and I came to a road junction. There was a signpost for Krefeld, 5km. I felt relieved inside my heart; I was on the right track now.

I passed a graveyard; it was dark, foreboding and overgrown. It must have been old, dating to the Great War. Most of the gravestones were in the shape of the German cross. I heard a dog barking on the other side of the road. It was a huge bullmastiff, the sort of dog that placed a pathological fear in me. It could easily have vaulted the wall and mauled me within an inch of my life, but it was trained not to. It was trained to defend its master's property. I scuttled on quickly, with the feeling that there was something at my back. The experience soon receded to memory. I saw a town ahead, it was familiar, and it was Krefeld. My feet felt like corncobs, I was hot and sweaty. I had marched back. I got into town and made my way to the apartment. I looked at my watch, it was past noon.

Ewen let me in. He was on his own, doing some painting. He was producing his own version of the truth. There was a sharp contrast between our two states. He was relaxed, almost laid back. I was hot and agitated. Ewen said, "We were worried sick about you, we came through in the morning and you had vanished." I was emotional; I described the route I had taken to him. Ewen got out the map and roughly traced the journey. I had walked in a complete circle, almost 30km. I had completed a cycle, physically and as I was to come to realise it, mentally too. I took my shirt, shoes and socks off and lay on the couch. I was exhausted. Ewen made me some food and coffee. I sucked on a cigarette greedily. Ewen came through with the food. He said, "That was a very courageous thing you did today to undertake that journey." He reflected for a moment and said, "It is the sort of physical statement that true art should be founded upon." I wolfed down the food, my appetite had returned. My spirits buoyed. I replied to him that, "I don't know if it was courageous or not but my journey was fruitless, I didn't find what I was looking for." Ewen was cleaning his glasses; he looked totally different without them. Almost vulnerable and afraid without his defense against the world. He said, "We are all human Cal, as you know there isn't always a pot of gold at the end of the rainbow, but you were searching for something, with all the inbuilt flaws of the Human condition, and most importantly you returned safely." I should have listened to him then, reached into myself for some insight, stability. But I could not. As it was I just wanted to curl up on the settee. Besides I was going back to Aberdeen the next day. The experiences I had had would perhaps one day serve to inform my life in some way. For the moment I was keen to move onto the next stone crossing the infinitely wide river of life.

I fell asleep; I must have slept for 5 or 6 hours. It acted like a soothing balm on my mind and body. I woke about 7pm. There was a programme on TV about Goethe. Katie was watching it avidly, she had her glasses on. I said to her I had read one of his books, "Elective Affinities." She asked me what it was about. I was still curled on the couch, semi naked in abandonment. I said, "A modern interpretation would read it as a tale about wife swapping where all the spirit and sexuality gets mixed up." I added, "What starts out as on the physical plain, becomes bound up with a spiritual nether world, the mind." Ewen came in from the balcony. He said, "Sounds like a typical modern parable Cal." He had a joint going and he handed it to me. I smoked the rest of the joint and it hit me, feeling stoned, feeling strange again. Acute paranoia, the feeling that everyone is watching you. A feeling of intense alertness, as if the cannabis has the opposite effect on me than anyone else. I should be laid back and soporific but I was not. I went to get a shower and have a shave. I could taste the salt on my skin in the shower. I got dried and dressed and came out of the shower. Ewen had joined Katie in front of the TV. Ewen said, "Tonight we will go to the local bars, for your last night." My episode this morning was forgotten about now, not mentioned. Society finds it far more convenient to brush these distressing incidents under the carpet. To maintain the decorum, until something happens that you cannot be held responsible for. Only punished.

We went into a pub in town about 8pm. The place had an urban working class, beat up feel to it. The only thing that made the place stand out was the quality of the beer. Everyone spoke exclusively in German. There was a waitress service. Ewen said he had never been in here before. The barmaid took our order and then came over with the drinks. Suddenly the drinks spilt all over us. A glass smashed on the table angrily. It was as if she had done it on purpose because we were British. The barmaid had a mischievous gleam in her eye. She went to get a cloth and bucket. We agreed that she had done it on purpose. I said, "It is incredible how parochial insularity seems to be the spirit of our times. If you aren't part of the culture you don't belong here somehow. It doesn't embrace an outsider's trade. It is almost hostile." Ewen replied, "That sort of inward looking narrow mindedness is dangerous. It creates a false sense of superiority amongst the population. There are some forms of aggression that may or may not be universal. But they are specific to regional culture." Katie said, "Like here now you mean." I had a small shard of glass stuck in my hand. When the barmaid came back to clean up, I pulled the glass from my hand symbolically. It was my turn to be malevolent, and react to the situation. I said to the waitress, "Crystallnacht eh." She seemed to shrink visibly. Ewen looked at me humorously and said, "Come on let's get the fuck out of here." We rose and made a quick exit, the "Ladies from Hell." The pattern for the evening had been established.

We went along the road to another bar. The place was filled with tropical plants and fake palm trees. It looked like a set out of Casablanca. We went and got a drink and sat down under the fake palm trees. The leaves were dripping with cigarette tar. It soon filled up with "The Africa Corps." Young German guys who seemed drunk and boisterous. The young men came together and gathered. They started singing drinking songs. The atmosphere became charged, almost hostile. And there we were a small group of the 8th army, incognito, deep behind enemy lines. I said to Ewen and Katie, "Hitler would have been proud of their patriotic nationalism." We drank our drinks and decided it would be wise to leave. Safety in numbers. Fear is the key. Walking back along the road now in the quiet dark that I had now become accustomed to I said to Ewen and Katie, "Nowadays the outward mass manifestation of trouble is at the last gathering of the population, football. It shows that humanity still has a primordial need for war." Ewen had lit his pipe he seemed calm, puffing peacefully. He said, "There is something very chilling about a sense of superiority coupled with the physical group, ultimately the message is oblivion." Katie looked at the ground ahead of her as she walked home holding Ewen's arm tightly. I asked her if she was okay. She said, "I was just dispirited with the atmosphere of the pubs. The reason that brought us here was the urban melt down in Scottish society, but that seems to be ubiquitous just now. There seems to be bad vibrations wherever you go in the world."

We got into the apartment. Katie said she was going to bed. She wished me a good trip home. We embraced briefly, with warmth. She looked into my eyes and said intuitively, "You look after yourself Cal." It made me feel apprehensive about the future, not reassured. Katie went off to her bed. Ewen brought me a bottle of beer, and we sat on the couch. I took a long pull on the pilsner lager. It was chilled. I said to Ewen, "Sometimes civilization seemed like a thin veneer, papering over man's instincts." Ewen replied, "As they say in Scotland you can take the boy out of the scheme, but you can't always take the scheme out of the boy." I said, "There's good bad and plain indifference wherever you go in the world. You just hope that you can embrace goodness if it comes your way." Ewen said, "If all people are artists you have to learn to recognize this human potential and understand there is no substitute for daily experience." I was reflective, I said, "I have almost sacrificed everything recently including my health. I have reached the point where all I can turn to is the love of my family. Even that can fail ultimately." Ewen had reached the fag end of his drink. He said, "Cal, just be thankful that you have a family to turn to." I was silenced; it had been a funny holiday. I felt fine tonight, rational and composed. I had been spinning up and down like a yo-yo. Everything was quiet, there was nothing left to say. Ewen locked the doors, and we both withdrew into ourselves, finishing our drinks in silence. Finally Ewen said he was going to bed. Alone now my cough started up again, a constant fiery tickle. I lay curled on the couch; I couldn't summon the effort to pull out the settee. It was as if I was broken now. All the years of winter days, all the years of cold water flats. All the years of making ends meet. All the years of toiling in life instead of enjoying myself had left me unable to look after myself anymore. I thought I had spent my entire life giving so that when something was given to me back I took it readily. I was born with a metal spoon in my mouth. Although I didn't realise that this alloy had created in me a unique genetic inheritance. It was just that material and spiritual inheritance hadn't gelled in my own existence. I had been cheated somehow, way back, way down the line. I could feel weak and vulnerable now, it was only human. I turned off the lights, pulled off my boots and pulled a blanket over myself, and dug myself into the recesses of the couch. Trying to escape, trying to come in from the country. Sleep laid her gentle caress around me.

I woke early the next day. I heard Katie leaving for work. I had a racking cough. I got up and packed my bag. The train to Amsterdam was at 10am. I had some coffee with Ewen. There didn't seem to be much now to say, there was a distance between us. I thought perhaps the only reason Ewen was my friend was because just occasionally Cal outshone Ewen the Artist. Perhaps Ewen liked to bask in the reflection of that light, whoever it may be. Ewen walked with me to the Railway Station. It was a fast non-stop service. There was a stall selling flowers, I bought some roses for my mother, who would be waiting for me in Aberdeen. I said goodbye to Ewen, we embraced in a manly fashion. Ewen had a bovine odour about him. I thought Ewen didn't show any warmth embracing. It was just another perfunctory act in his painter's repertoire. An empty ceremony. Elaine's recent words to me came to my mind. That Scotsmen were about the most repressed sexual beings in the Universe. The perfect recipe for homophobia. At least in that regard I was liberated. I had had an unusual upbringing if nothing else. One way or another I had encountered just about every nationality on Earth in my short life. This coupled with imagination also led to problems in my life in Scotland. The expressive Scots of my generation had either left or made a name for themselves, and had risen above my social standing. I did not encounter much compassion from this latter group who had stayed. I had become increasingly stranded. Like here on an empty railway station platform. Waiting for a vehicle to take me somewhere else. But as I knew myself I had to carry my own baggage also. Maybe it was sentiment that I possessed. It was in me not of me. I was born that way. I was thinking about this and I suddenly said to Ewen, "It is funny how reason has become more important than emotional response these days." Ewen piped back immediately, almost gleefully, "It is a grey utilitarian world we live in." I thought that Ewen's reasoning was that as a result he the painter would stand out, shine somehow. I lit a fag; the train would be here soon. I said, "All that I'm saying is that people like me have been left behind, our spirit is of another simpler, less cynical age." Ewen looked at his watch, he said, "Your train will be here soon." I felt gloomy almost in a panic. I said, "I feel like I am about to fall through a net. Like one of those grotesque ugly prehistoric fish on the seabed. I have almost become one of the dispossessed, the lonely, the unfulfilled." Ewen just looked at me from behind the anonymity of his glasses. He said to me, patting me on the back as if I was his child, "As the song goes everybody hurts, don't be sour with life." It was the closest Ewen could come to compassion. His linguistic talent was for expressing himself in a rhetorical empty way. He was unable to understand sympathetically my anguish.

That was the third facet of my character that caused me problems. In addition to sentiment and inward imagination I was filled with anger. Often like now this anger was legitimate. I didn't like to be thought of as sour. At other times my anger would pour out of me like black pitch. I would destroy things and be self-destructive but my essential honesty as a character had enabled me to start again. Now everything seemed futile, everything seemed without hope. The train snaked into the platform. I got on the train with my bag. I shook Ewen's hand through the open window. I asked him, "Do you think you will return to Scotland?" Ewen said cynically, "The shell suits are sitting pressed in the wardrobe." I laughed bitterly. I wouldn't forget Ewen's comment about being sour. It confirmed what I thought of him.

I said finally, "There is an inevitability about returning to Scotland if you were born there. There is a pull that takes you home, it is greater than the reasons that led you to leave." On that note the train moved off with a sudden jolt, and Ewen was left with a quizzical look on his face. For once he was unable to reply. I waved and went in and found myself a seat.

Public transportation on the continent was clean, modern, efficient and reliable. It was a smooth transition to getting aboard the flight to Dyce in Aberdeen. I was strapped in my seat with my roses stowed above me. Soon we were circling the city preparing to land. I looked out of the window. I recognised the familiar plain quality of the place. Yet I still felt sentimental. It was all I could base the idea of home upon. The memory of my own childhood tugged at my heart every time I returned here. The local scene I reflected as the plane touched down with a hard bump. Some Aberdonians viewed me as an outsider. I had not been born here; I was not one of them. This antagonism of my character hurt me. I had encountered this insularity throughout the North East of Scotland. Warmth of character was not a universal quality here. My Mother Lorna Moone was waiting for me at the arrivals gate.

She was not unlike me, in that she was unusual. Sensitive, gifted and naturally creative. She was not enmeshed by the rigour of the North East. She was of the place but not in it. She possessed innate warmth of character that had led many people to be attracted to her. It was hard to place her roots in any one place. She was a pearl amongst a handful of hard grit. She could be my sternest defender and also my fiercest critic. She was a teacher. Children seemed to place their trust in her. She gave freely of her time and creative confidence. In turn she believed that human potential was not just confined to an elite. She was a beautiful woman for this reason. There was simplicity and a complexity about her. She would greet like a small child when a cherished animal came to the end of its own life. She could loathe another human being pitilessly. Always though she would find it in her heart for forgiveness. Life was a kind of poetic symmetry to her, where if possible it should be experienced in the round and not endured alone. This latter condition she found utterly heartbreaking. Lorna Moone had encountered many different people in her life. She could make a home anywhere. She took her innate sense of beauty with her. I saw her smiling honestly at me.

I thrust the roses into Lorna's pointed artistic hands, I said, "Mum, these are for you." She looked back at me long and silently.

People everywhere were rushing to get away from the Airport into the city. She could tell that my brusqueness was masking something within me. How I was feeling inside. I said I wanted to get back to the flat. She had walked upon broken glass many times before. This experience was not unique to her relationship with her son. We walked out to the car. Girls were at the foyer selling things. If it wasn't credit cards, it was mobile phones. If it wasn't deregulated power and gas deals it was bogus scratch cards. Things that weren't essential. The material despair that had led our lives to becoming increasingly fraught and stressful. My Mother and I walked on past the heavily made up vendors. I remarked to her casually that, "The vendors are the greatest victims of the whole process." I pointed and said, "Death of a salesman." Lorna was smelling her roses. Lorna was oblivious to the salespeople. She had a love of nature but her father James had protected her from the cruel necessity of country life. Just then the shrill tone of a mobile phone rang, the tune of "Colonel Bogie", under the harsh artificial light, within the metallic interior of the terminal. It kept on ringing. Both Lorna and I found it the most intrusive repellent noise in the world. Finally we escaped through the rotating door into the fresh air. The vibe though seemed flat. A grey sea haar hung in the atmosphere. We got into her old car. It was a Morris Minor, and I felt like a character from Noddy whenever I rode in it. Lorna asked me, now that we were on our way, "Did you enjoy your holiday darling?" She was hunched slightly forward. It was her natural driving position. I had wound down the window. I said, "I don't feel altogether well. I feel extremely depressed. I felt strange when I was in Germany, as if there were unknown forces acting over me. I don't think I am quite myself." I was at the lowest point, the nadir of what my emotions held in store for me. I had, in the past few years been skinned and gutted and hung out in a public place to dry. I was stripped bare of any protection from the world. My reservoir of hope was now almost empty. Lorna Moone realised this. That it was better to do as I asked. She was not in the habit of poking a stick into an open wound, particularly not now.

We got to my flat; Lorna said she would phone me tonight. She wasn't quite sure where to proceed from here. This was new territory. I kissed her and took my bag from the car. We said goodbye. I went upstairs to my flat and locked the door. I didn't check my mail or even my phone messages. I simply turned the heating on, stripped to my underwear and took to my bed.

CHAPTER THREE

A s I sat in the waiting room there was a whistling noise from a tap. It was as if someone had forgotten to fully turn off the faucet. I was in the waiting room at the Mental Hospital waiting to see the Clinical Psychiatrist. The constant fluid noise was boring into my skull like a drill. Suddenly the noise stopped and the Doctor beckoned me in. His name was Wells. He shook my hand and I crossed the threshold of his surgery. I was crossing the threshold into a completely new world. Of often stigmatised misunderstanding, of sometimes little compassion. The world of the mind. The terrifying spectre of mental distress. The unwanted, the fetid. The dark side of the moon. I was taking the first steps into an altogether different phase of my life. The clinical chromium scrubbed clean world of rest and palliative care. The perceived imagination of lunacy in parts of the hospital that were abandoned. The reality of madness in all its physical and mental manifestations on the ward. The echoing of footsteps. Evaluate, hospitalise, diagnose, stabilise, then evacuate back out into the world, and move on to the next patient, the previous one is now an integral part of the pattern. Caught in the spiders web, terrified of a relapse back into madness, or acutely, totally unaware of anything wrong at all. It was a universal thing, the unknown element of human behaviour that was restrained with medication. The human spirit that was snapped like a rod of cane. I imagined it was a regional thing, mental illness, that it was caused by our inbred reckless identity. This had created a genetic flaw. Was I wrong? That is why the birds sang no longer at Auschwitz.

The Doctor said to me, "You were referred to me by your GP. You have been depressed by a particular set of circumstances, and now you are confused as if you cannot cope and do not understand what is happening to you." He went on in a quiet sympathetic voice; he said, "Can you describe to me the feelings you are having just now, honestly Cal?" It was as if the tap inside me was turned on in a gush. I was anxious to unburden myself. I thought my condition was like World War 1. It would all be over by Christmas. I gathered my thoughts; I looked at the closely cropped red nylon carpet. The soft bright blue plastic seats, at the dictionary of pharmacopoeia that sat on the desk. It listed all the different medications. Which in addition to listing the efficacy of each drug for a specific condition also listed the harmful side effects. I was still oblivious to all of this-that there was a nasty kick back to pay for having become mentally unwell. Some drugs were subtler than others. I looked in Dr. Well's face. He was younger than me. It was difficult for me to compromise in this respect alone. I had always until now associated medicine and wisdom with a greater age than my own. This was part of me growing older. I would increasingly have to accept the greater experience of professional people younger than myself. I didn't feel there was much left to look up to. The Doctor was dressed expensively. Pale blue shirt, silk tie, Rolex watch ticking away in perpetuity. It was a Friday midafternoon. It was the time when I in the past had looked forward to Friday night. But now I felt a void inside myself, as if the structure of friends and partner had been removed from my life. I was acutely aware of this for the first time. It made me feel uneasy. I was faced with myself. I inadvertently squidged in the blue plastic seat, I made a farting sound. I started giggling like a child standing in front of the headmaster in his office who is staring out of his window simultaneously giving a parable on morality before he administers corporal punishment. It was still funny for me; the punishment of more than just a long weekend in the heartbreak hotel was still to follow on. Dr. Wells noted my laughing. He was watching me closely for signs. It was all part of his evaluation of me. I was on parade.

The doctor repeated himself, beckoning me on, "Describe to me how you are feeling Cal." I began. I said, "I feel that I am being watched as if someone is filming and taking note of my every action. Everyone in the street seems to be laughing at me. I feel acutely stigmatised and paranoid. It makes me feel frightened and unsafe." Dr. Wells had a concerned look now in his face. He took meticulous notes with a thin gold propelling pen. I looked out of the window in a moment of self-reflective lucidity. Like my mood, the trees were changing to autumn colours. Summer was over. Winter was on its way.

I went on solemnly. I said, "My mood alternates between bouts of depression and these other unknown feelings when I have no sense of self control, when I feel uninhibited." Wells asked me, "Do you ever have suicidal thoughts Cal?" I looked at the box of Kleenex propped on the table. I then looked into the doctor's calm collected face and replied, "I have never consciously harmed myself, but yes when I am at the bottom of the dark pit of depression I can see no future. At that point there is not a day goes by when I do not think about taking my own life." The Doctor looked out of the window for a moment in repose. Weighing up what I had said about myself. He said, still looking out the window, "Do you have feelings of elation, when literally you feel on top of the world, are you aware that this is strange or unusual." I replied, "Yes, when I feel elated everything's moves at great speed, I have no insight into myself. I am filled with humour, but also extremely irritable. I feel as though I am someone of superior intellect that defies conventional wisdom. I have an angle on everything; I could talk on for hours. My consumption is increased for both alcohol and cannabis. I get messages from the TV, it is speaking to me personally." Wells had a slight look of alarm in his face. He had seen these symptoms many times before. It was his job to administer the lint and bandages. To stem the flow and try to heal the wound. His job was not just in the patient's interests but also primarily to protect society. He asked me if I ever had feelings of physical aggression. Did I want to harm someone else? I thought about it for a few moments; my feelings of aggression were born out of frustration. The slowness of everyone else, their inefficiency, their crudeness. I replied. I said, "I do not think for all the education, all the civilisation I may or may not have acquired, that as a Scotsman I have never had feelings of aggression towards another person. This roughness, the specific hardedged brutality is common to some extent to the whole of Scotland. I react to this as much as the next person, I contain the same reservoir of black pitch, the same anger."

Dr. Wells crossed his legs; he was wearing white towlon socks. It kind of spoiled his upwardly mobile image. He was taking notes silently. I went on, "Somehow though I don't think that Scottish culture, this parochial roughness has ever been an essential part of my character. Rather it feels as though it has been imposed upon me in some sense. I do not have a sense of belonging wherever I have lived in Scotland." The Doctor looked up, what I had said forced him to reflect on his own identity in this small land. However he could not betray his emotions, how he felt to his patient. He directed his gaze straight at me and said compassionately, "Would you be prepared to come in here for a few days so we can assess properly your state of health?" The way the doctor said it seemed like an invitation to something truly good and wonderful. The idea appealed to my racing mind. The voice inside me told me I had to come down, I had to come down. I was tired, I was exhausted. I couldn't carry on. I was sensitive to the drugs, I was sensitive to the medication, and my piercing blue eyes would always squint at the light. My physical constitution was inherent and strong, but my nervous framework was bare and exposed to the maelstrom of life's forces. I was crumbling from the inside out; my sense of self-preservation was destroyed from the outside in. I blurted out "Yes" to the Doctor's request. In my eager childlike state I was anxious to get to the root of this problem of mine. This minor inconvenience to my health, that I thought could be swatted like a fly. I was in for the long haul; the hard road I was embarked upon would often lead me towards the "twa corbies" sitting on the fence. They would often swoop and dive towards me, but I never quite became enveloped by their black sleek wings. That road was the crow road. I never quite lost sight of that difference, between dark and light.

The doctor said to go home and pack a bag and come back to his office. The territory was still virgin. There was still an element of trust in our budding patient/doctor relationship. I was prepared to place my faith squarely behind the Doctor. Until that faith would be broken by confusion between good and evil. It wasn't usually individual evil that permeated places like this. It was the notion that society in some sense punished you. Mammon was more concerned with the status quo of society than individual recovery. I made my way out of the benign natural tree laden grounds. The dry autumnal leaves rustled in the stiff easterly wind that was a forewarning of the cold brutal winter that was to follow on soon. I thought about the events that had led up to this point. I brooded silently as I trudged home alone late on a Friday afternoon, to my alone flat under the leaden sky, reflected in the grey slabs of tenements, occasionally looking into the faces of passers by for some creature warmth, some imagination. The ethos here was simple, there was a time to be born, there was a time to grow, then live, and now as I felt chilled and depressed, a time to die. Things at work were a disaster. I had taken to drinking every night. In a lucid sense I had realised the futility of my meaningless job, in this meaningless recession. I took to listening to the TV and radio, to try and blot out the loneliness of my life. I quickly came to realise that the anodyne, androgynous picture the BBC presents of this country was slanted in favour of just maintaining the status quo. They were an organ of the state. An "Enid Blyton" view of the world. The perceived reality of journalism was the output of middle-income people, for middle-income middle class people. The truth was no longer universally true. I imagined that people who worked in the media were most likely the least informed members of society about what was really going down. It was a curious, pernicious contradiction. Freedom was a metaphor for being stuck at the terminus unless you had the enabling factor of money. And if you did it was a version of freedom that chooses to ignore those who don't, at our peril collectively.

I was bumping along the bottom, groping my way in the darkness. I was signed off work. I had been in front of the area manager. I had just sat there and looked at him without any sense of motivation or even enthusiasm. I was cunning though. The man let off his spiel about me smelling of drink, how I was impossible to be around, and finally how my work had suffered. I said nothing, the ethos of employer dictating to employee did not now mean much to me. I had a healthy disrespect for authority. Until now I had bent the stick as far as I could without breaking it. But now I was broken myself. Without my health I was nothing. I reflected silently. I wondered how many people spent their lives doing jobs they did not enjoy. I wondered what it was like to be paid to do something you loved. Perhaps that was what lay at the root of my illness. I was at the "fin de siecle" of one stage of my life and one way or another thing would never be the same for me again.

I had tried to contact Selina. In the past month I had been caught up in the scummy parties and nightclub scene that I liked in a sense. I was like my father Norman in that way. We both liked to partake of the urban, social vernacular. We were both informed of the scene. At the end of the day intellect and sensitivity marked you out for something better. Or so the theory goes. Perhaps I was less condescending than my father, although I could mark my own territory if push came to shove. I realised something about myself in that month of steady descent. I had a serious drink problem. I wasn't so much an alcoholic as a dipsomaniac. I would spend my time alone drinking. It was the only escape I could imagine for myself. Into the place within, inhabited by my imagination. In the absence of love, like my father, in the absence of worthy companionship, I turned to drink. I was at this party all night. Two young guys at the party had been jacking up smack in the toilet. I burst in on them and caught them injecting. I had thought of Selina, what she had said, and became morally superior. I wouldn't have normally reacted, but I was irritable. I became verbally angry with the guys, they were teenagers. One of them burst into tears, (as if he didn't know he was killing himself). He didn't need to be reminded. I didn't realise then that skag had become the social convention amongst teenagers in the North East, along with the hot hatch, the sub-woofer and ecstasy shite music. The question remained though in my head as the boy sobbed pitifully, was there something more? Is there something out there? Scotland these days, a wrap of skag is cheaper than a packet of "Regal" king size. It is a cheap throwaway society; the temples seem littered and bare. No one cared about us, on the scrap heap, programmed to fail at birth.

On the one hand there is this view. It is contradicted in the North East by the fact that the majority earn good incomes, enjoy stable employment. Aberdeen has always been a rich city, agriculture, fishing, paper, spinning, and shipbuilding. The city had been founded on these staple industries. The largest man-made hole in Europe had been quarried to build the luminescent granite infrastructure of the city. On the back of the rich natural resources that were reaped from the sea and the land. Then had come the oil, "Welcome to the pork and beans capital of Europe," it might as well proclaim. The only place in the world where you are turned away as a potential trouble maker from a Country and Western night because you are wearing cowboy boots and jeans. And relentlessly, omnisciently the herring gulls screech on. A mocking, hooting, chorus from behind cold light yellow imperious eyes. The sense of utilitarianism that was pervasive in the North East had not come easily. The elements and the strict sense of discipline in the workplace was etched into the faces of Aberdonians. There is an honesty about Aberdeen, yet a strangeness too. A distinct point of view that lies behind quietness. An inward spirit that is most apparent in the male character. This thoughtful sometimes-vacant state is common to some extent to all Scots people. Maybe we feel bad about ourselves; increasingly we crave an original, individual identity but collectively struggle to find a voice. A way of expressing ourselves that is not destructive. We have forgotten the place where we first broke the earth and water sprang forth. Most decline in Scottish society is as a result of this puzzle. Because that is the final truth of utilitarianism, it has been constructed as a result of an unequal compromise, which keeps people where they are largely intended to be. How we value ourselves becomes confused with the infrastructure we have inherited and which we inhabit. We have come to accept physical aggression, drug abuse, and loneliness. There is a meek submission that dwells amongst us numbing our souls. In light of this do we still have something valid to say? Is there any point in trying to say it? We are in danger of forgetting how to express ourselves altogether.

Perhaps Aberdeen suffers less from not having a sense of belonging than other parts of Scotland. It is still inhabited by the same Pictish Beaker peoples. The largely unknown ancient people of Northern Britain. There is an insularity to Aberdeen, sheathed as it is mostly in grey permacloud, that gives it some sense of vast Continental drift pattern. It has bred predominantly amongst itself. Resultantly come the bit Aberdonians look to one another for mutual understanding and this has only created a self-limiting perception. It is known as native provinciality or some other condescending phrase. The paradigm is the same; birth, school, work, marriage, retirement, death. That is the basic pattern upon which the wheel of existence hangs. You either conform to that domestic or get out. The institution of Humanities plays little or no part in the everyday lives of working class Aberdeen. Of course amongst the native song of Aberdeen folk there is a rich vernacular, an oral dialect to be found in both language and music. To an extent the coming of the oil industry has eroded the parochiality of the city. It has brought material wealth to Aberdeen. It has created many institutions. Still though most cultural wealth remains elusive, catch it on the wing, as she flies. Aberdeen's hard exterior is often confused with a parsimonious dour population. Industry and pejoratively industrial dwarfism continues to remain the status quo. I suppose the quietitude of the people of Aberdeen is in the face of an inherent inferiority at being on the Northern periphery of Britain. People's imaginations need to be stimulated, not with drugs, not with fringe living, but probably normality. Just that, normality. Full realisation and acceptance of our own potential is the only way that we will achieve zero need and a greater tolerance of what others already know to be their own shortcomings.

I made my way back up to the Doctor's room. The ward was upstairs, a nice little homogenous package of co-existence. It was called Blair ward. Wells explained to me that all the wards were named after different areas of the region. Just like the patients, at the head, a balanced cross sectional view of the community. I arrived finally at the head of the stairs, almost bumped my nose at the transparent reinforced glass door. It was electronically locked. I peered above myself at the CCTV camera looking down at us. Wells pressed a buzzer to let us in, and spoke into an intercom. I asked him why the door was locked, and he replied to me, playing with the elastoplex strap of his watch, "It is nothing to be alarmed about, it is just for all our safety." He grinned at me weakly as though he were grimacing through pain. I felt as though I had encountered more sincerity from a wasp just before it is about to sting you. A nurse came to let us in, she was butch, used to trudging, she was though malleable, and that is what institutions do to you. Puddled clay. She had a kind face. She introduced herself as Christine, she was wearing civilian clothes, photo id, (like all the staff), and a huge bunch of keys on her belt. She opened the door and I went in across the threshold, slinging my bag higher up my shoulder, closer to me. I wonder what is sanctuary? Is it inside here, like being within some kind of harbour wall, head upright but your arse end hanging out because your hold is empty, or have I crossed over the fall from the harbour into Ocean to exchange ballast for nourishment. However I like staring straight ahead at polar North across the sea, with the Port Pier winking red and rapping a hand at my heart. There is no turning back to childish things any more.

The first thing that struck me about the ward was the smell of urine; it was pervasive. Christine took my bag and showed me round with Wells. Like all hospital wards it was basically a long corridor, we could have had a great game of carpet bowls, I couldn't see the Jack anywhere yet though. Two male wards led off to the right, one private room between them where a severely disabled, emaciated man with a beard was lying. This was the source of the smell of urine. Christine introduced him to me as Jerry. She said he had Huntington's chorea, but you could tell he understood everything; his eyes were bright blue as glass buttons. Just then as if in glee Jerry emptied his bladder through a catheter into his bag with a pouring sound. Momentarily I reflect on the joys of the wheel chair philosophy, as if gracefully gliding round the dance floor in multitudinous chrome wheeled embrace to Iggy Pop's "The Passenger," and I go and spoil it all and get a slap when I say to their able bodied friend, "Your mate looks a bit legless tonight." Further down a female ward leads off to the right. Tan nylon ankle stockings, baffies and gowns are the sartorial dress of the day. On the left of the ward was the staff room, pharmacy and treatment room. The toilets and bath/shower room were also on this side. A stack of commodes sit stacked and ready, their grey cardboard bowls thoughtfully attached. At the far end of the corridor was a small kitchen/dining room for us the patients. It was beginning to sink in, it was us not them, us. At the exit of the ward was a day room for the patients with a TV on. Several people were sitting around. One older man was sitting in a vacant way, but at the same time his body was restless, as if anxious to be on the move. I noticed how his hair was the colour of a young boy's, as if madness somehow precludes greying. His tongue was lolling carelessly out of his mouth, just like you would see it on a Butchers slab. Silent, he was scarred high up; he would withdraw his tongue and smoke on his cigarette, pinching the butt with forefinger and thumb, to get the maximum goodness out of it. The air of the room was fugged; the atmosphere of the room was feiched. There was a sense that our overwhelming despair had been masked by ennui, a kind of perpetual repetition, which we craved like nicotine.

Dr. Wells took me through to my bed. The ward contained three other beds where three young men lay asleep. He and Christine seemed almost purring with contentment, for this was where they could begin to place faith in the therapeutic powers of a rest cure. In addition to medication it seemed to solve some of the mystery of mental distress. If only momentarily it removed some of the burden that their occupation had placed upon their shoulders. It suspended their eternal sense of anxiety. Christine showed me my locker and left me to unpack. Dr. Wells sat momentarily on the edge of the bed, and said he had to go now; the nurses would take care of me. It was Friday around 5pm. And then he did it, like all Doctors seem to like to do once the work has begun; he gave me a playful pat on the back. He rose, said he would see me on Monday, and then he was gone, free to be anywhere he pleased.

Christine poked her head round the door and said supper would be in half an hour. She had a look in her face that seduced me into thinking somehow meal times were something to look forward to. I sat on my bed and almost timidly, silently, repetitively unpacked my belongings. This is real, this is crushed metal hardcore. Somehow it equated with being little, with being lonely, with feeling frightened. Of what? The grinding system of which I was becoming an integral member. Of the prospect of the rest of my life as a tiny speck amongst the vast colossus of humanity. What I was afraid of was the institutional welfare of places like this; the cure was as bad as the illness. I looked around me, in the cramped Victorian ward of the Lunatic Asylum, the ghosts, the spiritual fabric hiding some awful history; silently, reproachfully inanimate. Echo beach far away in time, and now I part of a tarry black residuum of society sitting thick and viscous at the bottom of the beaker. I was once clean and virginal but I wanted to scrunch myself up in a ball now. I had been thrown into the bin. I looked out of the vertical steel bars that protected the Perspex windows. The suffocating Perspex is worn dim by countless hands just rubbing. Just to see, only from the inside looking out at you.

Suddenly the guy in the bed next to me woke up; his eyes come on instantly like lights. There is an intense yellow somewhere in his blue Irises. It is feyness; it is wildness, like a wolf. He sits up on the bed, you can tell there is an innate energy about him, but he has a lovely smile. He introduces himself as Paul. He points to the other two and says in a deep Northern English accent, "They are still pretty well out of it." The way he says it suggests a compassion for his fellow patients; he seems to care. I introduce myself as Cal, still anxious to get to this minor inconvenience of mine, this minor health blip. Wanting to be on my way. I ask Paul, "Why do they look as if they have been hit on the nut with a sledge hammer?" Paul's eyes became even more animated and boisterous, he lets out a little chuckle, "ECT mate, kick start to the brain." My intake of breath was audible, my shock tangible. Paul was now rolling himself up a cigarette from a massive packet of Golden Virginia, I looked at the yellow on the packet, thought of the colour of gold and couldn't help but form the connection with the colour of Paul's eyes. He went on, "All mental illnesses tend towards the cyclical, and ECT is administered for deep seated clinical depression. You don't feel any pain; you get a muscle relaxant before they shock you. Afterwards once you wake up you feel animated, happy even. It seems to lift your mood." There were no smoking signs everywhere. Paul sparked up, and offered me a tickler, I accepted gratefully. Tobacco is a bond.

Paul asked me if it was the first time I had been in hospital, I stumbled hesitantly and replied, "Yes." Paul puffed on his cigarette and said, "Some of the fruit is riper than others, if you know what I mean, cool head warm heart." I thought of Kafka and Gregor Samsa's metamorphoses into a dung beetle, his family don't recognise him anymore and one of them throws an apple at him that sticks and rots into his back. I said to Paul, "So mental hospital is like some kind of cache', a licence to behave oddly, it is as if no-one notices you anymore, except as some kind of intangible to be afraid of." He looks at me with the sage gaze of the professional nutter; he smiles and says, "Worse than that Cal no-one cares about you anymore also." Paul went on. He said, "I am lucky to be ill in today's society, in the recent past I would have had my temporal lobes singed and chopped up like so much chicken liver pâté. When you are high you suffer from diminished responsibility, I have been in and out of Hospital for more than ten years. In a sense I have come to like it here."

Another male nurse called us through to supper. He introduced himself to me as Dougal. He had an air of normality, almost radiance about him. Of course they were trained to go about business as usual. To not so much gloss over our collective mental grief as get the job done. I went through to the dining room at the end of the corridor with Paul. Our other two contemporaries were left to sleep. Ticking away slowly in a deep place, lying like tossed aside rag dolls. Meal times were taken in turns, the dining room wasn't large enough. Eight of us were cramped around a small table, with the obligatory plastic tumblers and the large jug of orange squash, squarely in the middle. I sat down; everyone seemed to have a thirst, a need to slake unquenchable thirsts. The jug was soon empty and Dougal made some more. It is the medication you see, the damned medication. It increases your need to take on liquid. The person opposite me introduced herself to me as Suzy. I wondered Suzy Q? She had undergone a sex change operation and somehow the psychology of her physical change was comparable to a visit here. Her face was covered in downy facial hair, but she had breasts and a woman's voice. I sipped gently on my juice; I bet there was some omniscient narrator out there somewhere who was roaring to himself, "Can't wait to get Cal on some medication! What'll it be boy? A little Lithium salt sprinkled on your chips? Or what about a depot jag once a month just to keep the brain nice and regular. Some seroxat for the anvil of depression or what about a touch of chlorpromazine. Good old chlorpromazine the trusted grisly old friend of the psychiatrist. You will soon be glugging your juice like the rest of them Cal." I stared at Suzy and the other people but no one seemed to take much interest in me. Dougal served up the food from large age worn aluminium canteens, which had come up from the kitchen below on the dumb waiter. The meal was beef cobbler and I found it inedible. The meat was glutinous and fatty, and the potatoes seemed to be a reflection of the complexion of the people;

sallow and waxy. Everyone was positively wolfing the food down in automatic fashion. I couldn't understand how people could eat the most revolting food. Of course there is one thing if nothing else that increases your appetite and that is poverty. Because the vast majority of people who have chronic mental health problems are on the bottom rung of society, and in terms of society in here, out there through the barred Perspex, Thatcher is right, there isn't much of a society, just survival. Mental illness does not respect class division, but right here, right now below the wide meshed safety net I won't ever rub shoulders with a professional. I looked down at my plate; I would soon learn to slop in like the rest. Apart from Suzy Q, Paul and me, all the other people round the table were old men and women, they seemed all ravelled up like a ball of wool. This is real, this is hardcore. This was all the carcass of a life that they had. Dougal was caring and tender towards us, it was an innate thing, it made a difference to me to realise that he was decent towards the patients.

We had eve's pudding and custard for sweet. I liked that, I had always liked institutional puddings, and they served as a solace from your existence. After supper Paul and I went through to have a cigarette in the TV room. There was a tank with goldfish swimming around in circles; some of them were bottom feeding. I suppose it was perceived that the effect of the fish was calming and therapeutic. The walls were surrounded with paperback books and "Hello" magazines. It was all easy reading ephemeral stuff, because nutters can't concentrate, we don't have any attention span. Slushy romances, nickel and dime western type adventure stories. It all confirmed our lowbrow status. When someone breaks down they can't be repaired and reconstructed like a car. Invariably, nine times out of ten the recycled version is merely a shade of the healthy self. In a sense a completely different person. The only difference though from the reading matter on the shelf is that this reality, this heroism isn't rewarded at the end. It just either goes on or it doesn't. Paul rolled us a couple of cigarettes, the quiet time, the waiting huddled together. Across the room was a row of old women sitting patiently watching TV. They all had on their tan ankle nylon stockings, baffies, nightdresses and gowns. They all had their leather cigarette purses that would discharge a surfeit of blue Berkley Super kings smoke. The ashtrays were foaming like Jacuzzis. There wasn't much talk, just a kind of intimacy amongst them that was based on an awareness of the shared female human state. I noticed some of the women had burnt mottled legs from sitting too near the fire; some had distended whale limbs filled with fluid. Our declining Scottish genetic pool in gay abundance. The channel was on Grampian, it was the local news. The presenter droned on in a local Doric dialect. His message was flinty hearted, his accent mawkish and utterly parochial. Meanwhile the electric mock log fire glowed and swirled orange lending a surreal air to our little informal gathering. The presenter told us that a North East man had been lost at sea from a Peterhead registered fishing boat. The presenter's tone was dry, gravely and dispassionate. Meanwhile nothing stirred in the room except for the sucking inhalation of Berkley Super Kings. At least Paul let out a thick and noisy blow. You either laugh or cry but here nothing stirs in the dead zone. I went to turn the TV over to something else. Immediately I was stopped dead in my tracks by the shrill Doric tone of one of the nameless volcanic whales. She shrieked at me definitively, "Leave it on Grampian, Grampian's the best channel." The cuffs were definitely on now. I retreated crestfallen to my little square of existence. Paul looked at me and started laughing maniacally.

A young blonde woman came into the room. Her wrists were bandaged, and she sat down beside me. She was in a dressing gown and I could see her breasts flopping about underneath. It is funny how people have little or no inhibitions about their bodies when they are in hospital. She drew her feet up to her chest and started talking to me. She said, "They are coming to get me any time now, there will be a helicopter landing on the lawn and I will be going away to meet the President." I looked into her face; her skin was yellow and waxed like a Safeway lemon. Paul whispered in my ear, "That's crazy Carol, she is just a little bit disturbed that's all, she's harmless." A nurse came into the room; he looked around a bit, spoke to Carol and then left with her. You were never left alone long on the ward in case something bad happened.

Paul began to tell me what had triggered the onset of his own illness. His two only brothers had been in a car accident. They had both been killed outright. Afterwards when Paul was beginning to come to terms with a tragedy that is unimaginable for most of us, he began a University degree. At registration, on his first day the man who had caused the fatal accident was sitting in the class waiting to register on the same course as Paul. Call it twisted fate, call it cosmic chaos, but it sent Paul clean into outer space. "So you see Cal," said Paul, "I have more reason to feel cheated than most. There is that big word, never, and what might never have been if things had been called out different."

I could see that Paul was a sensitive person, in a sense like myself, he was fine grained. And here we were pegged up and strung out to dry. I said to him my problems were more prosaic than his own, "The eternal problems with girls accentuated with more than just a chance encounter with a few bottles of whisky." Paul looked at me flatly, he replied, "Some people are so emotionally retarded that they will in all likelihood not have it within them to acknowledge having caused suffering to another person. On the contrary they seem to see it as a boost to their own ego, hurting people in relationships." I thought about it, I was as guilty as anyone else in this respect, but I was quickly beginning to realise that life is unfair. I replied, "All you can hope for is that people can change for the better."

The scene had made me feel profoundly depressed, leaden and sad. I said to Paul I was going to lie down for a while. I looked into Jerry's room, Dougal was feeding him. The young man made a moaning sound, unable to articulate what he wanted to communicate. I noticed on his wall Jerry had a Pirelli girl calendar, what kind of sick joke was this I wondered? Seeing as whores weren't commonly available on the NHS. I went into the toilet to use the bog. One of the WCs' was choked with faeces, with other people's shit. The black linoleum floor was covered in a film of yellow urine.

Well I suppose there was a certain viewpoint to maintain. If you can't act carelessly in here where can you do it? I cowked as I peed in the urinal, man existing between piss and shit. I went and lay on my bed, the other two guys were still lying there motionless. I slept soundly, recuperatively for a couple of hours. I was woken by voices. For the first instant between wakefulness and sleep I felt acutely paranoid, fearful for myself. I wondered if I was going to get ECT.

The two men opposite me had woken up, they introduced themselves as Mike and Steve. They were both animated in conversation, but you could see somehow if you were to strip away the false work, you would be left with the form itself. Doing the best to hold themselves together, their outward appearance masked the hollow core they must have been feeling inside. Paul came into the ward and sat on his bed. Steve was telling a story about a man who had got his penis stuck inside a woman's vagina when they had been making love. They had locked like dog and bitch, and they had to be separated surgically. Steve said in a loud excited voice, "The guy broke his cock." We all burst into childlike endless laughter. It was a ray of lightness in bleak house.

The Medical Doctor came to see me at night, Dr. Ward. She looked beautiful, wan and exhausted. She took my blood pressure then examined my liver. Her hands were warm and sensual, my penis became tumescent, but it is painful to have your liver examined. Especially if you had been watering it as much as I had recently, it was the size of a watermelon. The Doctor dreamily felt how warm and soft my body was. Then she abruptly asked me about the drinking, and if I had been smoking cannabis. I said, "Yes to that and that, I haven't had many nights off the pints and joints since I was a teenager." She looked disappointed, I felt disappointed but not surprised. Instead of flintily looking at me in the eyes before administering a meaningless diatribe against drink and drugs she took pity on me. It was a fair compromise, was this not a complete shock to me so far? Why complicate things, little steps towards an overall recovery. She said, "I am going to prescribe you Diazepam tonight Cal to help you with withdraw from the alcohol. The psychiatrist will begin to address your mental state tomorrow." She then took a sample of blood from my arm. The rubber tourniquet velcroed tight, high up on my arm. The blood filled the styrette steadily. It was dark crimson and brooding looking. While she was doing this Doctor asked if I was going to have visitors over the Week-end, I replied, "I don't know, I think my Mum Lorna Moone will be into see me but in all honesty I haven't told her I am in here yet." The doctor removed the needle from the artery with a sharp scratch and said; "I think you should get in touch with her as soon as possible." I asked if I could go out. Perhaps out to the pub and back home on the ward in time for tea and toast. No such rosy illusions. This is a barred, combination lock safe, encased on five sides by concrete. Doctor replied firmly, she said, "There is never any liberty allowed in the first 48 hours." She put the glowing cherry red specimen in the glowing chromium kidney dish, and stuck a plaster on my arm. She pulled off the latex gloves with what seemed like an illusory post coital sexual slap. She stood up with the specimen and all her other paraphernalia. She smiled at me and wished me luck, drew apart the curtains and she was gone. I was paying the price for a crime I hadn't yet committed. However time ticks onwards, it constantly propels you forward in some kind of downward motion.

I decided to take the Doctor's advice and go and phone Lorna on the payphone. I had some coins. I rang the number and waited for her to answer.

"Hello," she said in that queer, inquisitive, plaintive way that she had about her. Lorna was a questful person. She liked to pose honestly felt questions in the hope that they would be answered. I said, "I have been admitted to Cornhill Hospital Mum, I am on Blair ward. I am not allowed out until next week. Can you come in with cigarettes and juice?" There was a slight pause before Lorna replied, a heart seas. When the phone had rung in her little cottage by the North Sea that resembled a whitewashed shoebox, she had been enjoying her supper. She was having porridge, taken separately with the milk, liberally sprinkled with sugar. Her little black leather high-laced booties were sitting in front of the little black metal range fire that heated her cottage. The wooden kindling was crackling and sparking as it attempted to ignite the black spluttering, sulphurous coal. The sea crashed and pounded foaming soda into the little harbour about 100 metres east of her front door, for it was the equinox, the time when the seasons change, and things will never be quite the same as they used to be. The air was full of tan froth bubbles, from the sea, scattering on the keen east wind. I wondered if I had intruded on her vision of micro happiness in her shoebox, with all her shoes, her books on natural health and spiritual aspiration amongst all her clothes. I said, "Are you there Mum?" She replied quickly, rubbing some flecks of oatmeal with her pointed feminine hands from her mouth, "Of course Darling. Perhaps this has been coming for a while. It is just such a surprise to me, but perhaps finally you have embarked on a path that will make you a happier person, if that does not seem a strange thing to say." George the cat was sitting curled up on the purple couch that had been christened the vulva by Lorna's sons. That had been in the days before she had moved to this kind of "Exile on Main Street", in the days when her sons had brought home so many different girls that she wondered whether she had enough food and conversation for them all. She looked across at George; he was grey brown like a ghost at the end of summer. Lorna had once been in love also with a deceitful man on that couch. George's sage green emerald eyes smiled warmly at her as they closed, realising how happy he felt to be with her here curled in on a Friday evening. I said, "I just phoned to tell you that I will see you tomorrow." Lorna replied quickly, "Yes darling I will be up tomorrow with fags and stuff for you." She put the phone down and let out a little sigh. In a sense she was relieved, she knew her son was being cared for. She ran her hand over her almost benign shiny white hair. It had once been lustrous black, although there were still one or two cobalt strands remaining: as in her character, in her temperament. The fire was beginning to take, throwing dancing ghosts onto the timber wainscoting.

When I put the phone down I reflected a little, I saw into a brief window of enlightenment on my recent, and perhaps not so recent past. I thought about Eva and my stormy relationship with her, I thought about my Mother and my stormy relationship with her. I thought about drink. Environment played more than a small part in landing me here. It always seemed to be cold in this country; you never seemed to be able to get warm. It was always a dark surreal world, dank and shiny damp, played out under the artificial light to enlighten our dim groping perception of ourselves, our identity. I was back to the spiny archaic fish again that has evolved in such a way to guarantee but at the same time self-limit its own reproductive worth. Here I was still sinking, still plumbing in order to achieve solvency in life. I had been descending a spiral towards this darkness with ease, now, all my life. I was a Civil Engineer, I knew that the spiral is the most beautiful but difficult project to set out and construct. It was purely geometrical. Here I was descending it with ease towards an inevitable conclusion. A collision between Earth and a moving body. Where I would have to remain standing still for a long time to come.

"Tablet time!" The words rang out like a battle cry, a call to arms. The words, shouted for the first time in my ears brought me firmly back into the present. It seemed like a novelty then, like a game of "cowboys and Indians." But I couldn't cope; my body had been sloughing off for a while now. People from all the different parts of the ward began to make towards the dispensary and congregate. Various stages of disrobement, various stages of chemical intangibility, but a common thread running through the crush, the melt. That curious "S" shaped silent scream that corded through our bodies. Phantasmagoria, incandescent ectoplasm. Each person giving off a luminescent glow like a Lamprey. We feel out of ease, not in ourselves, at times awkward in our own bodies, but not at this time of tension, waiting to receive your medication. The cheery careless chant of the nurses, under the neon light, like football fans outside in a beer garden. "Guinness is good for you," The pharmacy on the ward is wonderful. The orange rayon industrial carpet glows, the beautiful ordered coloured design of the drug packets, the tidy chrome, the blister packets, the green and yellow capsules, the cherry linctus for that troublesome cough that merely forebodes something worse that is wrong with you. Oh but no one remembered to tell you!

Once a point of acceptance has been achieved and if possible entirely realised by the patient the treatment can begin. The vast majority of us crave our medicine, are anxious to receive it and then go to bed. I stand in line with the rest. Behind me is Ella, who looks like an old bargirl. Wormwood spirit all right. Her flaccid breasts show under her black nylon nightdress, with its furry collar and cuffs (I imagine). No smell of Dior and Sobranies from her though, just stale food and Regal King size, and, can I make out the faint scent of Tweed? Her Tiara and Marabou feathers are firmly in the patient safe, she covers up her hand admirably, no scandal, no cheating here. She almost pushes me out of the way to get a purchase on the "Happy Valleys," and a shot of squash. I am still though a novice, mischievous. I take my two little tablets; slurp my squash and say, "Cheers." Admissions ward, mixed diagnoses, mixed problems. Ella's on the rest cure. In then out, in then out. Slowly sinking in sand. Imperceptibly sliding further down the scale of life. Nothing ever gets any better, there are only like now, moments of reprieve. My facility for judgment is impaired, I feel like doing a Waltz with Ella, but she just looks at me and pushes me out of the way to get to the tea and toast on the female ward. More freebies, something else for nothing. Take it! Take it while the going is good.

I resolve to use my heart more, but I feel deflated. I go through to the ward, everyone's bed was screened off and I could hear the brosy voice of a nurse doing the rounds. Normally I would feel funny about sharing a ward with total strangers, like being on barrack in the army. But not in here not tonight. Somehow I felt safe as if there were external not fully good factors acting upon me. I take off my clothes and get into my Hospital pyjamas, and get into bed. Suddenly the brosy voice has a face, and this fearful looking hag in a nurse's uniform pops her face round my screens waving an Industrial sized can of Johnson's Baby powder at me. She directs her firm glare at me and asks in the finest Doric dialect, "Has you bum been deen Cal?" I burst into laughter, she seems crestfallen. I thought I am not letting her near my arse. I said, "Yes it was deen quite some time ago." She seemed satisfied and then left. She turns off the ward lights. There would soon be a blue nightlight to replace the harsh glare of the neon strip lights in the corridor.

Waiting to drop off, white mice in a battery of wire cages. Jerry moaning up the corridor, doors shutting and opening, the metallic shoogle of bunches of keys. The nurses able to relax send out for a Chinese. The click of the thermostat on the kettle for coffee. The china clatter of cups grating on my nerves like a knife across a plate. Water flowing from the faucet, water roaring from the tap, reduced to flowing, to nothing. Think of the hundred of starlings I saw tonight at sunset on my way up here. Standing to attention on the telegraph wires, at their back the panoply of the glowing amber sunset. A sure sign that winter is coming soon. Coming soon. Nothing.

The next week spent in this routine of observation. I feel like Gulliver; lashed down by the Lilliputians while needles are stuck into my body. The curiosity of a great whale of a creature amongst the scurrying little people, waving their tiny arms about. The curiosity doesn't wear off. Food, television and above all sleep. My body was craving rest from the exhaustion that the world had imparted to me. We all slept a lot here. Medicine, the stifling unliberated atmosphere. It contrived to make us all want to sleep. Safety in absolute numbers, conforming to a pattern that suits the staff. Wells came to see me on Monday, he had stopped the script of Diazepam, it had helped the crash at least. I had retreated to a velvet lined cave. He said that at the end of the week he and another doctor would come to interview me. He said, "We want to conclude some kind of preliminary diagnosis of your condition Cal. I am starting you on a new medication today. You are to receive Sulpiride (400mg) three times daily." Just like that, he said it airily in a matter of fact sort of way, as if I had no choice in the matter of my own health. Which of course in the matter of medication the reconstituted sane person who has suffered a manic depressive psychosis does not. I asked Wells what Sulpiride was. He said, "It is a psychotropic drug, it is used specifically… for the treatment of Schizophrenia." He raised his voice a little, he said, "It will help to diminish the strange delusional thoughts you have been having." Well toss me a corded life ring, make my day punk. I looked out through the Perspex, the sun shafting in picking out the stillness of the dust in the air. I was shattered, I felt like shattering the plastic and doing a fucking runner. I felt like a piece of kindling that has just been lined up on the block and split in two. Immediately in my mindset a firewall of rebellion began to take shape, I thought I'm not a schizophrenic. The Doctor looked at me patiently, waiting for my reaction. The second hand on his watch ticking onwards in perpetuity. I blurted, "Will I be allowed out soon?" Wells said, "You can go out in the grounds with other patients, only in the company of the nurses meantime." I thought about it, a posse of nutters with Brown Owl. Perhaps we could have a picnic of snails and bluet mushrooms. Washed down by cherry linctus. If we were really good we would all get a "Jelly" for sweet. One little Indian, my canoe was sinking. I realised I was to remain inside here for the foreseeable future. Amongst the palpable pain, the decline. The sense of death forestalled. I suddenly realise that psychiatrists cannot just solely put the interests of their patients at heart, but must also consider society at large. It is not so much that the sane misunderstand the insane. It is rather that they fear us. That is why a stigma is attached to the insane. There is a gap in society between the suffering of mental illness and how others who are afraid of it themselves often persecute that illness. Wells could see that all this had swamped me so quickly like a tidal wave, he said, "I want you to remain here on this locked ward meantime for your own well-being."

That is how the week ahead of me progressed: a routine of food, medication and sleep. I told Paul that I was being interviewed at the end of the week to assess my condition. He said there was a two-way mirror in the room. Student Doctors sat next door and took notes on you. Detached fascination, the Lilliputians waving their tiny little arms around again. I suppose they had to learn somehow. I resolved in my own head to get away from this place as soon as possible. I didn't realise then that all I was doing was running away from my own sense of responsibility, my own well-being. Prolonging the problem. We got out into the grounds every afternoon, like a mournful, fuming procession, looking somehow gaunt and awry. Nails and fingers stained orange from the tobacco, moving around mostly silently in a group, at the head, at the stern, amidships; Nurses. Scrunching through the waves of hot musty leaves that had gathered on the lawns from the beech oak and ash trees. I retreated into myself as if embarrassed to be stigmatised as part of this slough. But it was more than that; it was my dignity that was being eroded.

Lorna Moone came up every day that first week. Bearing gifts of cigarettes, chocolate, juice and fruit. Like manna from heaven. I would violently rip off the cellophane, split the pack and proffer the tipped fags around. Not so much currency in here as sustenance. The sap that was now retreating into its branched silhouetted self to almost lie dormant throughout the long winter ahead. Lorna had been a little terrified that first visit as she sat amongst the human carnival alone in the TV room. I was taking a shower. She was wearing her patent leather black boots, her black velvet trousers and her waistcoat. The one she had embroidered herself with purple sworls, and golden autumnal leaves. She thought briefly about her own mother Betsy who had gone mad; at least Lorna had been able to care for her. The bulls tit was pinned proudly to Lorna's black cashmere turtleneck sweater, the one Norman had given her in one of his failed attempts at reconciliation with Lorna. The red central garnet glinted in the centre of the cut crystal, mounted in finest Perthshire gold. The fearful old women on the ward were disconcerted somehow by her presence, it reminded them somehow of their own particular female identity somewhere dimly in the past. Before all this began. The human noise started to rise audibly, not conversation so much as utterances and moans. Jerry's radar was picking it up; he began to moan louder and louder. For that was it, it was a rage against how unfair, how unequal life was, how little time there was for all of us. Lorna just sat there and faintly licked her lippies in a slightly nervous way. She raised her feminine pointed hand and rubbed at her mouth. Then like Sir Lancelot, Paul rode into the room high on a swell of mania and carbomazapime. He barked out at the hags, "Shut the fuck up, I can't hear the television." Simultaneously he was rolling a cigarette cowboy style from his massive packet of Golden Virginia. Lorna felt saved. There was nothing finer than the plain talking honest sentiment of a Northern lad. I came through in my dressing gown; my hair was tousled and wet. I introduced Paul and sat down. Mum gave me a bag with fags and fruit and juice etc. Jerry was still moaning. I said to Lorna, "It's alright, as Mary Whitehouse put it Jerry just needs despunked." Paul let out a laugh and said, "He's not the only one." Lorna was used to this sort of crude immature male talk, not only from her sons but also from the many thousands of adolescents she had taught. She didn't particularly like to encourage crudity but she did want to stimulate emotional literacy amongst boys. She asked me if things were all right with me, if I was settling in okay. I was taking a massive quaff of lucozade, replenishing my diminished body fluids, (my drug enriched metabolism). I asked Paul if he wanted some ale, he said yes and I passed him the bottle. Lorna said, "For goodness sake Cal get some cups," as if we were in The Dorchester or something. I just looked at her silently.

I decided to bring Lorna up to speed. I said, "The only thing of any note that has happened this week is one night I was up late alone here in the TV room. One of the old men on the ward next-door shit the bed, and the nurse discovered him. The nurse was of "the old school of psychiatry," he went berserk at the old man. Of course he doesn't know that I was sitting here alone in the dark. He was so angry with the poor old man who probably was totally confused and ravelled up. The nurse didn't seem to be acting rationally." Paul burped and said, "If you can't shit the bed on a mental ward where can you do it." Lorna let out a throaty giggle. I said, "Normally in any other situation I would have gone through and told the cunt to fuck off, but I am scared myself in this place; I don't know what can happen to you." Paul said quickly, "I'll tell you what would have happened to you. They would have put you on a section and thrown the key into the middle of a very deep pond." We all sat silently then huddled into our seats. Wishing that this drama were over.

The day of my interview arrived. There was a mirror in the room but it was covered with a screen. Wells was there and another older Doctor who introduced himself as Miller. He held out his hand and said, "Harry Miller, nice to meet you Cal." His blue eyes were twinkling benignly. I wondered if this masked an iron core. I wondered what palliative pleasures "Dirty Harry" had in store for me. First of all they asked me general environmental questions about the onset of my mental distress. Was there any history of illness in my family? Had I ever been unwell before? I decided to lie about my Gran. I shook my head and said "no" to both these questions, "We are your average lower middle class Britishers." I went on and said, "There were skeletons in the cupboard alright, things that aren't decently talked about, things that if they were discussed openly could serve to liberate our corseted souls." Dirty Harry looked at me interestedly and said, "What kind of things Cal?" I said, "Just the usual things, human disappointment I suppose, which in turn becomes the sin of the Father visited upon the Son." I said that on my Father's side, and indeed if I consider my Grandmother on my Mother's side, there probably was a clear history of nervousness, a highly-strung framework that suggested we were not a particularly well-balanced family. Miller was taking notes, he looked up earnestly from his note taking and said to me, "I am here to help you Cal, I want you to try and understand that. We are trying to make an accurate diagnosis of your condition." Wells then asked me to describe to him something of the strangeness I felt, the abstract thoughts I had been having. I said I felt as though some kind of canker had entered into my body, since that night recently I had met Selina, it was caught off the teeth somehow; it was a medical fact that is not widely understood. I said, "Obsession is manifest in my thoughts generally. The fantastic things that I think deeply about bear no relation to reality itself. I attach signs to reality; there are signs everywhere that point towards some greater unknown fantastic truth that lies ahead of me. I mean, doctors, in light of the mundane, cold world we have constructed and live in would you not attach some Technicolor, would you not feel inclined to go mad?" I went on and said, "The reproductive organs in some way represent the world. What was distilling in my testicles was merely a microcosm of all the weather patterns, the forces of creation and destruction that had resulted in our world. The canker that I thought had entered my body had changed me: physically and emotionally. I would never feel the same again. The forces of nature mirrored these changes. Selina and I meeting was the mutual recognition of two very old souls who recognise something they are afraid of in one another. Something that is utterly ancient and so utterly against the grain of ever happening that in a sense it is beyond just a material coincidence. Something that is beyond merely physical understanding but is spirit too." Wells had his pen in his mouth, he didn't know if I was making much sense, but I wasn't a dullard at least. Miller looked at me in an interested way and nudged the box of man size tissues closer to me cheekily. He said quietly, "Please go on Cal."

"I feel as though there is a fracture somewhere in all our souls, none of us are born perfect. Unlike democratic "Tabular Rasa" i.e. choice, it is our actual imperfection that individually sets us apart. Saying this though when you are confronted with this flaw it is as if someone is scoring a massive, vandalising, undemocratic weal through a smooth surface of bees wax. Laying bare to the world all your imperfections, all your vulnerabilities, forcing you to turn back to your archaic ascendancy and re-examine the evidence. I will be 38 years old, at the millennium. The world has come full circle once more, 2000 years after the birth of Christ. My star sign is Taurus, the second sign of the zodiac. I have one elder brother John who is 1 year, 1 month, 1 day, 1 hour older than me. Naturally his star sign is Aries the first sign of the zodiac. Symbolically I am the Tiger a natural ascendant and leader of men, in fact both my parents are also born Tigers. Obviously I share the same astral chart as the present Queen. My surname is Comyn; the circle; but how we choose to understand this creation itself is incomplete. Doctors what I am saying to you is that I am, no not chosen, just that I am born into this world as the Second Coming of Christ." A door banged loudly in the near distance. Miller looked at me compassionately with his bright blue eyes. Slowly but surely grinding down the meal I thought. I could detect a faint wry smile on his lips. Wells who had been silent asked me, "What about the cannabis Cal, how much have you been smoking, is it a regular habit?" I said I had probably been smoking more than a quarter ounce a week for as long as I could remember. Wells asked me, "Why do you smoke dope Cal?" I replied, "At first I found it slightly risqué because it was illegal, because it wasn't part of the mainstream associated with my teenage years. I suppose at that time the music, the literature, the art I was interested in were in some way connected to dope, but in a sense it was easy to confuse smoking and the often abstract hallucinogenic thought patterns it produced with creativity itself, as if naturally one led on automatically from the other. And of course I have since discovered that that is patently untrue. Pretty quickly the effects of dope were always a sense of paranoia that it creates in me. At first I used to enjoy this sense of danger, particularly on nights out into Town. But I suppose that was generally in the freedom of company." Miller interrupted briefly from his fastidious note taking. He said, "And now Cal, what part does dope play in your life now?" I thought about it quickly and let out a tremulous sigh. I said, "I smoke dope now to blunt my finer feelings, that is the point that I have reached. In association with alcohol I use it to fill in that damn gap, that sense of helplessness while I am drowning. You see Doctors I am definitely not just waving; it is much more than just self-pity. At almost every turn my creativity as a person seems frustrated, that combined with loneliness lies at the heart of my unhappiness. I am stuck in a lousy job being paid a pittance to help run the most fucking essential service utility in the country; Water and Sewerage. Dope and drink enables me to escape however briefly from what I perceive to be the finality of my life. Of course I realise that nothing stays the same, just like water we are in some sense always fluid, always changing, but I seem to have painted myself into a pitch black corner. Where no-one seems to even notice me anymore." I suddenly became restless, impatient. I felt as though I had spilled out my guts long enough. I said angrily, "When will I be getting out of here?" Wells replied calmly and clearly that they would like it if I remained on the ward a while yet, until my condition could be properly diagnosed and stabilised. I was anxious to be out, I had half-baked plans, ill thought out schemes to be carried out grandiosely. I had to resume my quest for the signs that were pointing to the greater purpose of my existence. Then the wheel turned rapidly one revolution. My heart sank; soon back on the ward, feelings of unbearable sadness welling up in my chest like a wood pigeon; it's split gizzard bulging with yellow corn. The interview was over. Doctors' Wells and Miller stood up. I rose to attention automatically, gentlemanly, with dignity and decorum intact.

Wells said he would see me again on Monday, I was to carry on as normal, and to remember that the nursing staff were there to help me. Miller shook my hand and said it was nice to meet me. The male nurse was waiting outside, waiting to take me back upstairs. His keys jingled as we went up the stairs. Too soon I was back on the inside, looking safely out at you through mesh reinforced glass. The electric lock nudged shut with a click. Roll up! Roll up! Welcome to the greatest show on Earth. Now inside the canvas tarp of the Big Top. It was easy to play your role in this circus of mental distress. There were frenetic times on the ward when some nurses would ride up and down angrily at our collective chemical intangibility; our haywire energy, and now thankfully times of quietitude. I looked into the TV room; Carol was sitting alone having a conversation with herself. Under the cold Technicolor of the fish tank, forever blowing bubbles. I asked her if she was okay. She looked up at me and said, "Did you know that it is possible to go beyond the I?" "How do you mean Carol?" I replied puzzled. She puffed repetitively on her cigarette taking deep lungfuls of smoke, as if she were auditioning for the part of Jim Morrison, "The Paris years." She said, "You can understand what someone else is thinking by using the 0." I looked at her even harder, concentrating on her form amongst the blue cloud of smoke. I said, "What is the 0 Carol?" She said it was a tight golden band around her head. The halo had been placed there to enable her to understand the inner voice in other people. God was communicating to her in his own voice, he was telling her what to do, what to say. I asked her if it was a good voice that she heard, but she wasn't able to hear me, something was preventing her from hearing me. She said, "Jonnie is coming back soon, Jonnie is coming back soon, he has been away but I don't care where he's been, Jonny's coming back soon..." She clutched the rubber hot water bottle she carried around everywhere close to her chest and resumed her conversation with herself. I left her alone and went to lie down on my bed. The door was ajar on the Staff room and some of the Nurses were in there eating fish suppers, the smell was wonderful. They were laughing and joking as if in some sense the road to happiness was barred from us the service users. I popped my head in the door and said, "Enjoying your dinner? Why aren't we allowed fish suppers...in this institution the harsh winter instinct of the Scottish psyche prevails alright." They just laughed even more, Scots on the rocks all right. The root of the problem lay in its solution; The Scots race ourselves.

I went on my bed and lay there like a party balloon with a slow puncture. I looked in the vanity mirror; I looked like a mongoloid; just like you and me. I lay and looked at the ceiling, there was a crack in the plaster that bisected the room, where the paint was all peeling away. What a fucking residuum all right.

The nurse came into the room and without any fanfare, in that queer drole North East way announced, "You have a visitor, he is sitting in the TV room." I wondered who it could be. Was I receiving visitors? I figured it was a result and put my trainers on and breenged on through. There he was sitting there with his oatmeal Ralph Lauren sweater on, his orange and purple wrap around shades, his baggy home boy denim shorts. It was Jack Killeen from Portland Oregon. Casually he was munching his way through a family sized bag of Cheesy Wotsits. He stood up and removed the shades, his eyes were blue and slightly awry looking, just a skeil of madness there. "Yo Cal how goes it old chap." Jack was an Actor. I had met him when I was in the USA with Eva, out on the coast. He had done his fair share of mining; TV advertising, amateur dramatics, bit parts in movies, painting, writing, directing and performing in his own play. He wanted to make it. We sat down and simultaneously stared at the mock glow off the fire for a few seconds. Jack said, "So what the fuck are you doing in here Cal?" I gave him a brief potted history of the mishaps that had conspired to overtake my life since I had last seen him, and of course Jack knew about my break up with Eva. He was still carefully and concisely working his way through the Wotsits. I supposed the American view of marital breakdown contradicts itself. On the one hand there is the transient nature of existence there, in a country so vast that you can confidently expect never to meet you're ex-wife ever again even by chance. Combine that rootless identity with Beatnik values of the "free spirit" generation; borne out of a deep desire to rebel against traditional white middle class respectability and you have some kind of argument. But in some overwhelming sense you get the feeling that America and Americans have never adequately answered the questions they have posed about themselves. Of course we get older, we trade personal liberty for security, we become afraid of the unknown, become more afraid to look towards the light. I said to Jack, looking down and over him, "You may start out in life as some kind of free radical, but in a sense we increasingly choose to trade that in for a deep sense of Conservatism as we grow older, it is the most profound form of parochiality there is."

Jackie had finished the Wotsits; he scrunched up the bag and landed it plumb in the middle of the steel bin. He hadn't lost his competitive edge. "God Yeah Cal, you should see LA. It is supposed to be at the heart of creative endeavour, but way up on Mulholland, up in Beverly Hills you will get booked for spitting in the street. And it is all going on behind the stucco, the white Venetian blinds, any amount of depravity." "Literally it sucks then Jack." He said he was working on a film script at the moment; it was going to be called "The Stepford Husbands." "All the men are automatons who act in groups except for the lone hero of the piece who represents our lost sense of humanity." I started laughing and said, "So all the actors in that one will just be playing themselves." I said, "When I was in America the thing that made me laugh was that in every town there was a wig shop, where you could get a hair piece or a toupee, or even the full bouffant", "Kinda cheesy Wotsits," said Jack.

So we were agreed on that at least, that was the problem; American cultural values were fairly thin on the ground, it was "Wigged out." I said to Jack, "It is as if in America you are all like plants that have been removed from their native soil and regrown elsewhere. Eventually it is only natural that you should become unique to your new climate. Evolve specifically." "But not suck the juice from the rest of the world as we tend to do and just assume America is the only way of life," said Jack. He was now munching into a Mars bar while yet another starving HIV positive child dies in her Mother's arms in Africa. I said, "You have to remember that in that transplantation process something of your identity was wiped, it is something that you can only be dimly aware of consciously at least. It is as if part of the jigsaw was removed and your quest in life is to somehow find a way of replacing that piece with something else that you actually care about." Jackie was tearing into his candy bar now, he said, "You know about the conspiracy theory Cal in USA? That mammon conspires to keep Americans in a childlike state, uninformed as much as possible, just papering the walls instead of raising the rafters. In a sense it has led to increased isolation and loneliness and that goddamn distance. It has acted in reverse to what it had set out to do; to keep the nation powerful, virile, healthy and strong." "And," I added hesitantly, "Familial."

Jackie had finished his candy bar, he had nothing to do with his hands now, and he seemed a little frustrated. He said, "There are five basic tenets to American culture; God, Food, Guns, Gasoline and Hollywood." He smiled at me with his calcium-enriched teeth, and held up his outstretched North American hand. Someone, somewhere way down the line had decided to enrich the milk in the USA with calcium. Part of the conspiracy theory I supposed. In the same sense almost all American men were circumcised at birth, you had no choice in the matter. I said, "There may be more of a sense of ethnicity in Europe but we mostly have a crap diet here in Scotland, we lead the world in having just about the worst health statistics in any developed country." Jackie seemed a little bored now, he looked longingly at the cold TV screen and said, "But there is more meaning attached to your culture. You are aware here of what has come before you." It was a complicated argument but I suppose Americans liked to simplify that argument where possible and cut to the car chase. I suppose that was what Americans were like: cunningly simple; stuck amongst all that big time society, driving around in those big time automobiles, having to deal with all that big time criminality in their own world, and not thinking twice when their new girlfriend goes down on them after five minutes flat. And resultantly taking that sort of attitude wherever they go in the world. I asked Jack what he was going to do; I said he could crash at my place for a few days. He asked me if I couldn't check out of the place for the night, as if it were in some kind of neon fronted Motel complex. Well I was at the crossroads all right, there was a question mark surrounding my immediate future. I said, "I feel like checking out of this place for good; it's funny how life throws these little challenges at you, nothing is ever straightforward, there always seems to be something holding you back." Jackie had got up and was now fiddling with the TV, desperate to get it on, so he could get his fix and stare vacantly at it in a childlike dumb way because what was invariably on every channel was crap. The notion of bad TV seemed to act as a placebo at the heart of American identity. Jackie couldn't get the TV to work, it was a matter of different systematic customs I suppose, and I wasn't going to put it on for him. He came and sat back down beside me, and looked at me with a mischievous gleam in his eyes; he said, "Why don't you just check yourself out then?" He didn't seem to have any sense of either guilt or responsibility for what he was saying. There was no crow sitting on his shoulder pecking him in the face. It was just a straightforward proposition, a straightforward turn of the screw. I said, "What the hell, Devil get thee ahint me. Wait here

Jack and I will go and check things out with the Staff Nurse."

As I walked along the artificially lit corridor set against the inky night outside, I thought about it; Jack had implanted the seed of certainty back in my mind; that I could be back on the outside looking in on you. Back on the exciting, exhilarating wall of death riding high on dope and drink. It seemed an attractive proposition to my mind; that I could not fail. I knocked on the Staff door, I said to the Staff nurse that I wanted to go out with my friend for the night. She looked thoroughly dismayed, she said it was out of the question; I was to remain on the ward on observations. I suggested an alternative, could I bring alcohol in then? "Not under any circumstances, if we find alcohol on you we will take it off you and put you off the ward for good!" The mercury was rising, shooting up inside me. She said alcohol or any other substance would be the worst thing for me right now, I was to remain on the ward in a stable condition. Of course she was right, but she served to aggravate me, she was taking my toy soldiers away from me in case I sucked on the lead. She was right, I was wrong. She was sane, I was mad, but I had clicked the revolver shut, I had spun the barrel onto the snub nosed bullet in the chamber, and my finger was on the trigger. I lost my temper, I said, "You can keep your poxy medication, you can keep your carnival of freaks, you can keep your pig slops food. You can't keep me here against my will, I am signing myself out." In hindsight it was not the most foolish decision I have ever made, just one of them. It just prolonged my diagnosis and also prolonged the most severe manifestation of my illness. Of course there are ways that Lunatic Asylums can keep you in Hospital against your will, but I was still to discover that. That lay waiting in the wings.

The Nurse was totally calm, she said if that was my final decision there was nothing they could do to stop me leaving but she implored me to reconsider. I said that I had my mind made up about leaving. I was a novice. I wasn't in complete possession of all the facts concerning my health. Because it was true mental distress is in some sense invisible, is in some sense an intangibility.

The Staff Nurse said I would have to see the Medical Doctor first and sign a discharge form. At the end of the day it discharged the carers from any liability if something went wrong. "Just let me out of here," I swaggered, with the false sense of bravura of some Daguerro type. I went through to tell Jack the good news. All the little sparrows had now assembled, in their crackled little nests. Their feathers fluffy and unpreened. The doyennes of TV viewing, incubating, sitting upon their own illness. Outside it was pitch black, it was funny how at this time of year nighttime descends and swoops upon the light like a thief in the dark, suddenly sometimes it seems irrevocable until the dawn returns. Jack reacted positively to the news, loudly and mock-heroic he announced, "You are the man Cal, lets ship the fuck outta here." Meanwhile nothing stirred in the ranks of the little disaffected sparrows. They were in the nether regions of the Styx somewhere amongst the swirling nebulous matters of the psyche. Tall Paul trudged through in his bare feet, he banged himself on the ear and said, "I wish I could get out of here but I'm hearing voices like fuck tonight." Perhaps it was a message of foreboding to me.

Doctor Ward arrived on the scene in her white coat and open black silk blouse. I could see Jackie undressing her with his eyes as if every woman you encounter in life was a possible conquest. I thought of the red blood coming out of my arm not so long ago. I said nothing. The Doctor and I went through to the ward alone. She sat me down on the bed, turned on the angle poise bed light and sat down beside me. Her black tights gave off a coiled sheen, the way that silk does. I could smell her perfume. As usual she seemed incredibly tired, harassed and short of time. Momentarily I felt guilty at adding to her burden on the front line. She said,

"You are extremely rash signing yourself out of psychiatric hospital at this stage of your treatment…anything could happen to you. This is the best place for you where you will remain safe." I added hesitantly, as if slightly afraid of her sexuality, "Safely locked up." She replied firmly that perhaps at the moment I was not in the best position to be in control of my own life. "You are not acting rationally or sensibly, but at the end of the day it is your decision if you want to discharge yourself." Maybe I was heading towards the waterfall and trying to paddle in the opposite direction but my mindset was decided. I said, "I want to discharge myself tonight Doctor Ward." She seemed resigned to losing me to the gothic city. She said, "I am giving you two weeks of medication and you will receive appointments in the next couple of days for your GP and the Psychiatrist. It is imperative that you continue to take your medication as prescribed and that you totally avoid smoking cannabis and drinking alcohol." She knew that I knew. My eyes had focused on an area somewhere to her side when she had said this. How often had this little drama been enacted before? It always seems to be at night, it always seems to be dark outside when these little dramas of classical proportions unfold. I didn't really want to stop and consider it all for any length of time. If I had I would have been terrified. I signed the discharge form and Doctor Ward rose and turned off the bedside light. She wished me good luck; she was silhouetted in the semi-darkness, at once I became afraid as if there would soon be sinister forces acting over me. The beginning of a season of discontent. She was gone.

I packed my bag quickly, stuffing it shut without thinking about it. The rest of the ward suddenly seemed afraid somehow. My leaving was forcing them to contemplate an environment they didn't want to think about. A world that had shit upon them. I said goodbye to them all quickly and went and got Jack from the TV room. The staff nurse gave me my supply of medication and went to let me out. She plucked a key from her bunch and opened the door. I could smell the freshness of the outdoors; suddenly it seduced me into believing that everything was going to be all right. The nurse gave me a perceptive look before we were gone, Scot-free. It was as if silently she was saying, "You'll be back in here before long my lad, just wait and see if I'm not right." It was no time for sentiment on my part though, just brusqueness. I positively cart wheeled down the stairs and out through the exit past the perpetual neon hum of the Coke machine, and the rolled up fire hose set into the wall. As soon as we got into the grounds Jack and I started running. Running through the scrunch of the late fall leaves. I shouted, "We're free," and did an air punch of victory. Jackie shouted back, "I'm as free as a bird," and we ended up in a giggling heap in a raked bunch of leaves. I could hear now the whoosh of the oncoming traffic outside the high perimeter wall, built of granite random rubble and lime mortar. Built to last. The city was seducing me in her glacial grip. I took out my supply of medication and defiantly threw it into the leaves. I didn't care; I was back on top of the world again. Jack picked it up and looked at it, he said, "Does this shit get you high?" I started laughing and said, "Don't be daft," and threw a handful of leaves at him; he said he would keep it for me anyway, "Just in case you change your mind." We walk up the grounds steadily now under an orange quarter moon, silently aware of the enormity of what we have done. Walking parallel to the obelisk that commemorates the founding of this Lunatic Asylum in Victorian Britain. We pass out of the grounds and cross over the passenger bridge that bisects the shiny black tarmac of the arterial highway. We stop on the hump of the bridge and look down towards the shoreline. The profile of the ancient stone houses surrounds the curve of the yellow beach and the North Sea at the bottom. Like now grey blue water enclosed in a test tube. The noise of the cars swishes, repeating themselves over and over. Their blue halogen headlights picking out their own path like a needle in the hem of a skirt. It seems to me a sophisticated exotic notion somehow. Apparently though here it is not. Jack pulls a cigarette from a soft pack of Camel and lights himself up, a rare smoke. He says, "This city is so grey and at once hard, it has a permanence, an ethereal quality." The moonlight is spotted here and there with the yellow of the tenemental windowpanes, lit vertically up. The inky black feminine pointed limbs of the bare, almost winter trees silhouetting the backcourts. I attach meaning to the landscape, and say quietly to Jack, "That is a large part of my identity out there." He nods in understanding. I am reminded of what I still long for in Aberdeen. I feel nostalgic for the certainty it once represented for me, but feel inhabited by a sense of spiritual unease.

On the way back to the flat we decide to stop and buy a bottle of vodka and a carton of tomato juice. We will have a little drink to celebrate the moment. In the Co-op skimming around. It is almost deserted. Suddenly I realise the aisles are not quite wide enough; perhaps I am reminded of the USA. We are not encouraged to think big in Britain. It is partly a question of the limits of scale, but there is still that nagging doubt, as you are forced to seek out every bargain, that our culture is an overwhelmingly utilitarian one. I say to Jack that the defining moment of John Major's premiership was when he declared that now there was so much choice of food on the supermarket shelves in Britain. "Kinda shabby thing for the PM to say," declared Jack as he greedily eyed the cuts of saucisson and pastrami on the deli counter. "In no sense is this happiness," I said as we strode purposefully towards the drink section.

There are distinct customer types who shop in here according to the time of day. Mornings are reserved for mainly the old people, clogging up the stream flow system. Now blissfully unaware of the frustration of the relative youth and sprite stuck behind them. In the afternoons the mother and child, the working people and inevitably the smoking teenager and children. And me popping up all over the place like a wild card. To use the American idea of alienation, like the single existential man sitting in an all-night diner sipping coffee, on the road, on the strip. I feel so fucking lonely.

There is a deal on vodka, (there is always a deal on vodka), still alcohol keeping the population down and me still keeping a firm hand on her crutch. A bewildering choice of 40% fine grain spirit alcohol. There is Totov, there is Chekhov, and there is Orlov. We settle for a bottle of Vladivar. It is probably distilled outside Kirkcaldy somewhere. We pay for the booze and walk round to my flat. I put on the CD player, low key, subdued lighting system and fire up the central heating.

"Cheers Jack," we slurped on our bloody drinks. I was out, I was home. It was late; it was dark outside in the most Northern English speaking City in Europe. I suddenly had a bright idea. I said, "Let's go down to the Bowery club in Market Street tonight. It's a basement club and the music is usually great, not like The Dandy Warhols or The Dharma Bums in Portland, but raw techno European acid house music." Jack sucked on his cocktail. It was funny how America made the distinction between beers and hard liquor. Perhaps it was a more conservative, healthy approach to drinking. Fuck that Jack. He asked me what the ecstasy thing was about. To him it seemed more than just taking drugs and music. It seemed to be trying to establish some kind of token counter culture. I said to Jack the whole thing was framed together. "Here we are a whole generation of disaffected adulthood. The product of marital breakdowns trying to construct meaningful lives for ourselves from the wreckage. Almost exclusively we live in a secular culture now but we still desire to attach some sort of spiritual identity to our lives. In a sense the music is new, attached to a new perspective of life. The music and ecstasy combined is attempting to question what is the point of our existence. In a sense it is primarily about communication. How we have almost forgotten to identify with one another, and also how we have forgotten to identify with creation. I mean is there really nothing else out there but us here on Earth? There is definitely something in the whole rave scene, there is a whole spectrum of colour." Jack said, "I think it sure is true that love has become less attainable these days, we seem more apart than ever." I finished my drink and went to get us both another one from the kitchenette. I said over my shoulder, "Life is a mystery alright. All Acid House music is doing is making its own contribution to the idea of union and the specific ideal of everlasting life."

I came back with the drinks and sat down. Jack said, "It is true that usually unless you have been very sick as a child you don't consider your own mortality until you reach the age of thirty, and thereafter there is not a day goes by when you don't think about your own death."

"And that's it Jack," I said laying the drinks softly down on the veneered cherry wood coffee table, "We don't now have much of a concept of death, and that the rest is probably just darkness. The only way we can express ourselves is to get trashed on cider and other stuff up on boot hill cemetery and then go and write a plasticine poem about it." Jack shook a flattened Camel out for himself, it was another moment of definition, he said, "Ya gotta spark Cal?" I fired him up. He inhaled deeply on the domestic and Turkish blend cigarette and then exhaled blue in enjoyment. "Yeah the whole thing Cal is just like plasticine now for us, we don't recognise the difference between shit and clay."

I said, "Have you noticed the fashion now. It is as if people are preparing for the new Armageddon, without ever having had their finger on the trigger. It is all action man kit: rugged trendy trainers, combat style fatigues and bejewelled in new age piercings." "Maybe they are hoping to make a quick getaway," said Jack. I said, "Perhaps it will be Armageddon time but I would like to think that we are in vogue by making a statement definitively against war." I got the vodka bottle and topped us up both a little. I capped it and stuck it in the fridge. I said, "No-one is spared from having to touch death at some point in their lives." "That is the problem with the fun-park, Technicolor pay and go concept of the USA, it fools you. It fools you into thinking that it will never end. Of course that was before AIDS, that has driven a wedge amongst us all like the four points of the compass," said Jack grinding out his cigarette. He had smoked it right to the butt. I reflected that some creatures had to die in order that the rest could live. Society didn't condone this set of affairs, didn't say it was either right or wrong. It is what we call primitive that the majority of those of us, who live, spend our existence in anguish, while a minority are consumed with self-indulgence. Many of this latter group assume our leadership. Art can be obscene, or rather Artists can. I said, "Do you think we are living in the age of the moronic inferno then Jack?" He started laughing,

he said, "That is like asking an American if he eats cheeseburgers."
"So you don't think it exists then?" Jack replied brightly, he said,
"I think it exists alright, it is ubiquitous in USA, and that is why
there is little or no basis for comparison with a philosophy of life
that is fairer and more humane. Jack Kerouac shortly before he died
thought well perhaps I have another novel in me. So he decides
to go back on the road one more time. He's standing on the New
Jersey Turnpike trying to hitch a lift. The most important post-war
beatnik contemporary USA novelist is standing trying to hitch a
lift and no one will pick him up. People don't generally stop for
strangers anymore they are too afraid, everyone else drives. So what
can he do, he has to get his rucksack and go back home to his
Mom." I said, "Back home for a little Wild Turkey, green bud and
Joan Baez?" "It is just that things have taken a turn for the worse,
we are all so damn corseted and isolated," said Jack.

I said to Jack I was going to have a wash and a shave and change
from my hospital clothes and then we could go out. We both got
ready, dumbed the flat down into dark cold-water mode and then
went out. I double-checked that the half core front door was locked.
I said to Jack, "That poxy door is all there is between me, Kermit
the frog, Miss Piggy et al," pointing around the shut up winterous
landing. "Thank fuck for the Housing Project Cal," said Jack.

We walked into Town. We stopped at MacDonald's and went
in. Looking like a pair of ravenous morons. The place was busy, it
was sad somehow this burger joint. Acting as a treat for British
Teenagers. It made me profoundly sad if I thought about it. It was
funny how at times like this I could feel responsible for my fellow
Aberdonians. As if their innocence was to be retained at all cost
despite all this. However we had bacon double cheeseburgers and
fries and watched the kids mucking around.

Jack and I walked into the Wild Boar, through the open glass
and pine green double door. Past the two spiky Tiger plants. Over
the coconut welcome mat.

I got us a couple of lagers and we took up stations on the smoking
side of the bar. There was a guy going around giving out fliers for

The Bowery. I knew him, it was "Leigh Loofah" to use his stage mic. Jack said, "That's a strange looking brother, he looks like a reject from the Simpsons, who figured a job out on the set of Clockwork Orange." Leigh was dressed in his usual moon bather gear; shaved slap head, black bowler hat and yellow and blue Helly Hansen fireproof coat. He had on long homeboy style black stitched denim shorts, just like Jackie. He had a big nose like Ebenezer Good. Leigh ran The Bowery and also fancied himself as something of a MC mixer, max waxer and "Jelly Bean" record producer. He came over towards our table, his long skinny calves were like pins stuck into soft black calf leather booties with the little white short socks just showing. You didn't really know where you stood with Leigh; it was hard to work out what he was thinking, if indeed it required much of a light to do his version of entertainment anyway. He smiled broadly at me, showing off his new teeth. He had just had them veneered recently. Leigh said, "Alrighty then lager maties, bit parkie out in the granola chill zone tonite. Coming down to the rumba clubbie for some ace esoteric tunes to beat da tomba to?" He had one of those hybrid Midland/Aberdonian accents of indistinct origin. Like one of those cod ex footballers turned commentators. I restrained a giggle and introduced him to Jack. Of course Leigh was totally non-plussed about meeting an American. It was as if his non-plussedness was an act in itself. They started chatting about the music scene out on the coast. Of course Leigh had been to San Fran many times. I blurted out suddenly, "Bart!" And started laughing. They both looked a little bemused at that little irony. He really was a fairly dodgy dude Leigh, a troubled and mysterious past it would seem that was all thrown like a blanket over most people. In a previous incarnation he spent two years in the Bastille for peddling coke. Or so he said. Let's just say that Leigh liked to exaggerate the truth, and that the length of his nose grew in direct proportion to the amount he lied. When he was on remand in Paris no one from Aberdeen would come forward and pay his bond. I once saw him at a scummy party rip off a poster on the wall of Boy George and shit on it. Leigh seemed a bit of an exhibitionist, he got a kick out of displaying his large genitalia. Once he had a one-night stand with an American ex-girlfriend of mine. Now this girlfriend was gorgeous when she took her glasses off. Part Native American, papoose breasts, exotic tattoos all over her New Mexican body. The sparks had flown off the ass of her tight little Levis more than once. After they got off, she told me he was scared in bed. He wouldn't have penetrative sex, no touching or intimacy. He treated her cynically like some kind of pole dancer, he just wanted her to touch his cock and balls and suck him off.

I suppose the strangest thing I could think about Leigh was when he set up an "operating theatre" in his promotion associate's flat. It was within Leigh's ambit of influence to provide a surgeon, (trainee), nurses, local anaesthetic and all the surgical paraphernalia. The patient or rather victim of this meaningless piece of schadenfreude was Clarke, Aberdeen's original Acid Casualty. He had picked up a rhinestone in Texas and he wanted it inserted into his foreskin, so he could give a little tickle on entry and withdrawal. Like Thai green curry on a stick; hot cock. Leigh's associate Sim was just as exotic as Leigh was. His party behaviour included enticing drunken young female students to his Bohemian residence where he would ply them with a heady mixture of extra chesty cough linctus, booze and hashish, and then seduce them. The last time I saw Leigh I walked in on him in the kitchen at this party, he was getting all his pubic hair shaved off for a bet. It seemed a bit dry down there so I got a hold of the "Squeezy" and squirted some on. Sleaze. I laughed my arse off. Aye it's strange up North alright. All those endless summer nights and Arctic Winter mornings. Infused by all that Radon gas that seeps from the granite and makes you "Feel" in the head.

Leigh drifted away to the next table, he didn't even mention my current problems with the head, and he was too self-centred to delve into that human orbit. After that we went to another pub for a drink then drifted down to The Bowery Club, down towards the docks. It was around midnight and we skipped down the stairs to the Bowery. We didn't have to pay. I never had to pay. The club was a bar with some tables, chairs and a small dance floor. Next-door was a larger dance floor where the MC sat high up above the crowd on a platform, protected by a mesh grill. Where the Sol bottles would rain if the music were shite. It was an Urban Techno Rap night. The music coming out of the sub-woofer system was laying down a thudding funky assed base line. We got a couple of Red Stripes. The place was a mixture, a heaving mass of students and regular no hopers like myself. Who came in here at weekends to define the rough pinnacle of our meaningless week. Jackie seemed impressed though, it was an experience. I said to him, "C'mon lets pop into the Chill room for a minute." There was a little room half way up the stairs with seating. The light was orangey red in there; the seats were clad in vermilion velveteen liberally spattered with "bombers,"(hash burns). Jack exclaimed suddenly, "It makes perfect sense; ambience, the colour we see in the womb." Keith the Artist was sitting there. He was a painter and I suppose he never refused a drink. He had chosen to scrape the bottom of the barrel for most of his adult life, and he figured, that is where you find it; life. Amongst the copper head blues, amongst the sediment. Keith seemed to always be hanging around, silent and mild, like a panatella cigar. He would never take the initiative himself, like walk into a bar in company first, but he would wait patiently alone and someone would always buy him a drink. He was harmless; there was nothing the matter with him. I said, "Hi Keith," he shot his hand up in the air silently in Fuhrer fashion. Keith had this kind of nervous affectation in the neck where he would make a facial contortion when he was confronted with other people. The stomach under his shirt looked as if it was waiting to give birth to the ambient child. The music was thudding from downstairs. I introduced him to Jackie who was by now banging away on a set of bongos in the room. Keeping a beat to the music, with a crazy moronic grin on his face. Perhaps Jackie thought he was like Marlon Brando, in "the early years," on a recreational night out. I suppose the only difference between the two actors was that Jackie had still to effectively shit on his own chocolate cake. Keith seemed dismayed by Jack. He said, "I heard that you were in the psychiatric hospital, up on the hill." I replied to him crassly, "I discharged myself." Keith's face was filled with a look of intense concern. He was genuine Keith; even with a bead on he wouldn't dismiss you. It was something that I was still learning, from other people's trade. Keith said, "You want to try and keep away from that place. You should stay away from drink and dope meantime." Keith must have meant it. I offered to buy him a drink but he demurred emphatically. I just shrugged, left the coomb and went down to the bar. It was hoaching, but I have a talent for snaking and slithering my way to the counter in no time. Someone had erected a shrine to Elvis behind the bar. It was like a rug thing with a tapestry of The King in his Vegas years, and two candles burning either side. I bought a couple more Red Stripe and went back upstairs with the drink. Keith had disappeared. Jack was sitting now finishing his drink He said, "This is great lager, and it's Jamaican, no?" I passed him a fresh can and said, "Yeah mon, Jamaican, just like the sensei mon." I said to Jack, "Do you want to hear a story about the Caribbean that kinda sums up the shabbiness of this country." Jack said, "Fire away I'm all ears." I said, "In the late 50s' and early 60s' when just about every Afro culture was aspiring to Nationalism, the Caribbean was no different, and their Britain was still the colonial master. Parallel to that, back in the UK there was probably the largest post war investment in infrastructure there has ever been. Harold Wilson called it 'the white heat of technology'. There was a massive skills shortage in Britain, and those were the days when labour costs were proportionally marginal in the construction industry. What do you think West Indians are the finest in the world at apart from music, drinking and weed?" Jack said, "I dunno, multiple fatherhood?" I smiled and said, "Concrete, they are probably the best shuttering carpenters and building workers there are, and they were needed in UK." "So there was a kind of trade off went down; Britain got its skilled workforce and the West Indies got Independence," said Jack. "Crudely speaking yes," I replied. I said, "It is worse than that though in the long term. Britain had enough foresight to realise that leisure based upon increased income would become the aspiration of white Britain. But it didn't realise that in the Caribbean there were the finest resorts in the world, in a sense we should have been able to invest in the Caribbean and repatriate communities into a finer way of life but that didn't happen." "In a sense then Nationalism was the politics of the day in Britain, (and is once more), now we have what Enoch Powell described as the river of black and white blood. Crack and dope, gun-crime, rape, murder, prostitution. A break down in society in both Trench-town and London," said Jack idly while he listened to the next track and sucked on his tin. "Foresight is the first principle I was taught as a surveyor, and it is that which is most lacking in our Politicians," I said bitterly.

We decided to go down and sample the dance floor. We went into the main hall where there was a huge camouflaged canopy hanging from the ceiling, the walls were black and sweating. A panoply of people was dancing, battle scarred in the urban jungle by jah war. Two couples took centre stage on the dance floor-enacting psycho Billy slam dancing. It involved immaculate timing, elaborate footwork and energy from each partner. The style of dancing was filled with an expression of hatred, throwing and pulling back in towards, harnessed aggression from each partner. The room was dark except for the red, blue and yellow lights flashing in rhythm to the beat. The room was stinking of reefer; it was good and claustrophobic, intense. Just like the "Granola" chill zone outside there was a hard edge to our conscious expression of leisure in our country down in here tonight. I shouted at Jackie who had started doing his own little monosyllabic shuffle, "You been in a place like this before Jackie?" He just grinned sweatily and raised his can to his mouth. I should have known; he could fit himself through a keyhole and still think it was clever and worth the effort, standing intact on the other side. Pete the Punk was there, the only dealer that had made it on to the front page of the Evening Express for selling 2% pure speed. He passed me the communal joint. I blew hard for a couple of minutes then passed it on to Jackie who roached it. There were quite a few good-looking women around. Kind of hard looking with their high uplift bras keeping their titties proudly stuck up and out. Somehow they knew it, they were content to just dance. Their magnetism was silhouetted by the tickering of the strobe that came on periodically, picking out her auburn hair, picking out her sapphire nose stud. Her white Tee shirt shines brilliantly, the face of her Swatch glows. Discos had become Niteclubs, we had pudenda now. More unisex now if you didn't have a partner. No sex places. The late 90s'; straighten the back and take a look, take a suck on your tinny. HIV, post-feminist definition, dodgy guys, had driven some kind of fast setting concrete between the sexes. The scene had transformed itself overnight. Girls loved to dance with you but it was harder to go any further. Women had been reinvented now as in some way choosing to be alone from men. But at the expense of love, an ideal that seemed less focused and almost dead.

Jack and I danced away, becoming part of the sway, riding on the swell of the move mania. The music had the effect of pulling everyone to the same concentric point. We had more drinks and then suddenly it was 2am and time to go home. The house lights came on anti-climactically, and the bouncers started clearing from the back out the people and debris. It was funny how unglamorous people look in a Night Club when they are picked out by the ordinariness of reality. I said to Jack we should leg it upstairs and we would get a taxi. We managed to get a place in the rank near the head of the queue. Taxi ranks at club closing time in urban Scotland are no places for the faint hearted. Whether it is Paisley, Dundee, or here, Market Street. And now this is the setting; hard unforgiving granite. The orange halogen spotlights up in the eaves of the opposite building are swirled by a wind-blown phantasmagorical fog, creating a gothic ghostly pallor. The pervasive smell of fish "bree" hangs in the air exciting the super herring gulls to a starving frenzy. Swooping down to the damp shiny granite cobbled street they screech and squabble over a discarded kebab. No one pays them any attention. The minkers disgorge from the Country and Western night in the Metro, and the lap top bars. Everyone almost rubberised drunk. Everyone talking in the coarse working class Aberdeen dialect that evolved this way. Somehow, somewhere they forgot the glottal stop. The police hover in numbers at a safe distance in their lime green reflective jackets. People are being sick exciting the gulls even more, chittering and crowing up on the roofs. The scene is like Sodom and Gomorrah as the police move in to break up a punch up. They radio for the meat wagon while simultaneously cuffing up. Everywhere are people with surgical walking sticks doubling up as weapons. A stunted bastard race of Scotchmen. People with casts, our caste. Garish hard gallous women with blazing mascara laden eyes, and red gashes of mouths. Tights rip; people gather and come together in small loosely formed groups. Drinking beer, smoking dope, groping at one another's bodies in the bitter cold. Someone shouts the address of a party and the crowd cheers and begins to lurch off en masse. Let the beggars banquet flourish once more. Drop some tabs, do some beer, smoke a Lambert and Butler, (the crème de la crème of urban class cigarettes). In the lane opposite the rank a man is being harangued loudly and abusively by a prostitute, he is pishing in her spot, where she takes her punters. Jackie just stands there dumbly with his mouth wide open. He has never encountered this kind of urban vernacular in the USA. I say to him, "You have to stand your ground. You learn to make a fist in this country from an early age." A taxi pulls up. It's tyres making a piffling noise as it rides across the granite setts. We jump in, it is our car. Dark intimacy. The familiar smell of vanilla and Ford plastic. The glow from the instrument lights, the fugged heat. As I am getting in the front seat a man emerges from the shadows where he has been lurking and shouts at me, "Hey min, fat boy slim that was my Taxi." I look over my shoulder at him for a couple seconds, the door still ajar. I shout back at him, "Away and fucking walk in the shadow of your Mother's own pish you stupid looking cunt." He visibly retreats back into the shadow. I slam the door and we take off at speed. The driver clicks on the meter casually and smiles at me. He says, "Don't worry about people like that, they are just the little people."

CHAPTER FOUR

I woke up early the next day; the light was streaming in the window, bathing me in therapeutic sunshine. I am awake but trapped in that web of innocence when you have no past and no future, only present. I suddenly recall the events of yesterday and the black bird of guilt comes back to haunt me. I could hear Nigel upstairs creaking about in his lonely world of hermitude. I went through to the living room to make some coffee in the kitchenette. The room was draped in darkness. The noise of traffic from the busy thoroughfare was rushing in the window polluting the silence. Jack groaned at me from the settee, he had a hangover. He would like to have a lot of sleep today and get up feeling totally poxy. I made some coffee. I suddenly said to Jack, "Let's go down to Edinburgh." I said we could stay overnight with my Gran. Jackie was enthused by the idea he shot upright in the bedclothes, he was naked except for his boxer shorts. A generous rug of hair covered his chest. It was funny how almost all American men had hairy chests as if it was an essential part of the red-blooded identikit. The Step-ford Husbands? I phoned my Gran's Edinburgh house, Lorna Moone answered the phone, she was never too far away, and sometimes I reflected selfishly never far away enough. She sounded concerned but managed to restrain the anger she was feeling towards her son. It was an illogical sort of anger that she displayed towards me at times. Her disagreement with me was based upon the fact that we loved each other but I was financially reliant upon her sometimes and consequently she liked me to abide by certain rules that were invisible but clearly marked out by her. She had set out the boundaries, not me. I liked to make my own rules. She said to me, "Why did you discharge yourself from hospital yesterday, what a foolish fellow!" I replied back to her calmly, "You can't begin to understand how much I hate that place, how good it is to have Jack here just now." I said, "We are coming down to Edinburgh today, can we stay with Gran tonight?" Lorna Moone brightened up at this idea, "Of course darling," she said, "Mama would love to see you and we can meet Jack." Lorna Moone was learning that you had to make allowances for sons with psychiatric illness. I mean it was my Father and she that had got me into this mess in the first place, but that reeked of self-pity. It was surely possible to change from within the person who you were. The parents somehow had to emerge blameless at the end of the day if like Lorna Moone you had all striven to do your best for your children. And Norman, was he guiltless? Maybe he was just reckless. I should ask his Mother Nora, my Grandmother later today. Nora and Lorna were very close; they both possessed an innate attraction for one another. The grace and modest wisdom of the older woman had rubbed off on Lorna. Nora had passed something essential on to Lorna that her own mother could not provide. It was a kind of middle class sophistication, an intellectual aspiration that seemed both exotic and attractive to both women. I said, "I will see you both tonight then around 6pm." I hung up the phone; the hard part was over.

Jack had leapt out of the bed into the bathroom. He was making noisy spitting and phlegmy coughing sounds into the WC, clearing his nasal passages of catarrh. He started brushing his teeth making an even more disgusting noise. White trash getting white teeth, there was no subdued tone to America's ablutions in the morning. He rinsed then poked his head round the door, "All set up then Cal for the Edinburgh trip?" That was it; life to him was an infinite carpet unfurling forward. There wasn't much point in looking backwards unless you had to. I was balancing a biro on my forefinger in a moment of familial reflection, all very clever but not quite worth the effort. I said, "Yup Jackie all set my boy." I slugged the end of my coffee and went through to get dressed. I got dressed and went back through to the living room; Jackie was eating a big bowl of cereal. He was shrouded in the blankets of his bed and was watching the television dumbly like a child. Transfixed by the images, every now and then the spoon would go from bowl to mouth automatically without looking. I shouted out in a mock American accent, "Right Jackie you've had your coffee fix, you've had your cereal fix, you've had your TV fix, time to get up." "Oh gee Cal can't I watch this, could I have a couple of slices of toast?" I just made him the toast and then pulled the heavy brown velvet curtains apart. The cold winterous light the colour of yellow ice cream flooded into every corner of the room destroying the notional romper pen that Jackie had constructed for himself.

We got ready and went to catch the bus to Edinburgh from Guild street bus station. I thought about the States and the time I rode from LA to Seattle and all stops in between. Twenty-six hours. The woman next to me offered me cool potable water from her jar. She was black; it was funny how there were clear lines of racial segregation in the States. She showed me the razor sharp hunting knife she had to protect herself. It was funny how when you waited for a coach in the States you had to wait inside the terminus until your stance number was called. And then you stood in line patiently until the doors were unlocked and you could climb aboard with your boarding pass checked. Here everyone just milled around. Sucking on a ten pack of Regal, scanning the Sun, eating crisps. It was a kind of antediluvian quaintness. It was a kind of real life parody of the innocence of experience in "Trumpton". With an edge. We got a seat on the bus at the rear, it wasn't too busy. Jack had his water, his peanuts, and his piece of fruit. We are on our way down the coastal back of the East of Scotland. Down towards the ancient capital city of Edinburgh.

We both chilled into the journey. Took a while to redefine our wakeful state after the excesses of the previous night. I began to tell Jack a story about Edinburgh when I was a student at a place there called Newbattle Abbey Adult Residential College. I had a holiday job as a Setting Out Engineer on a construction site at the Scot-mid Co-operative building in Fountainbridge, up in the North West of the City. Jack said, "What the hell is a Setting Out Engineer?" I replied, "It is probably the most crucial job on the site. It is the physical point from which all the other work can commence. Basically with the use of Theodolite and Surveying Level, the Setting out Engineer transfers the drawings to physical points on the ground, and the construction works commence from these building controls; of both line and level. In addition to this basic surveying the Engineer also has to supervise the Construction. It was a renovation contract; we were setting out massive areas of external car parking and permanent fencing boundaries. The guy who helps the Engineer is the chainman. While the engineer sets out from the surveying stations the chainman measures the distances, gets lined up by the instrument and bangs in Hilti nails or wooden nailed stakes. Brian was helping me. You didn't need much intelligence to be a good chainman; just accuracy and good at swinging the hammer. So I get Brian. He was totally humourless. The bitter lees of life's experience marked him out as in some sense resentful of anyone who didn't represent the narrow margin of life that he came from. He turned up for work in the same clothes every day. Blue umbro top, Heart of Midlothian FC tracksuit bottoms and safety boots. Of course Brian could barely read let alone read to measure with a tape. I had to go and point the distance for him at each setting out point. Brian's frustration at his own lack of education was translated into a sense of simmering hatred, which I was waiting for him to direct at me. His resentment was illogical, but then all resentment is. Okay so it is unfair that he couldn't do my job, but I had a Site Agent driving me on. The notorious lack of communication in the building industry had led to Brian working with me. At that particular point in time I didn't really consider whether it was fair that some people achieve their true potential in their working lives and others do not. I wanted to get on with the work. I would try and encourage Brian but it is almost impossible to educate someone who is too single minded and proud to admit he can't read. So we continue with our little rigmarole of me virtually doing his job as well. Brian had been well placed there to teach me something about Scotland itself. Eventually we get through the fencing, and the labourers and joiners move in excavating holes, concreting, plumbing and lining and jambing. There is nothing finer than seeing a series of arcs created on the physical plane. Of course Brian just stood and watched them working. He had shifted himself on to a different plateau of paid labour now. He was the Engineer's chainman.

"Our next task was to set out concrete "kerb log" for the car parking. It was a complicated job. I had to redesign all the black top gradients and the drainage layout and gully positions so the surface water would shed away into the storm water sewer. Brian didn't care that I put that effort in; he had been educated into the belief that spaghetti grew on trees. Of course that wasn't his fault either, but try getting that across to someone who is as tightly shut as an oyster-among the maelstrom, among the harangue of a building site in full swing. Well the sun had been growing higher and warmer on our cozy relationship, and that day it reached the apex of its curve. We had graded a section of sub-base to the correct gradient ready to receive the steel shutters for the kerb log. An experienced Engineer rarely makes mistakes. If he or she does, it is usually because they are under intense pressure from many different directions on the project. As a result of "fast track" building techniques it is the most stressful job on the site. Dave the foreman wanted me to go and mark out a "slap out" on an exterior wall. He said to get Brian started on the kerb log. I just looked at him and said nothing; the man was ignorant of his work force if nothing else.

"I showed Brian how to proceed, the only way. Pin the back forms; check the template between the pans. I set up a level string line for him, but at the end of the day you have to assume a little intuition for the work, some sort of actual experience. I went to mark out the slap out. I was relieved to be free of Brian's omniscient brooding presence. What happens here is that you establish the opening you want to take out. Position two holes above the opening at set points and then punch them out. Then by means of a transverse scaffold you underpin the masonry above. You take out an opening for the insitu lintel, put in your re-bar and construct an envelope shutter. You cast the lintel then take out your opening. You have your slap out. I went inside with the drawing to set out. The high ceilinged room was being gutted. It was massive with ornate round, Victorian cast iron columns. There was the stench of wet pissing plaster, lathe, and fungal rot in the air. In the corner of the room there was a huge pile of black steel voting boxes, there were literally hundreds of them. They all had written on the front in white enamel, "Scottish Midland Cooperative, Ballot Boxes." The boxes were long empty now, are still long empty. The importance of the ballot almost forgotten somehow. In a skip the demolition labourers were throwing hundreds of bound documents and ledgers. I picked up one of the ledgers; it was meticulously scribed in long hand Victorian writing accounting for each hapenny spent. Now it was worthless junk. People's collective toil amounted at the end of the day to little more than the contents of a skip. The ethos was democratic, but now the voting boxes lay empty and discarded. Somehow neglected like Scotland herself. We had forgotten about people like Brian. Politics should represent more than only a full stomach, a secure job and a warm home. That should merely be the springboard for potentiality. Politics was all about setting out in the right direction, but whereas the physical task was one of certainty, the political promise was merely a false goal of moral certitude. Invariably politicians proved to be poor Setting Out Engineers."

The bus had travelled, as far south as the countryside of Angus. The rolled up bales of hay lay motionless in the bristled, russet, barley and cornfields. Jack had been listening to me with interest. I looked out at the landscape, my Mother's heartland. I thought for a moment and said to him, "There is a Scottish word that describes most political ambition in this small fettered country; Scotland. The word is Torie." John asked me eagerly, "The word Torie Cal? The word Torie what does it mean?" I replied dryly with certainty, "It means; the grub of the Daddy Long Legs, the insect you know as the crane fly in North America. It is a seemingly innocuous, harmless bug, but the grub attacks the roots of grain crops and causes ruin, the crop becomes 'Torieat'. It is a direct metaphor for the damage that has been done to the people of this country." Jack was on a roll now, he said, "So what happened then with the guy on the construction site?"

"I came out from the building where I had been doing my work, and went to see how Brian was progressing. I was hoping against hope that I would be able to congratulate him. That even he might have taken pride in his work, an interest. I mean that is what everything comes down to. If you are able to comprehend what a task is you can carry it out with enjoyment. There is no greater enjoyment at some times than manual toil that interests you. I was hoping that it was going to be a point where at last Brian would show me just a glimmer of recognition, that he could now respect me. The air was reeking with the smell of brewing. Scottish and Newcastle's Brewery was just around the corner, the blue five pointed star pinned to the stack. It was the distinctive smell of the "Commons" that rises to the surface in the brewing process and is skimmed off as worthless scum. Spent worthless barley and hops. Their vitality given in order to give the beer body.

"Brian had misunderstood the point of what he was doing. He had contrived to lay the shutters in the opposite direction to the levels. Or was it malicious, was he set to antagonise me? His work was incorrect and incompetent. I just said to him that his work was wrong. No more, no less than that. He lost his temper and started shouting at me intimidatingly, we confronted one another. I thought of some of the young men at Newbattle Abbey College, the burning, violent indiscriminate anger they had within themselves. This was no different, it was the tide mark of our times. The fallout from the failed Miners Strike, social unrest like a rash on the streets of Toxteth. The Secretary of State for Scotland hiding behind Perspex windows. There is no point in trying to be on the level. Either rise above it all or wade in." Brian threatened to hit me, he said, "Ya radge whoore, I'll gie ye a slap sir." "Our relationship hadn't progressed any further than managing the first line on a Rubik cube. I just looked at him with cold, angry, intelligent blue eyes. He backed down. I got the boss and Brian melted like a chocolate watch. The rest of his time would be spent back on demolition. They are hard enough those Edinburgh boys."

Jack said, "It is terrible how industrial work tends towards brutalisation, no wonder people turn towards drink." I said casually, "My Dad Norman used to drink up there at The St. George in Tollcross. It was the only place in the late 50s' where you could get a drink on a Sunday in Edinburgh. It was a Scots/Irish pub." "Now there is a volatile firework of a genetic combination," said Jack with his eyes shining wildly. I said, "Norman used to drink in there with an Irish guy called Fitzgerald. All the men of my Father's age were demobbed at that time; they had all seen some action. The Scots/Irish boys used to be lined up at the bar, their bodies melded by bare knuckle fighting for money. The hair oiled sleek and the colour of lignum vitae wood. Everyone, except Norman, would be dressed in dark raytex suits, clean drip-dry white shirts where occasionally they would cut their blue jowled faces shaving. They all favoured thin shiny black ties, and they always wore a clean white handkerchief in their breast pocket. Bar time, standing in your own time wearing black leather slip on shoes, and gold elastoplex wrist watches. The perpetual faint whiff of Blue Stratos about the men. Norman and Fitzgerald drank "drams" of whisky, the amber cratur with occasional "scoosh" chasers of beer. My Dad told me it was a good, mixed atmosphere in that Sunday pub, everyone rubbed along. They just had to think of the immediate past to be reminded of how lucky it was. They all shared a love of gambling, women and drink."

I continued, "Norman and Fitzgerald both shared the blood of the Celt somewhere in their souls. It provided pointed intelligence.

It gave them a disdain of the merely ephemeral, but also an innate somnolent melancholia. An ability to stand apart from the mundane while at the same time rise above and be able to look into it. They both had a ruthless pitiless quality towards perceived lesser beings than themselves. There was a curious pecking order to the relationship between Norman and Fitzgerald. Norman didn't like to be reminded that the first Kings to unify Scotland and indeed name them the Scotti were the Irish Dalriadan kings. He didn't like to be reminded that his own Grandmother was a McDiarmid from Belfast. It had created an antipathy in him about which culture; the Irish or the Scottish could lay true claim to being "The Niggers" of Europe. It was at this point of shared identity that Fitzgerald held the edge. When he had met Lorna Moone for the first time with Norman, Fitzgerald realised that she was inherently much more interesting than either him or Norman. Primogenitively, she was a Mackintosh, one of the truly ancient Pictish peoples of Scotland. On her Father's Mother's side Lorna was Irish. Where Norman had seen her couthy roots as a hindrance to her intellectual development, Fitzgerald had regarded this as a positively creative virtue. He thought she was stunning."

The bus was approaching the Forth Road Bridge. I had been talking almost nonstop since Aberdeen. I was animated, my mind was alert. Crossing the Bridge I looked at the railed off fall that separated the North/South bridge flow. You could see right down to the water. It always made me feel afraid to look. We both marvelled at the Rail Bridge, like some kind of huge man made creature rising out of the Forth. Jack sucked on the end of his water and said to me, "What happened to Fitzgerald then Cal?" I said, "He worked as an Engineer in Petrochemicals, all over the world. As I said The Celts are an intelligent searching people, but they are also a doomed race. Fitzgerald returned to Edinburgh in the early 70s' and then he was diagnosed with cirrhosis. Or to use the vernacular, a hob nailed liver. He couldn't stop drinking. The last time Norman saw him was in Edinburgh Royal Infirmary where Fitzgerald was dying, in a private room. I went up with my Dad. Of course my Father brought a little present with him for Fitzgerald. A parting shot; 40 fluid ounces of Bell's whisky. So we are sitting there, Fitzgerald is in his sick bed and the tooth mugs have been broken out. An African doctor comes into the room and sees the scene. He starts to tell off my Father, but it was too late for that, it was just a question of time. After the doctor goes, My Father raises his mug and says to Fitzgerald in cut glass vowels, "Nigger brown old boy, nigger brown." Immediately Fitzgerald corrects him and says, "No, vitae negro Norman, vitae negro," and we all drained our glasses. He died a few weeks later."

The bus driver let us off at Davidson's Mains, an upper middle class Edinburgh suburb, where my Grandmother lived. You always could tell a difference in the money that was spent on the infrastructure in Edinburgh. The roads were all asphalted, with a red granite tread chip rolled in. She was quite a remarkable woman Nora. She was almost 96 and lived alone. She was a native Gael from Point in Lewis of the Outer Hebrides. Point literally meant the "dogs head" and the people there were indeed acerbic, quick-witted and at times pitiless, showing little false sentiment. As she got older and her body frailer, her mind accentuated. Confined to the interior, her quest for the external meaning of the world intensified. She was a contented person in herself but she had a desire for life that had not been extinguished. Nora had spent many years in West Africa with her husband Ian and this experience had served to shape her personality as part of Empire. A notion that was now confined to the faded photographs and mementoes that many different people had acquired in Britain in their service of Empire overseas.

She had one "gin and mix" before dinner. She had been a fiendishly good bridge player before her eyesight faded. Now she contented herself with a game of canasta with her grandsons, resting her feet up on the poufie. My girlfriends loved to meet Nora. She had looked a little like Colette in her younger days. A feminine cat like face. It was quite simply an incredibly fine genetic inheritance that she had been blessed with. She was a Mackenzie on her Father's side and a Macleod on her Mother's. The two most distinct and leading family names in Lewis. Where these people had originated still remains unclear. Thousands of years ago they had become Celtic and had settled in Lewis. Developing their own indigenous culture, and their own indigenous tongue; Gaelic. Making a home for themselves in one of the wildest, one of the freest, one of the last spiritual ancestral homelands in the world.

There was a distinct framework to the domestic routine of Redbank. A strict sense of discipline that had been eroded with the untimely death of her husband. It had been further eroded with her own children growing into adults and presenting her with their partners. With their children. Nora was of the opinion that a full stomach and shelter represented a happy heart. It was common for her to thrust £10 and a packet of cigarettes unseen into my coat, with her little extremely capable claws.

We went in through the immaculate garden into the house. Somehow we were seduced into the belief that our people would remain indestructible, and that nothing would ever change. Gran was in the kitchen sitting by the cooker with her walking stick. She was talking to Lorna Moone. She said, "Hello darling." She effortlessly managed to conceal the concern she was feeling for me. I kissed her and Lorna. Jack bowed and shook Nora's hand. It was naturally, always

At the forefront of Nora's mind to provide hospitality for a guest whoever he or she may be. Nora said to me, "Go and make us all some drinks darling. Let's get pissed!" Jack was already booming away in his pseudo Bronx accent, he was an Actor after all. Nora's hearing aid was starting to whistle which meant she was hearing him. I went through to the dining room to make the drinks. The table was set with the silver cutlery for our meal that night. I went into the drinks cabinet to make the drinks. I loved the spicy smell that had been imparted to the green baize by many different things. Lorna said to take the drinks through to the veranda. She used the time to ask me what the state of play was with the hospital. She said, "Are you seeing a psychiatrist soon? Will you be seeing your GP as soon as possible? How are you feeling?" Whispered conspiracies at Redbank. If the walls had ears we could have written a novel of epic proportions as a family by now. These questions from my mother were making me feel incredibly stressed. I could feel a physical tension in my head. At times it is better to say nothing, but we are all different. We all have our own way of showing our concern for another family member. I continued going through the motions of making the drinks. Ice, lemon, dubonnet, gin and beers for Jack and me. I said, "Everything will be fine Mum, let's enjoy our drink." She replied fretting, "That is just it, I wished that everything were fine but it is not." She was unwittingly picking at the scab that was my mental health. I said nothing and routinely went through to the veranda with the drinks.

Lorna resumed her routine of preparing the dinner. We were having soup, roast lamb followed by fresh fruit salad. My gran's soup was one of the wonders of the world. The secret was to use the vegetable boiling water as the basis for the stock. Trust Nora to be clever. Old stock, the full shilling. I said to Lorna that Gran would be after her with the wooden spoon if she hadn't followed her soup recipe. She laughed. In Lorna's character it wasn't at all apparent that she had learned a great deal about life from Nora. In some deep instinctive sense Lorna and Nora were alike. It was just their approach to life was different. They both believed in placing their family at the centre of their lives. Everything was just right with the food, it was the cocktail hour. We had our drinks out in the balm of the veranda and maternal concern was suspended for half an hour. Jackie was doing impersonations of Jimmy Durante and WC Fields to entertain the Ladies. He was an entertainer, and he had a receptive audience. Nora's eyes were sparkling with the combination of her gin and mix and Jackie's tomfoolery. Nora liked sophisticated humour, and also British humour of "the double entendre" variety.

We had an early night. Sitting watching television with Lorna Moone and Nora. My Grandmother would sit about two feet from the television so she could make out an image, the sound would be turned really loud. Because Nora was really deaf you soon got used to everything being far more accentuated audibly. I made sure the burglar alarm was switched on. Nora had been broken into last year, by "neds". They hadn't taken anything except her medication. While she was lying in her bed sleeping. A defenceless frail old woman. We all seemed to be alone as a family. Shattered schist, flung apart.

The next day Jack and I went into town after breakfast. We went up to the castle. The view over Edinburgh was spectacular. Jack loved history. He was imbued in the traditions of Europe that somehow seemed conspicuous by their absence in America. Yet that was a strange contradiction. Americans loved to point out that their country was a young country, and yet it is the oldest surviving democracy in the world. In light of this fact was it not about time they all grew up? Somehow cultural significance was immutable in Scotland. Part of our begrimed foetal existence. We made our way out of the castle and down the spiny cobbled high street. The palace of Holyrood lay at the bottom like a jewel. At any time of year this part of Edinburgh, the old town, was thronging with Nikon clad nationalities from all over the world. I said to Jack, "Let's stop at The Hebrides bar on the way down to Holyrood." My Father was a sleeping partner in the place. I suddenly had an image of him lying comatose in the foot well of the font. For as it would transpire there were plenty of people walking all over him in that place. Trying to push us into the gutter. A cold wind suddenly swirled like an omen. The drab watery sun shone through the clouds. Doing nothing to warm the marrow. Winter was close to its coming. Jack shivered. It was the cold coupled with damp that we couldn't take in Scotland. "Courage Jack, take courage," I said quickening my pace towards a perceived brosy indoors warmth. I told Jack that the only Scottish origin of my surname was in some sense obscured by history. But how we had chosen to interpret it was the distillation of alcohol. Jack started laughing and said, "Consummation by consumption Cal." I replied, "Yes that is true, in an overwhelming sense the gill of whisky, the imperial pint of heavy beer, was the measurement of

Scots aspirations. It has positive points; it is the largest industry by far in Scotland. A little dram is good for the heart. There is no finer feeling than those first two drinks in good company. However the image that Scots displayed of ourselves in drink is almost totally negative. Alcohol misuse is probably the most corrosive element in Scottish life. Alcoholism is endemic in Scotland. It is woven into the very fabric of our identity. We literally go from the nipple to the bottle. It is the example that we have been shown as children."

Jack pulled out a Camel from his crumpled flat pack. I sparked him up, cupping my hands against the wind. It was another moment of definition. He said, "Society uses alcohol as a kind of cutting tool in order to achieve some sort of social cohesion. It is literally, along with smokes, the drug of choice. During war years, times of crisis and depression, the consumption of alcohol increases. If there was no cigarettes and alcohol available to the population, there really would be a revolution." Jack rubbed forefinger and thumb together like a yid and said, "Virtue and vice rub along. They seem to need one another." I looked distantly into infinity and remarked, "It truly is a consumer society we live in now if that is what you mean."

We went down Coburn Street to the Hebrides pub around the corner. I hadn't been in since my Father had put the "thick end" of all his savings into the place. Norman had been unlucky with his money or rather it had been like water in his hands. His approach to money was linked to his abuse of alcohol. His heroic antics attracted more than its fair share of spongers and hangers on. Like moths to a flame. Super Nova burned brilliantly for a while now it is feeling all dried up and small. Norman was in the South West of Harris, where he was until recently bailiff of some of the finest Atlantic salmon and sea trout fishing in the world. Yet he hadn't dipped his rod once over the water in ten years. Was it a waste? He was content with the view. The frailties that his full life had delivered to him were: Lung cancer, heart trouble, two artificial hips, and psoriasis. Oh and just like old Errol Flynn the John Thomas was now limp and impotent. Norman was 68. I ordered a couple of pints and tried to think of him benevolently. The bar had taken a definite turn for the worse. Gone was the ambience that gave the place a highland grace. There were no haunting, plaintive pibroch tunes from the speakers anymore. The descending rows of amber languid malts had long since been drunk. The girl on the bar looked downwards, guilty somehow, wringing her hands. Perhaps the ones that had been caught in the till. I looked around, the place was almost empty. Sitting in the corner though I recognised one kent face, it was Sandy McRaw. Or to give him his full title Captain Sandy McRaw, formerly of The Scots Guards regiment. He was sitting there pouring over the obituaries in The Scotsman. It was his daily meat and drink. Start at the front, read to the back, and read to the front again. Then do the crossword. He saw me and raised his whisky glass, beckoning Jack and I over.

We went over. Sandy was dressed in what seemed on first inspection immaculate clothes. However look a little closer and you noticed the soup stained tie, the cigarette burns in the slacks. The worsted collar on his shirt, and his imitation leather slip on shoes. "Hi Sandy, ciamar a tha thu?" He held out a great strong shovel of a hand and said in a soft flat vowelled Lowland Scots accent, "Hello there Calum what brings you in here?" He looked at me over the top of his glasses from great poached egg eyes. His grey moustache bristled. I indicated to Jack with a fiver to go and buy a dram for Sandy. Jack said, "What kind of whisky would you like sir?" Sandy replied plainly, "Bells, large Bells son."

I asked Sandy if Watson was about, my Father's so called business partner. Sandy looked at me in a depressed way. He said, "The pub has just been sold to the brewers Maclays. Watson is in a bad way with alcohol. I'm sorry to be the bearer of bad news but it looks as though Watson has spent all your Father's money."

Sandy tapped his glass and said mournfully, "Landlord's ruin." Well at least Sandy wasn't a scrounger and he knew about the pub. The arcane arrangements that my father entered into with assorted macaronis and pseudo Celts in Pubs. Sandy said, "I don't think things were legal between your Father and Watson. Watson was the Licensee and he merely had a Gentleman's arrangement with Norman." I said, "That was £30,000, transferred by various ingenious drinking machines from alcohol into pish against a wall." "Not to put too fine a point on it." Said Sandy, sipping the last of his whisky. Of course, like Norman, life for Sandy had been transferred into an incredible disappointment in his declining years. A life of diminishing returns and a sense of felt foreboding trapped and isolated in a decaying body. Like Norman he felt as though he had done more harm than good with his life. Specifically to his children. I asked him if there was anything new. My mind was distracted now, realising the bitter irony of what I had been discussing with Jack on the way here. "Not much," he said, sticking out his bottom lip, "Just the broo." Jack came back with Sandy's dram and a jug of water. Sandy brightened up, he realised it would be tactful to change the subject. He asked Jack what he did. "I'm an Actor," said Jack proudly. Sandy said that he was once auditioned for the part of "Geordie" in the film of the same name. It was eventually played by Bill Travers. "I didn't get the bloody part, because I wasn't big enough," said Sandy ruefully. Rien, rien, life is full of regrets. Like Norman, Sandy had been something of a womaniser in his own day. There was a difference though, whereas Norman also possessed charm, good looks as well as intellect, (which made him something of an old trout to Sandy's Ferox), it was like an illness to Sandy; sexual desire and conquest. He had been something of a sexual drunk. Just then the barmaid went past with a large tray of clean glasses in her hands. All our eyes were drawn to the switch of her derriere. Sandy blurted out in his refined Lowland vowels, "Nice wiggle Anne." She heard him, crashed the tray down on the bar and rounded on him. She said, "I'll gie ye nice wiggle Anne; they'll be carrying you out on the Red Cross, McRaw." That was the essential difference between Norman and Sandy. The Norman Conquest was always a success. He would have had her sitting on his shanky knee by now. Sandy was a Medieval Scots Scholar; he had a First from St. Andrews. I told Jack this little piece of news. I said to Sandy that Jack was very interested in Scottish history. Sandy looked at his glass, lifted it up and said, "Gory son, gory."

I was curious now; I was not in my Father's thrall in here for once. I said, "What part did my family the Comyns play in high Medieval Scotland?" Sandy looked a little stifled as if he couldn't find it within himself to recant this story yet again. To another dimmer generation. He was tired; he was old, what was the point anymore? Valiantly though he removed his glasses, took a sip of Bells, lit up a fresh Windsor blue and replied. "The Comyn clan it has to be understood were symbolic in what they creatively represented in Scottish affairs. Their century was the 13th C. They were early Socialists within a general feudal framework. In a sense they understood power and influence in the round, and actively pursued "the political game". It was for the benefit of the entire Scottish community. They were probably the most powerful family that came to the fore in early Medieval Scotland. In this respect it is important to understand that they came first. Literally and figuratively. Hence the symbolism of their origin." He raised his whisky glass. "Themselves, the Comyns did not aspire to Kingship but did support the existing monarchy. It is important to distinguish this from the ambition of "The Brus". Who along with the Red Comyn had a legitimate claim to the vacant Scottish throne. The Comyns were deeply intuitive people who had arrived here as part of The Norman Conquest. It is thought that the Comyns would have been originally of North West European/Celtic origin, in a sense they were returning to their homeland. Mostly they were a family of clerics, which ties in with the creative meaning of the name itself. In 1306, The Brus met The Comyn in the church of Greyfriars in Dumfriess to decide what to do. They quarrelled and The Brus murdered The Comyn. The outcome of the ensuing civil war was that The Brus was victorious and was crowned the first king of Scotland; the Brus effectively destroyed The Comyn power base and their influence on the European stage was at an end. However the foundation of much of modern Scotland; what we understand as law and the upholding of the law; order, liturgy, equality, democracy itself was instituted by the old lead in Scottish affairs by The Comyns."

Sandy took a long sip on his Bells and returned effortlessly into the clear and present. He said, "Excuse me lads I have this little prostate trouble. I have to go for a widdle." He got up with his stick and went off to pish on the plastic coated characters out of Angus Ogg that were screwed behind the rusting, ammonia reeking hulk of a urinal. Jack drained his pint. He said, "That was quite a story. This country seems to have so many aces up its sleeve. Who would have thought that Sandy would know all that stuff." I nodded my head slightly. I said, "We are like one of those spiral fossils, here in Scotland. Utterly ancient and ingenious in our production."

I went and bought Sandy a dram for the ditch, on my hat, just for old time's sake. When I went over with the drink he was back from the cludgie. I said to Jack we should be going down to Holyrood. Jack stood up, we were both over six feet tall. Sandy had been six feet tall before he found himself stooping. It was funny; I noticed he had a big head, just like me, just like Norman. A distinguishing physicality that only a few Scotsmen now shared, since they had all died in the wars. "Ceann mor." Sandy seemed a little afraid of our relatively youthful vigour. Now that he felt old and in decline. He raised his glass and said, "Remember me to Tormod Calum, and you keep the head," pointing to us both. "Remember boys, brown bread." We made our way out of the saloon and Sandy faded into the blue smoke and grey ashes of memory.

We walked down to the palace. The palace was closed to sightseers at this time of year. We went and sat on a bench in the palace garden. I said to Jack that Scotland was now to regain its own parliament. Not outright progress; independence as many wanted, but a devolved Scottish Parliament. With its own legislative power and tax raising ability. "Do you think Independence will be the outcome?" Asked Jack. I said, "I dunno, why don't you ask that question to the people of Shettleston in Glasgow, the population of Lesmahagow in Lanarkshire. "What do you mean Cal?" "Those are the sort of places where ameliorative change is desperately needed, and without it the memory of the community will be confined to a set of meaningless statistics, a set of jumbled up hyroglyphics on abandoned Estate walls. But perhaps that is exactly the point. Those kind of places should be razed to the ground." "So you think then Cal that Scotland is set upon some sort of terminal decline, that it is simultaneously both dying and killing itself?" "It might just be that Independence could reverse that poverty; the poverty you find also in the North of Scotland: in places like Banffshire; in places like the Isle of Lewis." I said. Currently Scotland was an unbalanced equation, based upon an uneven set of principles. The compromise was perverse. It was designed to keep the majority of people where they were already. The question was why? I looked at the Saltire flag flying high above the eaves along with the Union Jack. I said, "When you think of the stars and stripes Jack what images are conjured up in your mind?" He said, "I suppose the words that come to mind are, power, modernity, looking forward confidently and technologically into the future." I replied to Jack, I said, "When I see the Union Jack I think of the past, the begrimed post Industrial and empirical military legacy that we have inherited in this country. The word that springs to mind is decline." "So you think that in an essential way the preservation of The Union is in some way sinister. It is an attempt to reverse that decline by subverting democracy," said Jack. All I said was, "It is mammon, society itself that is sinister. It is far greater than the finite span of any one person."

I pointed across to the clean, massive abandoned Brewery site, across the road. I said, "That is where the parliament is to be built. It is from that site that the institution of home rule is to either flourish or die. Our parliament, our ubiquitous way of expressing our national identity. Slainte." Jack said, "So in a sense things have come full circle since the first influence of your family in Scotland. At least in a way you have been vindicated by history in a way that we Americans are not, we are like your child. It is creation itself we are talking about here. You are only trying to ascribe meaning to that process of creation. That is all. The future of every man, woman and child in Scotland. The community." "I just hope that the politicians behave as guardians of that fragile thing we call democracy," I said with a ray of pessimism. "What I understand as coming is merely that. The grey watery substance that constitutes union with a woman and leads to childbirth. It is spermatozoa, it is virility. Our future. It is what I want for myself, a child. I fear for that very organic, that essential vitality of male and female that nurtures and has taken for granted, our natural behaviour. Couple that with the bizarre nature of global behaviour, mirrored in the bizarre natural world. The demographic trend of decline that points towards sterility in our country. Those are the reasons why I fear for the hard heartedness of the so called educated who want to fill those chambers."

CHAPTER FIVE

I staggered up George Street in Aberdeen. It was the coldest December I could remember. The ice on the pavement crackled under my feet like brandy snaps. My breath was hoary and reeking of alcohol. That was it all right. Scotsmen like the stink of alcohol on our freezing breaths. An attempt to escape from a winter interior of force-fed television. An appetite for appalling food and loneliness. Scaling an abyss of fear that is mainly a reaction to this inevitable regime of doom. Descending now into oblivion. Jack had hit the road to Germany a month ago, with a flourish of the hand and a skeiled grin. Onward onward ever onward. I had been cracking the screw tops on more than just a few bottles of Lermontov vodka. With chilled pilsner chasers. A hero of our times, riding bare foot down the river of life. My conscious thinking struggled to give some meaning to my life. I was still signed off work; I had been spotted out on the small town by colleagues, written reprimand. Who gives a fuck; the structure of modern work in society was just a con anyway. Designed to keep the wheels turning, designed to keep me swimming round and round the bottom of a briny barrel with the rest of the eels. Until I am chosen for consumption. The insularity of my environment, the repetition of my life here was throttling me to death.

I get up George Street as far as the Butcher's Arms and the concrete high rises on the other side. The definitive Scottish urban picture. Freezing cold, the mist swirling around the omniscient stillness of the halogen spots high up in the eaves of the no-fines high rise. Concrete, tangible, grey, black night. A sense of gritty realism. Are we in Poland, is this Krakow? Nothing moves, nothing changes. It is only hard. Just when I think nothing can pierce this bunded concept a woman appears around the corner, having an altercation with two men. She is only wearing falmers stone washed jeans, gutties and a vee neck blue sweater with "Scotland" written on the front, in white letters. It is well below zero, freezing. "Scotland" on the front. It seems a futile gesture somehow, but a fashion statement I have always admired amongst Scots women. Tough chicks flying in the face of Scots machismo and their unhealthy adult male obsession with football. I stopped; one of the men had her by the throat now up against the wall. I stepped in, filled with the stuff that courage is made of. I said to the men, "You two can fuck right off now, or else you can come ahead and deal with me." They scattered like pig slurry out of the back of a spreader. I wasn't surprised, it all clicked in like Lego. Like some kind of plot. She and I the remaining dramatis personae were left alone in the sub-arctic floe of George Street under the constant hum of the orange neon. I asked her if she was okay. She said, "Aye, they twa radges were aifter ma money." She said, "My name's Rosie".

I could tell by the way Rosie spoke that she was a tinker. A little bit of this and that in the genetic makeup. Scottish blend. Rosie spies at me from the corner of her eye and lets out a little giggle. It is not often you meet people like Rosie now in the dream Scotland is constructing for itself. A glitter about her. The hard mica of the road is etched into her features. She is a "macatink, boltweech, and feicher." That is the mistrustful, stern judgment from the blue pulpit of the tacit North East cast. Grit, mottled redness, black shiny eyes covering me now intelligently. Her second eyed skeil, her drink swollen distended features. She is dark and cunningly interested, she is slightly fey. Her dry hair sits awry.

I wonder why we are forced to turn into one another to replicate our identity. Shoot pontoon, shoot pool. It is the game we play for high stakes that has gone dreadfully wrong. Way down the line. Added expectations of material distress and you have a perfect recipe for the daily tragic spectacle that unfolds upon the map of our land.

She said she lived out in the caravans at Bucksburn. I said I would get her up the road. She seemed attached to me now, she held onto my arm tightly. I told her my name. I told her my Gran; my mother's mother was a Caird. Rosie said, "They were the Irish Romany's that made tin pots and pans and sold them around the villages." I said, "Sometimes my gran felt a need to connect with her father's people, it was like an urge." Rosie said, "Blood is stronger than stone." I said, "She once took me and the dog up into the wooded estate above the South Esk River in Brechin. It was the summer that Amazing Grace was at number 1 in the charts. It was never off the radio. My Grandfather had been Grieve of that Estate. He was paid to find the gin traps, the wire snares. We went into the verdant green of the wood. It was filled with fern, silver and copper birch, Scots pine, beech and rowan trees. The forest floor was soft and dappled in moss and brown. Sally the collie dog started barking up ahead. She was a working dog that hardly ever got off the leash now. Betsy was held on to me with her red hands that were sturdy from work. Ahead was a group of people sitting around a campfire. They had built a bender of haps and sticks. They were talking in a dialect that I couldn't understand. They were drinking black tea; there was a carcass of a rabbit cooking above the fire. The woman in the middle of the group had massive distended hands. Her fingers were swollen like beef and pork sausages." Rosie said she probably had leprosy. "My gran said to me," "Dinnae be feirt loon, they wilnae herm ye." "We stood around for a while and my gran spoke to the women in their strangely rapid dialect. We hadn't consciously sought out those people but my Gran understood a lot about the country ways of Scotland that I never would." Rosie said, "That way o life fer the travelling folk is ower now. There isnae muckle kindness in the world for tinks." She gripped my arm tighter. She looked up at me and asked, "Hae ye been wie a hoor before?" I said, "No as it happens, I haven't." I blurted it out like like a little toffee nosed virgin. This added an air of anticipation to our friendship now. An exciting edge of the unknown. Rosie had her trap. We got to Kittybrewster, the abandoned traffic lights at the crossroads. The colour changed from green to red. Suddenly round the corner swung a cattle float. It was filled with Aberdeen Angus beasts. Wailing and moaning. Their detritus skittered out the back of the float as it headed north to the abbatoir at Dyce. I felt acutely distressed for the animals. I indicated to Rosie, I said, "Bloody hell that is a terrible fate, in the middle of the night in the middle of winter." She just said, "You just have to face it. A lot worse things than that happen around here. Food is necessary for life." I said to Rosie, "You had better come in, I have some wine." I beckoned her in from the freezing rimy road up to the flat.

We sat down and I put some music on. I liked Rosie; I had come to her rescue. She was grateful to me and she wanted to repay me. I started to tell her about Selina and my manifestly strange, obsessive night with her. Rosie said, "The lady of the house doesnae ken what is happening to the horse fan the stable door is left unbolted." Rosie then asked quickly if she could stay the night. Sleep with me in my bed. I said yes. My sexual desire for her at this point feels like an illness that only has one cure. A combination of alcohol and excitement has heightened my mental state. My conscious awareness is accentuated to a sharper point. We went next door. We got undressed and went to bed. She had wonderful breasts; I cuddle her for a while, and then suckle her. All the while she is whispering in my ear in this strange dialect. I entered her vagina. It was good and tight. When I was riding her she suddenly groans in pain. I ask her what is the matter. She says to keep my weight off her right leg; she had just had the cast removed the other day. This piece of crucial information adds a certain finite mortality to the proceedings. I orgasmed inside her. I could feel the hot seed coming from my penis. I ask her if she orgasmed and she guides my hand to her clitoris. I masturbate her and then she climaxes. Digging her nails into my arms. "You are good," she says, "You could sell yersel onytime."

We both suddenly realise the forbidden barriers, the taboos we erect around sexual intercourse are a load of nonsense. In order to procreate we have to have sex. It is a part of life that cannot be ignored. We make love once more. Really slowly this time. It was nice and warm in the flat. A few hours reprieve for both of us. Rosie asks me to hold her into self with my arms. Sleep.

I woke up the next day with the sunrise and the noise of traffic rushing in the front window. Rosie was lying there on her back snoring. She doesn't look so good today as she did last night. Funny how alcohol blurs the edge. I had been wearing my vodka-tinted spectacles. Her body was covered in red alcohol blotches and plukes. There were childbirth scars across the generous beer fat on her stomach. I got up to make us some coffee. There was a letter for me. I ripped it open, it was an appointment to see Dr. Miller at Cornhill next week. I didn't realise that he was there to help me recover. I still thought that I was being sucked into a vortex of darkness. I brought some coffee and cigarettes through to Rosie. She had put her "Scotland" jersey on and she was sitting up. How vulnerable we are, despite the fact, flying in the face of the fact that Scotland is a special country. It doesn't seem to make any difference now. How vulnerable we looked in my pitiful little bedroom. Rosie sucked on her cigarette deeply and noisily. Sustenance. She had a daily hangover also. She smiled at me and ran her hand down the side of my hair as if she was taking pity on me and the general situation. She said, "How auld are ye Cal?" I told her I was 32. She replied ruinously. She said, "I am only 36, look at me." She knew it herself that the outlook was decidedly blue. Mornings were the time for bitterness and recrimination if you are on the game. If you are on the margins of loneliness and abandonment. Rosie just looked away and silently looked out the window. Holding her cigarette in a poised practised way. After a couple of minutes Rosie went to the bathroom, and I got dressed. I offered her some money, she said she just wanted a taxi out to "Bucksy." She said, "You were sweet to me, I was kind to you. I don't want any money for last night, we are even." I phoned the taxi for her. When it came Rosie was ready. I stuck £5 in her pocket and said, "That is for the taxi." I didn't think she would be any happier out there, but I didn't feel either that it had been a meaningless encounter. We had enjoyed our few hours together. That is what my life had become; brief windows of snatched pleasure amongst a general sense of unhappiness. The intercom buzzer sounded, the chirpy Doric voice said, "Rainbow," Rosie said, "I'll mind on you Cal, you take care." She kissed me let herself out and was gone. I heard the front door slam and the taxi takes off. Like a rainbow coming colours everywhere. The honey pot though is empty. I went back and lay on the bed and tried to gather in the threads of my hangover.

The phone rings naggingly. I had fallen asleep, I feel ratty. At moments like this having to talk on the phone is like the sperm of the Devil. It was my Father Norman. He has picked his moment immaculately to reappear in my life. He is sober; he is as dry as copra. His voice is like the crackle of dry tinder taking in a fire. His character is the complete antithesis of the "Cavalieroch" that is measured out in amber drams, cigarette butts and smudged lipstick. He feels this is the time for action. I said I was lying in bed. He said, "It is about time you are getting up, it is mid-day." The imposition of a half understood set of principles. His total lack of respect for the fact that my life was still in the main a mystery to him. I thought of the days on end he had spent lying in his mother's house drying out before returning abroad. Appearing briefly at the dinner table to face down food and his family with equal loathing. Like some kind of child, chasing the butter across the table with the shakes. Cowking with the dry heaves so bad that we all became paralysed by the spreading poison of his unipolar depression. "Le grande malle" that he was unable to talk about. So in light of this I sat around smoking dope all day. I wanted to avoid the mainstream of life. He was ill, I was ill. Norman in his heart realised that his relationship with his children required more than just money to make us more content as a family, but this agenda was denied by him unless he had a bead of whisky on. At moments like this he concentrated on the negative. Warm emotions were not universal in my Father's character. He had been deeply damaged himself as a child to the point where the common adjective that people used to describe him was "poor." I suppose all this did was to increase his sense of self-pity; it damaged him even more completely. Today he was trying to find a way of bridging the ravine of guilt that he felt within himself for the way he had behaved towards Lorna Moone. It was unfortunate though, his view of me was crystallised at that moment when she had left with the children. When he had stuck his head in the oven only to realise it was electric. He behaved towards me as though I were still aged 4.

In light of this best to stick with the mundane. The framework of a plot that drives our lives forward. I say to him, "I have an appointment at the psychiatric hospital next week." He replies, "You were bloody stupid to discharge yourself in the first place, charging around like a bull." The hackles are rising already, I say, "Well I am taking positive steps." He says, "You had better keep that appointment you stupid young bugger." I still allowed Norman to hold the rods of power in our relationship. It would only be when he died that the male conch of responsibility would be taken by me. Misunderstanding followed closely by anger. This is the main form of ignorance of mental health. I wasn't going to mention the Hebrides Bar, for it seemed to me that that sort of behaviour by my Father was the sign of someone that was not quite all there himself. I said, "I would like to come and see you in Harris soon Nono." I hardly ever called him by his Christian name let alone the pet name his Mother had given him. Our conversation was like a bar chart going up and down. He audibly shrinks on the other end of the line. He says, "You will get yourself better and go back to work, back into the mainstream of life. I'm not having you coming up here with your piss artist mates and firing off like a loose cannon." Now if ever there was a loose cannon with piss artist mates that stalked the streets of Edinburgh it was Nono. It was funny, it was unbearably sad the way he was behaving towards me. It was this dichotomy in his character that had made Lorna Moone realise that she did not really love him. That she was not prepared to make placatory little high protein meals for recovering alcoholics the rest of her life. Make placatory little squeaks and forgive him his gross behaviour. I should have told him to grow up and also to fuck off. Then quietly put the phone down. But I couldn't do that. I loved my father, despite his loathsome side. I loved the fine feelings that had never found a home for creative output. Or if they had it was totally unknown to me. My father had spent his entire working career abroad. Apart from his family. He chose to be alone.

I asked Norman how he was going to spend Christmas and New Year. He said the house doors would be locked up. More indications of self-pity. Sitting alone wallowing in it through choice. Mind you what was the alternative; a wailing congregation of the rags of South West Harris. The Hebridean character to a large extent is imbued with alcohol. It is more than that though; it is part of the culture in a way that I do not perceive as entirely negative. My Father and I were agreed on that much. In order to understand the Hebridean drinker it is important to understand the part that drink plays in their life. Whether the Hebridean has particular strength of character or not say in comparison to someone like James Mackintosh, Lorna Moone's father is another matter. All you can say is that they are very different people evolving from very different cultures.

In reality Norman the self-proclaimed "Laird of Obbe" was mostly glad for the human contact. The drink, his drink, gave him power over them in their relationship. Or perhaps it did not. For a Hebridean with a bead on does not need an invitation to drink more whisky than is good for him. I asked my Father, "How's the fishing been this year?" He replied gloomily, "Very poor; not enough water and too many gill nets." At one time we had owned fishing rights on the lochs. Something like that didn't have a monetary value.

Something to be looked after and passed on down through the generations. Norman had sold it for an undisclosed sum. In the Hebrides business is conducted with humour and politeness while you are being robbed blind. Norman was gamekeeper turned poacher. The Hebridean locals, many of them poachers, came into the house. Flattered to deceive as they poured generous west coast drams from Nono's bottle. They prayed on his weakness for whisky and dubious company with their native guile and cunning. Their hands, their amber filled glasses shimmering in season now with silver fish scale. Poaching was the common currency whispered in Gaelic. It was what we had given them, illicit prosperity. Norman knew it, they all knew it, the whispered Gaelic conspiracy. The late night anonymous visitations. Guiltily rubbing those shimmering hands, stinking of fresh wild salmon and sea trout. At the back of the mind fearful of the divine retribution that would follow as surely as night follows day. If there was such a thing as an honest thief, it was the Gael sitting in front of the blazing coal fire of Tormods'. Norman had the Gaelic, his mother was from Lewis. He had nothing to prove. Enacting the same political game that involved human aspiration, that had deprived our ancestors of all their wealth and power. In his cups, quite simply Norman liked to give it all away. And it didn't really matter to him who the recipient was. With one hand he was taking from his sons, he was returning something else with the other. Our independence and honesty to take responsibility for ourselves. It would be up to me ultimately if I wanted to go down the same path as Nono. My Father said he was going to ring off now. The call had not been a success. It came back to his self-guilt for the mess he had made of his own life. I felt pity for him. I was being forced to pay the price for displaying arrogant pride. Hubris was something he and I shared in common. It is just that I had the chance to find a solution to this human dilemma of classical dimensions. There were two qualities my father shared with his two sons; sensitivity and courage. It was where morality was concerned Iain and I were different. I said goodbye and put the phone down.

I went for my appointment with Dr. Miller. It was the day before Christmas. The mall was filled with people cramming in as much food, drink and anything else into their trolleys, into their cars. The final countdown. Less is best, the ritual was obscene. Christmas was part of the social calendar, part of the once Christian paradigm of existence that most people take for granted. I felt in a sense now free of being traded off with this burden, but I wasn't sure how to replace it. It was still freezing hard, there was no sign of a come in the air. It started to snow, a peppering of soft snow that swirled in the wind and obscured the car headlights. Trying to attach some sort of creativity in the North East. The courageous existential hero trudges alone past the happy office workers in their Santa Claus hats. He pulls his tan corduroy and sheep fleece coat close into his thin body and sucks on his cigarette. The black cat sits in the warm window and purrs contentedly out at him. There is a spirit that inhabits every corner, every wakeful second. It inhabits the entire environment and acts upon the people's actions. A cold Presbyterian spirit of righteousness, of controlled parsimony, a strange spirit of canker. A careful way of not spilling emotion, of holding it within. The cold, the white icy cold drives me on towards hospital, to Cornhill. Clean snow turned by footsteps into dirty brown freezing slush. Were we not made mostly of water? It perturbed me, it pestered my thoughts. I went into the hospital. I feel stress immediately. The gravitational pull of all the forces of lunacy that had been contained here. Were contained within me. I am nervous and agitated. I light up another fag. I felt in a panic. You suffer in silence. The look of concern from staff, the inward holding together of silent shuffling patients looking out at the blizzard. Medication is the key, to overcoming your fear.

There wasn't a cure for my illness except medication and time. You have to live with it. I sat outside Dr. Miller's consulting room. A guy is sitting there. He has his head in his hands and he is quietly weeping. He is wearing a shiny shell suit. I always wonder what people wear under shell suits. He must be freezing. He must be waiting for an admission. He had cauliflower ears, a flattened nose. He must be a boxer. He noticed me and stopped crying, he nodded at me and told me his name was Mark. He said,

"I'm one of the McAllen clan fae the Boulevard." "Oh aye," I said, "I ken your family." They were scrap metal merchants. I knew one of the ramifying clans' daughters. It was as synonymous with the Northeast as tubs of fish guts. Ferrous and non-ferrous metals. Enormous pitch pine breakfast bars, studded leather three-piece suites, eight pack vac formed sirloin steaks. Chained Alsatians. A liking for Johnny Cash, Tammy Wynette and Patsy Cline. A shelf of hair curlers and Bell-Air. A drinks cabinet stuffed full of Spanish Brandy and red Martini. The physical appearance of "crepe suzettes" because they were the first to pioneer the sun bed. Of course it all sits silently most of the time because everyone is out working, doing deals to fill the Chubb home safe. Mark said, "I'm a boxer masel." His declared state of independence. "Former Scottish schoolboy ABA welterweight champion," he held out his small, fragile boxer's hand. I took it, and felt I was passing on some good warmth to him. I asked him if he was waiting to see a doctor. He said, "Aye I suffer fae DIP." I wondered what that was, he could see I was lost, he replied, "Drug induced psychosis, I hear voices, get hallucinations, I'm a schizo." He looked at me with a combination of cunning and hopelessness. He said, "You got ony smack? Have you got ony dope to sell?" I said, "If I had ony gear I would share it with you." I asked Mark if he was in here. It was a Friday, tomorrow was Christmas. The nadir night for the lonely, the dispossessed. A night to go crackers for. Washing the knickers in a basin of Biotex. "Aye ahm on the ward just now, but I really look forward to Saturdays," said Greg. I said, "Why is that then?" Thinking he was looking forward to some kind of Xmas. He replied with a genuinely happy smile on his face. He said, "Because the TV is brilliant, there is 'Stars In Their Eyes', 'Play your Cards Right', and oh aye, 'The Premiership'!!" I said ironically, "Aye right enough Mark it's pretty good."

I asked Mark why he used drugs, I was trying to work out why I used drugs. He said, "Because my life is grey. It is pish being Scottish. No job, no girlfriend, no future. Everyone telling you your useless. But I train for my boxing. I feel a success there, in the ring. All that happens in here is that you come off the smack and hae yer condition stabilized. You get discharged, you get a Social Worker, and you see a Drugs Counsellor. But you still feel the same inside nothing ever gets ony better for you, so you go back on the Horse." As a group within, and as a large part of society, we the mentally ill felt as if life had shit on us. Disenfranchised, feeling powerless. Just take the fucking prescribed medication. What is the effort of protesting our intolerance? To our mental condition, to the injustice of life. I say to Mark, "It is just that some of us Cannae hack it onymore, and we go mad." It was for the others though, that you had to take a stand. We ignore the suffering of other people like us to our collective shame.

Dr. Miller came out of the Surgery and beckoned me to come in. I said cheers to Mark. He just said, "I'll see ye on the ward sometime and we'll go for a nip." Miller was dismayed at this final piece of information. It was beneath his dignity and professional conduct to issue any reprimand to either of us. Miller beckoned me to sit down, in his antrin, couthy dialect. "How have you been Cal?" He said quietly as he opened my notes. He asked me if I had been taking my medication. I lied and said I had. He knew I was lying because he immediately asked me if I had been smoking dope. "A wee bitty," I giggled out furtively. I imagined there was some sort of informer who had been party to my behaviour. The same informer who spotted me out on the town. Small town insularity. Meanwhile the huge blizzard outside pelts down diagonally. Nothing seemed straightforward. Miller said he had made an informed diagnosis of my condition. He didn't want to upset me but he wanted me to pay attention, if I could, to what he was saying. He tapped the table with the retracted stub of his pen and began. He said, "Stress and the manifestation of this in recent relationships which have seemed strange to you has brought on the onset of illness…mental illness. I would say you are an articulate person, that you are both sensitive and creative. You have had a kind of emotional breakdown, which physically manifests itself as a chemical imbalance. You are suffering from Manic Depression with schizoid tendencies. This illness involves wild mood swings with periods of both depression and mania. You say that you have been feeling as though you have been suffering from delusions. That there is a voice inside you. That you can hear voices running through your head. You feel paranoid as if everyone is stigmatising you." I was hoping that he was going to say next congratulations you are different and you have just secured a movie contract with MGM. Within a week you will be riding down Sunset Boulevard, with Jack Nicholson at the wheel of a cream and gold Bugatti Royale. And you will be in the back smoking a finest Romeo et Juliet havana stroking the knee of a very famous Actress. But it doesn't work that way in Aberdeen. Miller said, "The term that is professionally used for your condition is Bipolar Affective Disorder." So I was BAD, I'm bad. Light me up dirty Harry, make my day. I said to Dr. Miller, "What is mania? Is it connected to manacling people up because they are uncontrollably manic?" My blue eyes were shining like tractor lights by this point. Miller looked at me with a sweet benign look on his face. The iron discipline was within, it had to be within him. He said, "In a manic state a person appears totally euphoric and strong. The sufferer appears to share a high and a low pole of mood. When manic he is more than usually sociable, active, talkative, self-confident and perceptive. More creative than usual. In a manic phase the sufferer may experience increased energy and decreased sleep pattern. In addition to this you can be extremely irritable and violent. You can also suffer from a heightened sexual drive and appetite, poor judgment, racing over active mind, overspending, increased alcohol intake." He took a small sip of water from the plastic cup of volvic on his table and paused.

He took a brief note and said without looking up, "Incidentally we do not, contrary to popular belief, manacle patients." I blurted out, "Aye but you used to; now the manacle is purely palliative." Dr. Miller chose to ignore the both offensive and angry tone of my remark. The evolution of psychiatry was all about looking ahead, through the doors of perception, into a world free from illness. He went on, "In the depressed phase, which I would diagnose in your case consists of the majority of your illness, you suffer from a deep sense of worthlessness. You have a deep-seated sense of low esteem and are lacking in confidence. At times you feel as if there is no alternative to this condition and that you have felt condemned to contemplate suicide." I looked at him clearly. It was people like me who paid his salary. Even the nutters were making a valuable contribution to the economic well-being of the world. I said to Dr. Miller, "What about the environmental factors in my illness? I don't feel as though I have it easy. Living in a council house, amongst the sourness, the hardness. Not having much money or support mechanism around me. I am signed off work from a job I find extremely stressful and unrewarding. I do not feel as if I am achieving any of my potential. It is little wonder that depression is widespread among men my age." Dr Miller said sympathetically, "I know, I know Cal," but at the end of the day in the great UK middle class tradition we were just talking about it and nothing ever gets any better. He said, "Taking your medication as prescribed is essential to achieving a balanced state of your mental condition." He knew there was a gap in the system, but he was part of the system, an integral part. If he could provide the social fabric of life that I craved there would be fewer people in his waiting room. There was little sense of democracy in our relationship. He wasn't there to punish me. He knew I was in denial that I was still clinging on to my pride. The notion of my former life. Which if I chose to consider it was as disorganised and full of turmoil as the present. Miller said to me, "It is just bad luck that you have become unwell, but the key to managing your condition and moving on is stability." Now was not the moment to pose to myself the question, "What do I want from life?"

He rapidly moved on to the clincher. "I am prescribing you a new medication. It is called Trifluoperazine, brand name, Stelazine." He said I should start taking the medication immediately, (if I were you). Almost nonchalantly he said there were side effects. Commonly; uncontrollable movements of the body; mouth, tongue, cheeks, arms and legs. The most pronounced side effect was lockjaw. He was prescribing another drug procyladine to counter these side effects. Stelazine was a drug given for acute schizophrenia. Fight fire with fire. Extreme medication for extreme times. The whole notion of mental illness now began to terrify me. The things that happened in this hospital. It is human nature to be illogical. It is human nature to attach blame to the mentally ill. Dr. Miller took me up to the pharmacy and we got the medication. He wished me a happy Christmas, he said to take the medication as prescribed and totally avoid cannabis. This was my special present this year. A healthy dose of reality. Or rather unreality. I was left standing, helpless, not sure what to do next. All Miller was saying was play your cards right Cal and it'll be alright on the night. But that was like leading an alcoholic blindfold into a bonded warehouse on Hogmanay and locking him in alone with a glass and ice, for company.

I started taking the medication that night. Little blue and yellow capsules from the blister pack. A satisfying combination of colours, blue and yellow. The night was crystalline still and extremely cold. There was a crust of frost on the ground. The gritters had been out spreading sand and salt. Still the cars had shone bright, shiny tracks in the road with their tyres. Like we used to do at Mile-end primary School, making sliders with our cherry brown shoes. I woke up early in the morning, it was Christmas, and I was giving birth to a cold. My chest was thick with phlegm. I expelled great globules of it from the chilled bank that night had laid upon my chest; the seeds of an idea were germinating in my mind. A wild notion that in some sense creativity itself was linked to my own health. What swirled around in the external world was linked to my interior metabolism. In a sense just that, creation was greater than merely human design. There had to be a creator. And I was like some kind of shaman. That the North East of Scotland had produced. And this was some kind of truly odd place that is only partially understood but intuitively observed by all its' natives. At that moment I adored the darkly gothic spiral of our sub-Arctic city. Coldness and darkness pierced by the short and brilliantly bright window of winter sunshine. Icicles hanging for days on end from frozen rone pipes and guttering. Abandoned cars left under frost and snow. Permanently damp feet. Chilblains, hands thawing out red and numb in warm water. Going into the steaming brosy warmth of the boozy rubicund pub, but not much encountering that warmth in the people. Just an informal edge. Just dressed stone, horizontal and vertical hardness. Little or no beautiful arcing curve. Throwing snowballs over the top, hearing them thwump on the bonnet of an unseen car. Thank God it's Xmas.

Lorna Moone arrived at 10am to take me down to her house for Christmas lunch. I was inhabited by a strange mood; the spirit was twisting and coiling within me like a serpent. We had to make the most of the dawning of the light. Before it soon waned on the day. Lorna Moone looked pinky and healthy. She wisely knew how to counteract the effects of lack of sunshine at this time of year. I looked at my own face in the mirror. I was wan, sallow and tired looking. I needed to shave. I always needed to shave every day or I ended up looking like a coarse tink brute. I made my mother some tea. She liked her tea black. She liked to dunk the tea bag herself. I gave her some biscuits, she always liked something sweet with her "jew's tea". I sat down and started mumbling to myself. Lorna Moone sipped on her tea and looked at me. She said, "When you start mumbling to yourself Cal I really start to feel concerned. If you have something to say, say it out clearly." I looked at her; she was enjoying her sweet chocolate biscuit. It was her vice; sweet shit. Like booze and fags were mine. I suddenly said, "I know what the old beat was." Lorna Moone asked me innocently what that was. She was licking the crumbs from the corner of her mouth like a cat. A nervous reaction. I said, "We are filled with anger and sadness which is choler and melancholy. It is because the sadness of our existence became too much to bear that we left Europe and founded the New World." Lorna was cradling her tea in her hands like a warmer. Her nails were manicured and filed to rounded curves. "There is a lot of sadness in the world wherever you go just now darling." She said. We could hear the people scrunching on the icy snow outside, with their carrier bags filled with gifts.

The shoppers of Petrograd take a holiday. Lorna Moone drained the last of her tea and said in a pseudo American accent, "So what are you saying then numero uno?" I rose to my feet and said in an energetic, totally humourless outburst, "I am the second coming of Christ. He died on the cross he rose again, (I sat down, rose again, then sat down). To prove that after death there is rebirth. The wisdom of his soul is what swirls in my veins; blood flecked with purely healing platinum and gold. The lord binds the wounds. I hold the key to the procreation of Christ's spirit." Lorna Moone looked at me with focused concern. She would widen her eyes in innocent astonishment and then they would return to normal. She repeated this as she stared at me silently. I looked back at her grey blue irises and mocked the big eyes routine at her. Bad move Cal, it was like putting out the fire with gasoline. Both Lorna Moone and I had a violent temper and I was setting a course towards collision with her. She suddenly shrieked at me like a Gatling gun. A bit of Xmas high spirit. She said, "Are you paying any attention to Harry Miller? Are you going to take the medication and keep away from that bloody dope and drink?" I went all bendy in my seat and started laughing at her. The mere triviality of what she was saying. It was of no real concern to me; my health. I was an "Ubermenschen" invested with the most incredible, the most profound insight into life. The fantastic thoughts I was having were not the stuff of mere mortals. Lorna Moone was just my Mother. She said to me, "You may be filled with choler and melancholy Cal, but yes I am a mere mortal, and I only have a few coins in my tin to rattle. At this moment I am filled with sadness. Sadness because I feel very concerned about you and I love you. I feel almost powerless to do anything to help you." It shut me up like a box. I mentally digressed and lit up a fag and enjoyed the smell of the exhaled smoke. It was funny how it smelt different from the inhalation. A silent moment of singular reflection. "Come on Cal you can lead your generation to world peace and harmony later. Come down off your perch. Listen to Dr. Miller and let's get it right this time. I would love above all for things to work out for you. Let's get down to Johnshaven and get the dinner on. Oh and remember that bloody medication." I was moving. I washed, shaved and dusted down in rapid time, commando style. I dumbed the flat down into cold graveyard mode. I had a plastic bag of gifts. Jesus with a carrier bag. The well of the tenement was cold, gritty and empty. Under the constant glare of the communal lights the carpet was stained. It disturbed my aesthetic, that is why I favoured a low-key lighting system. It seemed as though everyone had shut up shop and taken this day off. From the grind that was the rest of our lives.

We were soon out of the city. Heading south in the white Morris Minor, with the red trim. The red hot, thin tail pipe farted and pooped, propelling us on, looking forward. The landscape was white and frozen, peppered here and there with blackcurrant. It was just like the seed of creation. Cryogenically frozen until the creative power of replication is harnessed from it. The ground was frozen hard to a depth. Like tundra: Movement. The sky was a pinky red. Everywhere in movement I was taking the weather with me. The cycle that was taking place in my body, and in my mind. Replicated patterns of low pressure, high pressure and meridian. I was like a flaming pie, racing through the air.

We arrived down in Johnshaven. It was not such an extreme place as the communities further West by North East. Isolated and out on a limb. It was more loosely knit now, although it was still bound by the common link of the sea. There was not such a fearful sense of sin and redemption that looked down and over the people and characterised much of the North East Presbyterianism. Although many a soul in Aberdeenshire would be in a state of perdition this Xmas. In the face of secular erosion of the church, of the perceived notion of community, there was a sense of caricature. Although there were still a few boats built in the village. Boats still landed lobster and parton crab. Yet there was a sense of decline. At the bottom of the hill the peeling ancient yellow and black SNP posters hung against the derelict church building as if defining the impotence of much of Scots aspiration. The ghost of the old railway line ran through the village on its fictional journey between Stonehaven and Montrose. We got along Main Street to Lorna's self-imposed exile. She lived in the old Library, which was whitewashed and roofed in slate.

Iain was in the kitchen basting the duck. The huge flat dish of smoked salmon and brown bread lay waiting to be consumed. Iain was wearing his red turtle-neck sweater and blue jeans. He had on his black motorcycle boots. It was almost impossible to describe the colour of his hair; it was the colour of blue tinged porridge. I shook his hand and said to him, "I see you have your motorcycle boots on, ready for some rough riding?" He looked back at me with a whimsical smile playing across his closed lips, circa "Last Tango In Paris". I said, "Get the butter out," he said, "You would know more about that than me seeing as you were the last person to have the 'buftie' behaviour." Iain's sexuality was something of a mystery to me. In a painting he had once characterised himself as a hermaphrodite, although I think he was showing off, it was part of a fashion of the 80s'; dare to be different. He was capable of understanding male friends confidentially as people. Well that was all a long time ago, the rough sex of the army blanket. He had a steady woman now who he lived with in Glasgow. He was Airean and he was a Ram alright. He was defined by his Martian ruler i.e. Mars, although I couldn't think of a less warlike person. He liked to follow the recipe. For the moment anyway his days of experimentation were behind him. The set routine of not straying too much from the path that he had laid out ahead of him. Recently he had taken to smoking after dinner cigars, and the smoke would curl round his top lip. I suppose if I was to consider my own sexuality there was a time when I would have shagged a hairy Paris bun. It is funny how we become more alone, conservative and distanced in matters of sexual libido, as we grow older. It is not necessarily the way you would like it, but it just seems to be the way things work out. Iain was an artist. He took after his Grandfather James Mackintosh. Iain had worked out a lot of things for himself; he was trustworthy if sometimes unreliable on account of his lousy timekeeping. I left Iain to make the gravy, everything else was ready. I couldn't wait to guzzle on the Cava Brut champenois. I took it out of the fridge and dried the glasses. I have never learned properly to sip alcohol. I've always guzzled.

I took the drinks tray through to the micro happiness of Lorna's living room. She was raking the ash from the fire and putting on coal. It was nice and warm. Amongst my Father's people there was definitely a sense of one upmanship. They liked to score points off one another. Personally I found this savagery ghastly. Pitiless, cruel sardonism. Lorna Moone and I were agreed on this much. The hackles would rise if it were directed at us. It was hard not to be duped by this form of humour, perhaps that is why increasingly I separated being here from my father's people. Although I wondered now how my father would be spending Xmas day. In turn, Norman too had chosen to remove himself from the domestic routine. But you cannot spend your entire adult life on the wing. In a sense now he had reaped what he had sown with regard to the nucleus of his family; Lorna Moone, Iain and me. I popped the cork and poured out three glasses of Methode Champenois. Iain came through with the salmon and we had some food. Three was my perfect people number; naturally it was the number of people I felt a logical part of. James Mackintosh and his Brothers had all been born in Johnshaven, in a sense we had a local connection. A reason for being attached to the place.

There was choice faced by them when they were young men come of age. Either to look east towards the sea and the sunrise, or turn their back and face the West and the land. They all chose the freshly ploughed smell of the earth. James was feed to a farm at the Stonehaven "feein market". People of this era were not just tied by employment and housing. There was a deep familial bond between employer and employee. This descendent of a form of feudalism created a kind of peasant class amongst my Grandfather's generation. A class which Lorna Moone was part of. We drank some wine, had our meal and pulled crackers. It was a book Xmas and some cash from Lorna Moone and Iain. After lunch I went through to take my medication alone in the kitchen. It was an act I still liked to perform secretly. I somehow imagined that people would not know I was manic-depressive. This new label that had been attached to me as though I were some kind of shrub. I tanned the pills with water. I imagined the medication had the effect of pruning back the worst excesses of my condition.

In the afternoon we went and walked on Lunan Bay. It was a 3 mile stretch of beach to the South of Johnshaven. Lorna took some snaps and Iain and I horsed about. Perhaps the Xmas day represented the 'fin de siecle' of the state of our post nuclear family. The end of a little era. We three had been forced to suffer. It was not any one person's fault but I felt as though I had missed out on something growing up, i.e. a father. Nothing could replace that lost time. It was like one of Lorna Moone's paintings. Standing naked in the Garden of Eden she shakes her clenched fist at the tree of life. Anger that would be sustained for a short while yet. To be replaced with a new sense of purpose. Striving towards a feeling of happiness. Yet in the face of this Lorna Moone was a happy person. She felt angry for her children that is all. The only way ahead was to make a concrete sustainable plan and act upon it rationally. In her heart of hearts as she looked at me setting up a pose for the camera, holding a piece of drift wood up Iain's rectum, while he looked like Frankie Howard. She knew that I would learn to manage my illness. That I would overcome this obstacle that life had flung carelessly in my face.

After our walk I took the notion that it was important to get back up to the city. The weather was beginning to close in. It would be dark soon. I said goodbye to my brother. Like the weather my mood felt ominous and uncertain. Lorna Moone and I began the short trip to Aberdeen. It began to snow, and simultaneously my mood lifted. The heavy pain in my testes lifted, in the same way that the sky was releasing its burden. The snow blew in across the road in horizontal bands. We were both enjoying the exciting uncertainty of the weather. The canker that had entered my body was releasing itself. The canker that was like a thumbnail pushed forward through the Tabular Rasa. Nature was purifying the world of the imperfection, the fault line we had laid across it. Like some kind of flawed genus. In some way creation had originated to an extent in this part of Europe. I said to Lorna Moone that in a tangible way this part of the world had influenced much of what we understood as spiritual truth. Lorna Moone smiled at me in a placatory way, she asked me what I meant by that. I said, "Take Hollywood, it is like a huge family, all the different stars had different surnames according to the significance of their origin. How we perceived them suggested the existence of some kind of meaning. If you consider my surname you come up with a tub of alcohol. If you consider Madonna's surname: 'Ciccone' you find a tub of fat. It is not too dissimilar. It was now clear and the moon shone. Lorna said intuitively without thinking. "As one waxes the other wanes." I said, "That suggests just that perhaps in some essential way we are related. A LIT CANDLE FOR PEACE. When you consider the world in this way, the energy of the massive movement that it creates is far greater than any one person. In a sense it becomes a kind of cult of the personality. A force for purely good change."

Lorna Moone replied, "Cult can be a dangerous thing, for the individual. It is perhaps best to take one step backwards in these situations. Surely at the end of the day Hollywood has more to do with talent than the meaning of surnames." We had reached the outskirts of the city. The dual carriageway was repeating itself in orange under the overhead lighting. We were safe now. I mumbled on, I said, "Hollywood tries to mirror in some way our pattern of existence. It tries to describe the state of the Ark. In a sense that is a spiritual truth." Lorna Moone just nodded in agreement. A nod I would get used to when my uninhibited bursts of insight tried to penetrate the dour tundra that Scots people had created around themselves. Something that was elementally true. I asked Lorna Moone to drop me off on Union Street. She was dismayed. I was a precious little "gowk's" egg that should be swaddled in cotton wool and put inside a matchbox. I asked her to drop me off at Zig Zag, the only place in the city centre open. Lorna Moone stopped the car and kissed me goodbye. She said, "Remember those tabbies now." I got out and scrunched across the pavement.

Aberdeen on Xmas night was like a ghost town. It seemed dark, gothic and impenetrable. Like an abandoned huge dormitory city with little or no aesthetic attached to its meaning. I went into the pub, it was quiet. The music was on, techno, repeating itself over and over. I had a beer and wondered what to do next. Someone was handing out free tickets for the club upstairs. I went up to the club and had another couple beers at the bar. I relaxed into the situation. I went through to the dance floor and stood on my own over the bear pit that was the dance floor. I was standing next to a speaker. Suddenly a voice, a raunchy American woman's voice overdubbed the track that was being played and asked, "Are you going to work?" I became excited, attached meaning to this voice as if it was addressing me. I was someone of vast importance surely. I wished her a happy Xmas, as if this disembodied voice could actually hear what I was saying. She replied, "Happy Xmas," in a dispirited way as if there was nothing in the world to rejoice about. There was no harmony; there was no world peace. There was a sense of moral outrage. I suddenly imagined that I was part of a movement greater than any one individual. I became ecstatic with excitement, I started gibbering. I said, "All the awful things we have been seeing on TV recently aren't true, it is just fantasy." The voice replied back, "It's going to make us all join." I looked around to see if anyone else was noticing the voice. Suddenly a drunken young man came up to me and started shaking my hand profoundly, as if I was someone very famous and cool. The bouncers grabbed him and threw him out. Then as quickly as the voice had begun she disappeared. The Immaculate Conception. All of a sudden the adrenalin stopped pumping. I felt a bit drunk and foolish. I just wanted to get the hell out of there and get myself home.

As people we suffer, and keep on suffering. Alternation between majority daily depression and the false elation that alcohol provides. The gap of New Year is spent alone. On my own with over proof Highland Park whisky and cans of beer for company. Looking at the goggle box in the corner. Loneliness can drive you insane. A dialogue conducted with myself. No choice this year.

When I was with Eva, I once saw in New Year locked in a Motel bathroom in Newport Oregon. Home of the State Mental Hospital. A strangely uninhabited, blank, lonely, swirling town. Travel North on Pacific highway and it steadily gets poorer, and the strip advertising gets gaudier, seamier. Until finally you will end up in Tacoma bay in Washington State. Rust belt culture, project shell housing, proud black Americans. Is there no way out of here said the joker to the thief? Industrial depression, burger and fries, (and pickled jalapeno peppers). Eva and I wind up in this Motel room in Newport. It was as far as I could drive. The combination of driving, cigarettes, booze and junk high carbohydrate food leave me feeling permanently exhausted. Eva was being childish. She is bulimic, the illness of plenty. She don't want Taco Bell, she don't want Arby's roast beef, How about Submarine sandwiches my little lima bean? She stops smoking that day, she would fidget and ficker then start again tomorrow. Meanwhile she rips up my carton of American Spirits, to punish me and my habit. So we drank 3 litres of cheap Californian red wine in the Motel room. Both our mouths were red from the wine, like Coco the clown. We burst into laughter then at that one. So we fucked on the double bed, then picked another fight. I could take so much. I lay there drunk smelling the dried saliva of the many previous guests on the pillow. The room was panelled in marine ply that had turned the colour of oak from all the cigarettes that had been smoked in there. There was an ancient mesh shaped oval electric coil fire that glowed orange like the end of a cigarette. In the UK this sort of junk would be called quaint and of period interest. In the States it was just like the wig shops. It was necessary tack. The stuff of urban mythology. The TV hummed on in perpetuity. I looked at The North West Bell phone longingly. I would love to make a collect call home but Eva would resent that. We ended up fighting again around midnight; the wine was finished, who was going for more?

A sense of malice between us. Locked into a fatal battle. I go to piss in the bathroom. Eva locks me in with a chair and I hear her taking off in the car. I kicked open the door. On the TV they were celebrating New Years. January 1st 1992. I was lonely, I was sick for my own environment. I since realised that environment is only where you find yourself at any given moment. I just sat on the bed straightening out the remnants of my rumpled American Spirits. Eva came back a couple of hours later. She was very drunk, weepy and full of contrition. I felt like slapping her hard across the mouth but I said and did nothing. Drink driving was a very serious felony in the USA; she had form in California for Dope, for underage drinking. It was her one eye culture; it was her choice to wring herself by the neck like a chicken. She had been in a bar with other Americans, she phoned her ex-boyfriend collect. The guy is dying from AIDS. She was as sad and deflated by the coming of the New Year as I was. They talked for an hour, and she was drinking these high balls, vodka martinis. I wanted to get away from the notion of Eva and me. I had just spent New Year in a place where not one person who cared about me knew where the hell I was. Sitting on the edge of the bed realising my marriage is dead. She had come to me in Scotland to find her own Scottish identity, and I would now have to return home to heal alone.

Into the New Year in Aberdeen, into a bright fresh routine. Like taking the cellophane wrapper off a fresh pack of bonded manila envelopes and smelling the wonderful clean, virgin paper. Fastidious ingestion of the Gumby head palliative medication. Shave, toothpaste, shower every day. Clean clothes, hoover, and dishes.

Just a wee wank once a month. Saving up my strength, storing up my seed. I decide to go back to work. My mind is curious. In addition to this the con side. Benefit culture, bumping along the bottom getting skinned and chaffed. My reward for making a significant contribution to the economy of the country. All those dark winterous mornings, all those years spent amongst the droning dwarfism of Industrial culture, while my Brother and his piss artist mates attempt to emulate Alcibiades in vain. They will face their turn on the treadmill. My plain staple contribution. In recognition of this I receive a reserved place in the poverty trap. Where do the spiders go in winter? Do they hibernate or do they continue to hatch their plans and spin out a web. To catch filthy flies like me.

———

I get the green light to return to The Water Board. Chocks away, but I still wasn't completely well. I associated things in my head, I interpreted signs everywhere. There was an inner voice talking to me. First day back, my contract will not be renewed. Six weeks and I will be finished forever. I was to spend my last period locating and renovating buried manholes in the shire. I shouldn't have bothered coming back, but it was that work ethic kicking in. We feel guilty in some sense. But all that had in fact actually happened was that my sense of resolution and determination had been humiliated. Was I being freed because of my mental health difficulties? Suffice to say it is a fucking disgrace the wages that are paid to staff that work in Public Service Utilities, considering how stressful the job is. It was just another turn of the screw for me. The Archimedes spiral had just lifted the shit and piss of my life onto another higher plain of conscious awareness. That is all.

The two guys working with me are Private Sub-Contractors. It is classed as minor capital works. These works aren't done by the utility authority operative anymore. The subs don't have the correct safety gear; they don't have the correct road signs. The authority ends up doling it out. We trace a foul sewer system at a Free Masonic Hall in Laurencekirk. The spire is twisted because the foundation had subsided. I say to the men loudly, "Truly crooked spires are founded upon twisted crooked hearts." This sort of thing doesn't sit too well amongst the Pictish brethren. They just say nothing, simmer for a while and keep on labouring. My time came to an end. The boss took me for a meal and on the last day I got a lift to Aberdeen.

I had been tempered, but I didn't feel as though I had come through the threshing mill yet. There was more bile to come out. I wanted to know from where this anger within me came? Change was not common to most Scots. It is anger at this inertia, which becomes pejorative decline and gives us a sharp edge as a race. A violent reaction to one another's anger. Seasonal unemployment, declining housing waiting lists. How is it that I can live in a Band A council flat with gas central heating, double glazing, fitted bathroom and kitchen and pay £90 per month. I rent a private flat Band A, no central heating, no double glazing, no fitted kitchen and bathroom, chronic dampness and pay £300 a month. Why is the gap between public sector and private sector housing so iniquitous? Particularly when you are receiving housing benefit. Is that what you call the acceptable face of advanced capitalism? The Scots are entitled to feel angry. We still have to kick against the pricks. Increasingly though, because nothing ever gets any better in this crucial area of housing, it just gets worse. We numb our souls with alcohol and drugs. The aspirations for our country are as narrow minded and parochial as the voices of the small 'feart' individuals who govern this country. Scotland is a post conservative land; we should rejoice for that much. But until some leadership of charisma arrives, until some excitement is generated that will dispel the inertia in both rural and urban Scotland we will remain where we are, stuck in the mire, gossiping, with our heads looking back over our shoulders, afraid of a Torieat. The most talented Scots will either remain cynically locked in obscurity or will continue to leave. We crave a dynamic in Scotland, if we are not to become blind. Light and tone that shades space enough for everyone. We need to be given the space to find freedom within ourselves. To go ahead and achieve our full potential. This involves a fundamental sense of self-discovery. However the material trade off continues in service of existing Mammon. The new icon of society is fake celebrity. Couple that with wealth, and a material culture has virtually replaced creative endeavour as something worthwhile, as something attainable and universally good. In a sense we are all in service of Mammon in Scotland. The creative statement we make about ourselves is that of the oxen, castrated and domesticated. Kept to work its life out, continuing to work its life out in the hope of a better life. That hope is extinguished when it realises it is of no use any more. The wild spirit of the Scots race has been harnessed so as a race we have submitted to consumer led capitalism in the hope that "It Could Be You". As a nation we huddle together and look consistently inward, ignoring the considerable influence we have in the world. The ox yoked to the plough, turning the straight stubbled drills in the park into loam.

Depression is the heaviest emotion. Like a load of barium rock dropped on the quayside. It is used to make drilling mud on the oilrigs. Because it falls to the bottom and lubricates the grinding process. You are debilitated by grinding depression, as if all your actions are in paralysis. That and loneliness, but that foe eventually becomes a friend of a sort. Nothing to get up for, an effort to wash your body. Simply going through the motions, get up and do it again. You are isolated; you have retreated yourself, to a place within where no one can ever harm you. Truly worthless, cast back to the ocean floor like a clinging starfish. Cudgelled into accepting the limited economic future of the rest of my life. Feelings of loneliness are replaced by a kind inevitability that things will never get any better. You learn to identify with the security of your own flat, your own company. Does anyone notice anyway? I merge in towards the right, just like everyone else. The gap in the system lies open, like a door ajar banging in the wind. The repeating bump becomes emotional pain. Call it anguish; call it a frustrated bewilderment, but the end result is that your identity is slowly erased. I am pigeon holed into a neat little box, as long as I take the medication, keep my appointments and only think about suicide that is okay. It is not just about money. Essentially it is about the redistribution of infinite happiness. Do a statistical survey of alcoholism amongst people like me with an enduring mental health problem and I am sure it will shock you.

Filled with despairing thoughts, at the bottom of my cycle. My daily ablution was eating food and the enjoyment of having big solid craps into the toilet bowel. Emptying my bowel, purifying my body. Watching the water well up in the lavatory bowl until the sump flushed away the faeces. I was always on my own. Watching a lot of television. A single candle burning, but not quite snuffed out yet. Paranoia. Afraid that someone is talking about me, that they can hear my waking whisper. Best to keep my own counsel comrade. Or I will find myself running away from rough violent men who want to abuse me. Paranoid of my own actions, that in some sense I worry about disrupting the status quo. That it will come back to lay a torieat across my life. Hateful poverty, to use "DSS speak," an either increasing or decreasing pot of money. The guy comes round and reviews my case. A Machiavellian scribe who tries to label me now as depressed instead of manic-depressive. I correct him frightened. Ration resources neatly like a row of sardines laid out in the open can. A budget becomes a way of life. I start going into my local pub. I sit on my own amongst the winey red darkness with my pint of dark heavy beer. I sit silently thinking amongst the dourness and glacial hardness of urban Aberdeen men. I pretend I am watching Sky One Sports, to fit in. The only thing I would like to do is fuck the presenter Kirsty Gallagher. But no one seems to be intolerant to my oddness. I don't seem to stand out. I have found myself withdrawn inside the small circle that could be my life. Potential there for danger, better to abstain to this point here. Pretending to enjoy a repeat of the midweek premier league action. I really have come to loathe the culture of football. For all that it aspires to in the faces of the fans, for all that it continues to erode majority British aspiration. Ennui for me.

My hands had developed a shake. It was a combination of the medication, my mental anxiety and alcohol. Benign essential tremor. I am prescribed beta-blockers. I was a time served Engineer, an MA graduate and I can hardly sign my own name. Zombified appearance, weight gain as a result of prescribed medication. Inside I writhe and wring in torment. Lorna Moone does not give up on me. Cooking, washing, guiltily snatched £10 notes from her cat like hands. Meanwhile Norman contents himself with his isolated view. The swan came back this year, to nest on his lochan one final time. He had lost his mate. He would gladly exchange his frail existence for the eternal freedom of the Gael. Norman had lost Lorna Moone when she still cherished his love. She had brought forth two eggs; the twin sons of Pollux and Castor. We shared the same fate in a sense; Iain and I. Living alternate days in the underworld. If we were one he would be an ideal mate. As it was Lorna Moone shared her Gemini/Tiger with Marilyn Monroe, and Lorna would have aborted both her sons if Norman had got his way. Yet he was born in the same year as Monroe, he was a Tiger also. And I was born in 1962, the year she died. Like a candle in the wind that was now almost burnt out. Lorna would say, "The world is still out there, it hasn't changed." I didn't want to be part of it because it seemed to ignore me. I was paying the price for arrogant pride I kept repeating to myself. My hubris was as a result of this fault. Lorna Moone would merely say, "Better to realise that now Darling than end up like Norman." For she had realised long ago that Norman was a lost cause. Not that he was a complete washout; she would not let that notion intrude upon her idealistic view of heaven. But she would sit looking at him in his Kilt-rig, awry, drunk with much whisky, his cock and balls hanging out. His cruel puckering mouth, snoring loudly. And she would think, "Him weak man, would bring destruction on almost anything."

I stopped taking the medication, the cure was more unpleasant than the illness. I was to go up and see my father in the next two weeks. Just like Norman my timing was immaculate. His style; turn up with food and drink, a grand gesture played with the flourish of the hand. I wouldn't describe him as in any way a traditional Scotsman but rather something that predates all that. Something ancient and ingenious in its production. Yet he wasn't able to understand my mental frailties. Not the part of me he was proud of but the whole of me. That was like having to eat a can of "McConnachies mince", cold with a hangover. I had tried to tell him how I loved him in my letter from Germany. He had told my brother that it was maudlin rubbish. The great highland tradition of hedging your bets and playing one son off another. So, I just stopped taking my medication one day, as simple as that. I threw it away and smoked a joint to kick in my sense of imaginative awareness. Confusing the abstraction of creativity with intoxication again. Norman told me once when I was a toddler I wouldn't stop crying. He was looking after me. He came into the room in a blind rage. The kind of rage you can only really understand if you are born under the sign of the Tiger. He smashed me across the face in the same way he would have another man. He felt guilty. If they were handing out medals for guilt Norman would have been the most decorated ex-serviceman in the UK. Well as it was he had seen action in Korea and in Suez. Tough toys for tough boys. So in my eyes it was man to man now. I decided to stop worshipping false gods. I decided to concentrate on the substance of my father's character. Until now I had only ever seen glimpses of that. Lorna Moone had managed to earn her independence all her adult life and still care for her children. But where she could be all air, light, whimsy and caprice Norman was intensely fatalistic. That his search for destiny in life would lead him only to one final resting place; the most beautiful, plaintive cemetery in Britain. A plot at the Braigh in the Eye peninsula where he had spent the happiest, childhood years of his life. Death and it's intimation was such a selfish, final act of contrition.

CHAPTER SIX

I don't know how it precipitates, but it is like a light switch being flicked on. Suddenly there is light where there had been darkness. Light floods into every inky corner of the mind. Intense feelings of premonition for several days. Incubating a sudden chemical twist. Leaping like a salmon. My energy levels are increased. I feel restless. Thinking intensely of the most profound insights into the fundamental truths of life. This is the truth of my life, this is a reality. I am within hours entered into a manic phase. The full lock has been snapped. The handbrake is off. The words, "Keep off the dope and take the medication," rang somewhere at the back of my mind. I just brush them off like dandruff. A minor inconvenience, an itch that I won't scratch. Mania had become my approximation of happiness. Interpreting messages from the TV again, part of a greater plan contributing towards world peace. My input is valued. The need for copious amounts of alcohol and cigarettes. Not to deaden and numb my soul, but to stimulate my creativity. My appetite for food is confined to eating on the hop, when I can, if I can. I start to listen to music again after months of pop celibacy. Rushing headlong in to embrace the two beats, where before there was only one.

A tight halo around my head like a band of gold. It was my brain trying to cope with, reacting to the disturbed electrical activity going on inside the spongiform mush. Jesus, I was feeling good again. The dawn would rise into my bedroom and I would be up with it. I thought as I loved myself in the full-length vanity mirror, "this boy is going all the way." Strange things do happen when you are strange. You give off a positive radiant glow of health that is only apparently true. Your eyes glow like gems of sapphire. I am on a high, springing, almost running along. Like a racehorse, nervous, highly-strung, sweating up a cob. On the move, restless, no concentration. I just need a drink again. In this pub and then onto the next. The barmaid says, "Not at work today?" I reply, "No I'm on the beach," she nods in understanding. I mean I'm not about to spill my guts and say I'm a manicker, am I? Limited expectations from the limited potential of Aberdeen. Fuck the money I think in erroneous judgment. Rushing on, ever onwards, no feeling now of being paranoid, in the town centre moving in a spiral towards the concentric point. Like stuck in a maze where there is no exit there is no choice. I cannot turn off the switch in myself. I'm a victim, the alcohol has no intoxicating effect, and it just increases my high. Standing talking to myself, mumbling to myself, the inner voice is audible. Two guys in front. One shouts laughing, pointing his pint at me, "He's drunk," his mate knows better, shows me a look of concern and says, "He's not drunk…" Retreat back on up the road; I forget now what I was looking for. Just about enough digging in the dirt bucket of life today. Restless energy, superhuman strength, beef and heart. From top gear down the box using the engine to brake. Stop. The 525 Cocktail lounge, the criminal pub where all the "crim" dwellers of Froghall liked to hop into. Amphibian, cold blooded, disreputable people. A fondness for delving in amongst the low life culture, I walk in. The huge 120-ounce bottle of whisky stands to attention on the optic. The betting slips are neatly stacked. Quietness, total quiet. The barmaid, another male punter and me. He eyes me suspiciously from his stool in the corner. His legs aren't quite long enough to reach the floor. They dangle like kippers in a smoke house. He is wearing black ankle zip up booties. Oh the Scot in full aesthetic and genetic glory. An overflowing abundance of scrunted majesty. Hail Scotia, great nation oh the pudding race! I order a half pint. The therapy of the pavement is within me. The red spattered trail of dried blood drops lead me in this door. A voice inside me tells me, "You should fight that man, burn the anger out of yourself with a hot poker, quell the aggression." The little frogman hops off his stool and hovers menacingly towards me. Small wide and ugly. Antithesis of Dodge City. The jukebox cracks into life, "Sailing" by Rod Stewart. The man says, "You're the Comyn aren't you?" I just look at him and smile, waiting for it in this stinking little fluff hole. The coil is winding up inside me tighter and tighter until I have to pull the trigger. Apparent ease. I offer him a cigarette, a toasted tobacco class 'A' cigarette. I light him up. He smokes it as though it were bad medicine. Showing his distaste for the possibility of ameliorative change that I might represent. He tries to wound my credibility; he stubs it out almost immediately. The romance of the song, "To be near you once again," riding stormy waters. Norman hated rough Aberdonian men. Fights were usually the same for Norman, he would merely look at his watch, his omega sea master, and announce, "Fairly fairly, any time you're ready cove," Norman would straighten his tie and the guy would pounce. Norman would grab his head in a left arm lock and stiffen him a couple of hard rights to the face. The assailant would drop to the floor and Norman would boot his head a couple of times with his steel segged black brogues. Remembering to splatter his nose. He would then drain his drink, go to the urinal and fling up his ancient hunting Comyn tartan kilt and piss from his pintle. The only time it didn't work was when Norman got himself into fights with that big mouth of his. Crude, bauchled Pictishness. The barmaid breaks the tension. She says, "Awa back ahn sit oan yer perch Davey or I'll put ye oot." The creature slimes back roon the corner. I was calmer now. I finish my drink and leave, reputation intact.

I walk the remainder of my journey home slowly. My investigation for the day is complete. It is time for dissection of the evidence. Where did I belong? This country seems as though it is penned off, but by whom? And why? Emotional illiteracy granted but also trespassers are forbidden. If I was able to realise, it placed me in a position of freedom that I wasn't accepted as one of 'us'. It freed me from the diminishing spectre of breeding from an already inbred pool of genetic inheritance. My genetic inheritance was a kaleidoscope of Scottish and Celtic roots. It is little wonder that creative sensitive Scots people feel the urge to leave if not altogether turn their backs on their native land. For that is where the pain lies, back here in the sod of Scotland. Tomorrow I journey to Lewis to see my Father. Perhaps being up in the North West will offer me some sense of both hope and compromise. Some sense of realpolitik. I am seeking solace from the internal and external forces that clash and create a kind of polar madness in me. My genetic inheritance was the full shilling. I was given it. But now I found myself a couple of bricks short of the full load. I got home and phoned Lorna Moone. She knew I was manic, but at the same time she was happy that I was going to visit my father. Perhaps she still felt that Norman somehow could make up for lost time. Both Norman's and Lorna's views of education were similar. As teachers they approached their profession from different directions, but the end result was similar; their former students universally adored them. It was a pity that this could not have been tangential in their marriage. As it was Norman was disappointed with himself. He had never had a novel in him, he had never been able to translate his warmth and depth as a person into literary output. Because of his own failure Norman resented literary success in others close to him. This was entirely selfish but understandable. In a sense Norman was Torieat himself, as a child he had been blasted at the root. The experience of his childhood was something from which he was never fully able to recover. As a child Lorna Moone had been incredibly shy and demonstrably loving only to her Father. She craved his physical love, and indeed she was a precious gift to him. One of those rare incandescent beauties that are sometimes born to strong, honest, caring peasant parents. Like Joseph and

Mary. Lorna Moone uttered her first words when she was six. She pointed at the cat and said, "Dad that's Whitey." Now she was an outgoing extremely sociable person with a gregarious nature. That is not to say that she did not have her moments of solemnity and silent repose. For there was that quiet queerness in her character also, that characterised the North and East of Scotland. In reality Lorna Moone had never met another man that quite captured the honesty, warmth and also imagination that James Mackintosh had shown her when he was still living. Her final words to me on the phone before she hung up were, "Look after your Dad Cal."

The journey to Harris is not a great one in distance but an enormous leap in faith. It takes a full day to get there from the East coast. Unless you have a car you have to get the ferry to Lewis then hitch a lift down to South West Harris and Leverburgh where my father lived. In practice, like Lorna Moone, his life was spent in exile, except she didn't live life as a ruinous endurance. Running out of time to put things in order. Postponing the inevitable as he wondered where all the years had gone. He had chosen to confine himself in isolation, at Obbe, subconsciously punishing himself for all the mistakes he had made in his past life. Imbued with the blurred edge of a dipping Hebridean twilight, beneath the astral zodiac in all its brilliance. A clean cutting wind was calling to him; the white pure shell sand picking clean the skulls of the animals. Norman sipped gently but consistently on the gill of whisky. Moist exhaled breath. Fresh wild game fish. Open the gills and a red pink fauna aquifer is exposed. A fanning filter for extracting oxygen from water. An exact measure of fluid, the Still is an approximation. An exact measure of life. A constant mechanism that is replicated perfectly by nature. The Scots humors; the vices of cigarettes and alcohol hacking and splintering from the bundle with the poked head of an axe. A powerful addiction, cutting, calling to him. A sort of a friend. The points of the compass pulled at his soul, when the wind would howl. The flat raftered roof bucking on the wall head. It would drive most men mad. It just made my Norman restless, still taking youth on his side. There was more pleasure in the raised

Olympian narrative of his life than the holding down strap that binds the rest of us to this world.

I arrived in Ullapool. The East European factory ships were anchored in the bay. The mother ships sat there looking gaunt and grey. Their stacks, Polack, sputtering blue fume. Here for the pelagic species. The mackerel and the herring. The North Sea is grey blue, grimy and threshing. A sense of small time total wildness. Here the Atlantic is aquamarine, tranquil and slick. Big time sensuality. Complexity, specific paradigm. The smell of ozone and fish combines in the air. Everything has a quality of fragility. There is a sense of decay. Dampness and mildew in the breath is pervasive. The West coast. It corrodes everything made of steel. Streaked rust spews down the piles on the Ro/Ro terminal. Temperature is milder. It does not, the people do not, have an edge. Everything blends in more subtly, the gulls are passive and not as cadaverous as Aberdeen. Sense of tone to the landscape. The mountains rolling down and into the sea loch. Time seems to be on the ebb more slowly. Recognition of the remarkable. Both man-made and natural that will outlive my human experience. I arrive on the scene with my pitiful little holdall. Braying filled with exciting hopes for my trip to see my father. I am energetic. I have escaped from the bauchled rawness of Aberdeen. Ignorance that is fuelled by drink and picks out a fight with a complete stranger. I am picked out by my difference that is all. The numpty factor that with illiteral logic blights our land. I go in the pub following the mantra of Buddhist teachings and sit and have a pint. I stare into the perfect measure of real ale. Savour the moment before imbibing. Once drunk becomes strange. My own thoughts, my self. I take a long drink on the pint. Taking on ballast, bunkering the boat from the dolphins for the journey ahead. Medicament for my condition. Like paraffin lashed onto kindling by grandfather James before he sparks the fire with his tinderbox. Time for another pint before embarkation. When manic there should be a guardian angel looking over me, but come the nub, she flutters off. I do not feel alone when I am manic. There is some sense of shared intuition. I am entering the right world for intuitive thinking. The world of the Celtic, where everything seems more mysterious and less straightforward than the 3-4-5 triangle of Aberdeen. The dust shrouded horny handed Masons clutching their pints, clecking in the bar after work. Almost everyone here is bilingual, speaks Gaelic. I like the sound of it. The incredible difficulty of trying to pronounce it phonetically. I took a deep drink on my fresh pint. Alcohol played an essential part in the extremes of Gaelic culture. However I was beginning to realise my reaction to whisky was a polarisation of attitudes wherever you went in Scotland. There was little or no tolerance. But like most things Gaelic whisky was as arcane as the utterly ancient wailing at a Gaelic Sunday service. There is no person more damned than the fallen Gael. Upbringing in a traditional Gaelic sense is deeply rooted in family. Estrangement from this upbringing leads the fallen Gael further into an inferno of guilt. The ancient culture of Gaeldom, spontaneous song and originality of poetic Gaelic meaning means clinging on to this geographical wilderness, sustaining a livelihood in a pocket of material distress in the face of this generosity and native intelligence. The inheritance was within me somewhere. Day dulling down. Imperceptible waning of the light. Time to embark upon the boat and cross the Minch. Our departure was announced. Watch the stern of the boat scooting away at high speed towards Stornoway. Go up and sit on the observation deck. I spend the crossing pondering in silence. The whole ship is fairly quiet. It is amongst the sober nature of the natives to respect peace. The black headed gulls glide and arc, keeping up with the wake of the stern. The Atlantic waters look cold and specific to their own topicality. It makes me want to take a mad leap from here on topside. My fear restrains me. Down in the bar the vessel sails through the water silently. Only the occasional judder, and the repetitive tinkle of a glass. We would soon be in Stornoway. The drivers made their way to the car deck. The boat was approaching the Ro/Ro terminal. The town twinkled like "Hansel and Gretel". It would be dark soon. Darkly I would be immersing myself in the customs of the town. I was in the whisky capital of the world. I had no specific plans about how to get to my father's house. I just wanted to immerse myself in the acutely alcoholic atmosphere of Stornoway on a Saturday night. The deck hands shot the leaders and the fragile bow and stern hemp ropes were snared on the capstans. The boat winched itself into the quayside. I disembarked from the boat, amongst a few eager continental tourists. Tomorrow is the Sabbath. My imaginary message to them is don't come my way dancing on a Sunday.

Extremes of behaviour are associated with alcohol: specifically in Scotland, aggression. It is not good for any of us. Who can hold their liquor? It is a curious contradiction. Alcohol intoxicates you yet you are supposed to be able to hold it. As if it is a not altogether good thing to drink at all. But it is that damned gap. That gap between loneliness and happiness that the addiction to alcohol tries to unsuccessfully fill in. Extreme forms of behaviour are not just confined to the drinker in Lewis. The teetotal 'wee free' Christian will gladly pour her husband's whisky down the sink. The police who uphold the law maintain a regime of zero tolerance in the Islands. There is little or no compromise. It is the same form of utilitarianism that is designed to keep the peace, status quo unchanging and intact. Whether this is fair or not doesn't come into it.

I bar hopped, filling myself with bleeze. Carrying a burning torch of whisky that glowed inside me. Funny you could be anyone in Stornoway. Cosmopolitanism does not pick you out as a stranger. Only my distemper, the canker sitting on my brain serves to point a redemptive finger at me. I was in the County hotel at the bar. I got into an argument with guys at the bar. I had attracted the trouble upon myself. I was too excited, I was exhausted, I had to come down. I needed a sanctuary, someone to look after me, is there no alternative to this eternal "I". Must I always be alone with a millstone of stigma hanging around my neck? The manic mariner. I lost my temper and started shouting at anyone who would listen. I snapped, filled and overcome with bleeze. Next thing the barmaid has called the Police before someone hit me. Amongst the ghastly cruel bullying laughter at me. The whispered Stornoway tongue.

The animus of Hebrideans as if they had become whole formed from the silt. A face like a cod. Puce and roughly acned. Cold fish blue disc eyes. A purple chub of a mouth. The police arrive in their funereal long black shiny duster coats. Status and power of the dice caps. I thought thank god they are going to sort things out, as if it wasn't my fault. But the cops are making for me. I am the source of the trouble. I suppose I am a bit antiestablishment, but I hadn't done anything wrong. In my mind was the thought that the police here screwed the nut of law and order very tightly. I mean if you get caught in possession of dope here you are looking at a trip to Porterfield prison, or at least a very heavy fine. So the cop says something. I just make my point, I say, "You bastards fairly think you are something when you come up here." Bad move Cal. He replied in a heavy Glasgow accent, "Just you wait till I get you back to the station." He had my hand bent up behind my wrist, my arm up my back in an instant. I was in complete agony. I was marched out of the pub hopping like a frog towards the station. He could have cuffed me, but now he was enjoying hurting me too much. He was on a high of anger. He repeated his threat. The other cop just walked along quietly. It always seems to be the same, one is a complete bastard and the other is the people's friend. I don't think I'm better than anyone else, just more intelligent than most. My huffy arrogance had been punctured. I was filled with indignation, my dignity had been completely eroded in a flash of verbal insanity.

We get to the police station, inside the desk sergeant eyes me and I am cuffed. I calm right down; calm, cool, collected. Name, address, the charge sheet is read out to me. I look over my shoulder at my back. 'Auld nick' all right. It is the most fearsome gaol I have seen in my life. Vertical bars from concrete floor to concrete drop out beam in the ceiling protects the turnkey cells. An authoritarian reprimand if you break the law. Regional variation, regional dialect, regional law and order. It's a hard screw, more secure than a prison. I am searched, all my meagre possessions come tumbling out. I look at the hardman arresting officer, he is sitting by the desk sergeant and he is like shaking in a state of shock. He has come down off his adrenalin high. Pussy man. My shoes belt and tie are taken from me. No mention of my medical condition, no open cell while they arrange a bed for me in the psychiatric unit, the thought of a ritual beating at the back of my mind. Is this any way to treat the mentally ill?

The decent cop bangs me up in my cell. He says, "I like your ease big man, you should have talked to me first." The door slams and the turnkey officer departs the gaol. In the cell is a vinyl mattress, a urinal and a King James Bible, the Good Book. Walls covered in graffiti. Someone has scratched "Sly" on the Perspex fanlight. That's it; you have to be sleek and oily like a seal pup here. I was the only inmate tonight. I could hear the constant noise of people coming and going. Americans, Germans, Glaswegians. I strained hard to hear what they were saying. I could only imagine what they looked like. Lost liberty, solitary cell confinement. The cops would peep through the spy hole every now and again. A kettle keeps clicking on and off, making hot drinks, unwrapping cling film from food. Excruciating torture, I am denied food and drink. A glass of water. The "puddling" I had expected doesn't materialise. A long absurdly strange night. Every sound travels yet I am barred. Liberty that we take for granted. I fall into a couple of hours of sleep. I am awoken by sunlight shafting in the high cell glass brick window. The sun also rises on my new day, thank God. The beautiful sound of Lewis women singing in Gaelic from the kitchen. My heart swells up like a wood pigeon its gizzard bursting with yellow corn. The sound so poignant, so clear, strong and plaintive. They are singing for me, to me, asking forgiveness and salvation to Lord Jesus Christ. A troubled life but not a lost soul, thrashing in the maelstrom of life. They are offering me solace in song and in my faith itself. It is Sunday morning.

I get breakfast in the cell. It is good; bacon, sausage and egg. But only a mug of cold water, Adam's brew. I get out, I get all my things. I am given some friendly avuncular advice to keep away from alcohol. I will be hearing from the local Procurator Fiscal's office. Hostility is replaced with bright sunshine. The town is deserted. Everyone is either hiding behind the curtains under the duvet with a hangover from last night or preparing for the first of several Sunday church services. The Sabbath is the day for observing the Lord. The town seems desolate in the face of this seeming celebration of Christ's life. Religious belief amongst the community frowns upon hanging out your washing, even going for a walk. The churchgoers are dressed in funereal black as if in mourning rather than celebration of Christ. This small fiercely independent community retains its right to observe the Lord's Day and suspend all other secular forms of life. The status quo of extreme religiosity remains here even when the rest of Scotland is at ripe proletariat play in the ghastly drinking shops.

1919, the troop ship Iolaire foundered at the entry to Stornoway harbour. The boat packed with returning servicemen. It was New Year's Day. 200 men drowned. The plaid shrouded women folk were to be observed on their knees wailing on the shore. Husbands, fathers, sons all drowned. Hardly one family on the Island was not touched by this tragedy. The Lewis people had been bought and sold over many centuries but the deliberate perversion of this tragedy was an obscenity. Hardly a land fit for heroes. So the people turned inward to what they had left. Upon their faith. Turned into themselves and galvanised their idiosyncratic, unique religious belief. Preaching the Gaelic gospel all over the world. Seeking to convert the heathen mass towards the goodness of Christ's teachings. The influence of religion in The Outer Hebrides in general remains strong. On a Sunday, on days of Communion. To give thanks for and to educate others in the forgiveness of Christ.

I went and shaved in the public toilet. The running water was saline. Cold and tangy, the razor scarting my skin. Smelling of whisky and sea spray. In marine mode. I remembered being on the ferry to Shetland once. Sixteen gut churning hours in mid-winter. The guy in the berth above me was paralytic drunk. He had urinated himself. The smell of urine and Four Bells rum, a heady brew. I could remember for the first time being afraid of alcoholism in Scotsmen. The pain is there. Corrosive, endemic, chronic pain.

The purser puts me up on the deck with a couple of blankets. See the guy the next day, innocence, unshaven, hungover. He liberally douses his head under the quayside tap before heading to the first pub. Alcohol is the factor that leads to moral conversion. That and alcohol's social fallout. I am unreconstructed; I am still unforgiven. I head for the public bar in the County for a livener. The hypocrisy of being in a dry town. Legions of people coming and going for a half bottle and four red 'heavy' cans. Stepping backwards in time to a place that is totally outdated, before the flood. You can hear the Gaelic singing in the church across the road while standing at the font, in the spirit of Nono slurping on an Usher's gold tankard. I am stuck firmly, somewhere between piety and sin. The same barmaid as last night is working today. She doesn't bat an eyelid. She knows I have a drouth on me. I must go now and phone my father. I call him from the public phone. He is livid, he wants to know where I am. I tell him I'm in the County having a pint. There is a part of Norman that frowns upon breaking the Sabbath. He is like a scalded cat. No point in being mendacious. Another part would like to be here himself. The only way he knows how to show his concern is to lose his temper. It was the teetotal example that was set in stone for him by his own father. Except his father was a model of consistency whereas Norman was up and down like a fiddler's bow at the lee end of a peat stack. Well you can only pish with the cock you've got. He told me to get a taxi and he would pay it. I drained my last pint in leisurely fashion. The long good Sunday. The power of goodbye.

I'm in the taxi. The driver realises he has a bit of a looper here. The fare is £100. No point though in fazing the customer. He steps on the gas and very soon we are driving at high speed on the arterial link to the south of the island. On either side of the road is peat bog. Banks cut vertically. The peats sits drying in stacks. Like squares of finest "packy black". Fuel that turns to fine ashen grey powder. The bog rises tan and browns up to the increasing purples of the rounded gentle Hebridean mountainscape to the East. Sharp incisive peaks to the west scar the sky. Sunlight hangs like a haze rising the bog cotton into life after the hard cold slumber of winter. The lochans lie scattered amongst the peat bog abstracted by palettes of fresh water life. Wooden telegraph poles repeat their message silently like slumbering natives with an ear to the ground. I have a bit of a bleeze on me. What was in my system has been topped up. Like pissing in a car radiator. All very clever but hardly worth the effort. We pass deep peaty Grimista on the left. It curves to and fro slowly. The finest Salmon river in Britain. Frothy "collops" scatter the surface, like a pint of heavy. Moving slowly in the languid current. Lewis collies bark, yawn and wink a knowing eye. Stretching like ballet dancers in the sun. Red post boxes with their slats protected against the horizontal sleat of rain. Villages, churches, ruinous rubbles of townships. Loch Seaforth looking out into the ocean. Creels, fish farms, yellow wellies, abandoned tractors and fielded cars, decline. Lazy beds, crofts and above all the shanky Hebridean sheep with their golden eyes staring you down for food. Gathering and huddling together in the passing places on the road.

We arrive at the bridge that separates Harris and Lewis. One Island, two names unified by the common bond of Gaelic, Leodhas literally looks down upon na Hearadh. They say the invading Viking Norsemen turned their back at Harris. The whole east side is a lunar landscape. We Climb the Clisham, the highest peak on the Island. Rising, rising, rising. Then helter skelter down the other side towards the defunct whaling Station. Soon we are passing through Tarbert towards the fertile machair of the west side. Wonderful, abandoned white shell sand beaches, gulf-stream exotica. Some of the finest, least polluted in the whole world. The taxi arrives in Leverburgh at my father's house. It looks tumbledown and neglected. The man made fabric falls into decline here. It needs constant maintenance against the extreme weather. It is not in the Hebridean vitality to do more than is necessary to maintain the fabric of shelter. Decline is symptomatic of depopulation here. This decline is mirrored by the endeavoured world. Fishing, weaving, crofting. Everything constantly seems to be in crisis. Hanging by a thread, verging on collapse. So the people turn to God for spiritual faith, which grows more devout in proportion to the decreasing pool of the community. Scotland's cradle of Gaelic Christianity is neglected. A stoic acceptance by the Islanders of the trials and tribulations of life. It is a question of continuing to shape a life for yourself from the land and sea. The ghosts of previous generations, your people, your identity. They also worked a way of life, created a specific, unique culture from this bleak and unremitting landscape. Abandoned rumbles of rocks, dwellings scatter the islands like busted Cairns. Graveyards stand in manicured testimony to the successive generations who were born, lived and died here. Their Celtic influence, on the edge of our world. On the western rim of the old world.

The taxi driver comes in with me, to the back door. My father will pay him. There is the mild smell of wet fungal rot. The smell of coal tar, salt fish tack, shaving soap and urine from my father's bathroom. The delheat boiler is whirring loudly. The precious force pumped oil burning blue like a turbine through the spy hole. We go into the living room; it is warm. The smell of peat smooring smokily over the coals. The TV is on. Norman is sitting unsoporifically in his chair by the window. His bottom lip protrudes petulantly. His unforgiven, cavalier, military moustache bristles. He holds his hands in front of him like two chub fists. His fat sagittarian green eyes fix on me in an intelligent, cold broth, imperious gaze. Norman is wearing a phlegm coloured green roll neck jersey and olive green twill slacks. His clothes are liberally spattered with some old, some new cigarette burns. He is angry but he knows that he is spent. Like an old milted silver cock salmon; it's chin protruding out at the unfairness of life. My Brother is there, he is equally ill-prepared to understand how to cope with this situation. I sit down on the settee next to my Brother like a happy shiny person. Trying my best to hold it all together. My Father writes the taxi driver a cheque in his versical fine lined quirky style. An air of querulous resignation. Normally he would get a whisky as well but not today. Stony mood, flinty heart, peeled back and left humourless. Like a Celtic cross design, Norman finds it impossible to cut cleanly through and disentangle his own ego from that of me. The man disappears. There are not many subtleties that the Hebridean has not encountered here amongst family on a Sunday. My Father has resumed the same curmudgeonly look he had when I came in. He mournfully stares at Jim Delahunt and Sunday "Scotsport." Not much competition really. I feel like shouting out, "That's the fuckin' game with the round ball Nono," love child outta control. Iain continues to follow the Martian recipe and enacts the essential framework. He goes to make me a sandwich in the kitchen. When Iain leaves the room Norman snaps at me like a man-eating tiger. "Where the bloody hell did you get to last night? You know you are not well, why didn't you come straight here?" I looked closely at Norman. His broad, flat straight, almost ugly nose. Smashed. His fine alabaster skin that has a tan complexion. Dada's puckering expressive torieat mouth. Dada's classically round, big Hebridean head. Dada has all his own teeth. Dada's hair is fine and blue grey, once light brown blonde. And above all those eyes, those circle flecked phlegm green eyes like an alligator. No anger for me to expel. My heart feels pity for him. His life now was closely around himself. His low tar cigarettes, his rolling tobacco, his radio, his heart pills, his skin ointments, his pen and his comb. His bar of Lindt chocolate, his shopping catalogues, his fly spray, his books, his telephone, his assorted disabled implements. His reading light, his candle. His whisky, which had a froth on it as if he like "the guga" (gannet) had regurgitated it. Was he going to feed it to his young? He still had resonance, he still had an aura of magnificence. He was too old now that was all. Afraid of the light, afraid of change. I replied to my Father's question airily, "I got into some bother in Stornoway, I spent last night in the cells." He turns on me and says, "You cack handed fool do you realise the sort of disgrace you could bring on the family name, what a stupid young bugger." The family, that was a façade erected briefly against the dying of the light. A façade that was disintegrating rapidly in front of my own eyes. I said, "You have never spent a night in the cells then Norman." He was calmer now but still incandescent with rage. He took a sip of his whisky. I wouldn't have minded a wee nip of the amber cratur myself. He knew I had him there. Stalemate Nono. Iain came back with the sandwich and a cup of tea. I said, "Is there any drink, a can of beer?" He said, "No, there is no drink in the house." He was taking Norman's side. For once Iain was cast in a favourable light with his Father. He had learnt his lesson a few years ago when he had broken Norman's fishing rod and Nono went ballistic and threatened to take the poker over his head. The house with the green shutters all right, (phlegm green). Iain the "lowland Whig", Norman the Hielan monster, with a bloody clump of his own son's hair singeing on the poker. I stepped in then but I wasn't myself now. I chomped on the brisket sandwich and slurped the tea. Nono kept sneaking me little sidelong glances. As if the fucking North Pole might melt. The scene was set, a day of dry heaves, frosty silence, cigarettes. Norman coughing constantly with his one lung. Me laughing and mumbling to myself at the little parables I was constructing in my 'chemmed' up head. Norman hardly moved from his chair. I went to my bed and hardly slept. Insomnia the worst torture there is. Coupled with the voice that wouldn't leave me alone. Pressing in on me constantly. Morning, I have survived another night. Norman was in place in the chair next morning. He was surrounded in a shower of dried skin from his psoriasis. He had been scratching and shedding all night. The fire was cold. Iain came in to set it. They both behaved towards me remarkably the same as they did yesterday. Jude the obscure, please don't let me be misunderstood. The horror, the thoughts that woke Norman with a darting leap all night long. Harpies on the wind. I went for a walk after breakfast. I walked down to Rodel. The pub was down there. The only way I could earn my father's respect was to buy him a bottle of whisky. Crack the screw top, break out the Senior Service and talk to him man to man. He would respect that gesture. It was a brisk, fresh walk. A Northerly had brewed up, it was the equinox. Straight off the Arctic. Wind and rain. The rain sleeted in on horizontal bands. I walked down the little glen past the dead petrified trees. Sitting lifeless on the bare hillside like a scene from "Wuthering Heights". The medieval church of St. Clements lay crossed at the bottom. I went into the church. In the crypt was a bowl for donations for the National trust to upkeep the sanctified site. I took the money that was in it. Enough for a pint of Guinness. I went down round the corner to The Rodel hotel. It was little more than the finest example of an Edwardian ruin in the Outer Hebrides. A metaphor for Gaelic aspirations. Sin and redemption, decline and fall. I went in. An atmosphere of mild damp combined with the vapours of cigarettes and alcohol. The time in the bar ticked away slowly backwards. I thought that was true. As Norman had moved forward in life he had gradually retreated backwards to this point now. The bar looked out over the small tidal shelf harbour, where prawn boats still fished for the finest cold-water prawns in the world. Donny the boss was on the bar. It was silent except for the Sky TV. The dish outside was rotten from corrosion from the salt air and the insidious damp combined. Donny was far from being an alcoholic. It is just that he was imbued with it. He managed to hold the threads of his various business interests together. Books on a Sunday, (profit and loss kind). The mercy missions to Norman. The satisfying tear of a serrated edge from a stub. Donny greeted me, he could tell that I wasn't quite myself but he didn't see it as anything to be afraid of. I paid with the tarnished coins. Donny said, "You must have had your hand in the bottom of the gruel bowl for that pint." He had a knowing smile on his face. The vodka optic winked an eye at me. The bottle gurgled as Donny measured himself a dram. Point of common acceptance. This is the current situation, neither good bad or indifferent. Little preamble with Donny about the fishing, local gossip. No questions asked, three wise monkeys. Rain and wind bursting and polishing at the window. How's Tormod? Not so good, feeling his years. The clock taking us back around the face, back down the years since my last visit. The half bottles and bottles of whisky for off sale huddle together warmly. Slurp gratefully and deeply on my stout, a real minister's collar. Cheers God! So out with it Cal enough scratching at the dust pail of life. I say, "Can I get a bottle of scotch on Tormod's slate Donny?" No problem, who was his best customer after all if it was not my father. I watch closely, the proverbial salmon is in the bag, tie the handle and ready to go. Bells whisky too, nothing but finest Perthshire cratur for Norman. Who saw Donny alright for a case a week? The myth of whisky, dramming on the neck. Norman was not an alcoholic by Hebridean standard. He just liked a drink. The trade end of the knackers yard that it brought. His riches, his choice to have chosen whisky instead of life. Missed out on so much. You have ignored so much in life. The myth of whisky, that fills in the ennui so approximately and replicates it with black oblivion. Roamin in the gloamin, the eternal fountain of life. The false promise of a new dawn that whisky intimated. Up through the glen, to the brow of the hill, and the long straight into the village. The avenue of broken dreams, the myth of whisky. A myth that could only be sustained for so long, for the fluid measure of a bottle. The myth of whisky that had seduced Lorna Moone briefly. The myth of whisky followed by unsatisfactory sex. The false promise of a false God that could not be enacted. Reality. Norman's essential distaste for the corporeal. His middle class animated unenjoyment. Moving from one cardboard cutout hangover into the next. Sucking on eggs to line up the stomach. The vessels in the corner of the whites bloodshot. The albumen glue that carried human trace. The bodily fluid that Norman found distasteful but perfunctory to replicating the cut out dimension of his character. Slightly larger than scale. He only really took enjoyment in animal nature. His life had been an incredibly profound sense of loss. Otter's shyness, Salmon's instinct and their fight to rage against the dying of the light. The red deer's gentle omnivorism producing gamey flesh. Pissing a rabbit before you gut it, having shot it yourself. The cruelty of the yellow and spotted belly buzzard. The oily fish smell of beached minky whale. The creamy roe of the herring. The total uselessness of the raas fish, ribboned in colour like something from the Notting hill carnival. The myth of whisky, diving into the amber warmth like a black-throated diver. The natural world in decline. A fragile eco-system that has been upset by man's avarice. The island is overrun with North American currant eyed minks, (those Yanks will take over everywhere). Vicious predatory creatures that strip the otter of their native habitat. Farmed for their shiny pelts the mink runs wild. Cunning rough city dwellers, who supersede native guile with their wits.

I get to the house with the whisky. The starlings, thrushes and robins are scrapping cheekily. Roosting in the holly bush by the wall. Norman gives them shelter. Either unwittingly or not they have come to adore the man who sits always alone drinking, smoking and watching TV. Two Rowan trees protect the gate, a reminder of two of Norman's girlfriends. I should cut a sappy sucker from a rowan tree and ceremoniously present it symbolically to Norman. The red poisonous berries glistening. But which one to choose? The north wind blows crests up on Loch Steisevat. Norman's Orkney class boat sits bleakly upturned. The clinker is holed and untarred. It will sit there now until it rots to dust. The two model swans sit entwined in necks towards one another in the passage window. Another attempt by another woman who tried to understand Norman. Who tried to reconcile the wound in his soul? I go in with the carry out. The 'delheat' is still whirring. Quiet respect staring at TV glacially. My Brother is deeply ensconced in a book. He looks up, sees the live man in the bag and gives a skeiled vacant stare into the blue yonder. He seeks to avoid these confrontations. He seeks to enact a framework instead of live. I go over to Norman, he shrinks visibly in his chair. It is the last time in my life that I will try to please him. "Here Dada a bottle of whisky on the slate from Donny for you." A reaction time that could be measured out in milliseconds but seemed like a pregnant pause of the full duration. What should have happened then was that I got a couple of glasses and a jug of peaty brown water. I then sit down and have a close conversation about the nature of my mental illness and plan the best way forward from that. But in that moment as I look into my father's eyes, at this closest interface between life and death; my Father is afraid. He cannot cope. He reacts to the situation with volcanic but physically impotent anger. It is the flaw in his character. The fault line that I have tried to bridge. He snatches the bottle from me with powerful iron fisted hands. He says, "How dare you insult the locals and my hospitality in such a back handed way." My face turns to ash. I turn away from him dead and lifeless. I go and sit across the room. Consumption of vast quantities of whisky benignly here. It was the only way I had been shown how to communicate with my father. It was perverse, it is twisted. Damp mild soporific air conducive to exhaled moist whisky breath. Norman wounded me further. He said, "You are going back to the mainland with your brother tomorrow and go and get yourself well." This was Norman at his monstrous worst. He was the Devil. It was why Lorna Moone could not cope with his behaviour. The only thing to do was to leave. Iain turned further into his book. He was sensitive, usually mild mannered, but he also had a streak of bitter cynicism in him that had only really manifested itself when he had been confronted by the disappointments of life. As it was until the next day I was in a company of deathwatch beetles on the dry munch.

I was sitting on the bus, on the road. The mountains either side were still capped with snow. Torrents of pure water ran down the burns in spate. There was the spring come in the air. The release of potentiality. This aspect of creation was of significance to us and also perturbed me. Frost becomes snow and ice becomes fluid water once more. The cycle of replication. The inferred responsibility for creation is the mantle of responsibility that I wrestle with. I get back to Aberdeen. Atmosphere is specific to locality. A grey haar hangs over the damp grey granite. Vulnerability, depressed to an accepted point of familiar aloneness. Tired. Walking up the road to the cocoon of my flat. At the centre of a circle of nothingness. Difficult to keep a picture in my mind that contains the element of happiness. Pairing off is easier than the individual existence, living on your own. Aloneness as a man becomes more honest. The impossibility of trying to attach any romance to the British urban infrastructure environment. Everything seems ghastly. Is that why

Norman spent his whole life running? Trying to recapture the essence of romance as she flys, People are picked out into a sexed but mainly unimaginative life here. We are left to be alone. Always incredible sadness after seeing Norman again, only a half-life, briefly, snatched. I get into my safe flat. I don't even consider the everlasting ideal of love anymore. Profound depression. Suicidal loneliness. I wonder how my Dad is feeling?

CHAPTER SEVEN

The street is silent, waiting for the morning. All I can hear is the electric hum of the overhead streetlights. I hurl the heavy granite rock with as much strength as I can summon through the plate glass window. Ubermenschen invested with superhuman strength. Standing outside Oddbins window, it is a mild sultry June night. The window shatters in like a windscreen. I cave the hole in with the heel of my boot. Everything is still damped down, quiet. There is no alarm. It's the residential west end of Aberdeen. I want drink, I crave alcohol. Constant abuse since my visit to my father. When I can, when I get the money, I smoke dope and drink. I am worse than I was, more confused, more unravelled, and more alone. I am avoiding that goon in the white coat who could help me. High on a swell of mania that pounds like white horses onto the shore, the ebb flow sucking on the mineral goodness of the shale and shingle. I reach in my skinny wrist, the ones they can't get the cuffs on and steal two expensive bottles of red wine. I gash myself on the jagged edge. I feel the vein cut painfully. Blood oozes red all over the white shirt I am wearing. It smears the window. Globules of bright vermilion red drop from my fingertips splashing a crazy war dance pattern on the pavement. Another battle scar. What comes out of my mouth is a kind of monologue. Describing and animating the dialogue I am conducting inside my head. I disappear around the corner into the seclusion of the lane with my wine. Flee the surreal silent booted in scene. I take off my shirt and rip off the sark. I bandage the wound tightly. Physically my upper body is 'melded' and supple. My skin glows in a kind of incandescent orange brown. However I feel the limits of my own physicality. I am fit in a sense. All the physical walking and tramping, wearing out boot leather. Exhausting lungs and beating legs into shape. Suddenly I feel a sense of self-loathing. I fling one of the bottles to the ground. It explodes in a shower of red wine and green glass. I put my shirt back on and scuttle from the scene quickly like a weasel. My wrist continues to bleed profusely through the bandage like a pulped orange.

I stop at the denburn on the way to my flat. I can smell the bad smell coming from the water. I'm on a little grassy knoll overlooking my old school. The two are separated by the innocuous looking denburn. There are the remains of a tinker's bash amongst the ash trees. We used to raid it and read his viscous porno mags. He had a bed, and I remember he had "immac" to shave with. The bash was always empty but no one bothered him, it was his comfortable little snug. Those were more sympathetic times in Aberdeen before the coming of oil and the one dimensionality of thought that goes with it. I was in my element: cigarettes, alcohol, and my own company in the midst of a balmy night in Aberdeen. No one could touch me here. I whacked the head of the bottle on a rock and the neck came clean off. I hosed wine down my throat. My wrist pulsed in a constant throb. I could feel the old fracture in my back, like a corroded seam across my soul. I felt limited, I felt old. The wine went to work. A chemical reaction, so much satisfaction, I became renewed with vigour.

I looked across at the school where I didn't achieve my full academic potential. I wasn't happy there. Into adolescence with the full weight of a sledgehammer on me. From being in twos and threes to suddenly, inescapably single minded, self-reliant and alone. Following on from that the glamour of pubs when the olfactory senses were still intact. Dope, speed, then into the brown; winterous, arctic smack. Sado/masochistic male friendships and the occasional fearful fumble with women. Slow but quick-witted. Shit hot cyclist, National schoolboy amateur champion. It could have been me; I could have been a professional cyclist. But the alternative to that self-determination seemed far more interesting. The flaw in the Scottish psyche. The totally insane verbal diarrhoea of so much of Scottish formal education. It could have been me; I could have been a professional contender. Ruled with fear. The statue of Lord Byron sat in the courtyard. Well old boy you make a good metaphor for me leaving our school. Your potentiality was your lyricism. It became your poetic sensibility. But your physical journey is dogged by your malformed clubfoot. Not part of the crush, shunning the bun fight. Young Harold stood amongst them but not of them; in a shroud of thoughts which were not their thoughts. I slugged hard on the wine. My wrist looked like a red Indian ink paper blotter.

I don't fear death, it is just the process of dying that I am afraid of now. Serving an apprenticeship in construction then. Leaving my warm imprint in my bed on countless winter mornings, to face the damp blackness of dawn. Permanently exhausted, the whirly gig of the weekend. Constructing the largest private housing estate in Europe, on the back of oil in Aberdeen. On site for 8am. Gazing in wonder at the building site rising from the clay gravel moraine. Two orange coloured hymac diggers make their way down from the compound towards the no-fines concrete housing shells being fast track constructed. They are etched out starkly by the rising winter sun from the east. Set moving parallel against the stone dyke line of grey barked beech and ash trees. Tracked caterpillars. Their bent jibs ahead of them rocking with the contours, carrying the massive worn bright steel of the shoogly-toothed buckets. The hydraulic power rams glitter chromium in the rising watery light. These pterodactyls move slowly on their track. Clouds of blue particled exhaust fume up from the corroded vertical tailpipes. I can smell the rich red diesel. I want to scoop my hands into their tubs of lubricating grease. It appeals to my young mind. I want to immerse myself in the "glaur".

The conditioning of acceptance. Wellies, donkey jacket, scarf. A steaming cup of stewed sweet tea then go to set out. Form and function bridged by the human warmth of the men. Free will asserts itself. The country boys of the North East. A plainness of character that I respect. The kind of blue imprint of their consciousness throughout the winter months. Fresh poured concrete happed in straw hessian to protect it from frost. The smell of blue pokered fat in concrete, blue circle opc. Cement that binds with aggregate and water. Stripped form. The insitu concrete steaming as a chemical reaction heats the curing process. The washing away by rain and wind. The frost, the snow. The kind of log of a construction project from beginning to finish. Turning to the whisky bottle sometimes. Driven into a bottle by the honest brutality of the elemental work. I am staff. The men clock on and off. The white waxed paper pay packets for the men on Thursday. They prefer hard cash. I fell on ice one winter. Into the enormous frozen ruts that had been created by the "moxy" articulated dumpers. Fractured spine, one cat life erased forever. I wanted to hospital but the manager wouldn't let me away. At the fulcrum point of the most profitable site for the company anywhere in Britain. The down side of Aberdeenshire; cold and callous. He gnarls his knuckle into my freshly and partially fractured vertebrae and sends me back out to work. Like my mother Lorna Moone as a child I was unspeakably dumb with pain, seething with anger. Something there wasn't right. But I carried it. I carried that injury, it has calcified now, but it is still at the core of my skeletal self, that fault line.

Paradox. The wildness and the chaos of my home life. Smoking dope, drinking and taking speed at the weekends. My scrawny fit body. Lager was better then, not only was my olfactory sense still complete but there was a taste of honey in Tennents. A healthy dash of innocence and wonder. Then Deke would turn up, like a cuttlefish, squirting black ink at a white wedding. With his little wrap of powder, his sharp scratch on the artery of wilderness. It wasn't Deke's fault, his jaggered weakness; his essential incompleteness was what attracted his minions like moths to a candle flame. And I would burn all right. I was nearly a virgin, left up on the branch at seventeen. At a party we were gone stoned in the car to get cola, crisps and condoms, me and Deke. Passenger night, no inertia seat belt. Listening to the crappy "Buggles". Time to take the roundabout, wet autumn leaves under the wheels of the car. Deke loses control. Smack, hit a tree then a wall. The prop shaft flies up through the floor. I go straight through the windscreen. Skin graft to my left hand, broken shoulder, fracture to my skull. Stinking of drink and garlic. Bleeding like an orange everywhere. Shirt red. Boots red. Zero self-respect lying naked in casualty. I can take more Deke. Six months later serumed up with Hepatitis B in hospital. The person next door in isolation died last night. Ho Ho, duck's foot: She was a mongoloid just like me and just like you. Constipating clay pipe stools into a commode. I lose three stones in what seems like three minutes. I will never push a needle into my body again. Filthy skag what kind of friend is that? It was no wonder that we used flattened beer cans to tingle our building lines on the site from time to time. My life was a kind of multi-facetted personality in those days. It is little wonder I have schizoid tendencies.

And so I die a little each winter. I had drunk enough wine. I left a pint sitting for the twa Jakes. I got up to make my way home. I wobbled a little, light aero headed. My arse was damp from the sap rising in the grass. I looked at my wrist, throbbing gristle; punk as funk. I've been there myself, out of my brain on the train. Punk rock. I was last year's youth. Walking down the pavement it is beginning to get light. The swallows and swifts scream in the sky. 1977 to 1981 the most violent thuggish times I have encountered in my life. The anguished voice of a mass disaffected generation. No fun on the dole. The bitter, controlling cynicism of oligarchic government. Discovering pubs, discovering women, discovering drug fuelled punk rock. Sharing intimacy.

The Star and Garter pub centre for punk rock aspiration in Aberdeen. It was more than a fashion. It was a definitive moment. Masson gave the guy the money in The Starry to buy the petrol to set himself on fire in Crown Street. He went and bought, doused, then suffocated to death like a suicidal Buddhist. So good to be back home again. Farmer and me just laughed; callow, callous, feckless youth. Masson's claim to fame. Inhale on the "Zoff" sticky plaster remover, (it's on a scribe now), high and happy. Sucking on petrol fumes, dropping tabs of LSD, doing magic mushies, smoking dope. Scoofing lager. So good to be back home again. Alan and I like Batman and Robin in Gothic city. Farmer the farmer's boy labourer. I'm signed off work with the Hep. "B". And Farmer comes to pay a visit in his Massey Ferguson tractor. We get stoned out of our brains on hash oil. I ask Farmer what he was doing this morning. He says, "I was going round the Tattie Park killing crows. I go up with my shovel and flatten them from behind. I tied their outspread carcasses to the fence to warn off carrion from the seedlings." He tells me he is looking after cattle. I ask him what the difference between a stott and a bullock is. He says casually, "A stott has its knackers chopped off so it fattens more." He is going with Kaz just now, he says, "Fuck me Cal me 'Jap eye' is fairly hurting from last night, I had me feet purchased over the end of the bed all night." Farmer takes off in his tractor at 10miles an hour. He is totally stoned. Riffling along the granite cobbled street of Summerfield Terrace. Cars parked either side. I follow him on my Yamaha RD250. He catches a car and destroys the sides of five other cars ahead of it. He looks round and grins at me. It'll soon be Friday. It is the Cockney Rejects concert this weekend. Soon we will be booting a pig's head across the black, spumed stage. End message of entire movement. So good to be back home again. Farmer disappears towards the Bridge of Don at 15mph.

Standing with Alan Farmer pissing against the closed roll over shutter door at police HQ, Lodge walk. Just been to The Damned at The Student's Union. We're in vain, we're not sensible, the night is jet black and suddenly the rats appear. The automatic door rolls up and the squad car is facing us. The cops' think they are turning Japanese, they really think so. "On your way," they say or, "You're both fucking nicked." Getting ready for a Friday night. "Sees a shot oh yer eyeliner Farmer," I shout from the kitchen of my flat. Alan is in the bathroom with a plastic bag on his head with his corn hair coming through holes. He is only bleaching with the domestos. He comes through grinning, smoking a joint. He says, "The only problem with this stuff is it gives you a sore head." Meanwhile the Mekons are playing on the monitored turntable. "Gonna drive up your driveway baby with a neutron bomb a neutron bomb." Wishful, wanking, later I am thinking, afraid of the superior power of female sexuality. The door knocks. Its Snoz dressed in his air force jump suit. He is angry, he is quite upset. Farmer comes through looking like Ena Sharples. He says, "What's the matter did marmalade legs finish with you?" Snoz shatters his new Banshees single against the wall. All the three of us do a line of speed and Snoz rolls up a joint. The one bar amber orange of the fire heated the room to a tepid temperature. Snoz had by now almost forgotten what he had been posturing about. There wasn't the same stressful tension attached to flings in those days. Boys didn't cry, they just kept on laughing, hiding the tears in their eyes. I go and make us all a cup of tea.

I got back home. It was now early morning. And dawn had risen beyond a rosy glow to that state of yellow. Was this mindset I was switched on to permanent? Chemical attuned phosphorescence. No sleep at all. The distressing cruelty of insomnia. I have been taking refuelling stops. Feeding the frenzy of my mania. It is June, the earth is truly warmed through, now Jack Kerouac is back, Jack Kerouac is back. Free will overcomes despair. The disinformation, a random wipe of rationale. Insight into the human condition but none into my self. How I am perceived by the world. Quell this chemical imbalance, right my wrong. Physical deterioration followed quickly by death. An incredibly strong constitution coupled with an incredibly sensitive, hurt nature. Burning out like a red sunspot. The recurrence of images triggers some kind of dim recognition. Some kind of warning. No cure but lithium carbonate is effective in the treatment of mania. Nature takes its course in an episode of mania. Unfit for work, love goes into a polar climate. Steered into a silent place, until the day that I die? Sadness wells up in me, my eyes filled with bewilderment and fear. Burst into uncontrollable sobbing, tears rolling saltily down my face. I rage back against the hard light. Fragility; fuck that, small circle; fuck that. Trying to turn away from the hurl and aggression of this town. Safe in my council flat, safe in my bed. Locked door always.

The sun was up now. A hot summer day. That window of light seems disproportionately tiny to the black cold of the rest of the year. My wrist had stopped bleeding. Irrationally I take the notion to go up to A&E to get treatment. Change my shirt rinse my neck and face. My feet are beat up. Uninhibited, physical nakedness, affection, warmth, good fuck, iron strength, intellectual rigour. A worker, a long line of travellers, once drunk becomes strange. Jack Kerouac is back, Jack Kerouac is back, free will overcomes despair. No guilt, no paranoia.

Couple imagination with loneliness, and then start walking up to hospital. Rave on up the road. Are women afraid of me? Even trained nurses and doctors? The only person who cared a fuck about who I was and where I was just now was Lorna Moone. I wait in the queue at A&E and fill in the right form to satisfy their rules. There was a cop sitting there playing with the green hat band of his diced cap. He wasn't looking for me, not yet anyway. The nurse puts me in a cubicle she takes off the bandage and keeps asking how I did this to myself. Human nature is complicated by mania. She thinks I am trying to conceal from her that I have tried to harm myself. She cleans my wrist and bandages it up. And this goes on like in a vortex, like being lost somewhere in the interior yellow network of British Rail, confusion followed rapidly by panic and fear. Insecurity, I lost myself last summer sometime. My entire sphere of mutual influence, my entire life up to now is vanished. This is the aloneness now of my picked out reality. I didn't realise then that it is possible to get back to where I felt I had once belonged. In reality that had only been in the arms of my mother and her mother. The nurse goes to get the doctor; she wants to speak to me.

The goon comes through wearing a white coat. Her stethoscope sits across her shoulders like a pet snake. She is on full tilt, she asks me definitively, "How did you hurt your wrist?" I remain silent then start laughing to myself, the guardian angel is fluttering her wings again getting ready for take-off. Nothing finer than the clean burn euphoria of mania first thing in the morning. She says jokily, "Oh yes I know you," She then asks me if I am a patient at Cornhill. I swallow the bait and my mood turns to anger instantly like the flick of a windscreen wiper. I look her in the eye, I say, "Fuck off you are here to bandage my body not mess with my head." I get up to go, the doctor tries to restrain me. I look out of the screen, the cop has gone. I brush the doctor aside and make a run for it. A real gone kid out of casualty running freely into the bright warm sunshine. I ease down to a walk, down towards the town and go and sit in the Victoria park for a while. No sense of guilt, no sense of paranoia. Go into the toilet to piss. Guy standing next to me at the urinal, checking out the size of my cock. My brother once told me that your cock looks bigger if someone else is willy watching. Which makes me wonder how he knows? Think nothing of it, go and sit on a bench beside the fountain. Kid memories; conkers, learned to cycle here, first childhood-unsexed girlfriends. Fireworks, the denburn park across the road. My George Best wine red and black leather football boots. Healthy play. Now there are only men around, mixed ages like players on a "1984" chessboard. Everyone else is at work. I realise suddenly the park has become a pick up spot for gay guys. No time to be 12 anymore. Aberdeen is no place to be gay. The stigma attached to being a homosexual picked you out just like mania does. I got up and left bitterly. We have all been driven into a corner not entirely of our own making.

I got back to my flat; there was a Ford Escort Police car sitting there. I went upstairs. The front door had been broken in. I eased my way in gingerly feeling my way ahead with my outstretched palms as though I were blind. I saw two athletic policemen were standing in the living room. The mental hospital had alerted them to pick me up. Calm, friendly, tolerant policemen. Just picking up another mental case. They asked me to sit down. They were here to take me to the mental hospital. The police said to get some clothes packed and they would take me up. I made them a cup of tea and we had a cigarette. The cops checked my ID just to make sure they had the right person. That's the law, suicide is illegal. That coupled with their genuine concern for me. I mean nothing wants to die, not even the gasping airless fish you have just caught as you kill it on the head with the lead priest. I realised that, it was just a playful cuff. A scratch.

We went downstairs to the squad car. Intense feeling of people watching from behind the swish of the old lace curtains. This most traditionally essential Scottish furnishing item. Turn back inwards you old bag and check on your mince and tatties, or I'll come up and shite in the pot, and I'll not leave you any to eat, I thought. The cops asked me if I had been cuffed before, as they snapped on the bracelets behind my back. Just like the aroma off freshly laid asphalt delights my sense of smell, there is no finer noise than the ratchet of cuffs camming round someone's wrists, except when they were mine. My wrist hurt, I grimaced a smile. The cop makes sure I don't bang my head getting into the car. Interior, radio scouring "Echo, Tango, Foxtrot, Charlie…I said, "Yeah I was cuffed once in The States." Radio scours on again, "Make your way to the Lord Byron, Cummings Park Estate. Bar assault with surgical walking stick and broken tumbler, one female suspect, use caution against male." The cop turns the radio right down he wants to hear this. Diced green band caps are tossed casually on top of the black dash, seatbelts on, and slam doors, ignition fires. Cops look good these days in their Kevlar jackets, navy blue pullovers, and heavy metal accessories. All that's missing is the side arms. The criterion of excellence, the aura of power, she loves a man in a uniform. We take off for Cornhill. Me sitting over the fucked differential of the vibing, hardy splicer. The passenger cop asks me, "So what happened in the States Cal?" I said, "It was in Portland up in Oregon, it was the last night I spent with my ex-wife Eva. We had been rowing for months, up until the night the pot boiled dry. We lived above this Hispanic couple, there was always this number had been coming on the TV about domestic violence, a number to call in an emergency. We were having a domestic, Eva and me, hitting each other, punching, slapping and body gouging…my worst nightmare of myself, shit, so she ends up trying to attack me with a carving knife". The cop driving had put on his shades, like the LA cop out of "Colours". I said, "She went flaky, a bit mad. I took the knife off her." The shaded cop asked me pungently if I had been doing any of the drinking? Smoking grass? I said, "Just a little bit, a few cans of Coors, a bit of green bud." They both seemed excited by that, they looked at each other and smiled. Here policing in the USA was perceived as more glamorous, more dangerous, and there they were still the good guys. I go on, "Next thing the two cops burst in, I was cuffed and sat in the corner, and one of them spoke to me. I think they call it the chill down period. Eva was taken away in the squad car. The cop said I should get myself home to Scotland as soon as it was possible…Two days later I was on the plane home to the UK. I never saw Eva again." The passenger cop said empathetically in Doric, "It couldae been worse Cal, they could hae charged you and you could hae ended up with a custodial sentence and deported to boot." I felt a little chilled at that prospect. "Just lint and bandages in here Cal, they'll hae you better in not time." Said the mortal passenger cop. The car wheeled into the hospital compound. We all went into Blair ward.

When you are out of control, it is almost impossible to pull the various strands of your life together, strands that for most people constitute normality. Small things like paying bills, getting a broken washing machine fixed become an overwhelming burden. You become irritated and upset by minor and trivial inconveniences. You worry and cannot cope. There is no alternative to the atmosphere of sheer fatigue that hospital presents you with. Into the familiar routine of security, keys, chains, the shambolic and the automatic people. A man sits unable to stop his knees and his arms shaking. I hold his knees, his arms together. I release and they start shaking again. No self-control, smothered with mental distress. Stiff and unsupple, trying to retain morale and dignity in a secret place deep within yourself. Turning away from the stress and discomfit of everyday life. Into asylum, a whole intangible seething mass, coming, grouped together on this overcrowded claustrophobic ward. A sense of sameness though that does not perturb you as much as the everyday alternative.

I was taken into the treatment room. The nurse confirms my identity with the policemen. The two cops wish me luck. They uncuff me into the care of the hospital. They both swagger off the ward with the same sense of bravura that all policemen possess. Wells came in to the room. He still looked upwardly mobile. He wasn't angry with me. It was just that his concern about me discharging myself had been justified. He sat down in front of me. It was all coming tumbling out of me now. Wells looked at me hard and said, "At the present time your responsibility is diminished to the extent that you cannot act rationally. You are both a danger to yourself and society. Therefore Cal you leave me no alternative but to section you under the mental health act." The nurse that was witnessing this, glared ahead hard, like she had done before many times. As if the operation was at the gorey bit. My consent was not required for this procedure. It was the law. This meant I was to be kept here, against my free will. The section would either be rescinded or extended after 28 days depending on my progress. Time ticks onwards, it was a sentence of a sort. Wells said he had contacted Lorna Moone and she would be coming up tonight to see me. He held my notes and said to me pointedly, "You know the routine on the ward Cal, and you will be reestablished on medication tonight." But I couldn't take the situation seriously. Hospital liked to gather together all the bits and pieces of a person's life and try to arrange them together logically. This was done with medication and rest. Free will in life was another matter. It contained emotion, it contained pity. It was an intellectual response to your physical condition. I was ga ga, like a burst couch with all the springs spiraling out of it. Out of control. And something was incubating inside me, some kind of ominous illness that merely masked my profound unhappiness. This was the worst episode I had ever had. Wells just looked at me for what seemed like a long time. He said nothing. I said, "I feel afraid Dr.

Wells, I feel that I will spend a very long time indeed shuffling fluff along the skirting of this hospital. Is there no alternative to this I! Am I condemned to this fate for the foreseeable future…Doctor? I am in despair. I feel as if I can't get any peace…no peace from the maniacal energy…the searing burn out…the terrible thoughts that are only briefly knocked out to return." Wells gently laid his hands on my arms and said calmly looking in my eyes, "This is the worst moment Cal, it cannot get worse than this. Medication and rest is the cure. This is the only place you can be right now. I want you to go and have some food and settle onto the ward. I will see you again soon." He got up, smiled at me and left the room. The nurse then did my bloods and I was put on 24-hour observations. The nurse felt afraid for me, she was nervous when she did the phlebotomy on my arm. It took her three attempts to puncture the artery with the styrette. Rich red blood flowed into the vacuum with an audible sucking noise. Letting, out. She said finally, relieved, "Just you settle yourself in and you'll be well in no time." Infinite bleakness. An absence of not only emotional and physical love, but more profoundly, hope itself. I get set up in my bed. I go through to the smoke hole. Most of the faces were different but their expression of anguish remained the same. Scattered like spent shell cases. Grey activity stuck between sea and sky. Reality picked out by its moving, sometimes silent drabness. Paul was still here. He must have been here for 6 months; a sage nutter, a crackers conductor leading this barmy army. Paul looked at me intensely and said, "Hello old timer, what brings you in here? Is it the good food, good wine, good company." I uncoiled a little, his irony served as a balm. I replied, "As it happens Paul I'm off my Tattie." Jessie sitting beside him says, "Join the club my loony".

Pacing up and down the corridor, repetitively for an hour. Work that body; burn out that canker that is enclosed at the bottom of your soul. A nurse dogs my steps like a black dog. Observations. After Dinner Lorna Moone comes onto the ward. She had cigarettes for me. She had told Norman I was in here, he had said that in recent years he had come to regard hospital as a kind of sanctuary.

Something of an understatement. His sense of detachment was retinal all right. His entire life had become some kind of interior within the fabric of home, and within the fabric of mind. The black thoughts of depression keeping him awake all night. I can't get any peace! He had rolled over and turned his eyes away from the light quite some time ago. Radio 4 booming out 24 hours a day. I felt suddenly sad for him, sad for the unbalanced manufacture of my stated family. Lorna stroked my hand and said, "I bought some savlon for your wrist." I was a wild savage child in this crackled nest. All she could do was somehow try to soothe me. I looked at Lorna's hands, they were becoming mottled with age. Mottled with care and worry. Not only for her children but also for the many teenagers she had listened to over the years. She had shapely feminine hands, quite small palms. All she could do was imagine how I must be feeling. She felt relieved that I was safe. She had been praying for me. She had spoken to Dr. Wells. The thought of me being sectioned made her think that she would never see the real me again. The thought caused tears to well up in her eyes. She cried softly in shrill little sobs like a young girl. The same way she had cried when our pets died. They always loved her best, better than anyone else. They felt closest to Lorna Moone. In its final conclusion life was such a sad thing. Her fashionable warmth and affection was adored by all who had come under her benign, caring influence. In a real sense Lorna Moone did more good than harm in life. She was one of the most beautiful women in Scotland. Now though she felt that she had failed as a mother. That somehow my illness was her fault. The powerful bond of parental responsibility. I put my arm round her and she courried into me briefly. Jessie came into the smoke hole for a cigarette. She was a harmless little dottled old woman. She saw Lorna's distress and sat down beside her. Jessie had a deep rasping voice. She said to Lorna, "I'm that depressed, I cannae wait tae git ma peels and git tae ma bed." I gave Jessie some cigarettes. She put them inside her Superkings packet, inside her purse. Jessie said, "What a fine loon you hae." Lorna perked up and blew her nose, death forestalled. She said, "Aye he's a sweet, kind lad. He is being heroic." Jessie stubbed out her fag and saved the doup. She got up and said, "I'll be back through for Coronation Street." Lorna looked at me and thankfully back on the mundane again said, "Speaking of constipated crap how is your bowel motion just now…regular?" Nothing better than a little warble about shite. I replied, "I have been laying a trailing cable since I came in." "Oh well you can't be beyond hope then," said Lorna all chipper. I suddenly had a moment of insight into myself. I said, "Everything is going to be alright eventually, I'll come through this and find myself standing on the other side." But in the mean time I had to grab on where I could and roll with the punches. At least I was off the ropes now. Lorna ended her visit on a high, if that didn't sound too familiar in the circumstances. She left me some money for the phone, before she was liberated onto the outside, and into the chastity of freedom once more. She said, "I'll see you tomorrow."

The monotonous routine of the ward, broken only by visits from Lorna Moone. Trying to attach some colour to illuminate the drab view. Lying on my bed, viewing everything through the orange, slanted oblique pane of the lucozade bottle. Far out, nothing straightforward. Colours. The colour of medication, doled out like the food parsimoniously and in regulation. The colour of blood, the colour of piss and shit. Still on observation, not allowed out of the ward at all. Eat, shit, medicate and smoke. Above all smoke. Fatigue and claustrophobia. I was waiting in the residuum of life. Is there any point in trying to attach spiritual meaning? Is there something else beyond life except this blackness? The contradiction of moral philosophy that suggested there was a psyche intact and distinct from physical consciousness. In the futile meantime just waiting. Waiting to be consumed now that I am stuck in a flytrap. One afternoon a young woman came on the ward. It was a distraction to talk to her. In for detox, she was a "Dipper". I found her sexually attractive. It was excruciating, my lost libido now suddenly heightened by mania. Uninhibited and out of kilter. My brain had hit tilt and the safety flippers don't work anymore. Her name was Beverly, Bev to her mates. Teeth were pretty stumpy, they call it preorthodontic decay in Scotland. I want to dive into your gene pool Bev. She was fiddling with the window as if she could figure a way out. She had a homemade blue tattoo on her forearm, "Mom and Da," and a heart. Tough chicks flying in the face of male Scots machismo. I said, "You're a darling. I have a hard on, if I get you outside full cuddle and sex in the grounds, it's quiet out there." She wasn't paying any attention to me. Just as I was about to touch her this guy comes in the room, my moment of intimacy is broken. You can't tell when a dose of the 'horn mania' is going to come on you. It's her boyfriend. He drags her from the window and stands between her and me proprietarily. He's sane, I'm mad. Fuck the lot of you. My hard on wilts like a lopped daisy. The nurse comes in, the girl goes away. The guy is grinning. Sexual conquest is like meat on a slab sometimes.

You hear them at nights in their beds; wanking. I don't care, the creaking and impotent moaning stops me getting to sleep. I practise my art silently between shines of the torch discretely. Male frustration coupled with mental distress. A fair formula for any amount of sexual perversion. Lumped in the ward here together. Different types of fibre, different forms of clinical diagnosis. Let's come together right now, the energy from all sorts of different angles. Get up out of the bed shamble through in the mules to the smoke hole. Silence of a sort; repetitive snoring, the occasional night scream. Doors slamming. The smell of bodies. Feel that I am being treated like an animal. My face is lit like a "guy" by the amber semi darkness of the mock coal fire. The front security door buzzes open. The city never sleeps. Someone new is coming on the ward with a nurse. Disruption, external vibes that swirls the thoughts of freedom up in me, fresh air blowing in. She comes through to the smoke hole; she is high on dope and drink, the final sodden high before the crash. She can't stop laughing. She looks like a gothic punkette, her face white with pan stick, black lipstick, chrome studded leather, black nylon and those Boris Karloff boots. A look amongst young men and women that is specific to this queer "furry boot" city. Her wrists are bandaged, she has come down from A&E. I look out of the window. I can see the normality of life beyond the dark hospital grounds. The trees etched in cobalt blue and black. The orange sodium reflected panoply hovers in the sky in vast perpetuity. I stub out the cigarette butt and stumble back to my bed. Sunday; another watery grey consciousness day in here. Routine is set in stone. I am still sailing high as a kite; cartwheeling and dancing on the breeze. A conductor of lightning to earth. Until the flier lets go of my guy; then I will be spinning further out of control about to plough into earth. Sunday; the day of uncivilisation in the towns and cities of Scotland. Shit hits the fan when the pubs are at their roughest. From the nipple to the bottle never, ever satisfied. Pent up aggression and resentment at the way the routine of our lives seems to be set in stone. Lousy jobs tomorrow, lousy houses, drink and smoke to excess and banish the shortening window of time between now, closing time, and then. Utilitarianism: Britain has made an art form of your pitiless, bitter resentment. An inability to articulate this sentiment except through violent action and reaction. Feeling blasted at the root: Weak and impotent. A day for bitter recriminations, reflection, and beginnings amongst the swirling Sunday Mails and kebab papers of the weekend. Rod's crepe suzette face stares out at you dripping in golden tints. Sean's capped teeth flash at you. We all reflect bitterly over the dregs of our heavy beer. The common experience of our short meaningless lives. A shared small violent urbanised consciousness, full of small-urbanised violent individuals who talk in rapid monosyllables, punctuated with coarse expletives, and unpunctuated by the glottal stop.

He sits with his earring on, (left ear lobe), gold chain around his neck. Arms florid with tattoos. Tribal markings. Sitting in a haze of Lambert & Butler. You would think he would be cold in his tracksuit bottoms. He is obsessed with football and darts in the pub. He is obsessed with play station at home. Demi is back in the "no-fines" flat up on Beattie Avenue. She is making dinner: It is reshaped Co-operative chicken kiev, chips, beans followed by tinned fruit and ice cream. His favourite. They have two children;

Darren and Chelsea. Darren is hers by a previous partner. His mates have gone, it is time to go home. He enjoyed his game of darts. He thinks in England they have pubs, but in Scotland there are bars. High frosted windows that are inviting you into a culture of hell. Nothing intimidates him; he's mental as fuck. He has an ornamental sword coming down at home. He loves big screen Sky TV in the bar. He looks at The Mail on Sunday on the table. At the stories, and the pictures of the Scottish stars who seem to lead such blissful happy lives, so much money, so much time. He doesn't realise it's an illusion, he invests his imagination in thinking about the stars, and he thinks it could have been me. I could do that. He isn't pished; he's only had six pints of heavy. Graeme Souness comes on the TV, praising Rangers FC. He thinks Souness is a blue nosed bastard. He loves the Dons, he hates the Huns. He mouths a mumbled expletive at the TV, and he laughs, dragging on the end of his heavy. His teeth sit in his gums like a row of condemned flats. Pyorrhoea, smegma, personal hygiene is a foreign concept to him. But he wears a tracksuit, sun ra culture of a sporting aficionado, we are the people! He has a little zip up pouch he carries around with him. He keeps his mobile phone in there, and a few 1/2 quarters of "rocky" hash to sell in the pubs. He sells enough to pay for the family habit. He gets pains in his chest, he doesn't want to think about it. He won't go to the doctor. He is 38, he is two stones overweight. Demi had first phase cervical cancer when they met. They don't have sex much now, but he likes to get a "gummy", after a couple of joints and the beer. Demi likes a few bottles of vodka ice. Still he thinks it could have been me. He has to get up for work tomorrow; he is a pipe yard labourer. He always carries a black fingernail that is nipped by the down hole casings. He used to work offshore, a hombre roustabout, best years of his life. Work, women, drink, drugs. Two on then two off. Then he got caught smoking dope; he was blacklisted, not required back. It didn't bother him; he could never imagine that day when there won't be plenty of work in Aberdeen. He feels a confused resentment though like now late on a Sunday afternoon. He can't really write, he never kept it up what he learnt at school. Demi pays the bills, the HP, the catalogue, and the rent. He gives her housekeeping every week religiously. She buys the food, she looks after the kids. They both would like to talk about things, but they can't be bothered. He is tired, she is tired. He thinks that the world exists only in his time. He doesn't feel any sense of mortality. He just thinks that one day he is going to die, neither better nor worse than he is today. Now he feels tired and boozy. He smokes a fag, he is feeling bored. Time to phone Demi to say he will be home soon. He hates feeling bored; he can't stand being on his own, he has not made a friend of himself. He craves order, he embraces gratuitous violence when he changes after drinking too much. He never hits Demi, he stays quiet when she shouts at him and sometimes slaps him. If you were to show interest in him he would be suspicious. He would think you were gay. He hates gays, he hates gays as much as his xenophobic distrust of the Englishman; up here, creatures not in their native habitat. He adores his boss and looks up to work hierarchy, but he is already looking ahead to next Friday all poofed up out with his mates, part of the strange drinking ritual. Slowly, physically self-destructing. He has never been near Cornhill in his life. He punches Demi's number into his mobile phone. Simultaneously as she answers I feel a heart stop. I would like to be out of this egg carton institution. Vegetable soup is on the menu again.

After the Supper is finished and cleared away I notice that the doors of the dumb waiter have been left unlocked. It is my route to freedom. My scheming feverish mind would gladly succumb to the soothing balm of cheap and copious amounts of alcohol. I was a man with half a face. My rationale had been almost totally erased. My escape path. My 'napper' had just become dumber and dumber, down one floor out of the main kitchen to the ringing tills of the boozy knappy. I go through to the ward put on my red windcheater, my mirror shades and my blue marine style cap. I have £15, more than enough for a wee fiesta. I am wearing my Bally mules. I find Paul and enlist his help in my escape from Blair Britain. Sunday night in Scotland going down. I crawl into the lift. Paul becomes enthused by the idea. His Blue Yellow irises shining iridescently. He shuts the door on me and says, "Have a good trip Cal, because this is a trip." He bangs on the red neon tit and I hear the winding gear move me in a constant but shoogly downward motion. I am going down but my brain is going up into orbit with excitement and anticipation.

CHAPTER EIGHT

Break out, somewhere in this town. Tonight there's going to be trouble somewhere in this town. Back in normal land. Empty kitchen, sun is streaming through the open back door. I bolt for it and soon I am running through the grass and the trees of the grounds. Making towards the perimeter iron gate. Marvellous fresh air, cleansing me of the permeating smell of the ward. I keep on running, onward ever onward. I want to get as far away from here as quickly as possible. I leave the grounds and cut across the North railway line. The signal lights are shining red for stop. The blue steel rails gleaming like ice skates. I get up the other side, scrambling up the embankment. Vaulting over the piked fence to the street like a caribou. Stop now here, panting for breath. Bent over, my hands spread on my knees. I regain composure and slip into anonymous pedestrian walking, there is a slightly awry smirk on my face. My head is tilted back slightly, the mirror shades glint in the sun. My mules slap against the soles of my feet. Come and get me. It is a warm muggy night, the swifts' scream like stukas, the brown-eared bats squeak and dart low. The wood pigeons are cooing to one another. Harmonious nature, the setting for incalculable mania. I make my way into the city centre. Prince of Wales for beer and nips.

On the way there I see a scaffolded tenement being renovated. I see a short piece of putlog scaffold. I pick it up it feels the right weight to smash in an off licence window when my money runs out. I put it inside a carrier bag. It would make a lethal weapon. Nothing to lose, no fear, no sense of law breaking. I am on the run from the loony bin. Beyond a state of irresponsibility, in a strange, outside place. Mad, bad and ludicrous. I go into the winy red darkness of the pub. I order a pint of heavy. I drink it in deep gulped draughts, like gorging on a sweet ripe nectarine. Soon I am reassured by the moist exhaled breath of alcohol and cigarettes. The guy next to me at the long shop font is reassembling a gold watch. It seems an ominous metaphor for my sinister appearance, my internal disharmony. I keep it together in here. I couldn't measure condition in time. The division bell, a circle of hours, minutes and seconds. Inferred understanding of sunrise and sunset, rising and falling tide. The consistent judgment of time. The printed imposition of human time upon existence. As old as time itself. Something so old it was from behind the moon. The grains of sand were falling slowly but constantly in an hourglass of my own making. Brooding on that thought of responsibility. For me time is running out. I finish my pint. I decided to go somewhere where there was a bit more life.

There is something about warm muggy nights that is a bit foreign to Scotland. It is unusual to say the least. All peely wally, sunning your "plukes". In other cultures the heat tends to damp things down. Things are more relaxed, slow and laid back. Here, there is no stopping this. The one eye culture of consuming as much cheap quality drink as fast as possible. Pub drinking on a Sunday night. A carousel, a barbed wire carnival of hopes, fears and aspiration. The characters in this western seemed rough and unhewn. Virtually unknown to themselves as they staggered from the hole in the wall to the next pub. So in walks The Sundance Kid on the St. Andrew's bar on Market Street. Who would like to offer his little homilies on life like selling small bottles of fish-oil. Drink is half price here on a Sunday night. A saloon bar, a sense of the frontier as I cross the Rubicon of the slatted swing doors.

It is a karaoke night, the last oasis of alcoholic solace for the little people before Monday hits us with the full force of a 14lb hammer. Shore up the holes in that five strand borderline, then, not now. Anything goes, the spirit of the klondykers. The place is teeming with minkers. A middle aged blonde woman is belting out, "Like a Virgin;" you can see her grey roots. The tables overflow with empty tumblers and ashtrays foaming like Jacuzzis. The Scotsman at play giving full rein to free abandonment. Work gives you money and money buys you some time. There is me in my garb, a cross between Robocop and Jimmy Crankie. No one bats an eyelid. Two men are entwined in one another kissing passionately on the floor; the red neck reaction. Fuck mild middle class tolerance; let me genuflect on the working class hero. I have a pint of heavy and a triple whisky. Gorging on the malt lets. I wasn't setting myself up to be sacrificed on this x shape cross. I slurped my drinks steadily and with enjoyment. I contented myself with observing the ritual spectacle, like a philanthropic mad man. A dim awareness of the value of cultural significance in Scotland. We continue to soak our history in blood. The working class hero; you are still fucking minkers as far as I can see. People were hovering now, the quiet man had aroused suspicion. I wasn't in the mood for petty martyrdom. I finish my drinks. There was the usual chorus of super seagulls screeching in the street, as if mocking me. That mocking chorus I imagined was the definitive noise of Aberdeen as fish was the definitive smell.

My picked out reality in common time was where I found myself in a given set of circumstances. There is no going beyond that "I". But if then I had used hindsight it would have informed my judgment, and I would have realised my own diminishing height on this earth and made my way back to the sanctuary of hospital. Instead I ploughed on down towards the East end. Jesus and a carrier bag. Skewed vision, I went down to the Castlegate where all the jakies and homeless liked to congregate like pigeons, picking at the discarded crumbs of human existence. The heat was hard on them, permanently dressed for a sub-arctic winter. An alcoholic thirst, physical and mental impairment. Men lying around sleeping in a stuporific slumber. A glitter about them, the hard mica of the road is etched into their features. I went and sat amongst the jakies on a bench. Sitting facing the mercait cross sucking on super lager and tonic wine. Their faces looked toasted. Caked with dirt, a bleeze of alcoholic drink, simmering in the heat. They looked like the boys on the asphalt gangs. A light warm breeze blew in relieving the odium, it was starting to turn to dusk. A young wiry guy appeared from nowhere and came and sat beside me. He seemed to be an individual of some sort. "Aw right big man, you want a drink, mah name's Billy," he said. He passed me the brown bottle of Harvey's Bristol cream. I took a good scoof, and handed it back to him. Etiquette of the road, he cleans the neck before drinking himself. "Excuse me big man," he says and takes a drink. I said, "Are you from Glesga Billy?" He just says, "Aye," laughing… "Ah lost mah guitar last summer sometime." He goes on, "There is hard times and there is just tough; last winter was shit in Glesga so I come up here, ah had had enough oh lying like a starched piece oh cardboard in doorways, skippering is better up here the people are more generous to the jakies." He passes me the bottle again and says, "What are you daein sittin around here?" I said defiantly that I was on the run from the mental hospital. He started laughing, rocking backwards and forwards, his hands on his sides. "So yer tea's no oot yet big man?" I showed him my scaffold and asked him if he fancied putting in an off licence window. He replied, "Nah man ah cannae be bothered wi that the night." After a brief moment of repose Billy beckoned me to come with him. He said, "Come on big man ah know where we can go for some hot food and shelter, just dinnae look at the guy in the corner wie the strange blue eyes, he's just oot oh Carstairs." Billy walked with a leggy swagger, he was all legs ahead, a rock and roll hood from the Strathclyde plain. We were going to the night shelter in Lime Street, down at the quayside. Vagrants, prostitutes, the bankrupted.

Victims of domestics, mental cases like myself. The dispossessed and disaffected. We get inside, it is a vaulted granite sett grotto. There is a small kitchen, bibles, a few mattresses, chairs and a stack of blankets. One Christian man was running the shelter. He looked like Hercules and had a squeaky voice. We get soup and bread. Billy says, "That's Franco over there." He was the Scottish Charles Manson, empty blue eyes, straggly beard, carotid artery necklace tattoo, blue-black tattooed hands and obligatory chib mark to his face. He sat amongst his confederacy of dunces but not of this world. A psychopath. Billy was scraping his bowl; he whispered in my ear, "Aye he's bit the heid aff a few budgies oor Franco." We go into the body of the Kirk. Billy starts talking to his mates, settling down in a space for the night. Sniggering starts like being in front of the headmaster at school. There is silence then the sniggering starts again. Everyone is scared to look in the direction of Franco who is staring coldly straight ahead, wired on an electric vibe. I start sniggering, I can't stop sniggering. Someone would have to put a fist in my mouth to stop me. Franco suddenly realises that I am twanging his wire. Franco suddenly reacts, he is sitting against the wall. He is wearing a camouflage jacket. He reaches inside and puts his hand on the butt of a hunting knife. He says to me, "If you dinnae shut the fuck up ahm gonnae slit yer fuckin throat." Then everyone starts laughing placing Franco's light squarely at the top of the Christmas tree in Santa's grotto. I look at Billy, he just shrugs; an unwritten constitution can present us with problems of self-preservation. I get my bag and flee. Run for home, running man. Five minutes later the experience is history. Melting into the balm of the warm night. Vague thoughts of going back to Hospital stray into Rosie's bar, the biker's bar. All the Guys wearing their colours, "The Black Angels," "The Nomads." The guys have their chicks with them tonight. It is all petoulia oil, fringed leathers, red nail varnish, peroxide blonde curls, silver and onyx rings and black suede booty's. The lead singer of the band notices me in my odd garb and shouts across to me on the mic, "Hey look it's Jack Nicholson in Easy Rider." Either a compliment or a warning or even both. I grip my carrier bag even tighter.

It is around closing time, still caught up in the heat of the night. I get up to Holland Street; the heat combined with intake of liquor creates a sense of malcontent. The atmosphere intake of liquor creates a sense of malcontent. The atmosphere hour convenience store stacked high outside with potatoes and cellophaned cheap flowers. Every space inside is crammed with goods of all kinds; there is still a niche in the market in "furry boot" Britain. The police have been watching the owner for years. Illegal drink sales, cigarettes to underage juveniles. Hard-core porn and "poppers". Alleged sexual deviancy. Claim to fame, the first person to be convicted of driving under the influence of ecstasy in the UK. I wonder into the bright glaring neon, I am seeing dark cool colours. Empty except for the man at back of store. Jumby vibes. I stare at him pointedly from behind my glinting shades. I am standing still in profile head turned left. The noise of the luminous blue fly killer crackles statically. The tension is palpable. I look at some socks on the carousel. I pick up a pair and suddenly the whole lot falls to the ground. Suddenly I feel trapped, motionless under the ubiquitous glare of the strip lights. The man rushes round to the front of the shop. He accuses me of trying to shoplift and demands payment for the socks I am holding. His reaction has the effect of sucking me into the situation. I produce some coppers and slam them on the counter. I say, "Here is the money sleaze ball." He jumps round and confronts me. He is about my size but about 3 or 4 stone heavier. He is a deep sherry brown from the sun bed. I grip the scaffold hard and raise it in the air threateningly. I shout at him this is a stick up. I want drink and cigarettes. The man knows how to react. He picks up a wooden and brass billhook for shutting and closing the rollover shutters. He takes it around my head twice with all his strength. I don't go down, he didn't drop me. My turn now. I take the scaffold down on his head, striking him on the skull. A spray of red blood spatters me. I know my strength, I just blood him. One blow with all my strength would kill him. Just on the point of impact he cringes back waiting for the blow. Still no one comes into the shop. The whole incident lasted no more than two minutes. But time was frozen into individual frames. I had just been crowned Prince of darkness. A little wobble but the manic cord was intact. The man goes and presses the panic button, an alarm goes off and blue lights start flashing. When he crowned me my glasses and hat are knocked off. The human face is revealed. I drop the scaffold and flee the scene, as fast as I can in my mules. In seconds a cop car picks me up. I ease into the situation like a big man. I give them no trouble, no verbal. I am cuffed and taken to Bucksburn police station. I confirm my name and Cornhill mental patient status. Around midnight. Time for reflection, I wouldn't say it had been a good day, I was probably lucky to still be alive, although at that moment I didn't consider it. I looked at my jeans under the repeating neon of the overhead street lighting. They were spattered with his blood. The thought was exciting, this was real life, not acting; it served to stimulate and increase my high.

I get into the station and the cop takes the bracelets off me. It wasn't as if the Police were congratulating me, but I guess most of us have seen Marty Scorsese's Taxi Driver by now. I was sat down, got a paper to read, a cigarette to smoke and a cup of hot sweet tea. I haven't seen the guy in that shop again, and they lost their liquor licence. I was taken through to a cell, the door was left open and a police officer sat with me. I asked the officer if he had ever carried a "piece". He said he had done firearms training. His reply was circumspect; he didn't want to further excite me. I change the theme onto my favourite obsessive subject; alcohol. I sipped on the tea, I said, "Did you know my surname is a subtle way of expressing our national addiction that is not a crude imposition but is an ameliorative creative statement. That consistently is flung back in my face by the Scots race. You can lead me by the thread of my hair, but go back against the grain and you cannot force me to drink from the communal cup." The policeman just sighed, he said, "We have to pick up the pieces from all the fallout associated with drink." I knew that, it made me wish that I had joined the police when I had been younger. Perhaps everything would have been all right for me if that had happened then. His silence and complete tolerance made me feel better about the situation. Eventually a squad car takes me back up to Cornhill. The sun was beginning to rise on the start of another day. Back on the ward, and I thought back onto the same routine of food, medicate, and sleep, but nothing can ever be quite the same as it was yesterday. I have a cigarette and spill out my story to the nurse; a maniacal, guilt free existence.

I went to my bed and slept for several hours. Wrapped in the secure arms of Morpheus, warmth and comfort and suddenly you feel the black bird of reality pecking you on the shoulder. Being woken roughly and physically by the large male nurse Abbey. He seems angry with me, there is a sense of urgency. If there was one moment in my entire treatment when I wished R.D. Laing could have fluttered down to my aid from heaven it was then. As it is they have to use restraint, by law they are not allowed to hurt you. Abbey said I was to get dressed I was being moved to another ward Crimond forensic immediately.

We walked across the grounds to Crimond. I noticed a group of stone sculptures that had been pushed over onto the ground. Where there had been harmony there was strife. Where once there had been peace there was now trouble. Everyone on Crimond was on a section for something. I was released into the muscular arms of another nurse. It was a bigger ward than Blair. It held the same facilities except the dining/living room was combined, and of course there was the obligatory smoke hole. There was the oppressive ennui of hardcore sedation hanging over the place. The staff though seemed more professional. I settled myself in for the long shove. I didn't realise that first day that I was about to be psycho tropically keel hauled.

Blue is the colour of infinity, light more sharply defined as I move on diminishing earth towards the point of the upward poles. I am attracted, yet in no illusion. Like my kilted Dad once falling drunk into the stern of a fishing boat and I see his cock and balls for the first and only time. No mystery, not then, not here. No skimming softly rounded slate. Just great angry chunks of concrete and haywire steel dropping into the water with a mighty kerplunk. We sit and gobble our glorious luncheon, (I cherish meal times); in here secure that no one can harm us. The suffocating Perspex is

221

worn dim by countless hands just rubbing. Just to see, only from the inside looking safely out at you.

Today in our institution the harsh winter instinct of the Scottish psyche prevails. Emotional pain is bound up with psychological damage that became an imbalance. Some nurses' ride up and down angrily at all our chemical intangibility. I am the lucky one. Saint Michael comforts himself with a feast of self-conversation and guitar playing. Paul masturbates onto his white cricket shirt and flannels, always just sniffing the soap, examining it over and over. I watch him secretly. "Do you pish in the sink?" asked Auden to one of his Dons. In a sense W.H. Knew the game was up by then. We had retreated to the interior, the ray was not so bright anymore. A cuddle, an embrace to touch, we have tried to learn to live without your comfort now. I am attracted like a game fish to chromium and light, but others are not, why? Where will that lead to?

Some mad people will never grow grey. They are trapped in a world of anarchic innocence. In a sense Alice is happy there scurrying about on her visits from ward to ward. She cannot remember anyone. Is it base instinct to fill your pockets with the doups from the ashtray? We crave tobacco; you are my best friend in the absence of love. Joy in life cannot be soured if it can be reaped honestly.

The summer day moves on languidly and Paul moves position in his seat slowly to get more comfortable, smoking, watching the Ashes, in his white flannels. The sun tries to stream in through the sealed window. Mental well-being at the expense of our vitality. We are like slow turgid turds slithering and snaking. Parting our kilt and giving off a stench of corruption. Are we to be forgiven after all? It will be a wrench to leave. I have come to crave solidity. I fear and implicitly distrust human uncertainty. Distantly there is a sense that I want to be able to place all my faith in one person. Home visits are out. The wide-open space. The brass mechanics of the lock that contains our basket of eggs. Wearing thinner imperceptibly, on each day. Nagging doubt though, biting at the bottom lip constantly. This has become where I want to be secreted. Amongst my spiritual travelers, in Crimond forensic.

I was in the hands of a forensic psychiatrist now. Someone who specifically dealt with criminal cases. Lorna hurried down from Oak bank on that first day. She worked at the secure school with adolescent schoolchildren. For many of them Lorna Moone represented their only source of human kindness. Above all she was prepared to listen to the boys and girls. She devoted much of her teaching time to just listening and being in the position of being able to offer encouragement and hope. Like her own son these children had been hurt, mostly by the break up and absence of the family home. Like her own son they were also part of a system that seemed more concerned with punishing rather than leading people back into happy lives. This manifested itself mainly in her pupils in shoplifting, stealing cars, vandalism, alcohol and drug abuse and often-unwanted teenage pregnancies from natural experimenting. In a sense she would have liked to have been able to offer these children a home herself. If she had had the resources she would have liked to offer them more. The children responded to her natural warmth, although things could be difficult at times. It was as if these kids had been forced into having to take responsibility for themselves at an age when they should be cared for and about. So they found themselves in Oakbank. At least Lorna liked to work within the widest parameters of the system. She liked to educate the children in things that they were interested in. Often the children were able to show her affection, both emotional and physical. At times though she could feel bitter at the system; what did the future hold in store for the majority of these kids? This highly emotive thought had a galvanising effect on Lorna Moone though. It just made her realise how precious her time with them and also her son. For within the limits of exhaustion Lorna Moone gave of herself freely, warmly and with professional confidence.

Lorna Moone came on the ward that first afternoon. She could see it was nothing to be afraid of. She had come up last night but I had escaped. She let out a little chirpy chuckle. Lorna Moone had brought up cigarettes and a big bag of ripe cherries. She had prayed for me last night and her prayers had been answered. We just sat for a while and I raved a bit off my head, talking to myself. I pray and hope that I will never have to witness the distress of a loved one undergoing a complete mental breakdown as I was in the midst of. Lorna Moone said she would be back tomorrow. I suppose I felt more completely incarcerated now, there seemed no way out of here. There was a sense of foreboding when a visitor goes. As if you are being stripped of your self-identity. But like so much in life; what doesn't kill you makes you strong. You just have to hack it sometimes. Lorna Moone got up to go, she had started to cry. She could intuitively tell that I was upset, like all those times I said goodbye to my Father growing up. She left with the nurse. Five minutes later and I had forgotten that. I went through to the ward. Ron is sitting there. He is big and brawny and simple. He gets excited easily. I offer him some cherries. His vocabulary is a little retarded like that of a young child. He seems to be able to hide his fear of the system, he seems an integral part of it. I keep feeding him cherries and he gets more and more animated. Rich dark red cherries. I say they are a magical fruit associated with witchcraft. They are Lorna Moone's favourite fruit. He gorges on the whole bag, looking at me with glee. I wonder what he did to get sectioned?

I was called through by the nurse. The doctor was here to see me. I was led into the tiny consulting room. He was a little dark man with a manicured beard. He was wearing a dark, cheap check suit. He introduced himself to me as Dr. Riddle. He bid me to sit down. He paused and looked at my notes for a minute or two. I became agitated, irritated. It seemed very formal. He said my section was to be extended for another 28 days, I was to remain here. Held and restricted on the ward. I wasn't paying much attention, I said in truth our conversation was being bugged. Tension. Someone could hear what we were saying. Exhibiting strangeness in front of another new Doctor. Another lump of meat. Totally uninhibited. He says, "You are acting in a way that none of us can understand. There are powers at work that are not specific to any one individual state, but are manifest in an overall psychiatric diagnosis. These patterns of behaviour must be treated as a matter of urgency. I am acting upon the advice of Dr. Wells and others… who have been associated with your treatment. I am restarting your medication tonight and we… will see how that progresses before deciding whether any further palliative medication will be required. To return you to a mood of normality." The short interview was over, the doctor said he would see me soon. I was glad to get out of that windowless little room. I had felt paranoid and claustrophobic. Back on the ward. When Michael wasn't mooching cigarettes and money he was sitting strumming his guitar. His face looked shattered. Pale and withdrawn, his skin was sallow; he had rings around his eyes. His hair looked like a greasy plate of mince. That was the side effect of the medication at work. Drugged up, aimless, unreceptive eyes. Disassociation from reality leads to a divorce from domestic routine. An interior existence on the whirly gig of 'Dougal's magic roundabout'. It is just that I realise this ward is more acute, the patients are more sick. Supper of Irish stew, we all wolf it down. Our human condition makes us all ravenous for more. There is never enough food for everyone to have more. The welfare state is tattered around the edges. Always feeling hungry. I have a visitor after Supper. It is Gary Cumming turning up for a dose of schadenfreude. I haven't seen him for a few years; he always seems to appear when my life is at low ebb. As if somehow he goes with the territory. Like an unwelcome visitor that might embarrass you with your fancy sophisticated friends. Well I was beyond all that now. Just a reminder of a previous existence. Gary had bright blue eyes and flame red hair. He never seemed to be able to turn big ideas into a sustainable way of life. He felt worse than I did about himself. He managed to erect a façade of self-preservation though, up to a point. Gary had the big jobs but had always managed to blow it. He was running out of options but he didn't seem to dwell upon that. Gary sought solace in the hard Aberdeen bars, smoking dope and taking heroin. He had a strange fondness for never missing the F1 Grand Prix every Sunday during the season, the crushing ennui of which seemed to confirm his loser bachelor status. Here I was sitting manic, Gary had the edge on me. I told him about the shop, he said, "You could get five years for that," confidently. Alice came through and sat down beside Gary and started talking to him. Gary was reeking of drink. He was rough looking, pickled somehow in alcohol, but no beer gut, still looking the rock and roll road crew. Alice kept asking him to get her dope, she wouldn't let it drop. I suppose Gary didn't have many scruples left by that point. Situations like this for Gary were just self-insight into his own downfall, into his own sexed out guilty existence. If only Gary had been able to find love, just once, things could have been better. Well, as it was the Hospital was some kind of social scene. I get him a cup of tea and some biscuits. I used to go and visit Gary in his flat when I first came back to Aberdeen. The condition of the place deteriorated in direct proportion to his own decline. Jacking up; speed, smack anything he could get his hands on. I used to wonder what were the underlying reasons behind his drug abuse. Was it because everything under the influence of dope seemed more articulate than the sub-arctic landscape when you are not stoned? Was life more tolerable, or was it plain and simple weakness. Dope offered some kind of antidote to the bleakness of existence, and Gary bled Alice of £15 for a half score.

Gary said to Alice he would come back up with the hash. I looked at Alice; her wayward green eyes were shining brightly with glee. Her strong yellow broken canine teeth were locked in a manic grin of childlike implicit trust. She was totally oblivious of her hairy chin. All the women in here had facial hair, it must be the medication or something. Alice disappeared, probably, hopefully, to find her rizzlas. I said to Gary to bring me up some drink. I gave him £5, everything in my pocket. Even then he was probably planning how to spend the small money. His favourite cocktail was beers and hash, followed by a big slug of sickly green methadone in some shooting gallery in the dingy, omniscient, gritty town. The reality of this group of young men sitting around an electric two bar fire, all unenlightened into themselves, frustrated, smoking joint after joint and gagging on methadone. Delving deeper into some personal meaning in the ecstasy, shite music. Gary was older than most of them. He tended to ingratiate himself into these kind of situations if there were drugs available. An alternative to the solitary repression of his flat. Gary's nickname was Fish. He had been the Scottish schoolboy amateur diving champion once. Naturally his star sign was Aquarius. It was funny how Scots boys with sporting potential are invariably programmed to fail. In your teenage years when temper is not altogether your own. I too now found myself bumping along the bottom. Gary felt he was on a superior plain to me now. Gary didn't seem to be able to understand equality. He either liked to look down upon people in order to feel better about himself or sucked up to people for drink, drugs and money. Gary was anxious to be off now; at least he had picked up a little money at the mental hospital. I didn't see him again up on the ward. He went off out of the abyss that was my life, and into the abyss that was his own. He managed to buy himself some more time until little over a year later an accidental methadone overdose sent him into a drug-induced coma and his heart stopped. He was 32.

The next day the nurse said I was to get an injection. It is amazing how much trust we place in the caring services. Usually that faith is not misplaced. What they are doing for us in our own best interests. I was injected in the buttock with a large syringe of clear fluid. I asked what it was. The male nurse replied back happily, "It's Clopixol acu phase. It is just something to help you sleep; it's prescribed by the doctor." Of course, they don't give this medication anymore, it is now illegal. "Nasty, nasty stuff," as one Doctor later described it to me. I was entering the most acute phase of my treatment. You had better believe it Psychiatric hospitals have lots of human tragedies associated with their treatment. Administering an intravenous sledgehammer to crack my nut. The effects of the medication crept up on me. It was a form of fast administering depot shot. There was no going back, no. The chemical screw was turning slowly within me in a consistent fashion. It was like some kind of sick practical joke. This 'liquid cosh.' The movement of my limbs became quickly arrested. There was a horrible taste in my mouth. All I could do was lie down. My tongue swelled to twice its normal size, I could barely speak. I didn't sleep, I was knocked out.

That was interspersed with brief moments of lucidity when like Jerry in Blair ward I was unable to articulate what I was thinking of. I had been given a chemical straight jacket. It is not as if the sane have ever tried this stuff, but it is happily doled out to the insane. This is the sharp end of psychiatric care where anything could happen. How many deaths have there been under the auspices of psychiatric care in the UK?

I lay there for two night and two days, interspersed with pissing in a bottle. The element of the unknown that was designed to disintegrate the manic chord within me. Coming down with a chemical cocktail. Cycle of bodily dehydration followed by rehydration. Drink gallons of fluid, my body trying to maintain some sort of equilibrium. Lorna Moone comes up with a big bottle of juice. Sloughing words and continually gouging out. Her distress is suspended meantime, only place for me to be was in bed. There was no fix to this living torture except time itself. Distress, acute anxiety of the staff and the other patients. A medical doctor examines me. I get some other tablets but the process continues. The process of regeneration that will see this brand new chrysalis emerge from his dry husk. On the second night my condition climaxed. I dreamt of the figurehead of the Queen herself; only she could come to the aid of one of her subjects. I teetered there on the edge of a black chasm for a while. It wasn't my time to go, that is all. It was just a dance with wolves that is all. Third day it was over. The chemical reaction of the drug in my body was over. I woke up in the morning. I was calm, I was lucid. Mr. Hyde had just metamorphosed back into Dr. Jekyll. The strange, obsessive, manic energy had disappeared. It had been replaced with a sense of crushing depression. I had just come through the most death defying stupendous trip. My character had completely changed. I was overcome with a wave of guilty nausea at my recent actions, particularly concerning my assault. I just turned my face into the pillow, in towards the soothing darkness of the wall.

Fatigue, sheer fatigue; eat, rest, medicate. I will never forget the countless tubes of half squeezed "ray bright" toothpaste. Cleaning up and down, cleaning up and down, three times a day. I will never forget the little "Roman" enclosed courtyard at the back of the ward, where we threw the slops of our food for the pigeons. Encouraging them to gather like vermin, feeding on our neglect. In turn we the neglected margin, feeding off society. Loyally Lorna Moone visited every day bearing cigarettes and fresh fruit. I listened to my radio, watched some television. I began to store up some new energy and could concentrate on reading again. I read Bob Geldof's autobiography. I clung to his words. They offered me solace, and a strategy out of this predicament. I was interviewed by Dr. Riddle for a forensic report he had to prepare for the Procurator's Fiscal office, about the incident in the shop. The man had received 14 stitches. I was remorseful about that until Dr. Riddle said to me that the man said I started the fight. Sitting in the same windowless, airless cocoon. Same tension, created by the forensic nature of the interview. Riddle is astounded when I tell him I have an MA degree; as if somehow educated civilisation precludes complete and acute mental distress. He is touching on the subject of societal taboo that surrounds mental illness. Wisely he skirts the subject. Riddle apologises to me profusely about the injection. "I didn't realise you were so sensitive to the medication," he said. If I had died that would have been another matter. As it was I never saw him again or heard anything about the incident in the shop either. Soon I will be transferred back to the relative sanctuary of Blair. My section is rescinded and I am allowed back out on the grounds, and also to go swimming. Eventually I was allowed out on my own for short visits to my flat. I was in hospital for six weeks. During this time I have managed to build up a small store of benefit money. There is that void though. On my discharge I get a letter for my GP and an outpatient appointment to see the psychiatrist. The ball had been firmly lobbed back into my court.

I am just glad to be out of hospital. I got home, but at the same time missed the safety of the place. Suspension of disbelief. The irony of my medically conditioned situation. Institutional values have replaced free will. So tired, so washed out. In a physical state of paralysis. I now enjoy a Spartan fare of budgeting on benefit. Trudging round to the Co-op to buy food and feed myself. The cycle of one day soon mends into the next. Medicate, reading.

Radio, television, (no music), visits from Lorna Moone. Catapulted into my aloneness. The noise of "neighbouring" thundering up and down the stairs drives me further behind the barricade of my council flat. Spying out from behind the locked door at the crude, inarticulate canvas. I take to visiting the job centre every other day. The absence of reward in my culture confronts me with an overwhelming sense of self-determination. Going for the most menial jobs; labouring, working inside a meat chiller room. Life ought to give my sense of self-respect back to me. It owes me that, but manic depression robbed me blind. Something akin to a chemical imbalance and a chance encounter with pain fed by drink and drugs. I want to make a complete recovery. I do not want to spend the rest of my life in the world of balanced, palliative, unpalatable psychobabble. A complicated mess of serotonins, aquifers and neurogenic transmitters. Why don't they just hold up their hands and say the bald truth, the riddle of psychiatric medicine; that there are forces working in the mind beyond human understanding.

Trouble haunts me. It slithers and follows me around like a dancing, antrin light. Aurora Borealis. From somewhere up there in the North east. Do not seek me out walking down George Street. Do not stigmatise me with your finger of blame. People's faces seem so poor and anguished, coming towards me, always coming towards my steps in an "S" shaped phantasmagorical vortex. The working class struggle, which contains about as much unity and substance as slush on the ground. Come spring it will be vanished to be replaced with, I know not what scream. Summer became autumn and now November leaves us all on the hard cusp of winter.

Attempting to build on strange ground becomes wanking exercise as I wake, to sign on through flying sleet, an old role for the engineer, setting out to make the Job Centre. Saving a half smoked regal. Unlike the bank's distant drumming security, this shaky overall state, within this social margin that promises me back into work if

I follow the green line to satisfy these damned rules. Quietly I sign the claim form. After all this we go through then, pushed out like a Viking funeral pyre on a loch. Jobs check meditative faces, scan jobs scrupulously. Check identity thrust against other people. What! New shoes, I see paid for status. A man like me his Oxfam suit remains black and bruised serge. Our drowned dignity in a world of post-new age hope. A smart façade, a hanging lie erected briefly, as a staff against the naked truth of loneliness and actual uncertainty. Attempting to build on unknown ground, seeing people hard and glum, rimed and old. The prevailing mood over coffee and smoking. An outdated concept of steamy café luxury. Remarkably it is still at this age rationed for me. My page turns slowly on a flimsy paper day. If I could I would turn my eyes straight towards the sun. More happy meantime to enjoy a hungry British sandwich. To eat, to rip off the cling film. Pass the day off, dole the time out, in bitter grey November ashes I sit and wait.

CHAPTER NINE

I'm holding this wee Pole up against the wall next to the pub. He is disjaikit, he is forfeikit, he is mortalled. We are in Dundee: city of discovery. I keep trying to hold this little guy up but he keeps falling down on me; rubberised. He has the build of a neatly stacked and folded up ironing board. He is wearing greasy black "Diesel" jeans turned up. A grey leather bomber jacket and a jersey that is black with filth on the part that faces the world. Tony the Pole, he doesn't shave, in classic jakie mode. Saves water, soap, time and effort. He is almost 60 now yet his hair and beard remain jet-black. Henry Chinanski I think as he pishes down the side of his leg and all over me. So far so good in the New Year. I got back into the building game and wound up on a site here in Dundee. It is a tough city, not unlike the rest of the Scottish urban vernacular in that respect. But there isn't the same bauchled indigenous rawness as Aberdeen. More grit, more wry humour. Dundee is the poorest fucking city in Britain, (well maybe). Perhaps it is the colour of failed idealism but I always associate the 60s' with Dundee. The Tay does look silvery under a yellow sun. A sumptuous estuary of a river. It is funny how all the cities of Scotland have strong rivers at their backbone; all except the capital Edinburgh of course. It just has the ornamental, shitty, polluted "Water O' Leith", which is only use for dressing up like Lord Byron and committing suicide into it, from the Dean bridge, like a failed romantic. Very curious. The site I work on is the full Dundee industrial oasis of shite. Outdated working practices riven with the bureaucratic cronyism of "the neebor". A working class parochiality that follows the corrupt mantra of failed high socialism. This sort of structure lays itself wide open to opportunism, corruption and self-seeking greed. I arrive on the job as Site Engineer. The site has just re-opened again after an industrial accident. The contractor is negligent for the death of three steel fixers crushed to death by falling masonry. Form and function by these men was correct. It is just that to save time and money the contractor had adopted a building technique that is virtually illegal now, (if it isn't already). The contractor had been sand coursing walls to receive insitu stair landing slabs at a later date. You carry on building above the sand course, but the principle rule of this technique is that the masonry is constructed perpendicular and plumb. So, as it was built, three unsupported walls collapsed on top of the steel fixers who were down below fixing rebar for the insitu-landing slab. Solid 9" grunter blocks. All killed instantly. Grim determination coupled with economic uncertainty of the times ensured that the contract recommenced. I was in charge of external works on the site. I quietly had to wade my way through the chaotic interference of the incompetent managers. For example extras to the contract in the form of retaining walls were required to support part of a car park. I point this out to the Site Agent, and he replies that they will only carry out the work if instructed to. You have to work as a team I say. In some areas the shortfall of one of the members of that team can be negated by the help of another qualified team member. That was the way it was, a sense of guilty unease. As it was we black top the car park and the section in question collapses. So in effect the main contractor gets paid twice for doing the same job, and building the retaining wall required. That sort of thing is how the cost of construction projects keeps spiralling upwards. Gross inefficiency. In a couple of months

I had chased the blacktop round the site. It has a galvanising effect on the workforce. It boosts our morale, and makes us all realise we just want to get finished and get the hell out of there.

You get on a stress curve in work like that. You need to unwind a little at the end of the day. That was how I met little Tony in the Tay Brig Bar. Sitting there like a bar fixture on his stool reading, "The Scottish Daily Mirror". I went in for a couple of pints before heading up north at night. We got talking one night. He was in a private rented flat round the corner. Living exclusively on state benefits. That is hard enough, but somehow it appears harder in a place like Dundee. Tony loved talking about supermarket food. About the cheapest food available. All his prices were worked out down to the nearest penny. The food he liked was canned or processed. Choice sticks two fingers up to Scotland's natural larder when it comes to living on the bread line in Scotland. The proletariat crave something cheap and tasty hence the fish supper, but that no longer is cheap. Tony's "Coup de Monde" was stewed liver and onion gravy, instant mash and canned marrow fat peas. Tony was an alcoholic. When he had the money he would buy a fresh pint before his other was fully drained. As if someone was going to take it away from him. Tony smoked tobacco; he always saved the doups and mixed them in his tin. Tony said he could get me hash. They would deliver it to the pub.

So it is late in this afternoon and I am trying to get Tony the Pole up to his flat. He has known me a few weeks and already he has become adept at scrounging off me. He has latched on to me like some kind of parasitical micro-organism. Just a few pints and money for tobacco. He has a surgical walking stick now; he was bumped by a car at the roundabout a couple of weeks ago when he was drunk. They drove off without stopping. He has a severely bruised pelvis. Tony has told me about the jobs he has had. He'd worked in the jute; he'd been a bus conductor. He has a memory for the minutiae of these jobs. It's his line of patter to get a few pints. Spiel off about working in the purification works and the labouring. You would think that he would be bitter that the wealth of a nation hasn't filtered into his own existence. But he doesn't seem to be. Just a kind of gritty determination that defines his aloneness. Finally I get him upstairs to the flat. I am exhausted after a day of work. Tony only had a couple of pints of heavy with me, but he has been drinking the white star cider at home. Tony carries his benefit book around with him. He always looks in it as though he can't remember his next payment. Just confirming what he already knows deeply lodged in his skippering brain. It is also a sign to me to help him out. A silent bond between brothers, he imagines. I carry him up to the top of the tenement. I lean him against the wall, he looks rough. He gives me the keys and I open the door, and we go in. There is the familiar smell of feich. The smell of the uncared for and unwashed. Tony goes into the bathroom, I go into the living room. All there is is a black and white TV, a three-piece suite, and a small table. The room is bare of anything else except a well book marked bible on top of the gas fire. An old beer mat sits on the table and poses the Hollywood question. "Sean or Ewan?" Meanwhile Tony staggers through on his stick. I go to use the toilet. The bathroom is bare of anything except a sebum-encrusted comb. Tony has managed to shit down the inside of the front of the toilet bowl. I take a pish and wonder, maybe Poles have clatty front bums or something. When I get back Tony is sitting perched on his seat like some kind of gamin little black bird. He grins at me from behind his black horn rimmed NHS glasses. You can hardly tell all his teeth are false. He says to me he never takes them out and cleans them. He is always producing little notes of paper from his inside jacket pocket. Someone he met at the broo, the phone number of his social worker. His filing cabinet on life. I never get so much as a cup of tea here unless I provide some alcohol. Tony buoys a little when he is jaked on the heavy and the cider. He likes to talk crudely about women. He says, "It doesn't matter what size their mantle is, it's what's between their legs that matters." Then he makes a priapic gesture with arm and fist; something huge is coming up. In his younger days, between jobs, between stalking for accommodation when life was rough for Tony he liked to sit in the old slum houses drinking with other skippers, getting limed amongst the crumbling lime mortar. Sleep out, sleep over, it didn't really matter if you were jaked up on the Hawkhill in the summer months. In the winter you come to rely on the stopover, the night shelters. He told me a story about a B&B. The social are paying it. The next step up the rung from the working men's hostels. The lice, the thieving. Their pissing rooms, scaling walls and cockroach infested kitchens. The stinking shitey cludgies. Tony is staying in this house. The landlord is a woman. The picture he sets is one of dismal permanent semi-darkness somehow; Scotland in winter. Living under artificial electric bulb lighting, Terylene, peeling walls and yes that colour black. I look out the high-begrimed windowpane. We are the 5th wealthiest country in the world, or is that a con? Potentially then the fabric should be more enriched, more liberated. I will ponder that question tomorrow when the joiners squawk at me angrily from their hungry bird's mouths. Industrial works tends towards overall dehumanisation, and that tends towards humiliating the individual person into accepting a limited potential. Social aspiration becomes a kind of crude howl. The spark of the square mouth shovel, the song of the eastwing hammer. Tony likes to bitch on me. I just wish he would pass me his NHS spectacles so this Matt McGinn of Dundee can see more clearly. There isn't so much as a Kleenex in the whole house. Tony perches and tells his story. He still has a wee drouth of white star left to suck on. "Ah mind we were drinking Haig whisky fae tumblers me ahn the landlady. She telt me she did tricks for a few extra poons, ah wasnae gonna knoack her back was ah?" The old fashioned brown bottle and label. I can imagine him biding his time for the bottle and something better. Trainspotting for decreptitude, the cod liver oil and the orange juice. "So," I said to him, "Cut to the car chase Tony, what happened wie Hairy Mary?" His false teeth glitter, all natural like, his black eyes shining like buttons. He has lit a doup up, and he tightens his grip on the surgical walking stick. They went through to her room with the whisky to have sex. Tony says, "We went in to her bedroom there was all this old Victorian furniture. The window was twelve pane sash and case. She put on a record by Ella Fitzgerald, "The Moon Is Made of Gold". She poured us both a glass of Haig whisky. The room was kindae damp and badly lit. She was all over me, she was drunk, she fancied me. She thought the twa were the same. Ah didn't really want to kiss her but it had been a long time since ah had had ma ride. She undid my trousers and told me to kneel. I had a real boabby's helmet under mah under pants.

"She pulled down ma pants and she started tae suck me aff. At the same time masturbating ma cock. I was looking off into the distance somewhere and suddenly I felt a tingling sensation in my cock. I looked down she was dipping ma penis into her glass of whisky then sucking me off. Next door I could hear one of the lodgers and his wife arguing. Downstairs ah could hear a guy sleeping off a session of drink. When I came she swallowed ma muck in one deep gulp. I felt deflated and uninterested then. I gave her £2 from ma social money. I used to see her efter that at the breakfast, but she never took me ohwn. Ah left soon efter that."

It was time to go. Tony was now sloughing his words. He was ready for a sleep session in the bed. I give him a note the colour of which he does like; the money he would probably spend on drink, but no one could say I wasn't good hearted to him. He put up some mock resistance for about half a second before accepting it, and I was gone. Out of the door and drumming down the stairs, briefly, vigorously. Towards the honesty of light, and the freedom of my own company once more.

The job ends. The dole restarts. I was back in Aberdeen amongst that curious combination of slow paced and rough edged rawness. Sterile high-technical oil industry slickness and the couth of the John Deere tractor. The common parlance amongst the chatter of Scotland in general. Some comment in defiance of the abysmal climate. Imagination was not a concept I could detect easily in the Aberdonian. It is frowned upon in a realistic, non-abstract sense to be imaginative here. You are a "daftie" trying to fill in the slabs of your life with colour. Set amongst the damp, permeated, cold grey masoned granite. The culture knocks it out of you from childhood, like impacted wisdom teeth. I was back on the cycle of Benefits Agency, back into that feeling of despair, material need, that being part of an easily recognised social margin brings out in me. There is always however a hidden agenda in these compromises life throws at you. If I cut do I not bleed! Filled with self-pity. No feeling for anyone else, except for myself. I veer off track from time to time, beyond the rails to a little understood place. I dust myself down a little and hop back on the cattle train.

It is late in the summer of the same year. The year my Gran died, the year I began to lose count of the amount of times I had been in hospital. The year was to continue in this fatalistic mode. No turning back from the finite reality of existence. It must be confronted in the death of loved ones and become accepted. No point in causing a commotion, I had never reached the stage when I had given up on life. Even though sometimes I felt I was enacting a sham existence. Lorna Moone, Iain and I are up in Leverburgh visiting my Father "en famille" for what would be the last time, and at once, one of the only times we were together as a family. Norman knew it, I knew it; he was dying. Listening to him at night. Constant coughing. The kind of deep pleural cough that makes your spine tingle with pain for him. There is nothing to be done. His taxi is here, (not even one for the ditch on my tab), your tea is out. Norman has given up on a life spent giving up. His unipolar depression which spread from him sometimes like a cloud of gas is replaced with a determined frail finality. All his time spent in bed, surrounded by the tools of his trade. Countless spent lighters, whisky, tumbler and water. Books and radio and pen. Tangible silence, neither of us can find the words to bridge that gap that finality engenders between loved ones. I must find a way of saying what I have to say. My Father holds a metaphorical Browning revolver to his head, and pulls the trigger, (where are you now BritArt cronies?). For once he is just getting exclusively what he wanted. There is no trade off required. Foreign exile. Being abroad for so many years. The beating sun, the parchment of his life dried to a husk. The living beat amongst death and decay that seems so omniscient these days. At least, terminal decline, measured out in the bead of an amber glass; for Norman. For Scotland? I am not seeing anyone; my life has been barren and fruitless in this area for some time. My thoughts merely confirm what my Father suspects I am dwelling upon too much. He is able to be selfless and fatherly. He gazes warmly and intelligently at me, with his unique frown. He holds my arm and says, "It will all work out in the end for you, I am sure of that Cal." The visit has to come to an end. The point of divorce that Norman and Lorna Moone have driven between themselves. They have taught by example, they took things all the way. No 19th hole, no howffs in the air, only the power of goodbye. At these points I crave the abnormality of this arrangement. I don't want to leave. I would rather stay here, but like always in the past a member of our family has to return back to something else. Something that merely represents an individual's status quo. Something that in light of this is trivial and of little importance. I go into the bedroom to say goodbye to my Father. He is grizzled like a common seal. He takes my hand and will not let go. Norman still has a grip like a vice. His big Hebridean head is like a wild thing straining from the crackled nest. Not saying anything but looking at me with that strange wild look of untamed innocence. In recognition of kin, rigour and intellect counts for little. It was just an identification with me, as simple as that. A situation drenched in sadness and sentiment. My family was still blazing the trail in Scotland for the breakdown of the family. Too late for regrets. I had to go now and pick up the pieces and resume what I was doing until that call came.

On the ferry across the Minch we were all quiet. Filled with a shared knowledge now that this was no dress rehearsal for Norman. I wrote a poem about my family, thinking about my Dad.

With Forfar in sight I am born into this world, the first time that blue eyes cry tears for my abstinent Father in ordered sun sprawled Sudan. Scotland, a summer myrrh of purple, yellowing field, bog, natural cattle work, tar black roads, snares and rabbit carcasses. My young Mother embroiders spirals to hang at the fern spore of Newforebank. Little shafts of light that will become the Autumn harvest in time. Simple choices that were woven skillfully in the absence of her Norman. Cups of golden promise not bitterness bring a smile to her idealistic view of heaven.

The seeds of change were born out of this uncertainty, followed by tumult. Across the North Sea, the Red sea deserted on the machair islands resting place. All by the age of four, my family and I had foundered as individuals, as family. What we had embarked upon together had now become set out alone and in life. Grandfather James reflected on this gall as he worked at his task on an August day in the thresher. His common task comes out of the need to separate the chaff from the corn and distinguish between virtue and falsehood. His skill, patience, courage and determination were born out of the hand that feeds the mouth.

I have accepted pain in the physical sense, by today's standard unburdened self of cuts. How I carried the emotional madness of a corn haired, blue-eyed wife in cat/dog days. I suffered the pain of seeing her's and others' weaknesses lead me down the spiral to the spirit of our age: Dark, love beyond comparison. Will I reap the harvest I have sown, through whisky weakness and tobacco trait, drenched in polar moods? A place further onward and inward. A tiny crevice of light that will allow a blood orange harvest in time. A time of giving, a time for enjoyment in song, food, drink and body.

Certainty that growth in the soil will always constitute life. The pattern will continue regardless of our fearful human dance.

It is November now. I am in the sub-arctic hermitude of Aberdeen. Lorna Moone has returned once more to stay with Norman. She subsequently tells me the two days they spend together are essentially the same as the first few days of their relationship all those years ago. No acrimony, no bitterness. It is much too late for that. Suddenly he is taken ill with pneumonia. The scene is transferred to the hospital. It is a Saturday. My Mother phones me and tells me to get up there, if I can. I make the Ullapool ferry. In a sense both Norman and Lorna Moone were remarkable leaders of their generation, yet life conspires to blunt Scots aspiration. Life seemed such a short experience that can only be realised with regret in hindsight. In a sense the reductio ad absurdum of all our lives as a family seemed to suggest that we were prepared to accept our lot in life. How late it is, how late. Potentiality seems a foreign, exotic notion in the face of survival, in the face of often-elemental savagery. Perhaps we can only truly see when either it is too late, or if a shining epiphany takes place in our lives.

The ferry docks in Stornoway. My Mother is relieved to see me and grips my arm tightly. I am still not aware of the seriousness of the situation. When I get to his room in the hospital, (he has been afforded more dignity in dying than most), I see my Father is wired up to all sorts of life support machinery. He is on an oxygen mask. I am overcome with anger. As if, (in reality), another someone perennially was always to blame for the full, often careless way my Father had led his life. Now though, I was wrong in making that assumption. It was his time. My Father had withdrawn into a state within himself. He was curled inside himself like the chrysalis on the branch. His psyche intact and turning, ever turning. Rolling eyes, opening and closing. Intuitively though he recognises my kindred spirit. I am in the position of having to say these things to my Father. How I wished we had played in the beet fields with the rest of our family and rubbed purple war paint on our faces as we pulled the crop. I can't say these intangible "might have been" things. I concentrate on his life as it had set itself out. Try to make his time more easy passing. I say to the nurse he had led quite a remarkable life my father. He had been all over the world. Stunned unreality of the living sharing the final hours with the dying. He had seen action in the Second World War, Suez and Korea. He was mentioned in dispatches, had achieved the rank of Major in action in Korea. He had come through it all with hardly a scratch. He spoke Gaelic fluently, he spoke Arabic fluently. A smattering of as many other languages. He told me he had had a different girlfriend for each night of the year. It was his consummate charm. He had known all the Scottish intellectuals. He had a fine-grained intellect combined with physical danger, a certain presence. Connery without the ulcers, MacCaig without the objection. Wild as the wind. He loved this island place; Lewis. It was where he had been happiest. Norman thought nothing of taking off into the moors, with just his tweed jacket and fishing rod. He would sleep out on the moors, fishing the burns and the lochs. He was an untamed spirit. His general knowledge of the world was quite remarkable. A large part of his life had turned out as an adventure. He had drawn a great many people to him with the magnetism of his personality. He had presence. He possessed Hollywood good looks I suppose, which was all the more remarkable considering the ravages he had done to himself. The nurse smiled at me tenderly; she could see how much I loved him. More than anything my Father Norman had been loved by his students of so many different races and cultures. He had contributed something positive to their lives. In fact Norman was adored by young people generally all his life.

I had finished my monologue. I had managed to find a way of saying what had to be said. I had paid his passing due regard. I looked at Lorna Moone, she realised this was not a time for considering herself as some kind of imposition in the situation. In some sense all the important events in your life hang together in the final analysis of the dying of the Father of your children. She held his hand and stroked his brow. She asked Norman if he had liked what I had said. He seemed to nod positively from somewhere deep within himself. He seemed to be sleeping then, gently. His face was peaceful. I was taken to a room where I could get some rest. At about 6am, I woke up. I knew that my Father was dead. Someone came down and said I should come up now. It was time. Typical Hebridean NHS fiasco. He doesn't wait to lead me up to my father; I have to find my own way. It is as if he is afraid somehow. I stumble about and finally make it to my Father's room where Lorna Moone is. My Father has just died. Time to say farewell to my Father. The spirit is yet to depart the body; his skin is warm, it is waiting to say goodbye. I have no fear of death, in a real sense I embrace it and my Father's body and mix my live imprint upon him. I put my arms on him once more and kiss his forehead. I hold his hand for a few minutes in silence, and now it seems to be over. It seems to be begun. There is nothing left to say, there is nothing left to do in the face of his death. It is Sunday.

My Mother and I go to my cousin's house to sleep. My body frame is totally exhausted, physically and emotionally washed out. I sleep for a few hours in the pervasive damp of the room. I wake in the late morning; there is bright sunshine like an orange fire streaming through the closed curtains. I spread the curtains there is a covering of frosty snow on the ground. The first snows of the winter. A statement of natural change. I feel different somehow in those first few stuttering minutes. In the same way I had felt a mantle of defined responsibility on the first morning of my marriage to Eva. Reality seems more focused. The physical environment seems more realistic somehow. I listen to the news on the radio. There is commuter chaos throughout Scotland. It is as if with the passing of my Father nature is pouring clouds of coldness on the ground. Marking his tangential point of passing. Accepting his antrin, pan-like soul into the spiritual nether world. Where he will be reborn once more, where he may find peace, free once more of weary human experience. Maturity is gently resting more upon my shoulders now. A greater awareness of what I want to aspire to in life. Not just the futility, not just the struggle.

There is a hope that I will go on now and shape some sort of happiness for myself. I am more distinctly aware of my identity as a man standing on his own two feet, raking into the earth for sustenance, for stability. The snow sheets in on fat flurries, the frost penetrating living marrow. It is time to distinguish more clearly between falsehood and truth. It is my Father's message to me in a sense; do not confuse weakness of character with strength. Just focus on that which pertains to my individual sense of well-being, and those around me who do give a damn. There is a strong sense that I either want to leave Scotland to return many years later. Or if I am to stay, only to make some kind of positive difference. You have to give fate a hand sometimes and still retain a strong sense of sentiment and love. Even though you are a bona fide crown amongst other, some snide coins. Take life by the throat. Make a positive contribution to your own well-being. Direct yourself into a life that makes you happy.

Sick, full of spleen at the obsessive, narrow margin of perceived Scottish consciousness. Even sport. A healthy childhood pursuit that has become an unhealthy adult male obsession of viewing sport instead of participating in it. This has become a blind retinopathic spectacle. This tendency supports the inequalities in Scotland. Elixed in the Scots humors of alcohol, drugs and tobacco. Contentment springs from happiness. The reverse of that statement is not true. So far that pure spring has eluded me, I have had mere glimpses of the light. I have led an unconventional life bathed in the light of the narrow margin of perceived Scottish consciousness. All I am armed with is the truth of my own experience. Good, sometimes uneven, bad. I am not indifferent you see, I do care about other things except and including myself. Things happen in your life that you have no control over. You are part of the spectacle. It is time to build a place for myself.

CHAPTER TEN

A May Day reunion suddenly here. The cast link drag chains throw clouds of orange rust into the air as the alloy frigate consistently slides down the slipway. In the boat shed an infinitely mild breeze blows. Rustling the multitudinous bunting of Union Jack flags. Above, on my close left stand the Queen and The Duke of Edinburgh. She is wearing what seems like an asbestos powder blue skirt suit, and ugly stacked black shoes. He is in naval uniform with a liberal dose of gilt and scrambled egg across his left chest. The Secretary of State for Scotland eyes us with protest as immediately beside me, Stuart slips his half bottle of whisky from his pocket and offers me a nip. Yarrows, naval boatyard, Scotstoun, Glasgow. I am well now for more than three years.

The boat suddenly hits the water and the restraining spun steel hawsers lash like bull whips. With enough power to cut a man in two. The crowd cheers, filled with vigorously renewed hope, filled with renewed optimism. The Queen just looks on in perfunctory, detached fashion as we ask three cheers, for the head of state. The assembly stands in subjective order while the Royalty and assorted politicians make their way to their limousines and the next function. She is our Queen, Stuart and I can be heroes just for this day.

We both make our way out of the boatyard. I say to Stuart, "That was just about the most completely protagonist episode I could ever hope to encounter in Glasgow." Stuart reaches into the pocket of his wool tan overcoat, the one with the black velvet collar. He likes to keep it happed up like a stove piped jake. He has a hangover of biblical proportions and now lays his right hand on the half jack of Scotch. "Fairly surreal little scene," he says as he drouths an almost indeterminate quantity of whisky between his lips. Then his face lights up comically, his eyes indigo blue. From behind the walrus grizzle. From behind the dark greasy snaky locks. There is a hint that he has his own set of teeth in there somewhere. The alchemy of the Irish and the Scots. It was in Stuart, it was in me somewhere. This was the city to encounter it.

We walked up towards Partick away from Scotstoun between the leaned to tenemental sandstone flats. A thousand sashed Victorian windows utter their silent reproach to our close coming. Stuart is like still water. He rarely sets out to antagonise people. What does stir within him stirs deeply. He is a painter and he realises that if he were not able to express himself this way, artistically as well as creatively, he would perhaps be dead by now.

We stop at a partly demolished gap site and Stuart says, "Let's go in here and finish the whisky Cal. Then we can get a pint." We go up a concrete ramp and lean across a wall getting a good view of the river Clyde and the city. This site has probably been built upon and demolished several times. Sedimental layers of Industry; post-industrial, pre-modernity, post-modernism. An old hunched picker is scavenging on the site with a wheelbarrow. Looking for any pieces of metal that might fetch some small money. He sees us and doesn't pay any attention.

We both stand and look way out towards Clydeside. Where the silent jibs of the cranes make a dusty scratch in the air like dry pen nibs. Standing still, gunmetal grey pointing outward towards the North American continent. Where the petrels fly far out from land. Close behind us sits a derelict mill, looking over the ghost of the site. The building is brown grey, it is dour. It is impossible to attach any aesthetic to this site, yet I try. The high and low metal windows have all been broken; there is no dynamic here. Once water turned a wheel and generated some sort of light that became brighter as the turbine spun faster. I look in and down, it is almost dark in there now. Dwarf walls and concrete machine plinths are submerged in blue black water. Their set out ordered pattern a kind of intimidating drowned world. Stuart pokes his head in with the wonderment of a child. I can smell the combination of whisky and tobacco on his breath. I am reassured, I crave the whisky, and the smell reminds me of the memory of my Father. Stuart passes me the bottle and watches me as the sunlight shafts the gurgling copious amber liquid as it flows into my body. It reassures him as he instantaneously realises that our shared weakness can be a bond, at least today.

We resume our position lounging over the parapet of the wall. The whisky warms our bellies and runs fire through our veins. The already subdued Lowland light becomes more subterfuged as the tone of the Industrial landscape becomes increasingly sepia tinted. We start gassing away, buoyed. I say, "You know that expression that all Scotland is a village but Glasgow is a street. I suppose I agree with it but it is pretty damn hard to define." Stuart holds out his hand. A broad hand, and straight stubbed fingers. Rubbed down tips, the fingers of a glaury painter. He says, "It is rhythm that is what defines Glasgow for me. Heavy industry, and the legacy of the imprint of that upon the people has created a kind of beat." I think about it for a while and reply to him, "Do you think then that people here have sought out some sort of creative endeavour as an antidote to the brutality of their lives?" Stuart says, while at the same time realising the cure can be worse than the illness, "It is funny this place, sometimes there seems no roadmap out of here as if living here is some kind of shared universal experience." I reply quickly in recognition. "It is as if no-one actually belongs here, originally we are all from elsewhere, it is the imposition of Industrialism that created this city." Stuart gave me the heel of the whisky and said abruptly, "Finish it." I tanned it and threw the empty in through the broken window behind us. It echoed way down below with a splash. Stuart said looking straight ahead towards the city, "Industrialism has laid itself upon the geographical beauty of this place like some kind of massive silk spun web. That restraint seems to permeate every living moment. That is if you let it".

I think about his comment on Rhythm. I say, "Do you know that in North America people are convinced that there is some kind of connection between smoking weed from a pipe and some kind of shared, kindred spirit. That people often will plank pipes under the floorboards so somebody else can find them. So they can pass on some kind of shared karma." Stuart looked at me and said, "In Scotland we were forced to hide the Pibroch (bagpipes) after the failed 1745 Jacobite rebellion and Bonny Prince Charlie. Because all national things Scots were proscribed. I smiled and said, "Music is creativity whereas dope is mostly intoxicating; ultimately you can't stifle creativity." Stuart went on, "In an overall sense there is a deep sense of inferiority imposed upon many Glaswegians, because insular ignorance of other Scottish culture isn't of their own making. That is why there are so many people here who try to improve themselves and overcome the injustice of having had your identity swiped at birth." I suddenly realise what he is getting at and say, "So it wasn't the lead in the water that started them carving each other up."

Stuart says, "Come on then Cal let's go and get a pint." We walk off the site and back onto Dumbarton road up towards the Partick Cross. Looking like a pair of overweight became tired psycho killers, head and shoulders above the perfectly proportioned Glasgow bantams. The men look up at us in interest and wonder if it was the chicken and the loaf that caused us to grow so tall and strong.

I stop at a cash machine to get money. The screen has been graffiti into a saltire with dried viscous blood. Next-door sitting in the window of a butchers are rolled gigots of beef. Curtains swish open above me and a young woman in a care worn dressing gown pings a tab through the open window. Stuart makes a connection and smirks. The Asian shops are multitudinous, filled with exotic beautiful women, smelling of spice and ginger. Halal meat, fresh coriander, okra, and sweet condensed milk. Confectionary sits in the windows.

We go into a pub called The Croft for a pint. It is still pretty early, we are just about the only punters. We have a couple of pints of heavy and break out the ash. Suddenly a Glasgowegian about 70 rolls in the door. He is wearing a blue serge suit, emerald green polo neck sweater. He has on old fashioned highly shined black boots. Clean-shaven, about 5'5", the faint whiff of Johnson's baby powder about him. Rubicund shiny cheeks, and blue eyes like ice picks. Sober as a judge. He looks at us and suddenly says. "The last time I saw a pair like yous' was when I saw Jesus Christ walking up the Dumbarton road." Before and after the resurrection I wonder. The bar maid comes over and says, "Usual Sean?" He says, "Aye I'll have ma usual, a large sweet sherry and a half pint of heavy." I notice he is wearing a gold wedding band. It is designed like a belt with a buckle on the front. Totally naff. It is as synonymous with the Catholic Irishman as the shillelagh, or the lucky four-leaf clover. For every protagonist there was to be found in the drinking shops of Glasgow antagonism. It was just that they liked to get in on the act. That's all.

Sean shows us a betting slip; he says he has just put a line on a nag. "Gone To LA, the 2:50 at Catterick," he says. "Good luck with the horse," I reply raising my tumbler in assent. Sean looks at me and smiles from behind his perfect dental plate. "That's the closest ahm gonnae get to the sunshine state, I've been on a DLA for ten years." Stuart asked him interestedly why he was on Disability Living Allowance. Sean looked at him for a few seconds as if weighing him up, he replied, "Asbestosis son, I was a lagger in the shipyards all my life. The white, the blue stuff, I've gunnited more of that in my lifetime than movie stars have squeezed toothpaste on their toothbrushes. I can't walk far anymore. I get breathless. Nighttime is the worst, but oxygen in the house helps. I'm done boys, I just live for my horses, my wee dram." He looked at us smoking and said, "Enjoy your youth boys, you're nothing without your health, just nothing."

The barmaid came over and said, "Your dinner's ready on the bar Sean." A sense of realisation on my part that somehow there was a genuine tight knit sense of concern for the old yins, that their rigorous routine formed an integral backbone of the community in bustling, declining, Ned land neighbourhoods like this one. Their pride should be reciprocated with respect. Sean said, "No bad eh; tattie soup, meat and two veg and tapioca and prunes for £2-50." I could hear him wheezing now, labouring under his own breath. Slowly within drowning under the welter of respiration using his own system. Sean drained his sherry and said, "Take care big yins, I'm away for a riddle before ma dinner, I'm sittin on an oil drum." Sean beamed us a smile and he disappeared away slowly now round the back.

We came out of the pub. We walked in silence up to Partick Cross and then left onto Byers road, up into the heart of the West end. Where the University was, where the melting pot took place within the crucible of middle-class academia, proletariat endeavour only a stone throw away but somehow suspended in disbelief, but never forgotten, just coexisted, amongst the red banded sandstone, the green painted sash and case windows. I go into a newsagent to buy some cigarettes, almost £4-50 for 20 tipped cigarettes. I come out and say to Stuart, "What a price fags are now." He nods vigorously in agreement and says, "High indirect taxation pays for every fucking essential social service in this country but the same amount of people drink and smoke, the roads are increasingly clogged with cars and the NHS can't cope." I split the pack and say, "Aye if we stopped the booze and the fags and moved to Greenland, there would be no point to it anymore." We are in agreement on that, politicians are a bunch of thieves, and not content with that they will steal your soul if you let them. We are meeting Stuart's girlfriend in a pub called the Rowan Tree in Woodlands, and make our way there.

We walk up the broad tree lined University Avenue towards the Gothic spire and quadrangles that lay at the heart of the University.

The Dear Green Place, Glasgow. The fish, the tree and the bell. And it was true in some sense the fish that never swam because the water table was polluted with so much heavy metal elements; chromium, mercury, lead. You name it. The Tree that never grew because life had conspired to fuck up his and her chance of nurture. And the bell, perhaps that did peal out in some clearly tangible sense. In places like Barlinnie gaol at slopping out time, or to administer the formal psyche of The Dominies log in places of education like this. The bell that never rang but silently divided this city between Catholicism and Protestantism. It was an amalgam of all three in some fundamental sense. The bitter irony of this had not been lost on Glasgow's forefathers. Red was the colour of Labour after all. It is what had washed into the Clyde. Our blood.

We walked down to the junction with Gibson Street. A taxi was stopped at the traffic lights. Inside was a famous poet his arm entwined around a young woman. Dressed in his black cashmere sweater, his olive green Donegal tweed jacket and his white canvas slacks. His cadaverous old face bore down upon her like some kind of reptile. She looked at him fawningly, serving to fan his ego. It was like "Custer's last stand" and I imagined a premature wet patch was slowly spreading through the crotch of his slacks. He looked at her and smiled, exhaling the moist Chivas Regal breath of the drams he had enjoyed over lunch at Rogano's Oyster Bar. The Black cab lurched off up towards the University rooms the Poet kept there. Stuart just looked at me and said, "Let's get some food." We went into the chip shop, I was feeling pretty hungry. Stuart rubbed his hands together enthusiastically and looked at the deep fried fare. A young guy was battering fish behind the range. He said, "What can I do yous' for gentleman." Stuart chirped back comedic ally in a pseudo Geordie accent, "I'll have a 'Mike Tyson' supper please," the guy smiled at him and replied, "So that will be a smoked sausage and chips then big man." All three of us burst into raucous laughter. I had fish and chips. It was an Atlantic haddock, thin poor little fish that somehow was synonymous with Glasgow. Not like the huge juicy haddock you got up in the North East. Specifically you had to make do. Like continually shaving with an old rusty razor blade. Time did not afford enough to go round. Life was a compromise; a tradeoff was necessary here.

We walked down to the Kelvin Park across the bridge, over the river. The shallow polluted water was home to abandoned shopping trolleys, milk crates and old tyres. We stood looking at the water and finished our suppers. Down at the park Scotland stood on the elbow of summer. Everywhere, everything was now gradually colouring itself in green. May was the most beautiful and optimistic month of the year. We had survived another winter, it was all still ahead of us.

The park was like some kind of huge green lung, something that could never be taken for granted by the dwellers of this tired city. A place where it was possible to escape from the unpleasantness that life throws in your face. A wee guy was sitting all alone near the gate getting the sun. He had his shirt off. He was emaciated and pigeon-chested. He had his cigarettes, his little bottle of cider and his newspaper. He didn't seem bothered by the fact that he was a victim of his own conditioning, that in a true sense it wasn't his own fault. Stuart could tell that the shock made me feel heartsick. He lifted the sadness and said, "At least he's getting the sun Cal, c'mon let's get a pint."

We got into the Rowan Tree up on Woodlands Road. Opposite was the sculpted tribute to the cartoonist Bud Neal. The guy who had done much to highlight the poverty of Glasgow that is still endemic. His hero was "The Lobby Dosser." Those were in the 30s' when tramps, (dossers), were forced to sleep in the communal closes of tenements. We were both bursting for a piss. We went into the toilet. The urinal was cramped and totally open. You had to fully expose your strop here if you wanted a pee. In a sense it was a case of ergonomic semi publicity. The fan-light high above was crawling with insects, I watched them as I found water and emptied my bladder.

The bar was horseshoe shaped. With a small lounge at the rear. The bar staff all wore kilts. You always know Glasgow guys by their sideburns. The rest of Scotsmen mostly just grow shaggy doormats but Glasgow guys hone their sideburns down to the criterion of coolness. Just like Duane Eddie out on a date. Glasgow is a street. The bar was bathed in a kind of ethereal green light, in keeping with the Celtic symbolism of the place. We had Guinness. Here in Glasgow it was the best in the world, outside Dublin of course. I suddenly thought about my Dad, rowing Iain and I across Loch Steisevat in Harris. He was like king Lear; filled with pathos, bathed in pity, imbued with sentiment. Yet he rowed on in mechanical strong pulls. Just laughing in the face of the wasteland he viewed as his life. The clear pool was here somewhere for places like Harris, the pull was here somewhere for places like Ireland. Yet that kindness could only be translated in the Glaswegian as a fondly held ideal that would never be realised now. In light of The Highland clearances. In light of The House of Hanover. The Lords still bind the Peasants with strong rope.

Just then the door swung open and Gina walked into the pub. She came towards us and embraced Stuart fondly. She said in a strong Glasgow accent, "Hi Calum," and gave me a cuddle. Gina was Italian on her Father's side, she was a Rossi. There seemed to be some kind of natural affinity between the Scots and the Italians, the genetic mix was invariably a confident one, amongst the women at least. Gina had thick dark auburn curly hair and black brown eyes. She was as sweet as a Victoria plum. Gina asked us how our Ship launch had gone, "I hope you didnae have too many drinks Stuart." He grinned from behind the grizzle. I got Gina a glass of red wine and we went and got a seat.

Gina like Stuart was also a painter but she seemed to treat her occupation as a more 9 to 5 job. She had been in the studio all day, she was tired. As a couple they were at the point where they wanted to start a family. They not only realised the enormity of this for themselves, potentially as a family, but also now how urgent it was becoming for Scotland to create children. I said to Gina that we had walked past the University Café on our way here. It was in Byers road and sold the best spaghetti in Glasgow. I said, "How do the Italians manage to make the Bolognese sauce taste so good?" Gina expressed her point with her hands. She had beautiful hands. Straight long fingers, broad and long, closely cropped fingernails. She wore her paternal Grandmother's plain gold wedding band on her marriage finger. "Traditionally," she said, "Bolognese sauce is very simple. Tomato paste, fresh plum tomatoes, onion and just a little garlic. Some fresh basil, finely diced carrot and celery, sea salt and black pepper. The secret is the meat. Fresh finely minced beef, and fresh finely minced pork. That is how I would make it. Oh and a little slug of vino rosso." "Cheers Gina," I said. Stuart had been listening closely. He fancied himself as a bit of a galloping gourmet, "Dinnae forget the cheese baby," he said. He did a good fish stew. His piece de resistance was a half-bottle of malt whisky tipped in just before serving it up. Stewart started teasing his wife. He asked her what she had been working on today. Gina pretended to ignore him and told me she was painting a triptych; she had recently been commissioned to produce an altarpiece for Glasgow Cathedral. Stuart said, "Worshipping those idolatrous rites of Rome all day makes you hungry for some bread and games." I replied to Gina, "There is nothing sadder than worshipping the plastic icon of Jesus on the cold Scots fireplace, with made in Taiwan stamped on the bottom." I was forcing Gina to dwell upon the Scots in her character, the Glaswegian in her-which was unfair of me. She said, "If you have faith it cannot be broken, it can't be taken away from you."

Stuart went and got us all another drink. I looked at my watch. I would have to be leaving soon for my train up North. Gina and I shared a moment or two of conspiratorial intimacy together before Stuart returned from the bar with the drinks. She said, "I can't believe how well you are looking Cal, forgive me if I am dragging up the past for you but I think I can more than just glimpse the real you again. You are a sensitive person, you deserve the best from life." I reflected for a few glaikit seconds looking at the floor and said, "I just feel...more hopeful...that's all Gina." She lifted her glass and said, "Chin chin," and leant over and gave me a light kiss on the forehead. Stuart came back from the bar with the drinks and saw his wife's gesture towards me and smiled to himself softly.

I got the underground down to the East End. The clockwork orange, as it is known. Down into the subterranean world of Glasgow. The distinctive, stale, muggy air. The sudden whoosh of wind and increasing clatter as the train approaches. The wheels clack clacking on the track. The squealing of metal to metal as the air brakes come on. I get off the train at St. Enoch Square. I have an hour to kill. I walk down Argyle Street where the designer labels wear the shoppers, towards the Gallowgate and the East End. Down the murder mile. Walking East to the Gallowgate where the severed heads of the Calton Hill Weavers were stuck on pikes by the English troops to warn off workers from combining in Industrial dispute. The weavers are buried now in a mass grave in Bridgeton Cross in the heart of the East end. The graveyard is a party house for alcoholics. A sin bin for contaminated sharps. A commemoration of neglect and shame.

Across from the Gallowgate a young boy is playing alone with a white plastic football. Throwing up clouds with his trainers from the red blaze cinder. He has on a green and white hooped Celtic top, he is a Bhoy. Orange hair, freckled face. I go across. He sees me and kicks the ball towards me. I pass it back to him, and he says, "Dae ye want a kickabout mister?" He must be about 8, but he has the maturity, the street of someone older. I say, "Okay then wee man." We start practising headers. We make a goal with my jacket and jersey, and I chip in corners so he can head in on goal. He practises jumping while at the same time swivelling his head to bullet the ball goalwards. His wee face is filled with concentration. Sport is his future, it is a physical art. We take a break and I ask him who his favourite Celtic player of all time is, he quickly replies, "Charlie Nicholas, he's a God." Little boys were still allowed to worship heroes even in this a most unheroic age. I say we'll try some running and then tackling me if you like. He looks sadly down at my pockets and says, "You got any money Mister, for sweets?" I take pity and give him a couple of pound coins. His face breaks into joy and he runs up to the far end of the site with the ball and says, "Okay then any time you are ready big man." He dribbles the ball then breaks into a run, he does a perfect nutmeg on me and slots the ball low into the net. I am mystified at how skillful he is. I lumber and get the ball back from the bushes. I come back panting and say, "Right, you go in goal and I'll run in and play a shot into you." He replies, "Okay. I'll have to go soon though my mam will be making my tea." He looked just a little bit worried, he was after all still only 8 and still needed kisses and cuddles from his Mother. I said, "Okay then this will be the last one. You're Packy Bonner, and I'm Charlie Nicholas when he played for Aberdeen."

I go up the far end and build up speed, guiding the ball with my right foot ahead of me. I move infield. Singular freedom of movement, mutual freedom of physical expression. Enjoyment. I'm going forward now towards somewhere new. The sequence of events that led me here, are no longer recurring. I shoot an arcing shot. Malkie dives to his right and the ball lands in the back of the net. We both roar with laughter as all the pigeons flutter and take off in shock up into the receding, reddening Glasgow night sky.